Whispers in the Sand

BARBARA ERSKINE is the author of *Lady of Hay*, which has sold well over a million copies worldwide, the bestselling *Kingdom of Shadows*, *Encounters* (short stories), and *Child of the Phoenix*, which was based on the story of one of her own ancestors. This was followed by *Midnight is a Lonely Place* and *House of Echoes* – both were shortlisted for the WH Smith Thumping Good Read awards of 1995 and 1997 respectively – plus her second volume of short stories, *Distant Voices*, and a novel, *On the Edge of Darkness*. Her novels have been translated into twenty-three languages.

Barbara Erskine has a degree in mediaeval Scottish history from Edinburgh University. She and her family divide their time between the Welsh borders and their ancient manor house near the unspoilt coast of North Essex.

BARBARA ERSKINE

Whispers
in the Sand

HarperCollins*Publishers*

HarperCollins*Publishers*
77–85 Fulham Palace Road,
Hammersmith, London W6 8JB

www.**fire**and**water**.com

Special overseas edition 2000
1 3 5 7 9 8 6 4 2

ISBN 0 00 710304 2

Maps and chapter head illustrations by Rex Nicholls

Extract from the *Encyclopaedia Britannica*, volume 10,
1970 edition, 'Glass: Ancient Times to the 19th Century'.

Set in PostScript Linotype Meridien with Photina display by
Rowland Phototypesetting Limited, Bury St Edmunds, Suffolk

Printed and bound by
Omnia Books Limited, Glasgow

The quotations at the head of each chapter are adapted from
The Book of the Dead
edited by E A Wallis Budge

THE WHITE EGRET
ITINERARY

Note: alterations to the schedule are subject to change without prior notice

Most evenings there are film shows and talks in the lounge bar on different aspects of ancient and modern Egypt

DAY 1: p.m. Arrival
Dinner on board

DAY 2: Visit the Valley of the Kings
o/n Cruise to Edfu

DAY 3: a.m. Visit the Temple of Edfu
p.m. Cruise to Kom Ombo

DAY 4: a.m. Visit the Temple of Kom Ombo
p.m. Cruise to Aswan

DAY 5: a.m. Visit Unfinished Obelisk
p.m. Kitchener's Island

DAY 6: a.m. Aswan Bazaar
midday: Aperitif at The Old Cataract Hotel
p.m. Visit High Dam

DAY 7: a.m. Sail on a felucca
p.m. Free afternoon

DAY 8–9: Optional 2-day visit to Abu Simbel
(4 a.m. start)

DAY 10: Return late afternoon
Evening: Son-et-lumière, Philae Temple

DAY 11: a.m. Visit Philae Temple. Cruise to Esna
p.m. Esna Temple. Cruise to Luxor

DAY 12: a.m. Temple of Karnac
p.m. Temple of Luxor
Evening: Pasha's Party

DAY 13: a.m. Luxor Museum and bazaar
p.m. Papyrus Museum
Evening: Son-et-lumière, Karnac Temple

DAY 14: Return to England

There can be little doubt that the first vessels of glass were manufactured in Egypt under the 18th dynasty, particularly from the reign of Amenhotep II (1448–20 BC) onward. These vessels are distinguished by a peculiar technique: the shape required was first formed of clay (probably mixed with sand) fixed to a metal rod. On this core the body of the vessel was built up, usually of opaque blue glass. On this, in turn, were coiled threads of glass of contrasting colour, which were pulled alternately up and down by a comb-like instrument to form feather, zigzag or arcade patterns. These threads, usually yellow, white or green in colour, and sometimes sealing-wax red, were rolled in (marvered) flush with the surface of the vessel. The vessels so made were nearly always small, being mainly used to contain unguents and the like.

Encyclopaedia Britannica

Prologue

In the cool incense-filled heart of the temple the sun had not yet sent its lance across the marble of the floor. Anhotep, priest of Isis and of Amun, stood before the altar stone in the silence, his hands folded into the pleated linen of his sleeves. He had lit the noon offering of myrrh in its dish and watched as the wisps of scented smoke rose and coiled in the dimly lit chamber. Before him, in the golden cup, the sacred mixture of herbs and powdered gems and holy Nile water sat in the shadows waiting for the potentising ray to hit the jewelled goblet and fall across the potion. He smiled with quiet satisfaction and raised his gaze to the narrow entrance of the holy of holies. A fine beam of sunlight struck the rim of the door-frame and seemed to hover like a breath in the hot shimmer of the air. It was almost time.

'So, my friend. It is ready at last.' The sacred light was blocked as a figure stood in the doorway behind him; the sun's ray bounced crooked across the floor, deflected by the polished blade of a drawn sword.

Anhotep drew breath sharply. Here in the sacred temple, in the presence of Isis herself, he had no weapon. There was nothing with which he could protect himself, no one he could call. 'The sacrilege you plan will follow you through all eternity, Hatsek.' His voice was strong and deep, echoing round the stone walls of the chamber. 'Desist now, while there is time.'

'Desist? When the moment of triumph is finally here?' Hatsek smiled coldly. 'You and I have worked towards this moment, brother, through a thousand lifetimes and you thought to deprive me of it now? You thought to waste the sacred source of all life on that sick boy pharaoh! Why, when the goddess herself has called for it to be given to her?'

'No!' Anhotep's face had darkened. 'The goddess has no need of it!'

'The sacrilege is yours!' The hiss of Hatsek's voice reverberated round the chamber. 'The sacred potion distilled from the very tears of the goddess must be hers, by right. She alone mended the broken body of Osiris and she alone can renew the broken body of the pharaoh!'

'It is the pharaoh's!' Anhotep moved away from the altar. As his adversary stepped after him the purifying ray of sunlight sliced the darkness like a knife and struck the crystal surface of the potion turning it to brazen gold. For a moment both men stared, distracted by the surge of power released from the goblet.

'So,' Anhotep breathed. 'It has succeeded. The secret of life eternal is ours.'

'The secret of life eternal belongs to Isis.' Hatsek raised his sword. 'And it will remain with her, my friend!' With a lunge he plunged the blade into Anhotep's breast, withdrawing it with a grunt as the man fell to his knees. For a moment he paused as though regretting his hasty action, then he raised the bloody blade over the altar and in one great sweeping arc he brought it down on the goblet, hurling it and the sacred potion it contained to the floor.

'For you, Isis, I do this deed.' Setting the sword down on the altar he raised his hands, his voice once again echoing round the chamber. 'None but you, oh great goddess, holds the secrets of life and those secrets shall be yours for ever!'

Behind him Anhotep, his bloodied hands clutching his chest, somehow straightened, still on his knees. His eyes already glazing over he groped, half blind, for the sword above him on the stone. Finding it he dragged himself painfully to his feet and raised it with both hands. Hatsek, his back to him, his eyes on the sun disc as it slid out of sight of the temple entrance never saw him. The point of the blade sliced between his shoulder blades and penetrated down through his lung into his heart. He was dead before his crumpled form folded at the other man's feet.

Anhotep looked down. At the base of the altar the sacred potion lay as a cool blue-green pool on the marble, stained by the curdling blood of two men. Staring at it for a moment Anhotep looked round in despair. Then, his breath coming in small painful gasps, he staggered across to a shelf in the shadow of a pillar. There stood the chrismatory, the small, ornate glass phial in which he had carried the concentrated potion to the holy of holies. He reached for it, his hands slippery with blood and turned back to the altar.

Falling painfully to his knees, sweat blinding his eyes, he managed to scoop a little of the liquid back into the tiny bottle. Fumbling with shaking fingers he pressed in the stopper as far as it would go, smearing blood over the glass. In one last stupendous effort he pulled himself up and set it down on the back of the shelf in the darkness between the pillar and the wall, then he turned and staggered out towards the light.

By the time they found him lying across the entrance to the holy place he had been dead for several hours.

As the bodies of the two priests were washed and embalmed the prayers said for their souls stipulated that they serve the Lady of Life in the next world as they had failed to serve her in this.

It was the high priest's order that the two mummies be laid inside the holy of holies, one on each side of the altar, and that it should then be sealed for ever.

1

May there be nothing to resist me at my judgement;
may there be no opposition to me;
may there be no parting of thee from me
in the presence of him that keepeth the scales.

It is thirteen hundred years before the birth of Christ. The embalming complete, the bodies of the priests are carried back into the temple in the cliff where once they served their gods and they are laid to rest in the shadows where they died. A mote of sunlight lies across the inner sanctuary for a moment, then as the last mud brick is pressed into place across the entrance, the light is extinguished and the temple that is now a tomb is instantly and totally dark. Were there ears to hear they would distinguish a few muffled sounds as the plaster is smoothed and the seals set. Then all is as silent as the grave.

The sleep of the dead is without disturbance. The oils and resins within the flesh begin their work. Putrefaction is held at bay.

The souls of the priests leave their earthly bodies and seek out the gods of judgement. There in the hall beyond the gates of the western horizon, Anubis, god of the dead, holds the scale which will decide their fate. On the one side lies the feather of Maat, goddess of truth. On the other is laid the human heart.

'What you need, my girl, is a holiday!'

Phyllis Shelley was a small wiry woman with a strong angular face, which was accentuated by her square red-framed glasses. Her hair cropped fashionably short, she looked twenty years younger than the eighty-eight to which she reluctantly admitted.

She headed for the kitchen door with the tea tray leaving Anna to follow with the kettle and a plate of scones.

'You're right, of course.' Anna smiled fondly. Pausing in the hall as her great-aunt headed out towards the terrace, she stood for a few seconds looking at herself in the speckled gilt-framed mirror, surveying her tired, thin face. Her dark hair was knotted behind her head in a coloured scarf which brought out the grey-green tones in her hazel eyes. She was slim, tall, her bones even, classically good-looking, her body still taut and attractive, but her mouth was etched with fine lines on either side now and the crow's-feet around her eyes were deeper than they should have been for a woman in her mid-thirties. She sighed and pulled a face. She had been right to come. She needed a good strong dose of Phyllis!

Tea with her father's one remaining aunt was one of the great joys of life. The old lady was indefatigably young at heart, strong – indomitable was the word people always used to describe her – clear thinking and she had a wonderful sense of humour. In her present state, miserable, lonely and depressed, three months after the decree absolute, Anna needed a fix of all those qualities and a few more besides. In fact, she smiled to herself as she turned to follow Phyllis out onto the terrace, there was probably nothing wrong with her at all which tea and cake and some straight talking in the Lavenham cottage wouldn't put right.

It was a wonderful autumn day, leaves shimmering with pale gold and copper, the berries in the hedges a wild riot of scarlet and black, the air scented with wood smoke and the gentle echo of summer.

'You look well, Phyl.' Anna smiled across the small round table.

Phyllis greeted Anna's remark with a snort and a raised eyebrow. 'Considering I'm so old, you mean. Thank you, Anna! I am well, which is more than I can say for you, my dear. You look dreadful, if I may say so.'

Anna gave a rueful shrug. 'It's been a dreadful few months.'

'Of course it has. But there's no point in looking backwards.' Phyllis became brisk. 'What are you going to do with your life now it is at last your own?'

Anna shrugged. 'Look for a job, I suppose.'

There was a moment's silence as Phyllis poured out two cups of tea. She passed one over and followed it with a homemade scone and a bowl of plum jam, both courtesy of the produce stall at the local plant sale. Phyllis Shelley had no time in her busy life for cooking or knitting, as she constantly told anyone who had the temerity to come and ask for contributions of either to the church fete or similar money-raising events.

'Life, Anna, is to be experienced. Lived,' she said slowly, licking jam off her fingers. 'It may not turn out the way we planned or hoped. It may not be totally enjoyable all the time, but it should be always exciting.' Her eyes flashed. 'You do not sound to me as though you were planning something exciting.'

Anna laughed in spite of herself. 'The excitement seems to have gone out of my life at the moment.'

If it had ever been there at all. There was a long silence. She stared down the narrow cottage garden at the stone wall. Phyllis's cat, Jolly, was asleep there, head on paws, on its ancient lichen-crusted bricks covered in scarlet Virginia creeper. Late roses bloomed in profusion and the air was deceptively warm, sheltered by the huddled buildings on either side. Anna sighed. She could feel Phyllis's eyes on her and she bit her lip, seeing herself suddenly through the other woman's critical gaze. Spoilt. Lazy. Useless. Depressed. A failure.

Phyllis narrowed her eyes. She was a mind reader as well. 'I'm not impressed with self-pity, Anna. Never have been. You've got to get yourself off the floor. I never liked that so and so of a husband of yours. Your father was mad to let you get involved with him in the first place. You married Felix too young. You didn't know what you were doing. And I think you've had a lucky escape. You've still got plenty of time to make a new life. You're young and you've got your health and all your own teeth!'

7

Anna laughed again. 'You're good for me, Phyl. I need some-one to tell me off. The trouble is I don't really know where to start.'

The divorce had been very civilised. There had been no unseemly squabbles; no bickering over money or possessions. Felix had given her the house in exchange for a clear conscience. He, after all, had done the lying and the leaving. And his eyes were already on another house in a smarter area, a house which would be interior-designed to order and furnished with the best to accommodate his new life and his new woman and his child.

For Anna, suddenly alone, life had become overnight an empty shell. Felix had been everything to her. Even her friends had been Felix's friends. After all, her job had been entertaining for Felix, running his social diary, keeping the wheels of his life oiled, and doing it, so she had thought, rather well. Perhaps not. Perhaps her own inner dissatisfaction had shown in the end after all.

They had married two weeks after she graduated from university with a good degree in modern languages. He was fifteen years older. That decision to stay on until she had finished her degree had been, she now suspected, the last major decision she had made about her own life.

Felix had wanted her to quit the course the moment he asked her to marry him. 'You don't need all that education, sweetheart,' he had urged. 'What's it for? You'll never have to work.'

Or worry your pretty little head about anything worth thinking about . . . The patronising words, unsaid but implied, had echoed more and more often through Anna's skull over the ensuing years. She kidded herself that she had no time for anything else; that what she did for Felix was a job. It was certainly full time. And the pay? Oh, the pay had been good. Very good! He had begrudged her nothing. Her duties had been clear cut and simple. In these days of feminist ambition, independence and resolve, she was to be decorative. He had put it so persuasively she had not realised what was happening. She was to be intelligent enough to make conversation with Felix's friends but not so intelligent as to outshine him and, with some mastery, she later realised, he had made it seem enormously important and responsible that she was to organise all the areas of his life which were not already organised by his secre-tary. And in order to maintain that organisation uninterrupted it was made clear only after the fashionable wedding in Mayfair and the honeymoon in the Virgin Islands that there would be no children. Ever.

She had two hobbies: photography and gardening. On both he allowed her to spend as much money as she liked and even encouraged her interest when it did not conflict with her duties. Both were, after all, fashionable, good talking points and relatively harmless and she had allowed them to fill whatever gaps there were in her life. Indeed in combining them she had become so good at both that her photographs of the garden won prizes, sold, gave her the illusion that she was doing something useful with her life.

Strangely, she had put up with his occasional indiscretions, surprised herself at how little they actually upset her and suspecting but never admitting that this was because, perhaps, she did not, after all, love him quite as much as she ought to. It did not matter. No other man came along to whom she was attracted. Was she, she sometimes wondered, a bit frigid? She enjoyed sex with Felix, but did not miss it when it became less and less frequent. Nevertheless, the news that his latest girlfriend was pregnant hit her like a sledgehammer. The dam, which had held back her emotions for so long, broke and a torrent of rage and frustration, loneliness and misery, broke over her head in a tidal wave which terrified her as much as it shocked her husband. He had not planned this change in his life. He had expected to carry on as before, visiting Shirley, supporting her, and when the time came paying, no doubt through the nose, for the child, but not becoming too involved. His instant and genuine enchantment with the baby had shaken him as much as it had pleased Shirley and devastated Anna. Within days of the birth he had moved in with mother and child and Anna had consulted her solicitor.

After the uncontested divorce Felix's friends had been strangely supportive of her, perhaps realising that something unplanned and unexpected had taken place and feeling genuinely sorry for her, but as one by one they rang to give her their condolences and then fell into embarrassed silence she realised that in fact she had very few friends of her own and her feeling of utter abandonment grew stronger. Strangely, the one piece of advice they all passed on before hanging up, was that she take a holiday.

And now here was Phyllis, saying the same thing.

'You must start with a holiday, Anna dear. Change of scene. New people. Then you come back and sell that house. It's been a prison for you.'

'But, Phyl –'

'No, Anna. Don't argue, dear. Well, perhaps about the house, but not about the holiday. Felix used to take you to all those places where you did nothing but sit by swimming pools and watch him talk business. You need to go somewhere exciting. In fact you need to go to Egypt.'

'Egypt?' Anna was beginning to feel her feet were being swept from beneath her. 'Why Egypt?'

'Because when you were a little girl you talked about Egypt all the time. You had books about it. You drew pyramids and camels and ibises and you pestered me every time I saw you, to tell you about Louisa.'

Anna nodded. 'It's strange. You're right. And I haven't thought about her for years.'

'Then it's time you did. It is so easy to forget one's childhood dreams. I sometimes think people expect to forget them. They abandon everything which would make their lives exciting. I think you should go out there and see the places Louisa saw. When they published some of her sketchbooks ten years ago I was tempted to go myself, you know. I'd helped your father select the pictures, and worked with the editor over the captions and potted history. I just wanted to see it so much. And perhaps I still will one day.' She smiled, the twinkle back in her eye, and Anna found herself thinking that it was entirely possible that the old lady would do it.

'She was an amazing woman, your great-great-grandmother,' Phyllis went on. 'Amazing, brave and very talented.'

Like you. Unlike me. Anna bit her lip and did not say it.

Frowning, she considered Phyllis's words, aware that the old lady's beady eyes were fixed unswervingly on her face.

'Well?'

Anna smiled. 'It's very tempting.'

'Tempting? It's a brilliant idea!'

Anna nodded. 'I did actually suggest once or twice to Felix that we go to Egypt, but he was never interested.' She paused, aware of a stirring of something like excitement deep inside her. After all, why not? 'You know, I think I might just take your advice. I haven't exactly got a lot of pressing plans.'

10

Phyllis sat back in her chair. Closing her eyes she turned her face to the sun and a small smile played across her features for a moment. 'Good. That's settled then.' There was a pause, then she went on, 'This is heaven. There is no nicer time of the year than the autumn. October is my favourite month.' Her eyes opened again and she studied Anna's face. 'Have you spoken to your father yet?'

Anna shook her head. 'He hasn't rung me since the divorce. I don't think he'll ever forgive me.'

'For separating from Felix?'

Anna nodded. 'He was so proud of having Felix for a son-in-law.' She couldn't keep the bitterness out of her voice for a moment. 'The son he never had.'

'Silly man.' Phyllis sighed. 'He's got more and more impossible since your mother died and that's a good ten years ago now! Don't let it upset you too much, darling. He'll come round. You're worth ten of any son he might have had and one day he'll realise it, I promise you.'

Anna looked away, concentrating as hard as she could on the drift of scarlet creeper on the wall on the edge of the terrace. She was not going to cry. She should have got used by now to her father's insensitivity and his blatant lack of interest in her, his only child. She sniffed hard and turned her attention to the York stone slabs at her feet. Old lichens, long dried to white crusts had formed circles and whorls in the stone. She realised suddenly that Phyllis had levered herself to her feet. Glancing up, she watched as her great-aunt disappeared back through the open French windows into the house, and groping for her handkerchief she mopped hurriedly at her eyes.

Phyllis was only gone two minutes. 'I have something here which might interest you.' She did not look at Anna as she sat down once more. She had dropped a package onto the table in front of her. 'When I was going through Louisa's papers and sketchbooks I despaired of ever finding anything personal. If there were letters she must have destroyed them. There was nothing. Then a few months ago I decided to have an old desk restored. The veneers had lifted badly.' She paused. 'The restorer found one of the drawers had a false bottom and inside he found this.' She passed the packet over to Anna.

Anna took it. 'What is it?'

'Her journal.'

'Really?' Anna glanced down in sudden excitement. 'But that must be incredibly valuable!'

'I expect so. And interesting.'

'You've read it?'

Phyllis shrugged. 'I had a quick look at it, but the writing is very difficult and my eyes aren't so good these days. I think you should read it, Anna. It's all about her months in Egypt. And in the meantime I think you should ring your father. Life is too short for huffs and puffs. Tell him he's being an idiot, and you can say I said so.'

The diary was on the back seat of the car when it was time to leave. The last crimson rays of the sunset were fading as Anna climbed in and reaching for the ignition looked up at her aunt. 'Thank you for being there. I don't know what I'd do without you.'

Phyllis shook her head in mock anger. 'You would cope very well indeed as you know. Now, ring Edward tonight. Promise?'

'I'll think about it. I'll promise that much.'

She did think about it. In the queue of heavy traffic making its way slowly back into London after the sun-drenched weekend she had plenty of time to reflect on Phyllis's advice and review her situation. She was thirty-five years old, had been married for fourteen years, had never had a job of any description whatsoever and was childless. Letting in the clutch she edged the car forward a few yards as the streams of traffic converged from the motorway into the clogged London streets. Her mind glanced sideways away from that last particular memory. She couldn't cope yet with the idea of Felix as the father of another woman's child. She had few friends, or so it seemed at the moment, a father who despised her, and a terrifying vista of emptiness before her. On the plus side there was Phyllis, the photography, the garden and whatever Phyllis said, the house.

One of the reasons Felix had left her the house was the garden. It was large for a London property, at first glance narrow and rectangular, but by some vagary of planning back in the eighteenth century the end of the garden took a steep angular bend around the back of two other houses, whose own gardens were thus sharply curtailed, doubling its size. The garden was Anna's passion. Felix had as far as she knew never even walked to the end of it. His interest began and ended with its uses as a place for entertaining corporate clients. Drinks. Barbecues. Sunday tea. The terrace with its jasmine and roses, its old terracotta pots of herbs – that was the extent of his interest. Beyond it, the winding paths, the high trellis-topped walls, the intricate beds with their carefully planned colours, the occasional half-hidden piece of sculpture lovingly garnered from trips to country antique shops was her domain alone.

It had stunned her when in the divorce settlement Felix had specifically mentioned the garden. He had said she deserved it after all her work. It was the nicest thing he had ever said to her about it.

'Daddy. Can we talk?' She had sat by the phone in her bedroom for ten minutes before picking up the receiver to dial.

There was a moment's silence, then: 'I can't imagine we have much to talk about, Anna.'

She bit her lip. 'How about the fact that I might be miserable and lonely and need you?'

'I hardly think you need me.' The voice the other end was cold. 'After all, you did not need to consult me over the divorce.'

'Consult you?' The usual emotions of anger, incredulity, indignation and finally impotence swept over her. 'Why should I have consulted you?'

'It would have been courteous.'

Anna closed her eyes and began counting to ten. It had always been like this. Other parents might show affection or sympathy or even rage. Her father was worried about a lack of courtesy. She sighed audibly. 'I'm sorry. I suppose I was too wound up about everything. It all came to a head too suddenly.'

'It should not have come to a head at all, Anna. You and Felix could have reached some accommodation. If you had consulted me I could have talked to him –'

'No! No, Daddy, I'm sorry, but we could not have reached some accommodation. Our marriage is over. Our decision. No one else's. If you feel slighted in some way, then I'm sorry. It was not intentional. I kept you informed all the way, if you remember. Every day.' Her temper was fraying.

'I don't expect to be kept informed, Anna. I expect to be consulted. I am your father –'

13

'I am a grown woman, Daddy!'

'You are not behaving like one, if I may say so –'

Anna slammed down the phone. Her stomach was churning, and she was almost sobbing with rage.

Standing up, she walked across to the dressing table and stood staring down at it, unseeing. It was a small Georgian writing desk, transformed for its current use by an oval toilet mirror and the scatter of cosmetics and brushes and discarded jewellery. Focusing suddenly on her reflection in the mirror she scowled furiously. He was right. She was not behaving like a grown woman. She was behaving as she was feeling, like an abandoned child.

Her hand strayed to the small scent bottle standing by the mirror and she picked it up, staring at it miserably. About three inches high, the glass was a deep opaque blue, decorated with a thick white feathered design, the stopper a lump of shaped wax, pushed flush with the top and sealed. Phyllis had given it to her when it had caught her fancy as a child and it had stayed with her ever since. 'Take care of it, Anna,' the old lady had said. 'It comes from Ancient Egypt and it's very, very old.'

Egypt.

Anna turned it round in her hand, staring at it. Felix had had it valued, of course, and the antique dealer had been very sniffy about it. 'I'm sorry to disappoint you, Anna, dear, but I'm afraid it probably came from a Victorian bazaar. The early visitors out there were always being conned into bringing back so-called artefacts. And this doesn't even look Egyptian.' He had handed it back with a slight sneer, as though even by touching it he had somehow contaminated himself and his Bond Street reputation. Recalling that moment Anna gave a weary smile. At least she no longer had to put up with Felix's pretentious acquaintances, pretending they were so wise and acquiescing with their patronising dismissal of her too as no more than a decorative nonentity which he had picked up in a bazaar somewhere.

With a sigh she set down the bottle and stared once more into the mirror. She was tired, she was depressed and she was fed up.

Phyllis, as always, was right. She needed a holiday.

'Have you ever been to Egypt before?'

Why hadn't she thought of this when she asked for a window

14

seat? Five hours of being trapped into conversation with whomever destiny had chosen to be her neighbour, and with no escape!

It was nearly four months since that glorious autumn day in Suffolk but now, at last she was on her way. Outside, the ground staff at Gatwick were completing the final checks on the loading of the plane and still spraying ice off its wings as they prepared for take off. Sleet slanted across the airport, whipping the faces of the men clustering round the plane into an angry painful colour.

Anna did not look up from her guidebook. 'No, I haven't.' She tried to sound unenthusiastic without being downright rude.

'Nor me.' She felt him glance at her sideways, but he said no more, groping in the bag by his feet for his own reading material.

Beyond him the aisle seat was still empty as the plane began to fill and the flight attendants shoe-horned people more and more tightly into place. Anna risked a quick look to her left. Forties; sandy hair, regular features, long eye-lashes, clearly visible as he flipped through an already well-thumbed volume. She was suddenly sorry she had been so curt. But there was plenty of time to make up for it if she wanted to. All the time in the world. Beyond him an elderly man in a dog collar inserted himself into the third seat in the row. He leant forward to nod first to her and then their neighbour, then he reached for a pile of newspapers. She saw with a smile the *Church Times* was firmly tucked away beneath a copy of the *Sun*.

That morning, as she locked the front door and hefted her suitcase into the waiting London taxi her nerve had almost failed her. The quiet early morning streets were white with thick February frost and the pre-dawn light was strangely flat and depressing. All her resolution had fled. If the cab driver had not been waiting to take her to Victoria Station to catch the train to the airport she would have turned back into the empty house, forgotten all about Egypt for ever, climbed back into bed and pulled the duvet over her head.

It was hot and stuffy on the plane and her head ached. She couldn't move in the closely packed seats and she could feel the arm of her neighbour wedged tightly against her own. Beyond a nod and half-smile when she had looked up to reach for her tray and another when the drinks came round he had said nothing more to her, and the silence was beginning to weigh on her. She

15

wasn't looking for a full-blown conversation, in fact only a short time before, had dreaded it, but a casual remark to lighten the atmosphere would be a pleasant change to silence. The drum of the plane's engines was relentless and when she closed her eyes it seemed to grow louder by the minute. She had declined headphones for the film. So had he. As far as she could see he was asleep, his book upside down on his lap, his fingers loosely linked over the cover. The first guidebook had been replaced by another and he had glanced through it swiftly before sitting back, rubbing his face wearily with his hands and seeming to subside at once into a deep sleep. Glancing out of the window she could see, far below, the tiny shadow of the plane dancing across the intense blue ripples of the sun-warmed Mediterranean. She risked a second glance at her neighbour's face. In repose it was less attractive than when awake. The lines drew heavily downward, the mouth was set and sad, a tangible weight moulding the features. She turned her attention back to her own book, envying him his ability to sleep. Another two or three hours loomed before them and her muscles were screaming to be released from the cramped position into which they were squashed.

Reaching up to the control panel over their heads to try and find some cooler air she realised suddenly that he had opened his eyes and was watching her. He smiled and she gave a small grimace in return. It was meant to convey cautious friendship and sympathy over the tightly packed, too intimate seating. She was about to follow this with a noncommittal remark when once again he looked away and closed his eyes.

Shrugging, she delved into the bag at her feet and brought out Louisa's diary. She had been saving it to read on the trip. Perhaps this was the moment to start.

The paper of the leatherbound notebook was thick, deckle-edged and in places foxed with pale brown spots. Carefully she turned to the first page of florid italic script and began to read.

'February 15th, 1866: And so, the boat has reached Luxor and here I leave my companions to join the Forresters. Tomorrow morning my boxes will be transferred to the *Ibis* which I see already tied up nearby. The decks are empty, even of crew, and the boat looks deserted. It will be wonderful at last to have some privacy especially after the constant chatter of Isabella and Arabella with whom I have had to share a cabin all these weeks from Cairo. I

16

am sending a packet of sketches and paintings back with them on the boat and hope to start a new series of drawings of the Valley of the Tombs as soon as possible. The British consul has promised me a dragoman, and the Forresters are said to be a kind, elderly couple who will allow me to travel with them willingly, without too much interference to my drawing. The heat of the day which at first renewed my spirits after the long voyage out here is growing stronger, but the nights are blessedly cool. I long to be able to see more of the desert. The nervous excitement of my companions so far on this adventure has prevented us from venturing any distance from our boat and I cannot wait to begin my explorations further afield.'

Anna looked up thoughtfully. She had never seen the desert. Never been to any part of Africa or the Middle East. Imagine the frustration of not being able to explore because your companions were too nervous. It had been bad enough knowing there was no time, no possibility of visiting properly the places she had travelled to with Felix. Shifting a little in her seat to try and make herself more comfortable, she turned back to the diary.

'Louisa, dear. Sir John Forrester is here.' Arabella bounced into the small cabin in a froth of white lace and slightly stained cambric. 'He has come to take you across to his yacht.'

'It's not a yacht, Arabella. It is called a dahabeeyah.' Louisa was packed and ready, her painting things already neatly roped on deck with her trunks and her valise. She adjusted her broad-brimmed black straw hat and reached for the small portmanteau on her bunk. 'Are you coming to see me off?'

'Of course!' Arabella giggled. 'You're so brave, Louisa. I can't imagine how frightening the rest of the trip is going to be.'

'It won't be frightening at all,' Louisa replied tartly. 'It will be extremely interesting.'

Her voluminous skirts gripped tightly in one hand, she climbed the companionway steps and emerged into the blinding sunlight on deck.

Sir John Forrester was a tall skeletally thin man in his late sixties. Dressed in a heavy tweed jacket, plus fours and boots he turned to greet her, his white pith helmet, his only concession to the climate, in his hand. 'Mrs Shelley? How very nice.' His bow was courteous, his eyes brilliant blue beneath bushy white eyebrows and shrewdly appreciative. He greeted her companions in turn then instructed the two dark-skinned Nubians with him to remove her luggage to the felucca drawn up alongside the paddle steamer.

Now the moment had come, Louisa felt a small pang of nervousness. She had shaken hands one by one with the men and women who had been her companions over the last few weeks, nodded to the crew, tipped her cabin servants and at last she was turning towards the small sailing boat which would ferry her across to the *Ibis*.

'Bit of a test, my dear, getting down the ladder.' Sir John offered her his hand. 'Once you're down, sit where you like. There.' His sternly pointing finger contradicted the vagueness of his invitation.

Louisa wrapped her skirts around her tightly, holding them as high as she dared and cautiously she reached down for the ladder with a small brown boot. From below a black hand grabbed her ankle and guided it to the first rung. She bit her lip, firmly fighting the urge to kick the man who had taken such a liberty, and quickly lowered herself into the small boat with its flapping sail. She was greeted by smiles and bows from the two Egyptian crewmen as she slid towards the seat to which Sir John had directed her. He followed her down and within seconds the boat was heading across the turbid water towards the *Ibis*. Behind her Arabella lingered on deck, her face shaded by her pink parasol, and waved at Louisa's departing back.

The boat towards which they were heading was one of the graceful private vessels which plied up and down the Nile, this one propelled by two great lateen sails and steered from the back by a huge tiller that extended over the main cabin roof. The elegant accommodation, she soon discovered, included cabins for herself, the Forresters and Lady Forrester's maid, a saloon, filled with divans and a large writing table and quarters sufficient for the crew which consisted of the captain, or *reis* and eight men. The deck allowed room to sit and to eat outside should they wish it, and also an area for the crew, one of whom was an excellent and talented cook.

This time she was to have a cabin to herself. Staring round it Louisa felt her heart leap with delight. After the dark wood and brass fittings of the paddle steamer this cabin, tiny though it was, was beauty itself. Her narrow bed was spread with brightly coloured woven fabrics, there was a carpet on the floor, fine blue and green shawls were draped across the window and the basin and ewer were made of some beaten metal which looked like gold.

Tearing off her hat she flung it on the bed and looked round approvingly. From the deck overhead she could hear the pattering of bare feet and the creak of the masts and rigging.

Of Lady Forrester there had been no sign. 'Indisposed, my dear. She'll join us for dinner,' Sir John had said vaguely as he showed Louisa to her cabin. 'We'll sail as soon as possible. Not far. We'll tie up on the other side of the river so you can set off for the valley tomorrow. Hassan will be your dragoman. That is, he will act as your guide and interpreter. Good chap. Highly recommended. Very reliable. And cheap.' He smiled knowingly. 'And you'll have to share Jane Treece, Lady Forrester's maid. I'll send her in to you directly and she can help you settle in.'

And here she was, a woman of about forty-five with hair pulled severely off her face beneath her cap, dressed, like her, in black and with skin which beneath the cruel sun had freckled and creased into a tight map of lines and blotches. 'Good evening, Mrs Shelley.' The woman's voice was deep and educated. 'Sir John has asked me to act as your maid and chaperone while you are on his boat.'

Louisa hid her despair as best she could. She had hoped to be free of such formality. It would though be helpful to have someone unpack and shake out her dresses and fold away her underlinen and petticoats and lay out her hairbrushes and combs. Her sketch-books and her precious Winsor and Newton watercolour box, her paintbrushes, she would allow no one to touch but herself. These she put on the small table in front of the elegantly pointed cabin window with its latticed shutters.

Turning she stared at the evening gown which Jane Treece had already shaken free of its folds and laid out for her. Her vision of casting aside her corset and petticoats and the formal black which her mourning demanded and putting on the blessedly cool, softly

19

flowing dresses made for her all those long months ago in London by her friend Janey Morris, were beginning to recede once more. 'I had assumed we would be more casual on so small a boat,' she said cautiously. 'And, though it was kind of Sir John to think of it, as a widow I scarcely think I need a chaperone!'

'Indeed.' The word conveyed shock, scorn and such superiority that Louisa was in no doubt at all that her assumptions had been dreadfully misjudged.

'Sir John and Lady Forrester keep every formality on the *Ibis*, Mrs Shelley, I assure you. When you leave the boat to go off and see the heathen temples I have no doubt it will be more difficult to maintain the niceties, and I have made it clear I am not prepared to go with you on those occasions, but while we are here Sir John's man, Jack, and I, see to it that everything runs as well as it does at home in Belgravia.'

Louisa bit her lip to hide a wry smile. Trying to look suitably chastened she allowed the woman to help her on with her black silk gown and pin her hair up in loose ringlets and loops around her head beneath a black lace veil. At least without the weight of her customary chignon it was cooler. The assurance that Jane Treece would not be going with her to visit the Valley of the Tombs had cheered her up enormously.

The main saloon of the boat was as exotic as her own cabin, but the silver and china laid on the table for dinner was English. The food itself though was Egyptian, and delicious. Louisa ate with enjoyment as she tried to explain to the Forresters why she wanted to paint the Egyptian scenery. Augusta Forrester had emerged from her own quarters looking as elegant and cool as if she were entertaining at home in London. A small silver-haired woman in her early sixties with huge dark eyes, she had managed to retain a prettiness of feature and a charm which made her immediately attractive. Her attention span was, though, Louisa discovered quickly, very short.

'When Mr Shelley died,' she explained as they ate, 'I found myself lost.' How could she ever tell them how lost without her beloved George? She had contracted the same fever which had killed her husband and although she had recovered it had left her too weak and too listless to care for her two robust and noisy sons. They had gone to stay with George's mother and Louisa had been persuaded finally that a few months in a hot climate would restore her to health. She and George had planned to come to Egypt one day. It was George who had regaled her with stories of the discoveries that were being made in the sands of the desert. It was George who had promised that one day they would go there and that she would paint the temples and tombs. The somewhat unconventional household they ran with its laughter and conversation and the constant flow of painters and writers and travellers had fallen apart when illness had struck. George's mother had arrived, nursed them both, taken away the children, dismissed half the servants, substituted her own and left Louisa devastated.

Glancing from Sir John to his wife, Louisa saw that the latter was no longer listening to her, but the mention of Augusta's nephew, Edward, brought her back from her daydreams and for a few minutes she sat, her beautiful dark eyes fixed on Louisa's face, as her guest described how that young man, a friend of George's, had rescued her, arranged her passage, booked the steamer from Cairo and persuaded his uncle and aunt to take her to see the excavations. Without his help she would have been destroyed.

His uncle and aunt were however not quite as unconventional as their nephew and she was finding out every minute that her dreams of conversation and laughter and the convivial travel which she and George had so often discussed were far from what the Forresters had in mind.

Anna looked up. Her neighbour appeared to be asleep. Over the back of the seat in front of her she could see the film in full swing. Most of the passengers seemed to be engrossed in the action. Surreptitiously she tried to stretch and wondered how long she could last before she had to ask him to move so she could go to the loo. She glanced back towards the rear of the plane. The queue for the lavatories did not seem to have grown any shorter. Beyond the thick glass of the window the distant ground had turned the colour

21

of red and ochre and gold. The colours of Africa. With a tremor of excitement she stared down for a long time, before leaning back in her seat and closing her eyes. She was almost there.

It was impossible to sleep.

She opened the diary again, eager to lose herself in Louisa's adventures and blot out her own less than romantic mode of travel. Skimming down the cramped slanted writing with its faded brown ink, she flipped through the pages, glancing at the sketches which illustrated the narrative.

'Hassan brought the mules at first light so that we could escape the worst of the heat. He loaded all my painting equipment into the panniers without a word. I was afraid he was still angry at my lack of tact and understanding of his role, but resolved not to speak of it. Instead I allowed him to help me onto my animal without uttering a word either of apology or of remonstrance at his outburst. He looked up at me once and I saw the anger in his eyes. Then he went to collect the lead rein of the pack animal and climbed onto his own. We rode all the way to the valley without speaking.'

Anna glanced up again, wearily rubbing her eyes. It did not sound as though Louisa had had a good time with Hassan. She turned on a few pages.

'I saw him again today – just a faint figure in the heat haze. A tall man, watching me, who one minute was near me and the next minute was not there. I called out to Hassan but he was asleep and by the time he had reached my side the man had vanished into the strange shimmer thrown by the heat of the sand. The shadows where I set my easel were dark in contrast but out there, on the floor of the valley there was nowhere for him to hide. I am beginning to feel afraid. Who is he and why does he not approach me?'

That sounded exciting. Exciting and mysterious. With a small shiver Anna looked up with a start to see the flight attendant hovering with a jug of coffee. Her neighbour, ignoring the woman, was looking down at the diary on Anna's knee with evident interest. She closed it and slipped it into her bag, reaching for the tray in front of her and letting it down onto her lap. He had already looked away. Outside, the sun was slipping nearer and nearer to the horizon.

Her neighbour appeared to have fallen asleep when she fumbled in her bag once again for the diary, and opening it at random was captivated immediately by the words which sprang from the page. 'I begin to love this country . . .'

Louisa set down her pen and stared out of the window at the dark river outside. She had pulled open the lattice shutters to allow the smell of it, the warmth of the night air, the occasional breath of chill wind from the desert to enter her cabin. It all captivated her. She listened carefully. The other cabins were silent. Even the crew were asleep. Gathering up her skirts she tiptoed to the door and opened it. The steps to the deck were steep. Cautiously she climbed them and emerged into the darkness. She could see the humped forms of the sleeping men before the mast and heard suddenly a brief sleepy snore as one of them eased his head on the cushion of his arm. Another breath of cold air and she could hear the rustle of palm fronds on the bank. Above, the stars were violent sparks against the blue-black sky.

There was a slight movement behind her and she turned. Hassan's bare feet had made no sound on the deck. 'Mrs Shelley, you should stay in your cabin.' His voice was no more than a whisper against the whisper of the wind in the reeds.

'It's too hot down there. And the night is too beautiful to miss.' Her mouth had gone dry.

She could see his smile, his teeth white against the dark silhouette of his face. 'The night is for lovers, Mrs Shelley.'

Her face burning, she stepped away from him, her knuckles tight on the deck rail. 'The night is for poets and painters as well, Hassan.'

With half an ear she was listening for sounds from below deck. Her heart was beating very fast.

Her neighbour was looking at Louisa's diary again, she could sense it. Anna sighed. He was beginning to irritate her. His glance was an invasion of her space, an intrusion. If he was not prepared to make a minimum of polite conversation he had no business being interested in her reading material! Closing the diary, she forced herself to look up and smile at the seat-back in front of her. 'Not long now.' She turned towards him. 'Are you going on a cruise too?'

He was an attractive man, she realised suddenly, but even as she thought it his face closed and she saw it harden and the warmth vanished.

'I am indeed, but I very much doubt it is the same one as you.' His accent was difficult to place, very faint – slightly Scots perhaps, or Irish – because that was all he said. He shifted his shoulders slightly, turning away from her, and putting his head back against the seat he closed his eyes once more.

She felt a surge of anger and resentment. Well, that had certainly put her in her place. How dare he assume anything about her! Turning abruptly towards the window she stared out, astonished to find that far below them it was already dark. In the distance, she realised suddenly that she could see lights. They would soon be arriving at Luxor.

By the time she had been through passport control and retrieved her suitcase among the teaming throng of other tourists Anna was exhausted. She hung onto her case, grimly waving away the offers of help from a surge of gesticulating shouting would-be porters, and joined the queue for the bus.

The White Egret was a small boat. The brochure had shown the Victorian paddle steamer on a separate page from the other cruisers belonging to the travel company, emphasising its age, its history, and its selectness. There would be only eighteen passengers. It was a long shot she had suspected, even to try and find a place on it but she had made the effort because it was the closest she was likely to get to the kind of boat Louisa would have travelled on from Cairo to Luxor, and to her enormous delight and surprise they had written to say that there had been a cancellation and she found herself allocated one of the only two single cabins.

A hasty glance round the bus showed her that her neighbour from the plane was not there. She wasn't sure if she was relieved or sorry. She had not enjoyed his rudeness. On the other hand his would at least have been a familiar face amongst all these strangers. She made her way towards the back and sat down, her small holdall and camera bag on the seat beside her. Was she the only person there on her own? It seemed like it. Everyone else was sitting in pairs and the level of excited conversation had escalated as the door closed and the bus pulled away. She gazed out into the darkness feeling suddenly bleak and lonely and then realised with an excited sense of shock which put all thoughts of her loneliness out of her head that beyond the reflections of the bus windows she could see palm trees and a man in a white turban, perched on the rump of a tiny donkey trotting along the road in the dark.

The boat – three storeys, picked out in lights with a huge paddle wheel each side – was moored on the outskirts of the town. They were welcomed with hot towels for their hands and a drink of sweet fruit juice, then they were given their cabin keys.

Her cabin was small but adequate, her case already waiting for her in the middle of the floor. She looked round with interest. Her new domain provided her with a single bed, a bedside locker, on which stood an old fashioned internal telephone, a dressing table and a narrow cupboard. It was scarcely luxury, but at least she did not have to share it with a stranger. Throwing her holdall, camera and shoulder bag down on the bed she closed the door behind her and went to the window. Pushing back the curtains and opening the shutters she tried to see out but the river bank beyond was dark. To her disappointment she could see nothing. Pulling the curtains shut again she turned back to the room. Half an hour, they had been told, until supper, and then in the morning they would be ferried across the River Nile and their first visit – to the Valley of the Kings, Louisa's Valley of the Tombs – would begin. A wave of excitement swept over her.

It took no time at all to unpack, to hang up the dresses and skirts

25

she had brought with her – there was no need of a Jane Treece to help her – and to lay out her few cosmetics on the dressing table. Amongst them she stood her little perfume bottle. It had seemed only right to bring it to the land of its origins, whether those origins had been in some lowly bazaar or in an ancient tomb.

There was time for a quick shower before dinner. Throwing off her clothes she turned and ducked into the little bathroom. She stood for five minutes beneath the tepid trickle of water, letting it wash away the weariness of the journey before forcing herself out of her reverie, and, stepping out onto the duckboard on the tiled, mosaic floor between the loo and the doll-sized basin, she reached for her towel.

Pulling it round her she stepped back into her room. The temperature in the cabin had dropped. Shivering, she stared round, puzzled. There was no air conditioning control that she could see. Perhaps there was some central system on the boat. Pulling on her green cotton shift and slinging a lightweight sweater round her shoulders she stopped in her tracks again, frowning. There was definitely something odd about the temperature in the room. She hoped she wouldn't have to complain about it; she had expected Egypt to be hot! Shrugging, she gave one more glance round the cabin and then she headed for the door.

This was the moment that she was dreading. She had to go out and meet the other passengers. This was her first sortie into life as a single woman once again. If she had imagined the people on the cruise with her at all it was as a homogenous group of which she would be a part, not as a collection of couples where she would be the only one alone. With a deep sigh she let herself out into the broad, carpeted corridor outside and, noting with relief how warm it was, began to make her way to the main staircase of the boat. Straight ahead lay the lounge and the bar and the double doors which led out onto the deck, and down the stairs, magnificently railed in brass and decorated with palms and Victorian spittoons was the dining room towards which everyone was now heading.

She found herself seated at one of three round tables, each of which accommodated six people. Beyond the windows she could see nothing of the land or the river she had come so far to visit. The only sign of Egypt was the appearance behind the semi-circular serving counter, piled high with fruit and cheeses in the centre of the room, of a solemn procession of waiters, dark-skinned, dressed in white – two or three per table at least.

Her companions were, to her relief, immediately friendly; the silence of strangers disappeared at once as on every side people began introducing themselves to each other. Next to her on her left she found herself shaking hands with a good-looking man perhaps her own age or slightly older. He stood up as he greeted her and she saw he was no taller than herself, but his broad shoulders and stocky frame gave the impression of size. 'Andy Watson, from London.' He smiled, hazel eyes bright with humour beneath dark lashes and bushy brows. 'Unattached, available, charming, with an absolute passion for all things Egyptian, as I suspect have we all, because that's why we're here.'

Anna found herself laughing. A little shyly she introduced herself as a divorcée also from London, recklessly meeting his eyes for a moment before she turned to greet the tall thin man with mousy hair, almost gaunt features and the palest blue eyes who sat on her right.

'There are five of us on the cruise.' Andy leant across her, reclaiming her attention. 'That's Joe Booth next to you, he's something in the City, and beyond him is his wife Sally, and this,' he indicated the slim, red-headed young woman on his left, 'is Charley, who is sharing a cabin with Serena, over there.' He nodded at a woman seated with her back to them at the next table. The sixth person at the table, the only one there apart from her who appeared to know no one on the cruise, introduced himself as Ben Forbes, a retired doctor. He and Andy were, it appeared, sharing a cabin. He was, she guessed, in his late sixties, a large, florid man with small bright observant eyes, a wild thatch of greying hair and a rumbustious laugh which within a few minutes had proved to be both infectious and a wonderful way of drawing attention to their table. The waiters unfailingly came to them first, as did their tour guide, Omar, who introduced himself as they were waiting to be served.

'Welcome. Tomorrow we start with our tour to the Valley of the Kings. Karnac and the Temple of Luxor itself we shall visit on the last day of the cruise. Tomorrow we get up very early. We cross the river on the ferry, and then we go on a bus. The schedule will be posted each day at the top of the stairs, outside the lounge.' A strikingly handsome young man, who, Anna discovered later, when he was not working as a tour guide, was studying history at Cairo University, he glanced round at them and smiled the most beautiful smile, his white teeth enhanced by what looked like a fortune in gold. 'Please, if you have any problems and questions come to me at any time.' He bowed and moved on to the next table.

Watching him, Anna saw him bow again and introduce himself to each of them in turn, then she noticed the man next to whom he was standing. Seated with his back towards her, his arm across the back of the chair as he looked up at Omar and listened to his short speech, was the man who had sat next to her on the plane; he must have been on the bus after all. He had changed into a dark-blue open-necked shirt and pale linen trousers and she saw him make some quiet remark to Omar which had the young man blushing and the others at the table laughing uproariously. So he was still being unpleasant. Obviously it was in his nature. She suppressed a quick feeling of triumph that she was after all on the same cruise as he was!

'Seen someone you know?' Andy was passing her the basket of warm bread rolls.

She shook her head. 'He sat next to me on the plane, that's all.'

'I see.' Andy stared over his shoulder, then he turned back to her. 'So. It's brave of you to travel out here on your own. What made you decide to come to Egypt after dumping hubby?'

She winced. 'It is as you said. I have a passion for things Egyptian. Well, perhaps that's putting it too strongly. My great-great-grandmother was a woman called Louisa Shelley. She came out here to paint in the late 1860s –'

'The Louisa Shelley? The watercolourist?' She had his attention completely now. 'But she is very well known! I sold one of her sketches not six months ago.'

'Sold?' Anna frowned.

'In my shop. I deal in fine art and antiques.' He smiled at her.

Beyond him Charley leant forward and smacked him on the wrist. 'No shop, Andy, please. You promised.' She surveyed Anna carefully, her eyes wary. 'Don't encourage him!' There was no friendly smile as she looked Anna up and down. 'What do you do?' She waited, eyebrows raised.

Not giving her a chance to reply Andy leapt in for her. 'She's here to spend her ex-husband's fortune, darling, what do you think? And I'll bet I can sell her some gorgeous things when we

28

all get home, but for now we're going to concentrate on Egyptian goodies, and first of all, Egyptian food. Did you know this boat is famous for its food?'

Anna glanced at Andy. His open cheerfulness encouraged confidences. She noticed suddenly that Charley's hand, resting on the table beside her plate, was touching Andy's. So, he was not as unattached as all that. She would have to be careful. 'If you're interested in art and antiques perhaps I should show you my Ancient Egyptian scent bottle!' She smiled.

Andy leant back in his chair, his head cocked on one side. 'Genuine Ancient Egyptian?' He waited attentively.

She shrugged. 'I have been told not. But it came from Louisa and I think she thought it was. I have her diary with me. I'll see if she mentions where she found it. I just thought it would be fun to bring it with me. Back to the place of its origin as it were.'

'Indeed.' Andy watched as a Nubian waiter approached with their soup. 'You must show it to me some time. I know a little about ancient artefacts, and I would love to see Louisa Shelley's diary. Are there any sketches in it, by any chance?' He had picked up his bread roll and was crumbling it between his fingers.

Anna nodded. 'A few, tiny thumbnail ones. She did most of her sketches in the special sketchbooks she had with her.'

She was aware suddenly that at the next table her neighbour from the plane had realised she was there. He was staring at her with such close attention that she suspected he had been listening to their conversation. She gave him a small quick smile – no more than the slightest acknowledgement – and saw him nod curtly in return.

'Your flight companion has spotted you, I see.' Andy's voice in her ear was amused.

'So it seems.' Anna wondered why the man's neighbour, Serena, was sitting separately and not at the table with her companions. So far she had not even turned to acknowledge them. Even as she watched the woman smiled across at her neighbour and began talking animatedly to him. He turned back towards her at once, and as his head turned Anna caught sight of the not unattractive smile.

She picked up her spoon. The soup was made of vegetables, lightly seasoned and thin but tasty. It was very welcome after the packaged food on the journey. 'He was fascinated by the diary.

29

I was reading it on the flight and he couldn't keep his eyes off it.'

'Indeed.' Andy's eyes narrowed slightly. 'Anna, you will take care of it, won't you? I'm sure it must be extremely valuable. It would be very tempting to anyone who guessed what it was.' His eyes on her face were concerned, sincere.

For the first time in ages Anna felt a small rush of grateful happiness. He actually seemed genuinely interested in what she was saying. 'You are not suggesting that he would try and steal it?'

'No, of course not. I'm sure he was just curious. A manuscript diary is not the usual airport reading that one expects to see on a plane.' He chuckled.

Anna glanced back towards the other table again and was disconcerted to find the man in the blue shirt still watching her. There was a look of faintly sardonic amusement on his face. She looked away, embarrassed at being caught staring and without thinking she smiled nervously at the tall Nubian standing behind the serving counter. He caught her eye and in a moment was beside her. 'More soup, madam?'

Andy chuckled. 'Go on. You'll have to have it now.'

She glanced up. 'Yes. Please. That would be lovely.' Watching her plate disappear she shrugged helplessly. 'They are going to think that I'm really greedy.'

'Or just hungry.' Andy laughed again. 'Just to make you feel better I shall have some too. You do realise that this is a four course meal,' he went on as her brimming plate reappeared.

'No!'

'Yes! And I shall order some wine to accompany it.' He raised his hand and beckoned the waiter back.

'I love their robes,' Anna whispered when the man had finished serving them and returned to his watchful pose by the counter. The waiters were dressed in long striped cotton shift-like garments, fastened round the waist with red cummerbunds. 'They look fantastically glamorous.'

Andy reached for the bottle. 'They're called *galabiyyas*.'

'What are?'

'The robes, as you put it, that the men here wear. Enormously comfortable. Cool.' Turning his back on the neighbouring table he leant back in his chair and beamed first at Charley, who was beginning to scowl at him, clearly resenting the attention he was paying to her, and then back at Anna. 'No doubt we shall have to don such apparel at some time during the voyage. Even the most salubrious and posh of vessels feel bound to humiliate their passengers with a fancy dress party of some kind, I gather.'

'I'm beginning to suspect that this is not your first trip to Egypt.' Anna watched as he squinted at the label on the wine bottle which had appeared.

'My first on a cruise like this.' He slopped a little wine into his glass and raised it to his nose speculatively. 'This may be a mistake. One should really stick to beer in Egypt unless one wants to buy French wine. Not bad, I suppose. Want some?' He reached for her glass.

Beyond him Charley was engaged at last in a lively conversation with Ben Forbes. Her long red hair had fallen forward over her shoulder and a few strands were trailing in her soup. She didn't seem to notice.

'I was a bit nervous, coming on a trip like this on my own,' Anna went on. 'I'll know who to ask for advice.'

'Indeed you will.' He winked. 'Now, eat that soup. I can see the hors d'oeuvres waiting to come in.'

When the meal was at last finished almost all the passengers made their way up to the lounge bar and some of them, thence, through the double doors out onto the deck. As she stepped out into the darkness, Anna shivered. She had expected the earlier balmy evening air, but a sharp breeze had sprung up. Threading her way between the tables and chairs she made her way aft and leant on the rail alone. Andy and Charley had stopped inside at the bar and she could hear their laughter through the half-open door. The river was broad at this point, though she could see little in the darkness. On the bank against which they were moored the houses, built with mud brick and clustered closely together were mostly without lights and the only sound, of distant singing, came from another boat further along the bank and from the occasional slap of water against the mud.

'So, it appears we are on the same cruise after all.' The voice at her elbow made her jump. 'Forgive me for doubting your good taste.'

Turning she saw the blue shirt, the sandy hair. He was leaning over the rail, not looking at her, lost in thought. He turned and held out his hand. 'My name is Toby. Toby Hayward.' Now that he was standing up she realised that he was much taller than she expected, his frame lanky, slightly stooped.

'I'm Anna Fox.' His handshake was firm but brief.

They both stared out into the darkness for several moments. 'You know, I am finding it hard to believe I am actually here,' Anna went on softly. 'On the River Nile. Somewhere out there in the darkness is Tutankhamen's tomb, and ancient Thebes and the desert and beyond that the heart of Africa.'

There was a quiet chuckle. 'A romantic. I hope you're not going to be disappointed.'

'No. No, I'm not.' Suddenly she was on the defensive. 'It is going to be wonderful.' Turning away from him, she made her way back between the deserted tables and ducked into the lounge.

Andy spotted her at once. 'Anna! Come on, let me buy you a drink.'

She shook her head with a smile. 'Thank you, but I think I'll turn in. We've an early start tomorrow, and I got a bit chilled out there. I never thought it would be cold in Egypt.'

'It's the night wind off the desert.' Andy caught her hand between his own. 'My goodness, yes. It's frozen. Are you sure a stiff drink wouldn't thaw you out?'

'No. Thank you.' She was conscious that the door behind her had opened and Toby had come in, leaving the deck outside deserted. Ignoring the other passengers he walked straight through the lounge and made his way out towards the cabins.

She followed him slowly, not wanting to catch him up as he headed for the staircase, but there was no sign of him as she made her way to her door and let herself in.

She paused, looking round. The cabin no longer looked bleak and impersonal. Nor was it cold. It was warm and inviting, the bedside light on, the bed turned down, the towel she had used before supper already replaced by a dry one. Her own belongings made the place look welcoming and friendly, the little perfume bottle, in place of honour on the dressing table, reflecting in the mirror, a small almost glowing patch of colour on the brown wood. Suddenly she was very happy.

The diary was waiting for her by her bed. Perhaps, before she fell asleep, she would stay awake long enough to read a little more and find out how Louisa had first experienced the Valley of the Kings, then tomorrow she would know what to expect.

2

The things which are abominated by the gods
they are wickedness and falsehood. If found
wanting, what future is there for those who
escape the blood grimed jaws of Ammit? He who
fastens the fetters on the foes of the gods; those
who slaughter in the shambles; there is no escape
from their grasp. May they never stab me with
their knives; may I never fall helpless into their
chambers of torture.
Better to return to the body in the silent heat of
the death chamber and wait.
I am Yesterday and Today; I have the power to
be born a second time.

*Thoth the god of judgement sees the human hearts and frowns
as the first is laid in the balance and the beam begins to tremble.*

*Ammit, the eater of the dead, licks her fearsome lips as she
sits beside the scale. Should this heart weigh more than the
feather of Maat, hers will be the reward. These men served
the gods. The one was a priest of Isis and Amun. The other the
priest of Isis and her sister, Sekhmet, the bloody-jawed lioness,
goddess of war and anger – and, oh strange and wonderful*

contradiction, of healing. They should pass the test; they should go on to eternal life with the gods they served. But there is blood on their hands and there is revenge in their hearts and there is greed in their spirit for the elixir of life. If they fail the test now, they will flee the terrors of Ammit and the tortures of the damned and they will return to the chamber of death to wait. All grows dark.

Louisa was ready at dawn. Hassan was waiting on the bank with three donkeys. Food, water and her painting equipment was loaded quickly and silently into the panniers on one and Hassan helped her onto one of the others, then, keeping a firm grip on the leading rein of both, climbed onto his own. Behind him the crew of the *Ibis* were busy going about their chores. Of the Forresters or Jane Treece there was no sign. Louisa hid a smile of relief. They were going to manage to escape.

The Forresters had not so far proved to be the hosts she had hoped for. In fact their regime was even more restrictive than that of Isabella and Arabella. They too could see no reason to visit the antiquities, and particularly not those which involved half a day's ride though the blazing sun. More importantly, they seemed to feel that they were responsible for Louisa's moral welfare. Though a dragoman had been hired for her, she was not to be with him alone. Though she had come to Egypt not only for the sake of her health, but in her own mind at least, to paint the antiquities, they did not consider that it was important or even advisable for her to do so. They were in fact due to leave for a gentle sail up the Nile as soon as the steamer had arrived at Luxor with the post from England. In near despair of ever visiting the Valley of the Tombs, Louisa had had to resort to secrecy. She had found Hassan sitting in the shade of the deck awning, writing in his own small notebook. He rose to his feet the moment she had appeared, and he listened

34

gravely to her whispered instructions. Well aware that Lady Forrester might at the last minute insist on Jane Treece accompanying her as a chaperone, Louisa had told them that she would not leave until mid-morning. To Hassan she explained privately that they must leave at dawn.

She had awoken while it was still dark, climbing into her clothes as silently as she could. Her first brief meetings with the man who was to be her dragoman – guide, escort, servant, interpreter – had gone well. He was a quiet, refined man, grave and very conscious of his responsibility. His loyalties, he made clear immediately, were to Louisa alone. Wherever she wanted to go he would take her.

'Does he have a name?' Louisa patted her animal's neck as they set off.

Hassan shrugged. 'I don't know. I hired them for the journey.'

'He must have a name. Perhaps I should give him one. Caesar. How does that sound?'

Hassan smiled across at her as they rode swiftly away from the river bank and turned between some square mud-brick houses out of sight of the *Ibis*.

'That is a good name. I shall call mine, Antony. And this our beast of burden shall be Cleopatra.'

Louisa laughed in delight. 'Then we shall be such an intelligent party.' He was a good-looking man, of middle height, slim, dressed in loose blue trousers and a striped robe. He had large dark eyes, fringed with long lashes. Looking across at him surreptitiously she wondered how old he was. It was hard to tell. His hair was hidden completely by his red turban. There were wrinkles at the corners of his eyes and laughter creases from nose to mouth, but apart from that his skin was smooth.

'How far must we ride to the valley, Hassan?' In spite of herself she glanced over her shoulder.

He shrugged. 'We will know when we get there. We have all day.' His smile was warm and without guile.

Louisa laughed. In Egypt, she had discovered, things happened when they happened. That was the will of God. With a contented sigh she settled onto the felt saddle and concentrated instead on trying to accommodate herself to her donkey's pace.

The track through the fields of berseem and wheat and barley was cool in the dawn light beneath the eucalyptus trees and the tall graceful date palms and she relaxed, enjoying the scented air, the greetings of the fellaheen they passed making their way out to the fields. It was all too soon that they reached the edge of the cultivated land which bordered the River Nile and struck out into the desert. In front of them rose the long red shoulder of the Theban hills, so visible, and so mysteriously close that they could be seen from the deck of the boat and yet now, shrouded in the misty distance.

They stopped briefly for a breakfast of slices of watermelon and cheese and bread before the sun was too high, then they rode on. Ahead the hills at last drew closer. Louisa stared up, fanning herself beneath the shade of her broad-brimmed hat. A kite circled overhead, a dark speck against the brilliant blue of the sky.

'Soon there. Very soon.' Hassan reined back his little donkey. 'You are going to draw pictures of the mountains?'

Louisa nodded. 'I want to see the mountains and the tombs of the pharaohs.'

'Of course. What else?' Hassan smiled. 'I have brought candles and flares for us to see them.' He gestured towards the pack animal. 'Not far. Then you can rest.'

She nodded again. Perspiration was trickling down her back and between her breasts. Her clothes felt heavy and stifling. 'I expected to see a lot of visitors along this road,' she called across to him. The loneliness was beginning to unnerve her.

'There are lots of visitors.' He shrugged. 'The steamer has not been here for several days. When it comes they will arrive again.'

'I see.' She smiled uncertainly. The barely distinguishable road was empty of other riders. There were no tracks.

'There are no footmarks, no signs of anyone else.' She gestured nervously.

He shook his head. 'Last night the wind blew. Poof!' He blew out his cheeks, gesturing with his hands. 'The sand comes and all things disappear.'

Louisa smiled. That was a phrase for her diary. She must remember it. The sand comes and all things disappear. The epitaph of a civilisation.

The road grew steeper as they made their way into the hills and eventually they turned into the hidden valley where she could clearly make out the square doorways cut in the brilliant limestone cliffs. Drawing to a standstill Hassan slid off his donkey and came to help her dismount. As she stood staring round, listening to the moan of the strange hot wind and the cries of the circling kites he unloaded her sketchbooks and paints and a Persian rug which he spread nearby on the sand. He also produced some poles over which he draped a length of green and blue striped cloth to make her a shelter, like a Bedouin tent, to give her some privacy in the barren valley. The donkeys and he remained in the sun, seemingly oblivious to the heat.

'I expected to see people digging. Excavating. Why is it all so empty?' She was staring round, still overwhelmed by the desolation of the valley.

He shrugged. 'Sometimes there are a lot. Sometimes none. The money stops.' He raised his shoulders again eloquently. 'They have to go away to find more. Then they return. Then you will see the wadi full of people. The local men are always here. We will see them, I expect. They dig in the night. If they find a new tomb they dig in the early morning, even in the heat of the day. They are supposed to take what they find to the authorities at Boulak, but . . .' Again the shrug of the shoulders she was beginning to know so well.

Digging into the donkey's pannier he produced two candles and a small flare. Flourishing them he bowed. 'You would like to see inside one of the tombs now?'

She nodded. The tombs would be blessedly cool after the endless sun. She reached for a bottle of water and Hassan hastened to pour some out for her. The water was warm and brackish but she drank gratefully, then she dipped her handkerchief in the cup and wiped her face with it.

When she turned to follow Hassan towards one of the square doorways in the cliff, there was a sketchbook under her arm.

'We will start here,' he waved at one of the entrances. 'It is the tomb of Rameses VI. This has been open since the days of the ancients.'

'You have brought other people here before. You know them all as well as a local guide?' she asked as she made to follow him.

'Of course.' He nodded. 'I have heard the guides from the villages a thousand times. I no longer need them.'

As they entered the passageway Louisa stared into the darkness completely blinded after the brilliant light outside. Then slowly her eyes began to acclimatise. The flickering light of Hassan's candle barely lit the walls of the long passage in which they found

37

themselves, but from its pale glow she could see the breathtaking riot of figures and colours stretching into the distance. Then he lit the flare and in the streaming flame and smoke she could see hieroglyphs and gods and kings covering the walls and ceiling in rich colours. Standing still on the steep sandy floor of the passage she stared round in amazement and delight. 'I had no idea,' she gasped. 'No idea at all that it could be so . . .' she fumbled for words, '. . . so wonderful!'

'Nice?' Hassan was watching her.

'Very, very nice.' She took a few paces forward, her shoes slipping on the steeply sloping passage. 'Hassan, it is more wonderful than I had ever dreamt.'

The intense silence of the place was overwhelming but far from being cooler in the darkness the tomb was hot and airless as an oven. She moved across to the wall and rested a hand for a moment on the paint-covered stone. 'It would be very hard to copy this. Even to convey this wonder. This mystery. I could never do it. My sketches will have to be so impressionistic, so inadequate.' She shrugged helplessly.

'Your pictures are very good.' He raised the flare higher so the light shone a little further into the darkness.

'How do you know? You haven't seen any,' she retorted over her shoulder.

'I saw. When I was loading the donkey the wind blew open the book.' He followed her with a grin. 'I could not help but see. Here. Be careful. There are steps now going down a long way.'

Behind them the small square of daylight at the entrance to the passage abruptly disappeared as they began to descend a long flight of roughly excavated steps. The candlelight condensed on the multi-coloured walls, then as they reached the pillared chamber at the bottom it spread and faded again, mixing and losing itself in the vast darkness. A further series of passages led deeper and deeper into the dark, then at last they reached the burial chamber at the bottom. Louisa stopped with a gasp. Soaring overhead in the flickering shadows two huge strangely elongated figures spanned the ceiling above her head.

'Nut. Goddess of the sky.' Hassan was standing beside her, holding the flare high and she found herself suddenly intensely aware of his closeness to her. She glanced sideways. He was gazing up at the figures, his face a silhouette in the soft light.

He turned and caught her staring at him. She blushed. 'May I have the flare?'

'Of course, Sitt Louisa.' For half a second their hands touched as her fingers closed round the wooden shaft. Then abruptly she stepped away from him. 'Tell me about the goddess of the sky.'

Anna woke with a start to find the light in her cabin still on, the diary lying open on her chest. Daylight poured through the slatted shutters, sending bright narrow wedges of light onto the floor and up the wall. Leaping out of bed she reached across to the window and slid the shutters back. Outside, the river was a brilliant blue. A Nile cruiser was making its way upstream, whilst across the broad stretch of water she could see the palm trees on the distant bank, a strip of brilliant green fields and beyond them in the distance a line of low hazy mountains, pink and ochre in the early morning sunlight.

Dressing quickly in a blue shift she made her way out between tables and chairs in the lounge onto the deserted deck and stared round in delight. It was already hot on the afterdeck, but under the awning it was shady. She walked to the rail and leant on it, staring at the palm trees on the far side of the river. The cruiser was out of sight now, and for a moment the river was empty. It was several minutes before she could bring herself to turn her back on the view and head for the dining room and breakfast. At the door she met Serena, Charley's cabinmate, who the night before had been sitting at the next-door table. About forty-five, slim and attractive with short dark hair and huge green eyes she gave Anna a cheerful smile. 'See you later,' she said by way of hello and goodbye. She held the door open for Anna, then disappeared in the direction of the cabins. In the dining room only Charley was sitting at the table they had all shared the night before.

'Good morning.' Anna sat down near her. 'How did you sleep?'

'Not a wink.' Charley scowled. She was nursing a cup of black coffee. She sighed. 'I hate flying and I hate boats.'

Anna hid an astonished smile. She resisted the temptation to ask why in that case Charley had come on such a holiday. 'Can I get you something from the buffet?' Behind them the serving table was laden with cereals and fruits, cheese, cold meat and eggs.

Charley shook her head. Her long hair was caught back in a ponytail this morning and she was wearing a tee-shirt and jeans 'Just ignore me. I'll improve when I've had a couple of these.' She gestured at the coffee.

'Have the others had breakfast?' Anna eyed the empty places, already cleared by the waiters.

Charley nodded. 'All early birds.' She gave Anna a sideways glance. 'Andy and I are an item, we've been together for several months.'

Anna watched while the waiter poured her coffee then she stood up ready to go to the buffet. 'I thought perhaps you were.' She smiled. Charley's comment was a clear warning shot across the bows. Yet hadn't Andy said he was unattached? Piling up fruit and cheese and a delicate crumbling croissant onto her plate she turned back to the table. Charley had gone.

Returning to her cabin to collect her sun hat, glasses and guidebook, Anna stood for a moment staring round. She had left the diary on the bedside table. Hesitating briefly she swung her suitcase down from the top of the locker where she had stowed it and put the diary inside. Locking it, she lifted it back into place. As she was collecting a hairbrush and some sun cream from the dressing table to toss into her bag her eye was caught by the scent bottle. Should she have locked that away as well? She hesitated, glancing at her watch. They had been told to meet in the boat's reception area at six forty-five to leave at seven a.m. She did not want to miss the bus. The decision was simple. She would take it with her. Picking up the bottle she wrapped it in one of the fine silk scarves she used to knot back her hair and tucked the small scarlet bundle into her bag. Then, turning, she let herself out of the cabin.

A small coach collected them from the river bank and drove them to the ferry in Luxor. To her surprise as she sat down alone towards

40

the back of the coach and waited, staring eagerly out of the window, Andy came and sat down beside her, wedging his broad frame into the narrow seats with a familiarity which, she had to admit, she did not find entirely unpleasant. 'So. How are you this morning? Excited?'

In spite of herself she glanced round for Charley. Not seeing her she nodded. 'I'm fine. Very excited. Yes.' She recognised all the faces now. Near her were Sally Booth and Ben Forbes. And Serena, sitting next to an elderly lady in a cerise trouser suit. Then two more couples whose names she didn't know. And at the back of the bus on his own she saw Toby Hayward.

'Did you bring your precious diary?' Andy was looking at the tote bag on her knee.

She shook her head. 'It's locked in my suitcase.' She grinned at him. 'I'm sure it's all right, Andy. There wouldn't be anyone around who would want it. Really.'

He was still staring at her bag and she glanced down to see what interested him so much. Her scarf had worked free and the little scent bottle was lying on top of her guidebook in full view.

'Souvenirs already?' He smiled at her. 'Don't let the peddlers badger you into buying anything you don't really want. They're awfully persuasive.'

She shook her head, feeling suddenly defensive. He had clearly not recognised it as antique. Wrapping the bottle up again she pushed it to the bottom of the bag. 'I won't. I'm good at saying "no".' She caught sight of his raised eyebrow out of the corner of her eye and chose to ignore it.

As the coach lurched up the track from the river and onto the narrow dusty road she stared out of the window at the squat, square mud-brick houses on either side. They seemed to rise to two or three storeys then they would stop, unexpectedly, as though only half finished, with yards of metal reinforcements projecting from the top, like clusters of TV aerials. Huddled together they gave the impression of shanty towns clustered around the outskirts of the city itself, all built in a uniform yellowy-grey colour but some brightly painted, with wild designs and patterns, a contrast to the sandy dust which was everywhere, and many further decorated with the rugs thrown across the sills to air. Some had nothing more than a few palms or straw mats strewn across the top, instead of roofs, and all over the place Anna saw rows of amphora-like clay

41

pots lying on the rooftops or around the doors. She shook her head. 'I still can't believe I'm here, to be honest.'

He laughed. 'You are here, believe me. So, did you read any more of the diary last night?'

Anna nodded. 'A bit. I found the section where she went to the Valley of the Kings. There was a wonderful description of the valley. It was empty. Deserted. There was no one there with her accept her dragoman, Hassan. They sat and picnicked on a Persian rug.'

Andy laughed. 'I'm afraid it won't be like that for us. It will be packed with tourists. I've heard a lot of people say there are so many crowds there that it spoils it. No atmosphere, or not much. And no dragomen!'

'It's such a lovely term. I should love my own dragoman!' She clutched at the back of the seat in front of them as the bus hit a pothole and then turned sharply to the right, hooting furiously as it hurtled out onto the busy main road.

'Perhaps I can be of service?'

She smiled at him. 'I don't think Charley would approve,' she said gently. 'Where is she, by the way?'

'Up front somewhere. With Joe and Sally. She's been chatting up Omar.' The lurching of the bus threw him against her for a moment. 'Have you got your camera?'

She nodded. 'Photography is one of my passions. I'm not likely to forget that.'

'Good. You'll have to take a picture of me in front of some great pharaoh so I can brag about my trip at home.'

They climbed out of the coach to queue for the short ferry ride across the Nile and found another identical though older vehicle waiting for them on the other side. When Anna looked round for Andy as they climbed aboard, she saw that Charley was by his side. For this second part of the journey she found herself next to Serena.

'My first visit to Egypt.' The dark-haired woman was wearing a cool cheesecloth skirt and blouse of brilliant contrasting blues and greens.

'Mine too.' Anna nodded. 'You're a friend of Charley's, I gather?'

Serena laughed. 'For my sins. We're sort of flatmates in London. Well, in fact she rents a room in my flat. It was my idea to come out to Egypt and before I knew it Charley was coming too. She knew how long I'd wanted to come out here and I suppose I was so enthusiastic and excited I sold her the idea.' She shook her head

42

ruefully. 'She and Andy had been going out together on and off for several months and when he heard about it he half jokingly said he'd come as well. Charley was over the moon and he realised he might have committed himself a bit more seriously than he intended so he asked the Booths and there we were, a veritable wagon train!' She sighed. 'I'm sorry. Does that sound as though I'm complaining?'

Anna shook her head. 'I should think it's more fun coming with friends than on your own.'

'Perhaps.' Serena did not sound too certain. There was a moment of silence as the driver climbed into his seat and leant forward to turn on the ignition. The bus gave a shudder and settled down into a violent but steady rattle. 'You're on your own?' Serena's enquiry was almost lost in the noise of grinding gears.

'Newly divorced and stepping out for independence.' Anna had a feeling that her jaunty tone had a wistful ring to it. She hoped not.

'Good for you.' Serena nodded. 'My partner died four years ago. For a while it was like losing half of my own body. We had been so close there was a physical loss; part of me had died with him. But it gets better.' She gave a big smile. 'Sorry. That's a bit intense for a first conversation, but at least you know there's someone who understands if you need a chat.'

'Thank you.' Anna was astonished by the wave of warmth she felt for the other woman. It wasn't the same, of course. Felix wasn't dead. And her feelings for him – had they ever been so intense that she had felt him to be part of her? She wasn't sure they had ever been that close.

Conversation was impossible above the noise of the engine and they turned their attention to the passing countryside. Apart from the cars and buses the landscape was, Anna realised, exactly as Louisa had described it a hundred and forty years before. And, with its intense air of timelessness, it might for all she knew have been the same fourteen hundred years before as well.

She stared out of her window at the intense green of this narrow strip of fertile fields, watered by narrow canals, and at the shade of the eucalyptus trees and palms which formed darker patches on the dusty road. She caught glimpses of water buffalo and donkeys and even camels; of men dressed in *galabiyyas*, boys dressed in jeans and some on bicycles, but most perched on the rumps of small

43

trotting donkeys, whose ribs stuck out like harp strings. And there too were the fields of sugar cane and small allotment-like squares of onion and cabbages. Amongst them were scattered small, shabby papyrus and alabaster factories.

They stopped briefly to get out of the bus and photograph the Colossi of Memnon, two massive figures carved out of pink quartzite, standing alone on the bare rubbled ground, then they were back into the coach and heading once again towards the edge of the green fertile countryside. At last they were nearing the range of mountains she had seen from the boat in the early morning light. As they drew closer they changed colour. They were becoming less brown, less pink, more dazzling as the sun reflected off the dusty stone and the sand. They passed villages nestling into the cliffs with dark holes amongst the mud-brick houses which could have been modern or ancient, caves or dwellings or antiquities.

It was hard to tell, Anna realised, if something was two years old or two thousand. Here there was no green to be seen at all. The ground was everywhere a rubble of rocks and shale and scree.

The bus park in the valley dispelled all her visions of Louisa's lonely visit to the tombs. As Andy had warned it was packed. Acres of coaches, hundreds of tourists and round them, like wasps round a jam pot, dozens and dozens of eager noisy men, dressed in colourful *galabiyyas* and headscarves, holding out postcards and statuettes of Bast, Tut and souvenirs galore.

'Ignore them and follow me.' Omar clapped his hands. 'I will buy your tickets and photograph permits then you can explore alone or stay with me and I will take you into some of the tombs.'

Anna looked around in dismay. It was nothing like the place she had imagined. Nothing at all. For a moment she stood still, overwhelmed, then she was swept into a loosely gathered queue making its way alongside the barren cliffs, past a line of colourful booths and stalls where yet more souvenirs were being hawked. Andy and Charley, and Serena had disappeared. For a moment she wondered if she should try to find them, then she decided against it. With a smile she took her ticket from Omar and resolutely she set off to find her way around on her own.

The narrow valley absorbed the sunlight, turning it into a blinding oven. The mountains all around them were huge, ochre-coloured, awesome, rugged and uneven and deeply fissured. It was a landscape utterly untouched by time. The square entrances to the tombs were black enticing shadows scattered over the cliff faces. Some were barred with gates. Many were open.

'You look bemused, Anna, love.' Ben Forbes was beside her suddenly. 'Want to venture in with me?' His broad-brimmed hat flopped idiosyncratically to one side and the green canvas bag hanging from his left shoulder looked as though it had seen quite a few expeditions in the past. He had his guidebook already open. 'Rameses IX. This is a particularly splendid tomb, I believe. It is as good a place as any to start.' He led the way down a sloping ramp where they joined the queue of people wanting to go in.

'Interesting man, Andy Watson. We were both a bit late applying for places on this holiday and as fate would have it there was only a double cabin left so we're sharing. I don't find him irresistible, but I can see the ladies might.' He had taken off his glasses and was polishing them with his handkerchief.

'Yes.' She nodded.

'Seems to have taken quite a shine to you.'

'Oh, I don't think so. He's just being friendly.'

Ben nodded. 'Probably.' There was a moment's silence as they shuffled forward in the queue. 'I sat next to Charley on the bus.'

Anna glanced at him. 'His girlfriend?'

'According to her, yes. Forgive me poking my nose in, Anna, especially at this early stage, but I've been on cruises before and ours is an exceptionally small boat.'

Anna raised an eyebrow. 'Am I being warned off?'

'I think the lady could turn a bit nasty, if provoked.'

Sighing, Anna shrugged. 'Isn't it a shame when one can't just be friends with someone of the opposite sex? I don't want to get in anyone's way. He was friendly. I don't know anyone. That's all.'

'You know me.' Ben gave her a warm smile, his eyes crinkling into deep folds at the corners. 'Not so attractive, I grant you. Not so young. But infinitely less dangerous. Come on.' He touched her elbow lightly.

They were in front of a large square entrance, the heavily barred gate standing open but overseen by watchful guards, who solemnly took their tickets, tore off one corner and returned them to each tourist. Slowly, shoulder to shoulder with people of every nationality, they shuffled down the long slope into the darkness, staring at the walls on either side of them, and at the ceiling over their heads. Every available surface area was covered from top to bottom in

45

hieroglyphics and in pictures of pharaohs and gods – the overwhelming colours ochre and lemon yellow, green, lapis and aqua-
marine and black and white, stunningly preserved and covered
now in plexiglass. She couldn't take her eyes off them. So many
books, so many pictures – ever since she was a child she had seen
them, as everyone has, but never had she realised the overwhelming beauty and power they would present, or the sheer scale of
them. To her amazement she found she could ignore the people
milling round her, ignore the shouts and excited talk, the high-
pitched competitive commentaries of the guides, the laughter, the
irritations of people who, having come so far, to this wonderful,
awesome place, proceeded to gossip and talk amongst themselves,
seemingly oblivious to the beauty and history around them. The
incredible silence was overwhelming. It drowned out the noise. It
was all encompassing.

The further they walked into the tomb, the hotter it got. Used
to British and European caves, which grow colder as you penetrate
further in, Anna found it a shock. The darkness did not give respite.
The silence and heat grew more and more dense.

On they moved, through three successive corridors, towards a
huge pillared hall and then, at last into the burial chamber itself,
with nothing but a rectangular pit to show where the sarcophagus
would have been.

Ben glanced down at Anna. 'Well, what do you think?'

She shook her head, 'I'm speechless.'

He laughed. 'Not an affliction which seems to affect many people
down here.' Slowly they turned and started making their way back
towards the daylight. 'What about going to see Tutankhamen's
tomb next? He's back in there, you know, minus his treasure, of
course.' As they came out once more into the sunlight, he gestured
towards one of the smaller entrances. 'We're lucky. I think they
close his tomb every so often to give it a rest from all the visitors
who come here. According to my guidebook it's small and relatively
low key compared with some of the others, because he died young
and no one was expecting his death. He might even have been
murdered.'

Once more they queued, once more a corner was removed from
their ticket and slowly they made their way into the darkness. This
tomb was indeed very different from the last one they had seen.
Besides being smaller, it was simpler; there was no decoration,

46

but there was something else. Anna stopped, allowing the people around her to pass on, unnoticed. Staring round she let her eyes become accustomed to the low level of lighting. Ben had moved on and for a moment she was alone. Then she realised what it was that was so strange. This tomb was cold.

She shivered, conscious of the goosepimples on her bare arms. 'Ben?' She couldn't see him. A crowd of visitors were making their way into the inner chamber. She turned round, half expecting to find someone standing behind her. There was no one there. 'Ben?' Her voice was muffled in the silence.

Confused, she put her hand to her head, conscious suddenly of a group of tourists speaking Italian loudly, happily, as they filled the entrance behind her; in a moment they were all around her and she found herself being swept on in their wake.

She frowned. The tomb was no longer cold; it was as hot as the other they had visited and she could hardly breath. Suddenly panic-stricken, she pushed her way forward. She still couldn't see Ben. She wasn't usually claustrophobic, but the walls seemed to be closing in on her.

The people near her were anonymous black shadows, faceless in the dark. Her mouth had gone dry.

She stared round frantically and diving for the next entrance she abruptly found herself standing in the burial chamber itself, looking down at the open eyes of the young king Tutankhamen. He lay gazing up at the ceiling of his dark, hot tomb, disdaining the presence of the peasants who had come to stare at him, divested of the riches which had bolstered his royalty, but still he was awe-inspiring. How many of the people standing round him, she wondered, were as suddenly and as intensely aware as she was of the emaciated, broken body of the young king, lying inside that gilded wooden coffin? She shivered again, but this time not with cold.

'Anna?' Ben appeared beside her, his camera in his hand. 'Isn't he amazing?'

She nodded. The bag on her shoulder had grown very heavy. Why had she not taken out her own camera? She swung the soft leather holdall to the floor and was pulling open the zip when a strange wave of dizziness hit her. With a gasp, she straightened, leaving the bag to subside into the dust at her feet, spilling its contents over the ground.

'Are you OK?' Ben had caught sight of her out of the corner of his eye. He stooped, and hastily began pushing everything back into the bag for her. She saw a flash of scarlet as the silk-wrapped scent bottle was scooped out of sight, then his arm was round her shoulders.

'I felt weird suddenly.' She pressed her hands to her face. 'I'm all right. I must have bent over too quickly to get my camera. Too much excitement, and too early a start, I expect.' She forced herself to smile.

'Perhaps that is a sign that it's time to go and have a rest up in the fresh air.' He took her arm, glancing over his shoulder. 'These tombs are a bit overpowering, to my mind.'

'There's something down here, isn't there?' Anna could feel the perspiration on her back icing over. She was shivering again. 'I thought all that business about the "curse of the mummy's tomb" was rubbish, but there is an atmosphere. I don't like it.'

A shout of laughter near her from a party of Germans, and the earnest mumble from a group of Japanese photographers in the treasury beyond the burial chamber, seemed to contradict her words, but it made no difference. 'I do want to leave. I'm sorry.'

'No problem. Come on.'

Grateful for the strength of his arm she stumbled after him, back towards the entrance corridor and the blinding sunlight outside.

Once sitting in the shade of the visitors' resting area, she felt better. They both drank some bottled water, but she could see Ben was longing to move on. 'Go without me, please. I will be all right soon. I shall just sit for a few minutes longer, then I'll follow.'

He gave her a searching look. 'Are you sure?'

'Of course.'

She couldn't see where it was that Hassan had taken Louisa and pitched her a makeshift shelter on a soft Persian rug. She desperately wanted to get away from the crowds, to find the place and to experience the silence as Louisa had done. She stood for a moment shading her eyes, looking up one of the white, dazzling paths which led away from the noisy centre of the valley. Could that have been where they went? Glancing over her shoulder she saw Ben disappearing with another queue into a tomb on the far side of the well-trodden centre of the valley. Near him she recognised one or two other people from their party. She hesitated, then, resolutely turning her back on them, she began to make her way up the empty track past a dusty fingerpost labelling yet more tombs, and,

48

her shoes slipping on the dust and stones, she scrambled on upwards away from the crowds.

Above her the rock martins circled and swooped into holes in the cliffs but apart from that nothing moved. Almost immediately the sound of the crowds behind her diminished and disappeared. The heat and the silence were overwhelming. She stopped, staring round, scared for a moment that she might lose her bearings, but the path was clearly marked. Just empty. The colours of the rock were monochrome. Blinding. The sky the most brilliant blue she had ever seen.

Somewhere near her she heard footsteps suddenly, and the sound of scraping on the limestone. She frowned, shading her eyes as she scanned the cliff face. There was no one there. It was no more than a shifting of the sands.

But her mood had changed again and once more she began to feel uneasy. After the noise and bustle and colour of the main valley – the crowds, the shouting guides, the raised voices in a dozen different languages – this intense silence was unnerving. It was the silence of the grave.

In spite of the heat she found herself shivering again. She had the strangest feeling that she was being watched, a weird sensation that there was someone near her. She stared up at the cliff face, narrowing her eyes against the glare. There were other tombs in this direction. She had seen them on the plan. But no one seemed to be visiting them. Perhaps they were closed as the greater part of the tombs were, to protect them from the massive tourist interest. She took a few steps further up the path, rounding another corner. The cliffs were arid, silent, but for the birds. Far above she could see a dark speck against the blinding sky. Perhaps that was a kite, like the one Louisa had seen. The feeling that there was someone there at her shoulder was so intense suddenly that she swung round. Tiny eddies of dust swirled momentarily round her ankles in an undetectable breath of wind, then the air was still again.

Stubbornly she moved on. It was round here that Hassan had pitched the shelter for Louisa, she was sure of it. Here they had sat together on the rug and she had opened her sketchbook and, unscrewing her water jar, had begun one of her paintings of the rugged hillside.

'Do I gather you too prefer to be away from crowds?'

The voice, a few feet from her, shocked her out of her reverie.

49

She spun round. Toby Hayward was standing nearby. He swung his canvas satchel off his shoulder onto the ground and wiped his face on his forearm. 'I'm sorry, I didn't mean to startle you. I didn't see you until I came round the corner.'

Astonished at how relieved she was to find out the presence she had felt was that of a real person, she managed a smile. 'I was dreaming.'

'The right place for it.' He stood for a moment in silence. 'I find it hard to catch the atmosphere with the crowds down there,' he said suddenly. 'So many of them, and they snap endless pictures, but don't look. Have you noticed? Their eyes are closed.'

'The camera remembers. They are afraid they won't,' Anna said quietly. 'We all do it.' Her own camera was still in her bag.

'I'm sure you look as well.'

The anger in his voice disturbed her. 'I try to.' She decided to try a different tack. Her quest, after all, was not secret. 'I was trying to picture this place a hundred years ago, before it was commercialised.'

'It's always been commercialised. They probably brought guided tours here before the corpses were cold.' Folding his arms he stared up at the cliffs. 'Did I hear you right last night? You are a relation of Louisa Shelley?' No apology for eavesdropping, she noticed.

'I'm her great-great-granddaughter, yes.'

'She was one of the few Victorians who empathised with the Egyptian soul.' He had narrowed his eyes, still studying the rock formations above their heads.

'How do you know that's how she felt?' Anna stared at him curiously.

'From her painting. They have a set of watercolours at the Travellers' Club.'

'I didn't know that.'

He nodded abruptly. 'On the staircase. I've often studied them. She lingers over details. She's not embarrassed by form or feature. And she's never patronising. She uses a wonderful depth of colour unlike Roberts. He sees all this –' he waved his arm at the cliffs – 'as one tonal range. She sees the shadows, the wonderful textures.'

Anna looked at him with a new interest. 'You talk like an artist.'

'Artist!' He snorted. 'Stupid word. If you mean a painter, yes, I'm a painter.' He was still staring up at the cliff and she took the opportunity of looking at him for a moment, surreptitiously, taking

50

in the rugged features, the thatch of unruly greying-blond hair beneath the faded blue sun hat.

'Louisa loved Egypt. I'm reading her diary, and it's apparent on every page.' She gave a wistful smile. 'I almost envy those Victorian women. They had so much to contend with and yet they persevered. They followed their dreams. They worked so hard for them –' She broke off in mid-sentence, aware suddenly that he had turned his attention from the cliff and was watching her intently. She met his gaze and held it for a minute, but it was she who looked away first.

'It sounds to me as though you wished you too had had to work hard for a dream,' he said quietly.

She shrugged. 'Perhaps. But I'm not the intrepid type, sadly.' How could she be when she had remained so meekly in her marriage and at home?

'No?' He was still looking at her thoughtfully.

'No.' She smiled suddenly. 'Or not until today. Breaking away from the group and coming up here was pretty intrepid for me.'

He laughed and suddenly his face looked much younger. 'Then we must encourage your intrepidness. Which tombs did your great-great-grandmother visit? Not young King Tut, obviously.'

'No.' Anna's smile died.

Watching her, he raised an eyebrow. 'So, what have I said now?'

'Nothing.'

'Something about Tutankhamen's tomb?'

She shook her head. He was intuitive, she would grant him that. 'I was in there. A little while ago. Something strange happened.'

'Strange?'

She shook her head. 'Claustrophobia, I suppose. Nothing really. Only it made me need to get away from everyone and come up here.'

'And I spoilt your solitude. I'm sorry.'

'No. No. I didn't mean that.' She shrugged helplessly. 'The trouble is, it didn't work. The feeling, whatever it was, followed me up here.'

Again he gave her that long, disconcertingly direct look. There was no judgement in it. He wasn't laughing at her. On the contrary he was considering her words, mulling them over, scanning her face for clues. 'I think this whole valley could have that effect on people,' he said at last. 'In spite of the numbers of tourists who

51

come here, the atmosphere is extraordinary. It is uncomfortable. Have you met Serena Canfield yet? She was sitting next to me at dinner last night. You should talk to her if you're a sensitive. She is into Ancient Egyptian magic and stuff which might appeal to you. She has read all the books about star gates and Orion and Sirius.'

Anna raised an eyebrow. Was he being dismissive of her, gently taking the mickey or was he making the suggestion in good faith? It was hard to tell. Those steadfast eyes, the colour as clear as water, were impossible to read.

'I might just do that,' she said with a small touch of defiance. 'There is room for so much that is strange and out of the ordinary in Egypt.'

He shrugged, but the angling of his head could have been a nod of agreement. 'What I do hope is that she doesn't go too near our revered guide, who is a devout Muslim and will not hear a word about all that stuff on his ship. He has enough trouble with the ''legends'' of the pharaohs. Did you notice that? He will not allow them even to be history.'

Anna shook her head, laughing. 'I had no idea there was so much ideological conflict going on on the boat. It will make for an extraordinarily interesting trip. I have spoken to Serena. She sat next to me on the bus, but we didn't talk about Sirius. That aspect of Egypt's history seems to have passed me by. My interest stems from travel books, people like Lawrence Durrell, my mother's books about archaeology, even school where we had a teacher who was passionate about pyramids.'

'And Louisa.'

'And Louisa.'

'Can I see her diary one day?' He held her gaze once more with that disconcerting directness which seemed to be his trademark.

She looked away first. 'Of course you can.'

'Now?' He raised an eyebrow hopefully.

'I'm sorry.' She shook her head. 'I didn't bring it with me. It's on the boat.'

'Of course. Silly me.' He swung his bag back onto his shoulder. 'OK, I think I'm heading back down to the valley to see another tomb or two before we leave. I'll go and find Omar and plague him with some deep philosophical questions! Will you be all right on your own?'

She wasn't sure whether the question was posed out of real concern or was a subtle way of telling her that he did not expect her to walk back with him and indeed, no sooner had he spoken than he turned and began to lope back down the path. In seconds he had disappeared behind the rocks.

The silence and the heat flowed back over her in a heavy curtain. Standing stock still she found she wanted to call him back. The loneliness in the valley was intense. Shading her eyes, she stared round for a moment scanning the cliff face then she turned and looked after him. At her feet a few pieces of shale rattled down the path. The sound emphasised the quiet. She was trying to recall the diary, the picture of the valley as Louisa had seen it, trying to visualise the rug, the shelter, the simple companionship of the man and the woman as Louisa laid out her painting things, but she couldn't bring the picture into focus. The shadowy image of Louisa and her parasol, the click of the donkeys' hoofs on the stone, the tap of the paintbrush against the rim of the water pot had all faded into the silence. She bit her lip, fighting the urge to run after Toby. This was ridiculous. What was there to be afraid of? The silence? The emptiness after the crowds in the valley bottom? She cast one last look over her shoulder up at the sun-baked cliffs and then she began to retrace her steps, hoping at every moment to catch sight of Toby ahead of her on the path. Twice she glanced over her shoulder again and then suddenly panic overwhelmed her. She lengthened her stride and before she knew it she was running back down towards the valley as fast as she could, slipping and sliding in her anxiety to catch up with Toby. It didn't matter what he had said, she didn't want to be alone in that spot for one second longer.

But the path was empty. There was no sign of him. Arriving at last in the valley bottom once more amongst the crowds and the shouting guides she made her way panting to the shaded resting place where groups of other tourists were sitting, exhausted by the intense heat which seemed to pool in the valley. Closing her eyes she took a deep breath, trying to steady the thudding of her heart under her ribs. There was no sign of Toby anywhere.

It was Andy who found her. Sitting down heavily on the bench next to her he took off his hat and fanned his face with it. 'Hot enough for you?'

53

She nodded, struggling to steady her voice. 'I thought the tombs would be cool. In the darkness.'

'More like tandoori ovens.' He grinned. 'Are you enjoying yourself? You look lonely sitting here. I thought Ben was taking care of you.'

'I don't need taking care of, thank you!' Her indignation was only half feigned. 'But he was with me, yes. He's a nice man.'

'And so am I.' Andy raised an eyebrow. 'Can I escort you into another hell hole? We gather for our picnic in about an hour.' He glanced at his watch. 'Then this afternoon it's off to the Ramasseum and Hatchepsut's temple. There's no slacking on this trip!'

A shadow fell across his face. Charley was standing there looking down at him. 'I am sure Anna doesn't need an escort. If she needs someone to hold her hand in the dark, Omar can do it. That's his job, after all.' Her voice was acid.

Anna stood up hastily. 'I don't actually need an escort of any sort. Please, don't worry.' She grabbed her bag and slung it on her shoulder. 'I'll see you back on the bus, no doubt.' She did not wait to see their reaction, plunging back into the sunlight to make her way across the sandy path towards the shadow of another tomb entrance.

It was only when she was standing in the queue, her guidebook in her hand that she realised Andy had followed her.

'I'm sorry. That was embarrassing.'

'Not at all. Charley is right. I don't need an escort.' She glanced behind them. 'Where is she?'

'Still over there in the shade.' The queue shuffled a few steps closer to the entrance. 'Egyptology is not her thing. She feels she has seen enough for one day.'

'I see.' Anna glanced at him sideways, unsure whether she should feel triumphant or sorry for the other woman. She liked Andy. His good-natured friendliness had done much to put her at her ease amongst so many strangers. Not that they seemed like strangers now. It was her first day in Egypt and yet she felt as though she had known them for a very long time.

'Hello there.' As though to confirm her thought Ben emerged from the entrance in front of them. His face was pink with heat, a marked contrast to the whiteness of his hair. As the sun hit him he smacked his hat back onto his head and grinned at them hugely. 'One of the best tombs, this. Magnificent! The mind just boggles at the thought of how much work has gone into it all, and how many men it took to do it.' His face sobered at little. 'Charley! Are you going in too?'

Charley was suddenly beside them. Her face was tense, her eyes smouldering with anger. 'Yes, I'm going in too. Stupid thick Charley is actually interested.'

'Stay here!' Andy's hand on Anna's wrist was like an iron clamp as she turned to move away. Startled, she frowned. 'Andy, please –'

'No. I asked you to visit this tomb with me. I meant it. If Charley wants to come too, then that's up to her. She has a ticket, the same as the rest of us.'

Charley's face was red with fury. 'That's right. And I'm coming in.'

'Please do.' Andy's smile was, at least on the surface, as affable as ever.

When Anna glanced round for Ben, he had gone.

As they walked down into the darkness Anna spotted Omar ahead of them with some half-dozen of the other passengers from their boat who had elected to stay with him for the tour. With relief she hurried to catch up with him, aware that Andy was still at her side. Over the next twenty minutes or so as Omar talked to them about burial chambers and cartouches, *The Book of the Dead* and *The Book of Gates*, slave labour and the gods of death and retribution she slowly managed to distance herself from Andy and Charley in the darkness. By the time they had reached the inner pillared hall she had lost sight of them entirely.

It was as she was walking back, her concentration on the ceiling with its wonderful paintings that her arm was seized. 'What do you think you are playing at? You hardly know him!' Charley's hiss in her ear was full of venom. 'Why? Why are you doing it?'

Anna turned in astonishment. 'Doing what? Look, Charley, you've got the wrong end of the stick. I'm not trying to do anything, I promise.'

'You're encouraging him!'

'I'm not. Andy is a kind man. He has seen that I'm on my own and he is trying to make me feel welcome. So is Ben.' She paused for a fraction of a second. 'And Toby. And your friend, Serena. That is all it is. They are nice people and I appreciate their kindness.'

She glanced round hoping to see Andy nearby, but there was no sign of him. A long queue of people was shuffling past them as

55

they stood at the centre of the corridor leading from the depths of the tomb back towards the light. Someone jostled her slightly and she stepped back. 'We're in the way, Charley. We have to move on with the others.'

'I'll move on. As for you, you can get lost!' The viciousness of Charley's remark left her speechless. For a moment she didn't react and Charley, hurrying swiftly ahead was soon out of sight behind a sea of slowly processing backs. Anna shivered. The attack had been so swift and unexpectedly unpleasant that she wasn't sure what to do. She wanted to run after her, to argue, to defend herself, but at the same time some defiant corner of her mind was telling her to take no notice, to talk to Andy and, as long as she found him attractive, and she realised suddenly she did find him extremely attractive, to give Charley a run for her money. It was only a small corner of her mind though. A far larger portion was all for keeping the peace.

3

O keep not captive my soul. O keep not ward
over my shade
but let a way be opened for my soul and for
my shade
and let them see the great God in the shrine on
the day of judgement . . .

*Rejected by their gods, and fleeing retribution the two priests
sleep in the darkness of the tomb. The scent of oil of cedar and
myrrh and cinnamon hangs in the hot dry air. There is still
no sound. Far above them the cliff is the haunt of kite and
vulture. The call of the jackal rends the night sky as the stars
fade and the sun disc returns from its voyage beneath the earth
to rise again over the eastern desert. In the darkness time is
without meaning or form.*

*On the shelf between the pillar and the wall the small bottle
sealed with blood lies hidden. Inside, the life-giving potion,
dedicated to the gods, made sacred by the sun, thickens and
grows black.*

Tired and dusty they returned to the boat late in the evening to be greeted by fragrant hot towels, handed out at the door to the reception area by one of the crewmen from a steaming metal platter. Next they were given fruit juice and then at last their cabin keys. Anna made her way to her cabin without glancing round to see if Andy and Charley were nearby. On the coach she had sat at the back with Joe, relieved to be excused from talking by his instant somnolence. In her cabin she threw her bag on the bed, and as exhausted as Joe had been, she kicked off her shoes and began to pull off her dress.

Abruptly she stopped. Her skin was prickling. The cabin had grown cold and for a split second she had the feeling that there was someone in there close to her; watching her.

'This is stupid.' She said the words out loud, staring at herself in the mirror. The cabin was a scant ten feet by eight. The tiny shower had room for barely one person. There couldn't be anyone there. She pushed the door open with her foot and it swung back to reveal basin and shower, fresh towels ready on the rail.

She glanced up suddenly at her case on top of the cupboard. Had it been moved? She didn't think so. With a sigh she shook her head. She was just very tired. She had imagined it. It wasn't cold at all. On the contrary, she felt as hot and sticky as she had on the bus, after her day in the sun. Peeling off her dress she shook it to remove the creases and dust and hung it on the door, then shaking her hair free and sweeping it back off her face she stepped into the shower and turned on the blissfully cool water.

The only empty chair at her table when she arrived at dinner was between Ben and Joe. Slipping into it with a sympathetic smile at the now wakeful Joe Anna saw Charley link her arm through Andy's and give it a proprietorial squeeze.

'So, how did you enjoy day one?' Ben said quietly in her ear as he poured her a glass of wine.

'Wonderful.' She smiled at him and caught his wink. 'I could get used to all this very easily.'

'And so you shall. But today is not over yet. Did you see the noticeboard outside the dining room? Omar is going to give us a talk in the lounge after dinner, then the boat leaves at about eleven, so when we wake up in the morning we shall be well on our way up the Nile.'

There was a sudden roar of laughter from one of the other tables and Anna turned. Glancing up Toby caught her eye. With a sardonic wink he raised his glass and mouthed a toast at her, but in the general noise of conversation and laughter she couldn't hear it. She raised her own glass back and saw Andy turn quickly to see who it was she was smiling at. He frowned. 'So how did your visit today compare with Louisa Shelley's?' He leant across his plate, raising his voice so that it reached her across the table. 'Has the valley changed a great deal?'

'Out of all recognition in some ways.' She glanced from him to Charley and back. 'In others not at all. There really is a timelessness, isn't *there*?'

'As there is all over Egypt,' Ben put in.

'Louisa had the valley all to herself, of course. It must still be wonderful when all the tourists go and it's empty. That's a problem all over the world nowadays, I suppose. There are so few places left where one can get away from other people.'

'The cry of a true misanthrope.' Andy grinned at her.

She felt herself blushing. 'No, I like people, but I like to be able to get away from them too, especially when it's somewhere where atmosphere is part of the attraction. It's the same in great cathedrals. It should be possible to get away from parties of noisy tourists and uninterested school children who are just ticking the place off their list of trophy visits, or being dragged around by desperate teachers without the slightest genuine interest.'

'Hear, hear! Well said.' Andy clapped solemnly. 'A great speech.'

'And a sensible one.' Ben smiled at her. 'Which I think we would all agree with deep down in our heart of hearts.'

There was a moment's silence. At the table next door Anna noticed that Toby had turned to listen. She looked down at her soup in confusion. It was a novelty, she suddenly realised, to be listened to!

Exhausted, she went back to her cabin early. Glancing out of the window, shading her eyes against the reflections, she could see the dark river; they had not as yet moved away from the bank. With a shiver of excitement she got ready for bed, and at last reached up for her case, to retrieve the diary. She was looking forward to reading another section before she fell asleep.

'Sitt Louisa?' Hassan's shadow fell across the page of her sketch-book. Louisa glanced up. Her easel, her parasol clipped to the canvas, had been set up in the bows of the dahabeeyah as it slowly sailed south. Of the others on the boat there was no sign. Succumbing after their midday meal to the heat of the afternoon they had returned to their cabins, leaving her alone on deck with her watercolours. Only the steersman at the opposite end of the boat, the tiller tucked under his arm, had kept her company up to now. She glanced up at Hassan and smiled.

'Before we left Luxor I went to the bazaar,' he said. 'I have a gift for you.'

She bit her lip. 'You shouldn't have done that, Hassan –'

'I am pleased to do it. Please.' He held out his hand. In it there was a small parcel. 'I know you wanted to visit the souk yourself to buy a memento.'

Sir John and Lady Forrester on hearing of Louisa's plan to visit Luxor again had decided almost wilfully that now was the time to sail south.

Taking the parcel from him Louisa looked at it for a moment.

'It is very old. More than three thousand years. From the time of a king who is hardly known, Tutankhamen.'

For a moment the angle of the boat changed and the shadow of the sail fell across them. She gave an involuntary shiver.

'Open it.' His voice was very quiet.

Slowly she reached for the knotted string which held the paper closed. Untying it she let the string fall. The paper crackled faintly

60

as she pulled it away. Inside was a tiny blue glass bottle. With it was a sheet of old paper, crumbling with age, covered in Arabic script. 'It is glass. From the 18ᵗʰ dynasty. Very special. There is a secret place inside where is sealed a drop of the elixir of life.' Hassan pointed to the piece of paper. It is all written there. Some I cannot read but it seems to tell the story of a pharaoh who needed to live for ever and the priests of Amun who devised a special elixir which when given to him would bring him back to life. It was part of a special ceremony. The story on the paper says that in order to protect the secret recipe from evil djinn their priest hid it in this bottle. When he died the bottle was lost for thousands of years.'

'And this is it?' Louisa laughed with delight.

'This is it.' Hassan's eyes had begun to sparkle as he watched her pleasure.

'Then it is truly a treasure and I shall keep it always. Thank you.' She looked up at him and for a moment their eyes met. The seconds of silence stretched out between them, then abruptly Hassan stepped back. He bowed and turned away from her.

'Hassan –' Louisa's voice was husky. The name came out as a whisper and he did not hear her.

For a long time she sat still, the little bottle lying in her lap, then at last she picked it up. It was little taller than her forefinger, made of thick opaque blue glass decorated with a white, twisted design and the stopper was sealed in place with some kind of resiny wax. She held it up to the sunlight, but the glass was too thick to see through it and after a minute she gave up. Slipping it into her watercolour box, she tucked it safely into the section where the brushes and water pot lived. Later in her cabin she would put it away in the bottom secret drawer of her wooden dressing case.

Picking up her brush again, she turned back to her picture, but she found it difficult to concentrate.

Her thoughts kept returning to Hassan.

EGYPT

Anna laid down the diary and glanced at the slatted shutters over the window. The boat had given a slight shudder. Then she heard the steady beat of the engines. Climbing to her feet she went to the window and pushing back the shutter she opened it. Already they were moving away from the bank. She watched the strip of dark water between the boat and the shore widen slowly then the note of the engines changed and she felt the steady forward thrust of the paddle wheels. They were on their way. She stood for several minutes watching the luminous darkness, then leaving the window open she went back to her bed and sliding under the cotton quilt she picked up the diary again. So, the bottle lying there in her bag, had originally been a gift from Hassan. And what a gift! It wasn't a scent bottle at all. It was some kind of ancient phial, a holy artefact from the time of Tutankhamen, whose tomb of course had not yet been discovered in Louisa's day, and it contained nothing less than the elixir of life!

She shuddered. For an instant she was back in that dark inner burial chamber looking down at the mummy case of the boy king and she remembered how she had become instantly and totally aware of his body lying there before her, and how she had dropped her bag – and the bottle – virtually at his feet.

Pulling the quilt more closely under her chin she picked up the diary again, soothed by the gentle rumble of the engine deep in the heart of the boat, and she began to read on.

That night, dressed in her coolest muslin Louisa lingered at the saloon table after Augusta had retired to her cabin. Sir John raised an eyebrow. 'We sail as soon as the wind gets up a little. The *reis* tells me that should be with the dusk. The wind comes in off the desert then.' He reached for the silver box of cheroots and offered it to her. Louisa took one. She had never smoked before coming to Egypt. To know how shocked her mother-in-law would be to see her was enough reason. The scandalised lift of Lady Forrester's eyebrow had been a second. With a silent chuckle she leant forward and allowed Sir John to light it for her.

'Can I ask you to translate something for me?' She reached into her pocket for the paper which had been wrapped around the little bottle.

Sir John took it. Leaning back he inhaled deeply on his own smoke and rested it on a small copper ashtray. 'Let me see. This is Arabic, but written a long time ago, judging by the paper.'

He glanced at her for a moment. 'Where did you say you found this?'

She smiled. 'I didn't. One of the servants found it in the souk with a souvenir he bought for me.'

'I see.' He frowned. Laying it down on the table he smoothed out the creases and peered at it in silence for several moments. Watching him, Louisa could feel her first casual interest tightening into nervous apprehension. He was frowning now, a finger tracing the curling letters over the page. At last he looked up.

'I think this must be a practical joke. A piece of nonsense to frighten and amuse the credulous.'

'Frighten?' Louisa's eyes were riveted to the paper. 'Please, will you read it to me?'

He was breathing heavily through his nose. 'I needn't read it exactly. Indeed it is difficult to decipher all of it. Sufficient to say that it seems to be a warning. The item it accompanies –' he looked up at her, his blue eyes shrewd – 'you have that item?'

'A little scent bottle, yes.'

'Well, it is cursed in some way. It belonged once to a high priest who served the pharaoh. An evil spirit tried to steal it. Both fight for it still, apparently.' His face relaxed into a smile. 'A wonderful story for the gullible visitor from abroad. You will be able to show it to people when you go back to London and watch their faces pale over the dinner table as you recount your visit to Egypt.'

'You don't think it's serious then?' She tapped ash from her cheroot onto the little copper dish.

'Serious?' He roared with laughter. 'My dear Louisa, I hardly think so! But if you see a high priest on the boat, or indeed any evil djinn, please tell me. I should very much like to meet them.'

He moved his chair closer to hers as he laid the paper down on the table between them. 'There are real antiquities to be bought if you have the contacts. I could arrange for some to be brought to the boat when we return to Luxor. There is no need for you to send servants to the bazaar.'

'But I didn't –' She bit off the words before she could finish the sentence, realising suddenly that it would not be wise to tell Sir John that the bottle had been a present from her dragoman.

He leant closer to her. 'I have been looking at some of your watercolours.' He nodded towards the corner of the cabin where she had left a folio of sketches. 'They are very good.'

It was extremely hot in the cabin. She could feel the heat from his body so close beside her; smell his sweat. She edged away from him. 'That is kind of you to say so. And yes, I should like it if it were possible to have some antiques brought to the boat. I have as you know very little spending money, but if I saw something I liked I could at least sketch it.'

He let out a roar of laughter. 'First rate! Good idea! I shall look forward to seeing you do that.' His hand came down on top of hers, suddenly, as she rested it on the table and he gave it a squeeze. 'First rate,' he repeated.

Louisa pulled her hand away, her anxiety not to offend him fighting with her desire to stand up and put as much distance as possible between them.

A sound in the doorway made them both turn. Jane Treece stood there, her eyes on the table where, a moment before, their hands had lain together on the piece of paper with its Arabic script.

'Lady Forrester wondered whether Mrs Shelley would like me

64

to help her get ready for bed.' The voice was a monotone. Cold. The woman's eyes strayed to the ashtray where Louisa's cheroot lay, a thin wisp of smoke rising up towards the cabin lamp hanging from the ceiling beams.

'Thank you.' With some relief Louisa stood up. 'Forgive me, it has been a tiring day.' She moved away from the table, her black skirts rustling slightly. She could feel Sir John's eyes on her and her face grew hot again.

'Your note, my dear.' He picked up the piece of paper and held it out to her. 'You had better keep it safe. Your grandchildren will no doubt enjoy the story.'

Anna stopped reading for a moment. Beneath her she could feel the steady movement of the boat as it forged its way south. In the diary Louisa too was making her way over exactly the same stretch of river, heading towards Esna and Edfu. With her scent bottle. A scent bottle with a curse, haunted by evil djinn. In spite of the heat of the cabin Anna shivered.

She lay looking up at the shadows on the ceiling thrown by the small bedside light, the diary propped open on her chest. What had happened to that piece of paper with its story, she wondered.

Her eyes wandered over towards the little dressing table, where she had left her bag. It was dark there; she could just see the outline of the mirror, the glass faintly echoing the light the lamp threw onto the ceiling. She stared at it sleepily and then suddenly she frowned. Deep in the mirror had she seen something move? She caught her breath as a shaft of panic shot through her. For a moment she couldn't breath. She gripped the quilt tightly to her chest then she closed her eyes, trying to steady her breathing. This was nonsense. She was dreaming, frightened by a fairy story. She pushed herself up against the pillows and groped for the switch to the main cabin light as the diary slid to the floor with a crash. In

65

the harsh clarity the overhead lights threw on the scene she could see clearly that there was nothing there. The key was still in the cabin door. No one could have come into the room. Her bag was lying untouched where she had left it – or was it? Still trembling with shock she forced herself to push her feet out from under the sheet and, standing up, she went over to the dressing table. Her bag lay open, the scent bottle in full view on top of her sunglasses. Cautiously she touched her scarf. It had been wrapped round the bottle in the bottom of the bag, she was sure of it. Now the scarf lay across the dressing table, a swathe of fine scarlet silk against the dark-stained wood. She stared at it with a frown. Across the silk lay a scattering of some kind of brown papery stuff. Curious, she reached out to touch it and rubbed some of it between her fingers. Then she swept it to the floor. Under the scarf lay the hairbrush she had used before she climbed into bed, the hairbrush she had taken from her bag last thing before she rezipped it and put it on the shelf. She was sure of that too. She had closed it and put it away.

She glanced round. There was nowhere for anyone to hide in the room; nowhere. She threw open the shower room door and rattled back the curtain, still damp from her shower only a couple of hours or so earlier. She looked under the bed, she shook the door handle. It was firmly locked. But already she knew there was no one there. How could there be?

With another shiver she made her way over to the bed and bent down to pick up the diary. It had fallen open when it hit the floor, cracking the spine lengthways. Forgetting the scarf she ran her finger sadly over the leather. What a shame. It had lasted so long undamaged and now it had been broken. It was as she was preparing to climb back into bed that she noticed that an envelope lay on the floor where the diary had fallen. She bent to pick it up and saw that the strip of sticky brown paper with which it had been stuck in the back of the diary had torn away. The thick woven paper told her at once it must be contemporary with the diary and turning it over she saw a crest embossed on the flap. It depicted a tree with a coronet. She smiled. Forrester? Had it been she wondered part of the stationery they used on the boat? Forgetting her fright in her curiosity she opened it. Folded inside was a flimsy piece of paper. Already she had guessed it was Louisa's Arabic message.

If you see a high priest on the boat, or indeed any evil djinn, please tell me . . .

The words from Louisa's entry echoed for a moment in her head.

A high priest who served the pharaoh . . . an evil spirit . . . both fight for it still . . .

Anna found that her hands were shaking. Taking a deep breath, she put the paper back in the envelope and opening the drawer in the bedside table slotted it into her slim leather writing case.

Climbing back into bed and pulling her feet up under her she drew the covers up to her chin. The cabin was cold. A stream of sharp, night-scented river air came in from the open window.

She wrapped her arms around her knees and resting her chin on her forearm, she shut her eyes.

She sat there for a long time, her eyes straying every now and then to the bag still lying on the dressing table. At last she could bear it no longer. Climbing to her feet again she pulled the little bottle from the bag. Holding it in her hand she stared at it for a long time, then reaching down her suitcase from the top of the cupboard she rewrapped the bottle in her scarf, put it in the suitcase, tucking it into an elasticated side pocket where it would be safe, closed the lid, turned the key and hefted the case back into place. Helping herself to a glass of water from the plastic bottle on the table she stood for several minutes sipping the cold water, staring out at the blackness of the night as it drifted by, then snapping off the main cabin light she climbed back into bed.

Louisa was not sure what had awakened her. She lay looking at the ceiling in the darkness, feeling her heart thumping against her ribs. She held her breath. There was someone in her cabin. She could sense them standing near her.

'Who's there?' Her voice was barely more than a whisper but it seemed to echo round the boat. 'Who is it?' Sitting up she reached with a shaking hand for her matches and lit her candle. The cabin was empty. Staring into the flickering shadows she held her breath again, listening. Her cabin door was shut. There was no sound from the sleeping boat. They had moored as night fell, against a shallow flight of marble steps, where palms and eucalyptus trees grew down to the edge of the river. Water lapped against the steps and in the distance, against the fading twilight she had seen the outline of a minaret.

A sharp crack followed by a rattling sound made her catch her breath. The noise had come from the table in front of the window. It sounded as though something had fallen to the floor. She stared at the spot, straining her eyes in the candlelight then, knowing she would not rest until she had looked more closely, she reluctantly climbed out of bed. She stood for a moment in her long white nightgown, the candle in her hand, staring at the floor. One of her tubes of paint had fallen from the table. She picked it up and stared at it. The slight movement of the boat as it lay against its mooring must have dislodged it and allowed it to roll from the table. Her eyes strayed to Hassan's scent bottle. She hadn't seen him to speak to since he had given it to her that afternoon. While she dined with the Forresters he had been sitting on the foredeck with the *reis*, smoking a companionable hooker, both men deep in conversation.

She had tucked the piece of paper with its Arabic warning into an envelope and slipped the envelope into the back of her diary. Joke or not, the message made her feel uncomfortable.

The little bottle was standing on the table with her painting things. She frowned. She had surely tucked it into her dressing case? She remembered distinctly doing so before dinner. Perhaps Jane Treece had moved it when she tidied away Louisa's muslin gown and, not recognising it, had assumed it was part of her painting equipment. She reached out to pick it up and at the last moment hesitated, almost afraid to touch it. What if it were true? Supposing it was three or four thousand years old? Supposing it had been the property of a temple priest in the days of one of the ancient pharaohs?

Drawing in a quick deep breath she picked it up and taking it back to her bed she sat down. Leaning back against her pillows, the little bottle cradled between her palms, she lapsed into deep thought, her imagination taking her from the high priest who followed the scent bottle, to Hassan. Why should he have given her

68

a present at all? She pictured his face, the strong bones, the large brown eyes, the evenly spaced white teeth and suddenly she found herself remembering the warm dry touch of his hand against hers as he passed her the flaring torch in the tomb in the valley. In spite of herself she shivered. What she had felt at that moment was something she had never thought to feel again, the intense pleasure she used to feel at the touch of her beloved George's hand when he glanced at her and they exchanged secret smiles in unacknowledged recognition that later, when the children were asleep, they would keep an assignation in his room or hers. But to feel that with a comparative stranger, a man who was of a different race and one who was in her employ? She could feel herself blushing in the light of the candle. It was something too shocking, almost, to confide even to her diary.

Anna awoke to find the sunlight flooding across her bed from the open window. The boat was still moving and when she climbed to her feet and went to look out she found a breathtaking view of palms and plantations streaming steadily by. For a few moments she stood still, transfixed, then she turned and pulling off her night-shirt she headed for the shower.

Toby was just sitting down to breakfast as she arrived in the dining room. 'Another late arrival? I believe most of the others have already finished. Please, join me.' He pulled out a chair for her. 'This morning we go to the temple of Edfu. I gather we will be arriving fairly soon.' He beckoned the waiter with his coffee pot over to the table as Anna sat down. 'You look tired. Did the Valley of the Kings prove too much of an exciting start?'

She shook her head. 'I didn't sleep well.'

'Not sea sick, I trust!'

She laughed. 'No, though I must admit I noticed the movement. It did feel odd.' She reached for the cup.

'I expect it disturbed you when we went through the lock at Esna. It must have been some time in the early hours. It certainly woke me, but not enough to make me want to go up on deck and watch.'

She shrugged. 'Would you believe, I missed that. No, actually I was reading Louisa's diary until late and I think it gave me nightmares. I kept waking up after that.'

'What on earth was she describing?'

'She was talking about a scent bottle which her dragoman bought for her in a bazaar. It had the reputation for being haunted.'

'The scent bottle or the bazaar?' His eyes crinkled rather pleasantly at the corners, she realised, although he kept all traces of laughter out of his voice.

'The bottle. I know it sounds strange. A haunted scent bottle!'

'What haunted it? A genie, presumably. They seem to favour living in bottles.'

'She called it a djinn. Is that the same thing?' She smiled, hoping that would show she didn't believe it herself, that she could laugh it off as he had.

'Indeed it is the same. How intriguing. Well, you mustn't let such imaginings disturb your sleep again. Perhaps you'd better not read such sensational stuff at bedtime.' He stood up, pushing back his chair. 'What can I get you from the buffet?'

She watched as he made his way across the dining room and picked up two plates. She saw him carefully select two of the largest croissants from the basket on the counter, then he was on his way back. 'We've arrived. Do you see?' Putting down the plates he gestured towards the windows. 'Just time to eat, then we'd better go and claim our places in a suitable calèche. We drive to the temple of Edfu in style.'

A line of four-wheeled open carriages, drawn by an array of painfully thin horses was drawn up on the quayside waiting for them, each driven by an Egyptian in a colourful *galabiyya* and turban. Beside each driver a long, formidable whip rested against the footrail. Every so often one was cracked loudly as the horses milled about, jostling for position. The shouting was deafening, as around the calèches and between the horses' feet a dozen little boys shouted for baksheesh, and urged the tourists towards their own particular choice of vehicle.

As they assembled on the quayside, Anna found herself standing next to Serena and it was with some relief she saw that they were both bound for the same calèche. She became aware that she had been scanning the crowds for Andy and Charley almost without realising it, but there was no sign of either of them; with them when they were finally settled into their seats were Joe and Sally Booth. Their driver, whose name, so he informed them, was Abdullah, could have been any age between seventy and one hundred and fifty, she decided as she quailed beneath his toothless grin. His skin was especially dark, gauntly drawn into deep creases and his missing teeth rendered his smile particularly piratical. Anna settled beside Serena with a fervent prayer that they were not going to be whisked off into the desert and never seen again. They set off at a canter, passing the other vehicles and heading into the centre of town where the horses challenged lorries and cars with no fear at all. Holding frantically to the side of the carriage Anna wished she had a hand free to take out her camera. There was something deeply primitive in this mode of transport which appealed to her greatly.

The calèche lurched into a pothole and Anna fell sideways against her companion. Serena laughed. 'Isn't it wonderful? I am so looking forward to seeing Edfu Temple. It's very special you know. It's not nearly as old as somewhere like Karnac which we shall see next week. It was built in the Ptolomaic period, but it is famous for its inscriptions and carvings and they were faithful still to the old Egyptian gods even in Roman times.'

Anna found herself wishing suddenly she had spent less time reading up about the scent bottle and more on Louisa's diary entry on her visit here. As the calèche hurtled up the main street and over a crossroads she pictured Louisa and Hassan together in just such a conveyance. There was a shout from behind them. She turned in time to see another vehicle, drawn by a grey horse with hips that stood out like coat racks draw level with them. Its driver cracked his whip in the air above the horse's head and gave a shout of triumph as Andy leant forward to wave at them. 'Last one there pays for the beer!' His call rang in their ears as his calèche drew ahead.

Serena laughed uncomfortably. 'He's like a child, isn't he?'

Anna raised an eyebrow. 'I suppose you see a lot of him if he and Charley are together.'

Serena shrugged. 'Not that much. Not as much as Charley would

71

like.' She broke off and they both watched anxiously as a woman crossed the road in front of them, a watermelon balanced on her head. Abdullah cracked his whip just behind her with a malicious grin, clearly hoping to make her jump and she turned, melon still firmly in place, to shout and swear at him without losing an iota of poise and grace. It was impressive to watch.

'Aren't they wonderful?' Serena glanced at the camera which had finally appeared in Anna's hands now that they were in the thick of the crowds and the pace was less breakneck. She watched as Anna focused and pointed it at the departing woman. 'I wonder why we don't carry things on our heads. I don't know that it's ever been a western tradition, has it?'

'Perhaps it's the damp. Our belongings would get wet in the rain and we'd all develop arthritic necks.' Anna laughed. 'It could be a sign that global warming is with us for real – when all the people at the bus stop one morning put their briefcases and bags on their heads.'

Both women laughed. They fell silent again as a small boy passed them, a trussed turkey tucked beneath his arm. The bird's eyes were crazed. It was panting with fear. Anna raised her camera as Serena shook her head. 'I find it hard to cope with, the cruelty. That bird. These horses . . .'

'They don't seem to actually hit them,' Anna put in. 'Most of the whip cracking is for our benefit. I've been watching. My guess is that they know jolly well it would upset the effete western tourists if they hit the horses.'

'While we are here, perhaps not, but what happens when we've gone?' Serena did not sound convinced.

'At least they feed them.' Bags of bright green fodder were hung from every vehicle.

They left the calèches in the shade at the back of the temple and walked the final distance, its full length, towards the entrance. Anna stared up in awe. The temple was huge, a vast squat building, rectangular behind the enormous pylon or monumental gateway, forty metres high, carved with pictures of Ptolemy defeating his enemies. They stopped in front of it, their group forming obediently around Omar, as they listened to his summary of two thousand years' history and the temple's place in it.

A white robed figure stood near the entrance, beside the statue of the god Horus as a huge hawk and Anna found herself watching him. A black line of shadow cut across the dazzling white cotton of his *galabiyya* as he leant silently against the wall with his arms folded. She had the sense that he was watching them and she felt a sudden tremor of nervousness.

'What is it? Is something wrong?' Serena was watching her face.

She shook her head. 'Nothing really. I keep getting this strange feeling that there's someone out there watching me . . .'

Behind them Omar took a deep breath and continued his story. Neither woman was listening.

'Not someone very nice, judging by your reaction.'

'No.' Anna gave a small laugh. 'I think Egypt is making me a bit neurotic. Perhaps we could have a drink before dinner this evening and I could tell you about it?'

About what? A nightmare? A feeling that someone had unpacked her bag in the dark of her cabin and moved her little scent bottle? A scent bottle haunted by an evil spirit. She shook her head, aware that Serena was still watching her curiously. It might sound stupid in the cold light of day, but after all, Andrew and Toby knew about the diary. Why not someone else? And someone in whom she sensed she could confide without feeling embarrassed. Wasn't it Toby yesterday who had suggested she speak to Serena about her strange feelings in the Valley of the Kings? He had thought she might understand.

They were late back to the boat, exhausted and dusty and hot after their visit. Warm lemonade and scented washcloths were followed by lunch and then as the boat cast off and headed once more upstream, the passengers retired either to their cabins or to the sunbeds on the upper deck.

It was there that Andy found Anna a couple of hours later. He was carrying two glasses. Sitting down in the chair next to her he offered her one. 'I hope you haven't been to sleep without your hat.'

'No, as you can see.' It was hanging from the chair-back. She pulled herself upright and sipped the fresh juice he had brought her. 'That was lovely. Thank you.' The deck was deserted, she realised suddenly; while she had been asleep, one by one, everyone else had disappeared. 'What time is it?'

'No such thing as time in Egypt.' He grinned. 'But the sun disc is getting low in the west. Which means it will soon be time for another meal.' He patted his stomach ruefully. 'I suspect our excursions ashore, strenuous though they are, are not going to be sufficiently energetic to make up for all the food we eat.' He paused for a moment. 'Would this be a good time to let me see the diary?'

The abrupt change of subject startled her. He was, she realised, looking down at her bag, which lay on the deck beside her chair.

'It's in my cabin. Maybe later, Andy, if you don't mind.'

'Sure. No hurry.' He leant back and closed his eyes. 'Have you shown it to anyone else?'

'On the boat, you mean?' She glanced at him over the rim of her tumbler. It was impossible to read his expression behind his dark glasses.

He nodded.

'No. Toby is the only one who has seen it. On the plane.'

'Toby Hayward?' Andy chewed his lip for a moment. 'I've been thinking, I know his name from somewhere. He's a bit of a loner from what I gather.'

'As I am,' she pointed out gently. 'At least on this cruise. He is a painter.'

She did not miss the raised eyebrow. 'Indeed. Is he well known?'

Anna smiled. 'I've no idea. Perhaps that's why you know his name? I don't think I've heard of him, but that doesn't really mean anything.'

Andy drained his glass. 'Tell me to mind my own business, if you want to, but I do think you should take care of that diary, Anna. Apart from being worth a lot of money it's a piece of real history.'

'Which is why I have left it locked up.' She spoke perhaps more firmly than she had intended, but his tone was beginning to irritate her. There were shades of Felix in his manner. And it was patronising.

He laughed, which infuriated her even more. Putting his arms across his face he pretended to duck sideways. 'OK, OK, I'm sorry. I surrender. I should have realised you are perfectly able to take care of it and of yourself. You are after all, Louisa's great-great-granddaughter!'

A fact she reminded herself about later when she met Serena in the bar and they settled into one of the comfortable sofas in the corner of the room. Outside it was dark. They had moored alongside a stretch of river bank which was, so they understood, within walking distance of the great temple of Kom Ombo. Around them the

74

others were assembling a few at a time. She could see Andy perched on a stool at the bar. Charley stood near him and they were engaged in a noisy conversation with Joe and the barman.

'So, tell me about these strange feelings of yours.' Serena leant back against the cushions, her glass in her hand. She scanned Anna's face intently for a moment then she glanced back at the bar where a particularly loud shout of laughter erupted from the group standing around Andy.

'It sounds a bit silly talking about it in cold blood.' Anna shrugged. 'But someone mentioned you were interested in sort of psychic stuff.'

Serena smiled. 'Sort of? I suppose so. I gather this is to do with the man we saw at Edfu this morning?'

'Not him especially. He was real. But for some reason he made me feel nervous. He was watching us, and I keep getting this feeling that I'm being watched by someone. It's nothing specific . . .' She broke off, not knowing quite how to go on.

'Start at the beginning, Anna. I find things are much more clear that way.' Serena was giving her her full attention now. 'There is clearly something worrying you and that's a shame on what should be lovely carefree holiday.'

'You don't read Arabic, I suppose?'

Serena shook her head and laughed. 'I'm afraid not.'

'I have a diary in my cabin.'

'Belonging to Louisa Shelley, I know.' She saw Anna's face and laughed again. 'My dear, it's a small boat and there aren't very many of us. You don't surely expect it to stay a secret?'

'I suppose not.' Anna was taken aback. She was thinking suddenly of Andy's warning. 'Well, in this diary there is a description of how Louisa was given a little glass bottle by her dragoman as a gift. I have inherited the bottle. With it was a piece of paper, which I also have, written in Arabic, saying that the bottle, which it claims is pharaonic in date, has a sort of curse on it. The original owner, a high priest in Ancient Egypt, is following it and so is an evil spirit because a secret potion is sealed into the glass. I know it sounds ridiculous, like something out of a film, but it's worrying me . . .' Her voice trailed away in embarrassment.

'You have this bottle with you, on the boat?' Serena asked quietly. In the general hubbub Anna could hardly hear her.

She nodded, relieved that Serena had not laughed. 'I brought it

75

with me. I wish I hadn't now. I don't really know why except it seemed right to bring it back to Egypt. I've had it for years. I always assumed it was a fake. An antique dealer friend of my husband's said it was a fake. Andy thinks it is a fake.'

'Andy Watson?' Serena's voice was sharp. 'What does he know about it? Have you shown it to him?'

'He saw it yesterday. He says masses of fakes were sold in Victorian times to gullible tourists.'

'He's right of course. But you don't strike me as being gullible, and I am sure Louisa wasn't either, nor her dragoman, if he had any integrity at all.' Serena paused for a moment. 'And you are afraid of this curse?'

It wasn't an accusation, merely a statement of fact.

Anna didn't reply for a moment, then slowly she shrugged. 'I've only known about it since last night.' She bit her lip with an embarrassed little laugh. 'But I suppose if I'm honest it is beginning to get to me. Even before I knew the story I had the strangest feeling there was someone watching me. I've been jumpy since I arrived in Egypt. Then once or twice I had the feeling that someone has been touching my things when the cabin door was locked and no one could have been there. I've tried to persuade myself I was dreaming or hallucinating or imagining it. I was tired after the visit yesterday and everything, but . . .' Once again she tailed off into silence.

'Let's take things one at a time. Tell me what the note says as far as you understand it. I take it you have a translation?' Serena's voice remained quiet, but firm. It had an attractive deep quality which Anna found profoundly reassuring.

Serena thought for a while in silence after Anna had repeated it to her, staring down into the glass she had put down on the low table in front of them, while Anna anxiously watched her face.

'If Louisa felt there was a spirit guarding the bottle then we must assume the bottle to be genuine, obviously,' she said at last. 'And if it's the same bottle that you have brought with you then the chances are that it does have some kind of resonance about it.'

'Resonance?' Anna looked at her anxiously.

Serena laughed again. Anna was beginning to enjoy the deep throaty gurgle. That too was reassuring. 'Well, my dear, as I said, let's take this one step at a time. Presumably you know you are of sound mind. When you had this strange feeling, you weren't asleep; at least you can be sure you weren't asleep the first time, as you had just stepped out of the shower! You were sober. You knew where you had left your bag. You have probably had your eyes tested at some time in the not too distant past, so, why do you not believe them?'

'That's easy. Because if the bag was moved and the bottle unwrapped, someone must have done it. I don't believe in ghosts. I'm not psychic. After all, nothing has ever happened to it, or me, before. Oh no,' Anna shook her head, 'I can't cope with that idea, I really can't.'

Serena watched her thoughtfully. 'Will you show me the bottle?'

'Of course. Come to my cabin after supper.' Anna bit her lip. 'To tell you the truth, I'm a bit nervous about going back in there now. I don't know what I'm going to find!'

'If it worries you so much, why not ask them to put the bottle in the boat's safe with our passports and valuables?' Serena glanced up as outside the restaurant in the depths of the boat the gong began to ring.

They stood up and began to move towards the staircase which led down to the lower deck.

Anna shrugged. 'That's a good idea. I might just do it.' She shook her head. 'I can't believe all this! It must be my imagination. After all, nothing ever happened before I read about it. If it's true, why has nothing ever shown itself in London?'

Serena turned towards her. 'Isn't it obvious? You've brought it back to Egypt, my dear. It has come home.'

Unlocking the door later Anna reached in and turned on the light. The small room was empty. Beckoning Serena inside she closed the door behind them. They had lingered over supper with the others, but by an unspoken agreement had turned away from the lounge where the coffee was being served before Omar gave another talk to the assembled company. Tonight's topic was Egyptian history since the days of the pharaohs.

It seemed crowded in the tiny cabin with two people in there. Serena sat down on the bed whilst Anna swung her suitcase down from the wardrobe. Setting it on the floor she squatted down, unlocked it and threw back the lid. 'It's here.' She reached into

77

the pocket and pulled out the small silk-wrapped bundle. Without removing the scarf she handed it to Serena.

The cabin was very quiet. All the other passengers were in the lounge watching as Omar set up a projector on the bar preparing to take them through Egypt's more recent history. The two corridors on the boat, off which the ten cabins led, were empty. For the crew, it was their turn to eat. The river bank was dark and deserted. There was a gentle lap of water from outside the half-open window and a dry, quiet rustle from the reeds as the wind began to rise, stealing subtly in from the desert.

Very carefully Serena began to unwrap the bottle. 'It's smaller than I expected.'

Anna sat down beside her. 'It's tiny.' She gave a nervous giggle. 'So small, and it's causing so much hassle.'

'Hush.' Serena pulled away the scarlet silk and dropped it on the bedcover. She was gazing down at the bottle lying on the palm of her hand. She stroked it with her finger. 'It feels old. The glass is flawed. Bumpy.' Closing her eyes she went on stroking with her fingertip, gently, scarcely touching it. 'It's old. Full of memories. Full of time.' Her voice was very soft. Dreamy. 'This is real, Anna. It's old. Very old.' She went on stroking. 'There is magic in this. Power.' There was a long silence. 'I can see a figure with my mind's eye. He's tall. His eyes are piercing. They see through everything. Silver, like knife blades.' She was still, caressing the bottle with slow, gentle movements. 'He has so much power,' she went on slowly, 'but there is treachery there. He has enemies. He thinks himself invincible, but close to him there is hatred, greed. Someone, whom he thought a friend, is near him. Waiting. Drawing the darkness of secrecy around him. They serve different gods, but he has not realised it. Not yet . . .' Her voice trailed away into silence. Anna held her breath, watching mesmerised as the fingertip with its neat, oval, unpolished nail stroked gently on. 'There is blood here, Anna.' Serena spoke again at last, her voice a whisper. 'So much blood – and so much hate.'

'You're making it up.' Anna backed a step away from her. She leant against the door. 'You're frightening me!' Suddenly she was shivering uncontrollably. Was it this which had woken Louisa and frightened her in the darkness?

Slowly Serena looked up. Her eyes found Anna's face but she wasn't seeing it. Her pupils were huge; unfocused.

78

'Serena?' Anna whispered. 'Serena, please!'

There was another long silence then abruptly Serena rubbed her eyes. She smiled uncertainly. 'What did I say?'

'Don't you know?' Anna didn't move from her position near the door.

Serena looked down at the little bottle still lying in her hand. With a shiver she let it fall onto the bed. 'It is old. Very old,' she repeated, her voice completely flat.

'You said.' Anna swallowed. Her eyes were riveted to the bottle, lying on the bed. 'But what was all that other stuff? About the blood?'

Serena's eyes opened wide. 'Blood?' There was a moment's silence then she looked away. 'Oh shit!' She put her hands to her face. 'I didn't mean that to happen. Forget it, for goodness sake. I'm sorry. Don't believe anything I said, Anna.' She reached out towards the bottle, changed her mind and stood up, leaving it where it was. 'I have a tendency to be melodramatic. Take no notice. The last thing I meant to do was scare you.'

'But you did.'

'Did I?' For a moment Serena stood gazing into her face as if trying to read her thoughts. Then she shrugged and looked away. 'They must have finished the talk by now. Why don't we go to the lounge and have a drink?' She bent over the bed and reached out to the bottle. The hesitation was only momentary, then she picked it up and firmly rewrapped it in the silk square. She held it out to Anna. 'I should get Omar to put it in the safe for you. I think it probably is genuine.' Her voice was still strangely flat.

Anna took it reluctantly. She held it for a moment then she stooped and tucked it back in the suitcase. 'Later. I will. When there's someone at the desk.' She opened her mouth to ask another question, then she changed her mind. Grabbing her purse she reached for the door handle. 'Come on. Let's get out of here.'

Drinks in hand they made their way through the lounge where the others had settled in groups round the low tables and they stepped out onto the open covered deck where the tables and chairs were deserted. Anna shivered. 'There's a cold wind.'

'I don't mind. It's wonderful – cleansing. Such a relief after the heat of the day.' Serena shook her head. 'Let's climb up onto the sundeck.'

She led the way up to the front of the boat, where Anna had

been asleep earlier. All was in darkness up there as they looked down on the string of small coloured lights around the awning of the lower deck. Looking up they could see the velvety black of the sky and the intense brightness of the stars. They stood leaning on the rail looking out across the river. The night was somehow more silent for the sounds of talk and laughter wafting out of the doors below them.

Anna fixed her eyes on the wavy reflections in the dark water below them. 'How did you do it?' She took a sip from her glass.

Serena didn't pretend not to know what she was talking about. She shrugged. 'They call it psychometry. It's a kind of clairvoyance, I suppose. Reading an object. I've always been able to do it, since I was a child. It was what first drew me to the study of psychic phenomena. In children it's called a vivid imagination. In adults ... she paused. 'Eccentricity. Lunacy. Schizophrenia. Take your pick.' There was the slightest touch of bitterness in her voice for a second, then it was gone. 'It's not something to be cultivated lightly, as you can imagine, but it has its uses. Sometimes.'

Anna was still gazing down at the water. 'What did your husband think about it?'

'Ah.' Serena smiled ruefully. 'Another woman, of course, goes unerringly to the crux of the problem. He vacillated between thinking me delightfully scatty and certifiably insane. But to do him credit he never tried to get me actually locked up.' Her quiet laugh made Anna glance up at last.

Serena stood back from the rail and sat down on one of the chairs. Leaning back with a sigh she stared up at the stars. 'We were very happy. I adored him. I kept all this stuff firmly under the hatches as much as I could while he was alive. Then, when he died,' she paused, 'I suppose it was rather like coming out. I found kindred spirits. I read. I talked. I wrote. I studied. Charley thinks I'm mad, but she's not there much and frankly I don't care what she thinks. I began to study Egyptian mysticism two years ago and I came out here to get a feel of the place in a group before coming back on my own.'

Anna turned back to the river, leaning on the rail. She too was looking up beyond the low bank and the dark silhouette of the trees. The stars were so bright. So clear. She shivered. 'So, tell me about my bottle.'

'I don't remember what I said.' Serena took a sip from her glass.

She caught sight of Anna's face in the darkness and gave a rueful smile. 'No, honestly. I don't. Sometimes I do, but more often than not I go into some sort of trance state. I'm sorry, Anna. But that's how it is for me. You will have to tell me what I said.'

'You talked about hatred and treachery and blood.' The words hung for a moment in the silence. 'You described a man. The priest. You said he was tall, with piercing eyes.' She turned with a start at the sound of footsteps behind them.

'That sounds like me. Tall. With piercing eyes!' Andy had appeared at the top of the steps. 'Come on, girls. What are you talking about so secretively? Serena, old thing, I can't have you appropriating the most beautiful woman on the ship. It's not allowed. Especially if you're going to discuss other men.' He gave an amiable grin.

Serena and Anna exchanged glances.

'We'll join you in a minute, Andy.' Serena did not move from her chair. 'Now, bugger off, there's a good chap.'

Anna hid a smile. She said nothing, watching his momentary discomfiture. It was followed by a shrug. 'OK. Don't shoot!' He raised his hands in mock surrender. 'I know when mere males are not wanted. There'll be drinks on the bar for you if you want them.'

They watched as he padded back across the deck with a nonchalant wave of the hand and disappeared down the steps out of sight.

It was a few moments before Serena spoke. 'Andy is a scoffer. A non believer. I think it would be wiser not to mention any of this to him.'

'I agree.' Anna sat down on the chair next to her. She pulled her sweater round her shoulders with a shiver. 'So, what do I do?'

'You could throw the bottle in the Nile.' Serena tipped back her head and poured the last dregs of her drink down her throat. 'Then my guess is you'll be shot of the problem.'

Anna was silent. 'It was Hassan's gift to Louisa,' she said at last.

'And what happened to them?'

Anna shrugged. 'I haven't read much of the diary yet, but I know she came home safely to England.'

'It's up to you, of course.' Serena leant forward with a sigh, her elbows on her knees.

'You said you were studying Egyptian mysticism,' Anna said slowly. 'So, perhaps there is something you could do. Could you talk to him?' Part of her couldn't believe she was actually asking; another part was beginning to take Serena very seriously.

'Oh, no, that doesn't qualify me to deal with this.' Serena shook her head. 'Anna dear, this is – or could be – heavy-weight. A high priest, if that is what he was, would be way out of my league. Probably out of the league of anyone alive today. Those guys practically invented magic. You've heard of Hermes Trismegistus? And Thoth, the god of magic?'

Anna bit her lip. 'I don't want to destroy the bottle.'

'OK.' Serena levered herself to her feet. 'I tell you what. You read some more of that diary. See what happened to Louisa. How did she deal with it? Perhaps nothing happened to her at all. I'll spend the night thinking about this; tomorrow we go to the great healing temple of Kom Ombo. Who knows, perhaps we'll be able to appease the guardian of the bottle by making an offering to his gods.'

It was late when Anna let herself into her cabin. She stood for a moment, her hand still on the lightswitch, staring at the suitcase lying on the floor. Behind her the short corridor was empty. Serena had gone to her own cabin which she shared with Charley on the floor below.

Anna bit her lip. An hour's cheerful socialising in the boat's lounge bar talking to Ben and Joe and Sally had relaxed and distracted her. She had not forgotten that the bottle would still be here in her cabin, but had been able to put it to the back of her mind. Leaving the door open behind her she went over to the suitcase and knelt down. Opening it, she looked in. Only a small bulge in the side pocket showed where the bottle was hidden. Taking a deep breath she took it out, still carefully wrapped in its scarlet silk. Not stopping to think she left the cabin, hurried down the short corridor to the main staircase and ran down to the reception desk at the foot of the stairs on the restaurant floor. There, behind a panel in the wall was the boat's safe where they had all lodged their passports and any other valuables they didn't want to leave lying around in cabins or bags. The desk was empty and in darkness. Taking a quick, jerky breath, she punched the brass bell which lay on the otherwise empty polished surface. The sound resonated round the reception area, but the door behind the desk which led towards the crew's quarters remained closed. Agitatedly she put out her hand to strike the bell again, then she changed her mind. A glance at her watch had reminded her that it was nearly midnight. It wasn't fair to expect anyone to be on duty at this hour. Except for Omar. He had told them he was there for them at any time of day or night if there were any problems. But he had meant appendicitis or murder, not a forgotten trinket. That could wait until morning. Or could it?

Turning she hurried back towards the stairs. His cabin was on the same level as hers, at the far end of the corridor.

Outside his door she stopped. Was she really going to wake him at this hour of the night to ask him to put something in the safe? For several seconds she stood there, undecided, then turning away she walked slowly towards her open cabin door.

On the threshold she hesitated. She had only been away a few minutes but something in the cabin had changed. Her fingers tightened involuntarily around the small silk-wrapped bundle in her hand as she stood in the doorway peering in. The suitcase was still lying where she had left it, the lid thrown back, in the middle of the floor. She stared at it. It was empty but something was different. The obliquely slanting light from the bedside lamp threw a wedge-shaped black shadow across the empty case, a shadow in which something was lying. Something which hadn't been there before. Her mouth dry, her heart beating fast, she forced herself to take a step nearer. A handful of brown crumbled fragments of what looked like peat lay in the bottom of the case. She looked down at them warily, then slowly she crouched down and reached out her hand. They were dry, papery to the touch. When she drew her fingers over them they disintegrated into fine dust. Frowning, she glanced round the room. Nothing else had changed. Nothing had been moved. She rubbed the dust between her fingers then slowly she bent to sniff her fingertips. The smell was very faint. Slightly spicy. Exotic. For some reason it turned her stomach. She dusted her hands together and slammed the suitcase shut. Swinging it back onto the cupboard she rubbed her hands several times on her towel then at last she shut the cabin door and turned the key.

She undressed and showered in nervous haste, her eyes constantly searching the corners of the room. Wrapping the small silk parcel in the polythene bag in which she had packed her film she tucked it into her cosmetics bag and zipping it up tightly she put

83

it on the floor of the shower. Then she closed the door on it.

For several minutes she stood in the centre of her cabin, every muscle tensed, listening intently. From the half-open window she could hear a faint rustle from the reeds. In the distance for an instant she heard the thin piping call of a bird, then silence fell. Turning off the main cabin light at last she climbed slowly into bed and lay there for a moment in the light of the small bedside lamp, listening once more. Then she reached across and picked up the diary. She did not feel in the least bit sleepy now and at least she could lose herself for a while in Louisa's story and see if she could find any references to the bottle and its fate. Leafing through the pages she found herself looking at a tiny ink sketch, captioned 'Capital at Edfu'. It showed the ornate top of one of the columns in the courtyard she had seen only that morning.

'The Forresters decided yet again that it was too hot to do anything other than stay in the boat, so Hassan procured donkeys so that he and I could ride towards the great temple of Edfu . . .'

Anna glanced up. The room was quiet. Warm. She felt safe. Settling herself a little more comfortably, she turned the page and read on.

The donkey boy who had brought them to the entrance to the temple retired to the sparse shade of a group of palm trees to wait for them while Hassan led the way across the sand. He had commandeered two other small boys to carry the paintbox and easel and sketchbook, their basket of food and the sunshade. They set up camp in the lea of one of the great walls, Louisa sitting on the Persian rug, watching as the boys set down their burden and, rewarded with a half-piastre, scurried away.

'Come and sit by me.' She smiled at Hassan and patted the rug. 'I want to hear the history of this place before we explore it.'

He lowered himself on the edge of the rug, sitting cross-legged, his back straight, his eyes narrowed against the sunlight. 'I think you know more than me, Sitt Louisa, with your books and your talks with Sir John.' He smiled gravely.

'You know that's not true.' She reached for the small sketchbook and opened it. 'Besides, I like to hear you talk while I draw.'

Every second the sun rose higher in the sky. She wanted to capture the elegance and power of this place before the shadows grew too short, to record its majesty, the beauty of the carvings which had a delicacy all their own in contrast to the solidity and sheer size of the stone they were carved from. She wanted to reproduce the strength and wonder of the statues of Horus as a falcon, remember the expression of those huge round eyes surveying the unimaginable distances beyond the walls of the temple. Unscrewing her water jar she poured some into the small pot which clipped on the edge of her paintbox and reached for a brush.

'The temple has only recently been excavated by Monsieur Mariette. Before he came the sand was up to here.' Hassan pointed vaguely at a spot about halfway up the columns. 'He cleared so much away. There were houses built on the temple and close round it. They have all gone now. And he dug out all this.' He waved towards the high walls of sand around the temple on top of which the village perched uncomfortably over the remains of the ancient town. 'Now you can see how huge it is. How high. How magnificent. The temple was built in the time of the Ptolemies. It is dedicated to Horus, the falcon god. It is one of the greatest temples in Egypt.' Hassan's low voice spun the history of the building into a legend of light and darkness. The sands encroached, then receded like the waters of the Nile.

Louisa paused in her work, watching him as the pale ochres and umbers from her palette dried on the tip of her brush. His face was one minute animated, intense, the next relaxed, as the web of his narrative spun on. Dreamily she listened, lost in the visions he was conjuring for her, and it was a moment before she realised he had stopped speaking and was looking at her, a half-smile on his handsome face. 'I have put you to sleep, Sitt Louisa.'

She smiled back, shaking her head. 'You have entranced me with your story. I sit here in thrall, unable even to paint.'

'Then my purpose has failed. I sought to guide your inspiration.' The graceful shrug, the gentle self-deprecating gesture of that brown hand with its long expressive fingers did nothing to release her. She sat unmoving watching him, unable to look away. It was Hassan who broke the spell. 'Shall I lay out the food, Sitt Louisa? Then you can sleep, if you wish, before we explore the temple.'

He rose in a single graceful movement and reached for the hamper, producing a white cloth, plates, glasses, silver cutlery. Then came the fruit, cheeses, bread and dried meats.

He no longer questioned her insistence that he eat with her, she noticed. The place settings, so neatly and formally arranged, were very close to each other on the tablecloth.

Washing her brush carefully in the little pot of water she dried it to a point and laid it down. 'I have such an appetite, in spite of the heat.' She laughed almost coqettishly and then stopped herself. She must not get too friendly with this man who was, after all, in her employ; a man who, in the eyes of the Forresters was no more than a hired servant.

She slipped off the canvas folding stool upon which she had been sitting before her easel and sank cross-legged on the Persian rug, fluffing her skirts up round her. When she glanced up he was offering her a plate, his deep brown eyes grave as they rested for a moment on her face. There wasn't a trace of servitude in his manner as he smiled the slow serious smile she was growing to like so much.

Taking the lump of bread he offered she put it on her plate. 'You spoil me, Hassan.'

'Of course.' Again the smile.

They ate in companionable silence for a while, listening to the cheerful twittering of the sparrows which lived in the walls high above them. Another party of visitors appeared in the distance and stood staring up at the huge pylon. The woman was wearing a pale green dress in the latest fashion and Louisa reached for her sketchpad, captivated by the splash of lightness in the intensity of the courtyard. The figures disappeared slowly out of sight and she let the pad fall. 'We look like exotic butterflies one minute, and like trussed fowl the next,' she commented ruefully. 'Out of place in this climate. So uncomfortable, and yet for a while, beautiful.'

'Very beautiful.' Hassan repeated the word quietly. Louisa looked up, startled, but he had already turned away, intent on the food. 'Some of the ladies in Luxor wear Egyptian dress in the summer,' he said after a moment. 'It is cool and allows them to be more comfortable.'

86

'I should like that so much,' Louisa said eagerly. Then her face fell. 'But I can't see Lady Forrester tolerating me as a guest on her boat if I did anything so outrageous. I have gowns of my own which would be more comfortable than this,' she gestured at her black skirt, 'but sadly they are bright colours and the Forresters would not approve and so I decided I could not wear them in their presence for risk of offending them.' Janey Morris's gowns had, she noticed, been folded away by Jane Treece amongst her nightwear.

'Perhaps on our visits away from the boat we could arrange somewhere for you to change so that Lady Forrester need not be made unhappy.' This time there was a distinct twinkle in his eye. 'I can arrange for clothes for you, Sitt Louisa, if you wish it. Think how much more comfortable it would be for you now.' Although he barely looked at her she had the strangest feeling he could see through to every stitch she had on – the tight corset, the long drawers, the two petticoats, one of them stiffened, beneath the black skirt of her travelling dress, to say nothing of the lisle stockings, held up with garters and the sturdy boots.

'I don't think I can bear it a moment longer.' She shook her head. The tight wads of her hair, her hat, suddenly everything stifled her. 'Can we buy some things for me to wear here in the village, on the way back to the boat?'

He shook his head. 'We need to use discretion. I shall arrange it before we reach our next destination. Have no fear, you will be comfortable soon.'

Setting one of the boys to guard their belongings they strolled a little later through the colonnaded court into the hypostyle hall and stood gazing around them at the massive pillars. 'You feel the weight of the centuries on your head here, do you not?' His voice was almost a whisper.

'It is all so huge.' Louisa stared up, awed.

'To inspire both men and gods.' Hassan nodded, folding his arms. 'And the gods are still here. Do you not feel them?' In the silence the distant cheeping and gossip of the sparrows echoed strangely. Louisa shook her head. It was the sound of English hedgerows and London streets where the birds hopped in the road to scavenge between the feet of dray horses. Out here, amidst so much grandeur they were incongruous.

'Shall we go on?' Hassan was watching her face as the shadows fell across it. Ahead of them the second hypostyle hall was darker still. He was walking slightly ahead of her, a tall stately figure. On this occasion he was wearing a blue turban and a simple white *galabiyya*, with embroidery at the neck and hem. The shadows closed over him as he moved out of sight. For a moment she stood still, expecting him to reappear, waiting for her to follow him. But he didn't. The silence seemed to have intensified around her. Even the birds were suddenly quiet in the unremitting heat.

'Hassan?' She took a few steps forward. 'Hassan? Wait for me!'

Her boots echoed on the paving slabs as she moved towards the entrance where she had seen him disappear. 'Hassan?' She spoke only quietly. Somehow it seemed wrong to call out loud, like shouting inside a cathedral.

It was too quiet. She couldn't hear him. 'Hassan?' She reached the entrance and peered into the darkness, suddenly frightened. 'Hassan, where are you?'

'Sitt Louisa? What is wrong?' His voice came from behind her. She spun round. He was standing some twenty feet away in a ray of light from an unseen doorway. 'I am sorry. I thought you were still beside me.'

'But I was. I saw you go in there . . .' She spun round towards the dark entrance.

'No. I said we would go and look at the room of the Nile. It is the room from where the water was brought each day for the priests' libations.' He came towards her, his face suddenly concerned.

'I saw you, Hassan. I saw you go in there.' She was pointing frantically.

'No, lady.' He stopped beside her. 'I promise. I would not frighten you.' Just for a moment he put his hand on her arm. 'Wait. Let me look. Perhaps there is someone else here.' He strode towards the darkened entrance to the hall of offerings and stood peering in. '*Meen*! Who is there?' he called out sharply. He took a step further in. 'There is no one.' He was shading his eyes to see better. 'But there are many chambers further in. Perhaps there are other visitors here.'

'But I saw you. *You.*' Louisa moved forward until she was standing beside him. 'If it wasn't you, it was someone as tall, as dark, dressed the same . . .'

She leant forward on the threshold of a small inner chamber within the thickness of the wall and her arm brushed his. She felt

88

the warmth of his skin, smelt the cinnamon scent of him.

'See, it is empty.' His voice was close in her ear. Usually when she came close to him he moved deferentially away. In the narrow doorway he remained where he was. 'Without a candle there is nothing to see. I shall fetch one from the hamper –'

'No.' She put her hand on his arm. 'No, Hassan. I can see it's empty.' For a moment they stayed where they were. He had turned from looking into the darkness and was gazing down at her with a look of such love and anguish that for a moment she found herself completely breathless. Then the moment had gone. 'Hassan –'

'I am sorry.' He backed away from the door and bowed. 'I am sorry, Sitt Louisa. Forgive me. There is much to see yet, and we have need of light for the inner sanctuary. *Istanna shwaiyeh*. Please, wait a little. And I will fetch it.' He strode away from her, his face impassive once more, leaving her standing where she was in the doorway.

She glanced back into the darkness. Her heart was hammering under her ribs and she felt hot and strangely breathless. Turning slowly to follow him she found her fists clutched in the folds of her skirts. Firmly she unclenched them. She took a deep breath. This was nonsense. First she was having visions, imagining she saw him when he wasn't there, then she was reacting to him as though . . . But her thoughts shied away even from the idea that she was attracted to him. This could not be.

He had not waited for her. She saw him stride once more into the shadows and then out into the sunlight of the great courtyard in the distance. This time he stayed clearly in sight, and now she could see too, the other group of visitors. She could see the woman in the green dress, gazing up at something their guide was pointing out to them in a frieze far above their heads. She was bored, even from so far away Louisa could see it. And she was hot and uncomfortable in her chic flounced gown with its fashionable slight train dragging in the dust behind her. She could see the dark patches of perspiration showing beneath the woman's arms, the broad tell-tale stripe of dampness between her shoulderblades and suddenly she longed again for the loose clothing Hassan had promised or the soft cool fabric of the dresses folded beneath her nightgowns in the drawer on the boat. Wasn't that what she had come to Egypt for? To be free. To be in charge of her own destiny. To be answerable to no one now except herself. Not to her husband's family in

London. Not to the Forresters. Not to their maid. With a sudden leap of excitement she picked up her skirts and ran after Hassan. 'Wait for me!' She smiled at the other woman pityingly as she whirled past and wondered with a gurgle of amusement what she thought of this vulgar, hurrying baggage who had emerged from the holy of holies in pursuit of a tall, handsome Egyptian.

4

Thy servant hath offered up for thee a
sacrifice and
the divine mighty ones tremble when they look
upon the slaughtering knife . . .

I see and I have sight; I have my existence;
I have done what hath been decreed; I hate
slumber . . .
and the god Set hath raised me up!

In the silence comes the sound of scraping, faint and far away. It is an intrusion, a sacrilege in the thick heat of the dark where no whisper of movement, no breath, no pulse sounds inside or outside the linen that wraps the bodies.

On the walls the sacred texts spin their legends into the firmament. For those two men the prayers were hasty, they were quickly copied. The net of prayers to speed them on their way, to protect their souls, to direct their spirit is written in pigment, not carved upon the rock. In the corner, hidden, powerful, commanding, written by an acolyte, one single prayer begs for their spirits, if they lie ill at ease, to reappear in the world they left so suddenly. 'I hate slumber . . .'

EGYPT

Anna was awoken by a knocking on her cabin door. She stared up at the ceiling blankly for a moment, then squinted at her watch. It was eight-thirty.

'Who is it? Wait a minute!' Leaping out of bed she shook her hair out of her eyes, trying to defog her brain. 'Serena? I'm so sorry. I should have set my alarm.'

Turning the key she pulled open the door. Andy stood there, wearing an open-necked shirt and chinos. He grinned at her. 'I'm sorry. I thought I'd missed you at breakfast because you were an early riser.' His gaze took in her wild unbrushed hair, her short nightshirt and the long, bare legs and his grin widened. 'You were planning to come to Kom Ombo?'

'Yes!' Anna ran her fingers through her hair. 'Oh God, yes! I've overslept! What time are they leaving?'

'Ten minutes.' He stepped away from the door. 'I tell you what. Would you like me to fetch you some coffee from the dining room while you get dressed?'

'Would you?' She shrugged – impossible to stand on one's dignity dressed in crumpled pink cotton and nothing else.

She whirled into the shower, grabbed a dress and a cheesecloth shirt to use as a jacket, shoved her feet into sandals and was just placing films and camera into her bag when he reappeared in her doorway with coffee and a croissant wrapped in a napkin. 'Ali even spread it with strawberry jam for you!' He handed them to her. 'He seems to be quite a fan of yours. And there's no need to choke yourself. Omar said we could just follow them on down the track towards the temple. It's half an hour's walk, I gather, but we can't miss it. You can see the ruins from here.' He gestured at the window.

'You've saved my life!' Taking the coffee she sat down on the bed and sipped it gratefully. She was feeling awkward suddenly, having him standing there watching her. Then the ludicrousness of the situation hit her and she gave a burst of laughter. 'I'm sorry.

I'm not used to entertaining men in my cabin. Please, sit down. I'll only be two minutes.' The croissant was warm, oozing butter and jam. Not a thing to eat with dignity either.

He watched her, his eyes alight with amusement. 'You could have another shower before we leave,' he said after a moment.

She laughed again. 'Nothing so drastic. I'm sure a quick wipe round with a flannel will do! I'm normally quite house-trained.' She drained the coffee gratefully and turned to the bathroom. Her washbag was still on the floor where she had put it when she turned on the shower earlier. In such a tiny space there was nowhere else to store it. She glanced down at it, and froze. It had been fastened. She remembered. Only moments before she had opened it, forgetting the little bottle and rummaged for some lipsalve. Her fingers had closed over the polythene in the bottom of the bag. She had left it there, pushing it back, letting it nestle under the unused cosmetics and spare lotions. And now the bag was open and shreds of polythene were hanging out. For a second she was too paralysed by fear to move. She stared at it, her stomach lurching into her throat. Then common sense kicked in. She had been in a hurry. Andy had been at the door. The polythene had caught in the zip. There was no more to it than that. The bottle was still there. She could see where the shreds were sticking out between the metal teeth. Calming herself with an effort she reached for the flannel and wrung it out under the cold tap. Seconds later she was ready.

A cheerful crewman pointed the way along the river's edge where in the distance they could see their fellow passengers in a tight group, clustered around Omar as he gesticulated wildly ahead, and stood watching them with unashamed interest as they set off beneath the intense blue of the morning sky.

'Do you want to catch up for the lecture?' Andy glanced at her.

'Jog, you mean?'

'It's the only way.'

'I don't think so.' She grinned at him companionably. 'You go on if you want to. I'm happy to explore on my own.'

He shook his head. 'No, running is not for me. At least not in this heat. But I did read up on Kom Ombo last night. I'll fill you in, if you like.'

By the time they reached the crowded, colourful stalls clustered near the entrance to the temple, he had covered thousands of years of history, from its prehistoric origins, to its rebuilding in the Ptolomaic period. 'It's much older than Edfu; a double temple. Split in two down the middle. Half is dedicated to Haroeris or Horus the elder and half to Sobek, the crocodile god,' he instructed her as they walked. 'It was a temple of healing. People came from all over the place to consult the healer priests and it's far more ruined than Edfu. It's so close to the river, the water has damaged it, and then there was an earthquake not so long ago.'

The place was crowded with tourists and once more they found themselves shuffling forward in a queue of slowly moving visitors to present their tickets.

'I thought you must have decided to give this one a miss.' Toby was suddenly there beside her as Andy, distracted for a moment, and glancing from one side to the other at the temple, had drifted out of earshot. 'Dallying with our antique dealer, I see.' He raised an eyebrow in Andy's direction. 'Serena is looking for you, by the way. Do I gather that you decided to speak to her as I suggested?'

Anna nodded. 'She was most helpful. You're right. She knows a lot about mystical stuff and Egyptian history.'

'Enough to set your mind at rest?' He gave her a quick glance. They were walking slowly across the forecourt now, between the stunted remains of its stout columns towards the facade of the hypostyle hall.

'Set your mind at rest?' Andy had veered back towards them. 'About what? Is something worrying you, Anna?'

She shrugged and shook her head. 'Nothing serious.' Omar was close in front of them now, talking about the temple's position at the crossing of the caravan routes from Nubia and the roads from the desert where they brought in the gold, and pointing out winged sun discs over the two doorways. She moved closer. Omar was knowledgeable. Worth hearing. It was stupid to ignore the built-in lectures which came with the tour. Trying hard to concentrate on what he was saying, her eyes followed his pointing hand to look at the bas-relief carvings, but almost at once she found her attention straying. She was trying to imagine what this great temple had been like in the past. To sense whether any of its atmosphere was still there.

She had always done this, even as a child; felt the need to block out distractions, even when they were interesting and informative, so that she could concentrate on the atmosphere. Facts could come later. It was the feel of a place which brought it alive. That was what mattered, what would remain with her long after her visit was over; that was what counted, far more than finding out the date its walls were built. And that was the part of Egypt which she would take home with her. And anyway, she had never liked formal lectures.

'I thought I told you to keep away from Andy!' The whisper in her ear was sharp and angry. She spun round in surprise.

Charley stood only a couple of feet away from her, her eyes masked by large dark glasses. 'I meant it.' She glanced round and as the others shuffled after Omar into the hypostyle hall she stood with her back to them, barring Anna's way. 'I should concentrate on someone else if I were you.'

'I don't think it's any of your business who I talk to!' Anna retorted sharply. 'I can't help thinking you're over-reacting! I assure you, I have no intention of stealing your boyfriend, if that is what he is. After all, I have only just met him. But if he and I wish to speak to each other like normal adults, then I see no reason why we shouldn't.'

For a moment she thought Charley was going to hit her. The younger woman's face was scarlet with anger and her fists were clenched. She took a deep breath and visibly controlled herself, almost shaking with rage, then abruptly she turned away.

'Atta girl!' Toby, who had been eavesdropping with unashamed interest grinned at Anna broadly.

She blushed. For some reason she would much rather he had not overheard the exchange. She glanced round for Charley. She had vanished, then Anna saw her once more at Andy's side. As Anna watched, the young woman slipped her arm possessively through his 'I'm surprised she hasn't got him on a collar and lead,' she couldn't resist commenting tartly.

Toby made a face. 'I know a lot of women who would do that, given half a chance.' He didn't soften the words with a smile.

'That sounds very bitter.' Anna raised an eyebrow at his change of tone. 'Do I gather you speak from experience?'

His expression darkened. 'I am sure most men could, if questioned hard enough. Let's change the subject please. I'm sorry. I should not have interrupted your conversation in the first place.

95

Look, our trusty leader is holding forth once more and we should be listening to him.' Moving away he left her suddenly alone. Another crowd of people was approaching, engulfing her. Their guide, gesticulating expansively, was speaking French.

'Anna!' Serena was pushing towards her suddenly. 'There you are! Are you all right?'

'Of course.'

'You look shaken. I saw Charley speaking to you. I was too far away to get there. But you were rescued, I gather?'

Anna frowned angrily. 'In a manner of speaking. Tell me, is no one here interested in the history of Egypt? Everyone seems to have an axe to grind and no one is listening to Omar!' She paused, then she went on in a rush, 'I can't think, with all due respect, how you can tolerate Charley. I'm sorry, but she is impossible. I am not after her boyfriend, for goodness sake.'

Serena gave a comfortable laugh. 'I don't have to tolerate her. She's only my tenant, not my friend, or even my flatmate. Not really. And she doesn't see me as any kind of a threat. I'm afraid she has sensed Andy's interest in you far more quickly than you have. You're an attractive woman, Anna. He fancies you. It's the way he is. If you are genuinely not interested, she will see it in the end.' She paused. 'And in the meantime you and I have a task to perform.'

'A task?' Anna stared at her for a moment, not understanding.

'You can't have forgotten last night already! We are going to make a sacrifice to the gods, my dear. Remember?' Serena met her eye, then exploded into laughter. 'Anna, your face! I was not suggesting we make Charley and Andy draw straws and throw them from the highest column. I think we can be more subtle than that. More refined. If there were any I would suggest flowers. Perhaps, as it is, a libation will do. I brought something with me which I thought might be suitable.' She patted the large pale-fawn suede bag she habitually carried on her shoulder. 'We'll find a quiet corner. It's worth doing, Anna.'

They were threading their way through the French tourists, still heading steadily towards the heart of the temple. Their own group had vanished.

'I thought someone had tried to take the scent bottle this morning.' Anna followed her, close on her heels. 'I went into the shower where I had left it wrapped up in my make-up bag. I found the bag open, the polythene I had wrapped it in, ripped. It must have been me. I'm sure it was me. In my hurry I probably caught the zip and didn't close it properly, but I was, just for a moment, so frightened.' There was a small treacherous voice at work in her head. She could hear it distinctly pointing out, 'But you tucked the polythene bag out of the way. You know it didn't catch. You know you zipped it up properly . . .' She pushed the voice aside and became aware suddenly that Serena was talking to her.

'Don't worry about it. Not now. Did you look up the diary to see what Louisa has to say about it?'

'I did. But I'm afraid I was distracted into reading a bit about her and Hassan at Edfu. I will have another look for any references to it this afternoon.'

'And apart from the zip you saw nothing unusual last night?'

Anna hesitated. Some dust. Some strange, spicy dust. Just how neurotic was she getting? She shook her head. 'I read until quite late.'

'It was already quite late when we decided to go to bed, Anna!' Again the deep gurgle of amusement. 'Look, let's find a quiet place, if that's at all possible with all these crowds around.'

'And what good will it do?'

'If we please the gods, his gods, it can do no harm. And maybe, just maybe it will keep him away, whoever he is. Here.' She beckoned Anna away from the main stream of visitors towards a quieter corner.

'Omar said that the place for offerings was over there.' Anna gestured ahead of them.

'So it was. But there was another, where the priests served Haroeris through here, hidden in the wall. I think somewhere quieter would be better for our purposes, don't you?'

They ducked through the small doorway into a dark chamber. Inside two men were photographing the reliefs. They did not turn as Serena beckoned Anna towards the far wall. 'See here.' She groped in her pocket and produced a slim pencil torch. The thin beam focused on a group of figures. 'Yes.' Her whisper was triumphant. 'Haroeris with Thoth and Isis. We are in the right place. I looked it up last night. This is where we make our petition.'

She glanced at the two men. One was focusing his lens within inches of the wall, the other making notes by the light of a small lamp. 'Last one.' The words drifted across to them from the darkness.

Serena raised an eyebrow. 'The moment we are alone. Here.' She fumbled in her bag. 'These guys are used to a lot of ceremonial. I just hope the intention and our sincerity count for something with them.'

'If they're listening,' Anna couldn't help observing, somewhat wryly. 'After all, there can't be many people talking to them these days.'

Serena glanced at her quizzically. 'I think you'd be surprised.'

Packing up his camera at last the taller of the two men strolled towards them. 'Great place! You've found the Isis group, I see. Not many people know about it.' His accent placed him as German, Anna thought, or perhaps Swiss. 'It is beautiful is it not? We have already taken pictures of it.' His companion had shouldered a large bag of photographic equipment. He stopped behind them. 'The gods are still here, don't you feel it? They have fled the great temples and now hide in chapels such as this. Good hunting, ladies.' And with a chuckle he headed for the door.

'How did he know?' Anna breathed.

'A kindred spirit, maybe.' Serena reached into her bag and produced a small plastic bottle. 'Here, while we're alone. Pour some into your palm. Offer it to the gods, and then pour it onto the ground before them. It's red wine. The best we can do under the circumstances. I took it last night during dinner.'

Anna hesitated. 'This doesn't seem right.'

'Believe me, it's right. It's whether they accept it or not that we can't be certain of.' She unscrewed the cap.

Anna held out her hands. 'I'm sorry, but I feel like an idiot.'

Serena looked up at her face. 'Don't.' She spoke sharply. 'Quickly. I can hear voices. Make the offering.'

Outside in the distance Anna heard a guffaw of laughter, followed by a sudden animated burst of conversation in what sounded like excited Arabic.

'Quickly. Put your hands together.'

She did as she was told and felt the warm wine trickle into her palms.

'Hold it up! To the great gods of Egypt. Haroeris and Thoth and Isis, lady of the moon.'

Anna repeated the names, and then added for good measure, 'Please protect us and keep us safe.' She held out her hands for a moment, then slowly parting her two palms, allowed the wine to splatter on the stone at her feet. All desire to laugh had left her. The atmosphere in the small room was suddenly electric. She felt herself holding her breath and glancing at Serena, saw that she was staring at the wall, transfixed. She followed her gaze and gasped. Was that the shadow of a man superimposed upon the carving? For a moment she didn't move, then Serena brought her arms up and crossed them over her chest. Her bow towards the wall was deep and reverent. Anna hesitated, then copied her.

They had barely finished when two figures appeared in the doorway. 'I thought I saw you duck in here. What are you up to?' Ben's shape blocked out the light for a moment. He pulled off his hat and wiped his forehead with his arm. 'Have you seen anything interesting? Have you looked at the mummified crocs yet?'

Joe had followed him in. Both men had cameras in their hands. Anna surreptitiously rubbed the red wine from her palms on a tissue. She could smell it, rich and alcoholic in the air, and waited for the men to comment, but they seemed not to notice. Serena had screwed the cap back on her bottle. She slid it into her bag. In seconds they were back in the sunshine and the four of them were heading slowly further in towards the heart of the temple.

Anna glanced at Serena. 'Did you see it?'

Serena nodded. She put her finger to her lips. 'We'll talk later, back on the boat. Keep your eyes open, though. The gods are definitely around.' With a grin she linked her arm through Ben's. 'We've lots more to see, then Omar said we should look at the stalls down there in the village and buy ourselves something pretty if we can negotiate a good price.'

For the second time Anna made her way up onto the sundeck after their late lunch. She glanced round for the empty chairs and chose one at the extreme front of the boat. Clutching her hat and the bag which contained both sun lotion and diary she made her way towards it between the intrepid sun worshippers who were braving the afternoon's heat and, sitting down, she swung her long brown legs up on the leg rest in front of her. The air was very hot and she could feel the lethal bite of the sunlight on her skin even through the sun cream. Most of the others were below in the shade or asleep in their cabins content to rest after the strenuous morning.

She heard footsteps near her suddenly and feigned sleep behind her dark glasses. She couldn't cope with Andy and Charley at this moment. Lunch had provided Charley with several opportunities to clutch at his arm and pout in Anna's direction. The display had left her cold and Andy, she was glad to see, had ignored the woman almost completely, plainly growing tired of her petulance.

She half opened one eye and saw that it was Toby who had come up on deck. Ignoring the chairs he walked up to the rail and leant on it. There was a sketchbook in his hand, she noticed, though he hadn't opened it. He didn't seem to have noticed her, concentrating all his attention on the river where a graceful felucca was winging its way past them.

She lay still, Louisa's diary unopened in her bag. The hot air was heavy and it was hard to stay awake. Her eyelids drooped. She was aware of Toby putting one foot on the lower rail to rest more comfortably, then he opened his sketchbook and pulled a pencil out of his shirt pocket.

The boat would soon be leaving Kom Ombo to travel on south towards Aswan. Once they had started moving there would be a slight breeze. Stretching like a cat she closed her eyes.

She woke with a start as she heard the engines beginning to rumble in the depths of the boat and a slight tremor ran through the deck.

'We're just leaving.' Toby was still at the rail. He didn't turn round but she assumed he was addressing her; there was no one else within earshot. He was sketching swiftly and fluently, his pad resting in front of him, glancing up every few seconds to take in more detail of his subjects. This time it was a man in a turban rowing a small boat heavily laden with green animal fodder, *berseem*. Anna sat up and levered herself to her feet. She went to stand beside him at the rail. 'Those are good.' She had glanced down at the page of small sketches. He had made several of the boat, so low in the water there was virtually no free-board. And he had sketched separately the strange oars she had noticed everywhere – back to front compared with the ones she knew at home – with the broad end at the top for the rower's hand and the narrow part in the water.

'Thank you.' He drew for a few more seconds. 'That is the island where the crocodiles used to bask. Sobek's subjects . . .' He nodded at a low-lying sandy dune ahead. The temple ruins were above them now on the east bank.

'I was hoping we'd see some crocodiles.' Anna leant next to him, feeling the cooler breeze now on her cheeks.

He shook his head. 'Not any more. They disappeared from the river after they built the Aswan Dam.' He finished his sketch and flipped his notebook shut. Turning he leant on the rail, his back to the water. 'Are you enjoying the trip so far?'

She nodded. 'Very much.'

'When are you going to let me see the diary?' He wasn't looking at her. She followed his gaze and saw the old book, unmistakable in its worn leather cover, poking out of her bag on the deck beside her chair. She frowned. She couldn't explain her reluctance to show him, but already he had pushed himself off the rail and gone to squat beside her bag. Throwing his own sketchbook down on the chair he picked up the diary and without further delay, opened it.

'There aren't many sketches.' It was almost an accusation.

'No.' She was irritated by all this interest in her property and indignant that he had picked it up without her permission. She didn't want him to touch it. 'I'm sorry I can't lend it to you. I'm reading it myself.' She kept her voice steady with an effort.

'And you don't trust me.' He squinted up at her suddenly. His eyes were very clear in the blinding sunlight. His face had changed from a pleasant openness and had reverted to the hard closed look she had seen on the plane.

'I wouldn't trust anyone with it,' she said as calmly as she could. 'It is a personal document belonging to my family.'

'And pretty valuable, no doubt.' He was still leafing through the pages almost greedily. He paused when he reached one of the tiny cameo watercolours and turned the book round to see it better. 'She was good. Delicate. Her eye was fantastic. And her sense of colour. Do you see? She never falters – never hesitates. One stroke and it is perfect. You shouldn't bring this out in the sun, you know. Or put it near your sun cream. It's not some cheap paperback novel to cart around as the mood takes you. This is priceless!'

'It wasn't in the sun until you took it upon yourself to open it!' Anna retorted. She could feel her cheeks burning, and was suddenly furious with him. She was being patronised again. 'If you'd be kind enough to give it to me.' She held out her hand.

For a moment she thought he was going to refuse. He was holding it open, staring down at it as though he were trying to photograph it and fix it in his memory for ever. Reluctantly, he closed it and handed it to her.

'I'm sorry. I didn't mean to upset you,' he said quietly. 'Would you believe me if I told you that I'm not interested in its monetary value? It's the drawings themselves. They are unique. She captures the atmosphere as I would never hope to do in a million years.' Just for a second she saw through his defensive mask and glimpsed something of the spent-up frustration and anguish which seemed to be hiding there. He opened his mouth as though he were going to say something else, changed his mind and turned away. She watched as he disappeared down towards the lower decks.

There was no time to consider his outburst. Seconds later another figure had appeared. It was Andy. He saw her immediately and raised his hand. Hastily she squatted down beside her chair and returning the diary to her bag she pushed it out of sight under the seat.

'Was that Toby Hayward I saw up here with you?' His question appeared casual as he leant against the rail.

Anna raised an eyebrow. 'It was.'

'Wasn't he welcome?' He inclined his head towards her slightly.

'Not particularly. I was hoping to read for a bit in peace.'

'That sounds a bit frosty. Am I getting the brush-off too?'

She sighed. She enjoyed Andy's company, there was no denying it, but just at this moment she could do without anyone's, even his. 'It is not a brush-off, Andy. I am just tired after this morning. It was pretty strenuous, after all. We all had a nice lunch together. I was hoping now, to let the boat take the strain and enjoy some quiet leisurely cruising.'

She thought for a moment he was going to turn away and she gave a sigh of relief, but he changed his mind. He stopped and faced her again. 'Did he ask you about the diary?' he asked casually.

'He did.' She groaned inwardly, thoroughly irritated by his persistence. Was there to be no end to this questioning? First one then the other. Stooping, she scooped up her bag. 'Actually, Andy, if you will forgive me, I think I'll go inside. It's a bit hot up here for me and I might have a bit of a sleep before we all start eating again.' She didn't give him a chance to reply. Leaving him standing there she made her way below, heading back towards her cabin.

Reaching into her bag for her key she pushed open the door. The cabin was in semi-darkness. Before she had left it she had slid

102

the slatted shutters across the open windows to keep the sunlight out. She stepped inside and stopped, gagging. The air was thick with the same dusty spicy smell which had come before from the peaty substance in her suitcase. Choking, she staggered towards the window and throwing the bag on the bed she pulled off her hat and hurling it down she dragged back the shutters. Sunlight flooded across the small cabin. She spun round, scanning the room and then she spotted it on the floor, near the shower room door, a thin scattering of brown resiny fragments. She shuddered.

The shower room door itself was open and slowly she forced herself to move towards it.

Her cosmetics bag was lying on its side under the washbasin, the contents scattered across the floor. Of the polythene-wrapped bottle there was no sign. With an exclamation of alarm she bent and scooped the things back into the bag and looked round. It was only a small area. There was nowhere for the bottle to have rolled. There was nothing for it to hide beneath. Carrying the bag back into the cabin she emptied it onto the bed. She was shivering, she realised suddenly. Reaching for the sweater that was lying on the quilt she pulled it on and then stood looking at the collection of lipsticks and eye-shadows and the tiny travelling plastic pots of this and that cream. Irrelevantly she found herself wondering why she had brought them. She had used virtually none of them since she had come. But of the one thing she wanted to see, the little Egyptian bottle, there was no sign.

She sat down on the bed, running her hands lightly over the make up as though to fix it there, in her cabin.

Closing her eyes she took a deep breath, then she stood up again and went to kneel by the door to the shower. These fragments were not powdery like the last. They were sticky. She stared down at her fingers with a shudder of revulsion. She couldn't shake the stuff off. It clung to her skin, permeating her hands with the cloying scent of cedar and myrrh and cinnamon. Frantically she scrambled to her feet and throwing herself towards the wash-basin she grappled with the taps, turning them on full and rubbing her hands again and again on the tablet of soap until they were raw. Drying them at last she stepped over the rest of the mess and snatching up her key she threw herself at the door. Letting herself out into the corridor she ran towards the stairs.

There were six cabins on the restaurant deck, three on each side

103

of the long narrow corridor much like her own. Each was numbered like hers and all the doors were shut. Which one was Serena's? She stood there frantically, racking her brains. Had Serena told her the number of her cabin? She couldn't remember.

A door opened suddenly, almost beside her, and Toby appeared. She stared at him, startled, then forced herself to take a deep breath. Relaxing her face into a smile she greeted him. 'Ah, a friendly face at last!' Perhaps not the most appropriate thing to say, but the first that came into her head. 'I was beginning to think it was a bit like the Marie Celeste down here. You don't happen to know which is Serena's room, do you?'

He shrugged. 'I'm sorry. I think she's up at the end somewhere, but I'm not sure which one.' Closing his own door after him, he locked it and edging past her with a nod he made for the stairs.

She stared after him for a moment acutely aware with some part of her brain that he was still annoyed with her and that for the sake of her own peace of mind and probably his she was going to have to make amends somehow – probably by showing him the diary. She turned and made her way to the end of the corridor, listening cautiously for a moment at one of the doors where she thought she had heard a movement. There was only silence, as there was at the next. Then from the opposite side of the passage she heard the quiet murmur of a female voice. Raising her hand she knocked. The voice fell silent then she heard the clack of wooden sandals on the floor and the door opened. It was Charley.

'Well, well.' She looked Anna up and down as though she were some particularly odd form of low life. 'To what do we owe this pleasure?' Her voice was heavy with sarcasm.

'Is Serena there?'

Charley shrugged. She stepped away from the door and went to sit at the dressing table, leaving Anna in the doorway. 'It's for you,' she called.

The cabin was exactly like Anna's except that there were two beds and two cupboards crammed into a space barely larger than that of her own. The shower room door, an exact replica of the one in Anna's cabin, opened and Serena appeared, wrapped in a towel. Her short wet hair was pushed back off her face and her shoulders were covered in droplets of water.

'Sorry, I was in the shower.' She stated the obvious with a smile. 'What is it, Anna? Is something wrong?' Her smile faded.

'Something's happened,' Anna blurted out. 'I needed to talk to someone –'

Charley swung round on the stool and stared at her curiously. 'What sort of someone? Someone else's boyfriend, perhaps?'

'Charley!' Serena's voice was sharp. 'Don't be stupid.' She looked back at Anna. 'Give me five minutes. Wait in the lounge. Then we can talk.'

Numbly Anna nodded. She turned away from the door and made her way slowly back to the stairs and began to climb.

The lounge was empty. She stared out of the double doors towards the shaded deck with its awning and tables. It looked pleasant out there – cool out of the direct sunlight. The elderly clergyman and his wife were sitting beneath the awning, cold drinks in front of them, and near them a couple who had told her they came from Aberdeen. At one table she could see Ben. He appeared to be asleep. Toby was seated alone at one of the tables near the door, a beer in front of him beside the open sketchbook. He was working away at a drawing, his back towards her.

She watched him for a while, studying his profile as he reached forward, picked up his glass, drank and bent back over his sketchbook, his slim brown fingers moving swiftly over the page. From the direction of his gaze she assumed he must be drawing the graceful minaret she could see above the waving fronds of the palm trees on the opposite bank.

A large tourist cruiser was heading downstream past them. She could hear the beat of music over the pulse of the engines. Judging by the numbers of these huge noisy boats, she thought wryly, a large proportion of visitors to Egypt must be allergic to silence; probably allergic to history too. They were the ones who jostled and laughed at the monuments and listened to no one and looked at nothing. She felt a sudden quick surge of resentment. How was it they could all be so carefree? Many of them had probably come here on a whim, could have gone anywhere, probably had been on package tours all over Europe if not the world, already, whilst she, who had so passionately wanted to come to Egypt for so long, was feeling nervous and worried and very lonely.

'Why not come out here and join me?'

She realised that Toby had put down his pencil and was leaning back in his chair. He must have sensed that she was there. Reluctantly she stepped out through the doors. 'Thank you.'

He half rose. 'Can I get you a beer?' It seemed to be a gesture of appeasement.

'No. No, thank you.' She tried to modify her refusal by smiling. 'I just came out for a breath of air.'

'Noisy bastards, aren't they.' It was as though he had read her thoughts as he nodded towards the cruiser disappearing around the long shallow bend behind them.

'They do rather spoil the silence.'

'It's their way of enjoying themselves. I suppose we mustn't be judgemental.' He glanced at her, the trace of a smile on his lips. 'The birds take no notice. You see the egrets over there, on the trees at the water's edge? They just sit and stare and look enigmatic.'

'They're used to the boats. There must be hundreds of them every day, and I suppose they know the people never get off. Not just here, anyway.' Anna pulled out a chair and sat down at his table. His sketch showed the minaret as she had guessed, together with the palms and a group of flat-roofed mud-brick houses. Since leaving Kom Ombo the boat had been travelling through Nubia and there was a distinct change in the landscape. For one thing the houses were painted bright colours.

'You're lucky to be able to record the trip like this.' She indicated the sketchbook. 'I have to resort to the camera.'

'Are you not a good photographer then?' He was drawing again, cross-hatching a shadow on the page and did not look up.

She felt a quick flash of resentment. 'Why assume that?'

'I didn't. Your own doubt in the merits of your photography implied it. After all, this must be the most photogenic country on earth. You would have to be singularly inept not to be able to take a passable clutch of snaps home for your album.'

'My God, that sounds patronising!' She exploded, unable to stop herself.

'Does it?' His pencil hovered for a moment as though he were considering the matter. 'If so, I'm sorry.' He didn't look it. He merely raised an eyebrow. 'I see you are no longer trundling all your possessions around with you.'

'My possessions?' She stared at him, puzzled for a moment. Then she understood. 'Oh, you mean the diary.'

He gave an almost imperceptible shrug. 'Women seem to need to carry huge sacks of stuff with them wherever they go.'

'Unlike men we do not have voluminous pockets.'

He looked up at last and eyed her dress with, she felt, rather more than necessary care. 'I suppose not,' he conceded.

'Anna?' Serena's voice behind her made her look round in considerable relief. The woman was standing looking down at Toby's drawing. 'I don't want to intrude,' she said with a smile.

'No. No, you're not.' Anna stood up hastily. 'I'll leave you to your creative processes,' she said to Toby with some asperity. She did not wait to hear whatever retort he came up with next. Heading for the stairs to the upper deck she led the way up.

Serena followed her to the rail. Companionably she leant on it, watching the passing scene for a few minutes. At last she spoke. 'So, aren't you going to tell me what is wrong?'

'Do you think I'm mad?' Anna stared down into the water.

'I doubt it. Unless Toby Hayward has pushed you over the edge. You don't like him, do you?'

There was a long pause. 'He's too acerbic for me. I don't want to spend the holiday duelling. I don't see the need for it. He seems to have a massive chip on his shoulder!' She changed the subject abruptly. 'Serena, there is something in my cabin. It's weird. Horrible. I want you to come and look at it.' She shuddered. 'And the bottle has gone.'

'Gone?' Serena swung to face her. 'Are you sure?'

'Quite sure. I left it in the make-up bag, in the shower. The bag was open, emptied on the floor.'

'Then it has been stolen. One of the crew perhaps –'

'No. I think it was something – someone – else.'

Serena eyed her. 'Anna, sometimes when we're overwrought,' she said gently, 'we start to imagine things. It's easy to do.'

'No.' Anna's voice was bleak. 'Please come with me and see. I'm not overwrought. I'm not suffering from sunstroke. I'm not hallucinating.'

'OK. OK. This is me, remember?' Serena leant across and laid her hand on Anna's arm for a moment. She thought for a second then she went and sat down sideways on one of the sunloungers. 'Tell me exactly what you have seen.'

'Our libation to the gods didn't work,' Anna murmured sadly. She bit her lip.

'It seems not. But tell me what you've seen.'

Anna shrugged. 'Dust. Incense – in my cabin. I don't know what it is, or how it got in there – I can feel them close, Serena. Louisa's

107

good priest and the evil djinn. I can feel them so close.' She shook her head. 'I'm so scared.'

With a sudden crescendo of noise another cruiser drew level with them and began to pass them, churning up the turbid water. A line of figures on the top deck, all dressed alike in shorts and dark glasses and a dazzling selection of garish tee-shirts waved and yelled at them. Anna raised an arm reluctantly in acknowledgement of a race conceded without ever having been declared and turned her back. She looked down at Serena. 'I have this rather naïve, childish desire to pray. "Please God, make it all right. Make the bad men go away."'

Serena glanced up at her. 'Why is it naïve and childish to pray?' she asked gently.

'Because it never works, does it.' Anna sat down on the lounger alongside Serena's and faced her. She leant forward, her elbows on her knees. 'When push comes to shove, we're on our own. Aren't we?'

Serena looked at her for a moment, an expression of extreme sadness in her eyes. 'I don't think we're alone,' she said at last.

'Well, obviously not or you wouldn't be making sacrifices to Isis and Thoth!' Anna retorted. 'Although I did wonder if you were doing that just to make me feel happy.'

Serena shook her head. 'I don't believe in meaningless gestures, Anna,' she said sharply. 'We may not have known one another very long, but I hoped you would have realised that.'

'Yes.' Anna sighed. 'I'm sorry.

'I do believe, genuinely, that prayer works.'

'Does it?' Anna shrugged. 'For you, perhaps.' She stood up restlessly and moved back to the rail. The other boat, far larger and with powerful engines, had overtaken them and drawn away. The river was quiet again. In the distance a felucca headed for the bank. She could remember praying. Praying her father would love her and approve, just once, of something she did. Praying that Felix was really away on business as he had said, praying that her suspicions were not justified, praying that her mother wouldn't die. None of the prayers had worked. Not one.

'Maybe your prayers were heard, but the answer, for reasons you could not at the time comprehend, was no.' Serena leant back and swung her legs up onto the footrest. She folded her arms. 'It is perhaps childlike and naïve, to quote your own words, to expect the answer always to be yes. But if you pray for something which is right for you, then your prayers will be answered with a yes. Never stop praying, Anna.'

'But who do I pray to?' A large brown heron was flying up the river, only a few feet above the water, its slow wingbeats keeping time to the oar strokes of a small boat crossing their wake behind them. 'Isis? Thoth? The Jesus of my childhood?' She shook her head suddenly. 'I'm sorry. This is not the moment for deep philosophical discussion.'

'I think it is. It's very relevant. I have a rather unorthodox answer to your question. One that fits the Egyptian context very well. In my opinion they are one, Anna. Isis. Thoth. The Aten. Jesus. All different aspects of the one great God. Pray to any and all of them, my dear, but pray.' She smiled wryly. 'If my views were widely known I would probably be burnt at the stake by somebody even in our so-called enlightened age. No fundamentalist of any faith would put up with me for an instant. Perhaps you'd better not listen.'

'It's a comforting thought, though. Sort of covering all your options.'

'Think about it, Anna. In all the tens of thousands of years that mankind has existed and worshipped his gods, each successive generation has replaced the gods of the generation before with the gods to suit itself and they have all in turn said, 'Thou shalt have none other gods but me,' or words to that effect. But why should one be better than another? One be better than several? In my view each god is the manifestation of the one god in an appropriate form to fit his age. For our age and culture we had Jesus, a gentle healer, an idealist, but we turned out to be a far from gentle and idealistic people in the Europe and Middle East of the last two thousand years, so some of us have adapted Jesus accordingly and some have reverted to previous incarnations of the gods of the past; others have adopted gods from other parts of the world.'

'I think you're right. I think fundamentalists would indeed have problems with your views.' Anna shook her head. 'But the fact remains, we offered a perhaps rather superficial handful of wine to the gods of two thousand years ago in the hope that they would protect us from the ancient djinn and they have, probably quite rightly, ignored us. So, what do I do now?'

Serena climbed to her feet. 'Right. To the practicalities. There is something in your cabin that you want me to see. Let's go and look at it right now.'

The strange substance had gone, and with it the smell.

Searching the cabin and the small bathroom did not take long. They checked and double-checked and then sat down, Anna on the bed, Serena on the little stool she had hooked out from beneath the dressing table.

'I suppose you think it was my imagination.'

'No, Anna, I believe you.'

'But the smell has gone.'

'I still believe you.' Serena smiled.

'And someone has taken the bottle.' Anna shook her head. 'You know, in some strange way I'm almost relieved.'

'You don't sound too sure.'

'I've had it a long time. I treasured it.'

'Ah.'

'And I'm not convinced a ghost, even a cunning Egyptian ghost, can pick something up and carry it away.'

'But why should anyone else steal it?'

'It's an antique.'

They looked at each other for a moment then Serena shook her head. 'No. Not Andy. No way. Why should he? He thinks it's a fake. Who else knows about it?'

Anna shrugged 'No one.'

Had Toby seen it in her bag? She frowned. But surely even if he had, he would not have taken it.

Serena was watching her face. 'You've thought of someone?'

'No. No one on the boat would take it. The diary is valuable. That might be a temptation to someone, I suppose. Both Andy and Toby have warned me about it, but no one would take the bottle.'

They sat in silence for a moment, a silence that was intensified by the sound of the gong in the depths of the boat. 'Supper.' Serena shrugged.

'Do we say anything? Ask if anyone has seen it?'

Serena shook her head with a grimace. 'I'd say not. You're not accusing anyone yet – probably not at all. I'm sure the crew are trustworthy and all the passengers. No. If it was me, I'd keep quiet for now.'

110

She did. The meal was a cheerful one and it was easy to let the conversation flow round her, listening to the others. Once or twice she put in a comment, but it was hardly necessary. The visit to Kom Ombo, the afternoon's leisurely cruise, the throb of the engines as they headed towards Aswan had worn them all out. There was a general easy bonhomie interspersed with long friendly silences as one after another people found their eyes closing.

Omar had arranged a film for them in the lounge bar after the meal and gradually the passengers made their way up to find seats and sit sipping after-dinner drinks and coffee.

As they disappeared from the dining room Anna remained where she was. Ben leant down as he left the table. 'Coming with us, Anna, my dear?'

She shook her head. 'To tell you the truth I'm a bit tired.'

'OK.' He gave her a quick smile and moved on after Andy and Charley. Charley glanced over her shoulder as she left the dining room. The look she threw at Anna was triumphant.

She was the last passenger there, sitting alone as Ali and Ibrahim cleared the tables. It was Ibrahim who eventually approached her. He removed the final dishes from the table and whisked a brush across the tablecloth. 'You are sad, *mademoiselle*? Would you like a beer to cheer you up? Or a coffee, here alone? I can fetch you one.' He had a gentle face, deeply lined, and his dark brown eyes were, she realised as she looked up at him, very kind.

'I should like that, Ibrahim. Thank you. A coffee please.'

'But not Egyptian coffee.' His face creased into a thousand wrinkles as he smiled. It had already become a standing joke on the boat that Egyptian coffee was too strong for most of the effete British.

'No. I wouldn't sleep for a month. Weak English coffee with milk, please Ibrahim.'

Ali had finished his chores. He glanced round, satisfied, and reached to turn off most of the lights, leaving only the one above Anna's table.

'I'm sorry. I'm making more trouble for you by staying here.' She spoke to Ali, but already he had gone, disappearing towards the kitchens and the crew's quarters beyond. It was Ibrahim who answered, bringing her coffee.

'It is no trouble. I am pleased to serve you, *mademoiselle*. Please, sit as long as you like.' He bowed. For a moment he hesitated, as

111

though he were going to say something more, then he turned and left.

It was an odd feeling, sitting in the empty dining room. It was almost dark, save for the spotlight illuminating her table. The counter, with the empty polished coffee urn and spotless food containers ready for breakfast was in semi-darkness. There was no sound except the steady throb of the engine and the beat of the paddles as the boat slowly made its way upriver.

She sipped the coffee thoughtfully. Part of her was looking forward to going back to her cabin to read some more of the diary and get an early night; another part was, she had to admit, a little nervous.

She sat for a long time after her cup was empty, her chin resting on her linked fingers. Staring into space, half asleep, she did not at first hear the quiet creak as the doors swung open.

'Aha! So this is where you are hiding!' Andy came in, two glasses awkwardly held in one hand and let the doors swing shut behind him. 'I hope you weren't trying to hide from me!'

She looked up and smiled a little wearily, unable to stop herself glancing quickly at the door behind him to see if Charley were still in hot pursuit. 'As if I could. Or would!'

He put the glasses down on the table and pushed one towards her. 'A night cap.'

'Thank you.'

'May I ask why so thoughtful, all on your own in here? A trouble shared and all that? If it would help.'

It was strange how relaxed she immediately felt in his company. She glanced at him. 'I've lost something. Something rather precious. My little scent bottle. I know you said it was probably a fake but it's very special to me.'

'Could you have dropped it somewhere? Kom Ombo perhaps, when we were climbing around the ruins?'

She shook her head. 'It's gone from my cabin.'

'Stolen you mean?' He looked shocked. 'Surely you've mislaid it? Forgotten where you've put it?'

'I'd like to think so, but I've looked everywhere. Serena helped me. It's not there.'

'Have you reported its loss to Omar?'

She shook her head. How could she tell him that he, Andy, had been her chief suspect. 'I thought I'd look again before I say anything to anyone. It would create such a nasty atmosphere if I started throwing accusations around. Perhaps it will turn up.'

'If you're looking for a suspect I should ask myself about that Hayward fellow. He's been showing an inordinate interest in you and your diary and no one seems to know anything about him.'

'He's no more interested than you've been, Andy,' she retorted. 'No, he's fascinated by Louisa's drawing and painting. He's a bit abrasive, I grant you, but I'm sure he's not a thief.' She glanced at her watch, and sighed. 'So much for my early night. Has the film finished?'

He nodded. He was sipping his drink, staring at her over the brim of the glass.

'And was it interesting?'

'A lesson in how to be a good Muslim citizen of modern Egypt!' He smiled. 'Interesting yes, but I would rather learn more about the ancient history of the country if we have to have lessons at all.'

Anna chuckled. 'I haven't been to any of them. They're not compulsory.'

'They are if they're in the bar!' He leant back and folded his arms. 'So, how are you enjoying the cruise, apart from your loss? I get the feeling that for you it's been a bit stressful so far.'

She paused, considering. 'Yes, I suppose it has. I brought too much baggage with me. Not just Louisa Shelley and her diary and her scent bottle, but my own divorce and my worries for the future.' She shook her head slowly. 'Andy, can I ask you something?' She paused. She wanted to know if he had come across Louisa's paintings on the open market, if he had ever met Felix, if Felix had ever offered him any of her things for sale. Nothing had ever gone missing from the house permanently, but once or twice things had disappeared for a week or two, to be cleaned, he said, and then reappeared. Her suspicion was that he had had them valued. Or that once or twice when he had hit a bad patch at work he had been tempted. It didn't matter now. At the time of their divorce he had been rich enough to give her the house and leave its contents virtually intact. But part of her perversely still wanted to know just how much of a dupe she had been. She was trying to work out how to phrase her question when the double doors to the dining room burst open and Charley stormed in.

'So, this is where you're hiding!' She stepped inside, allowing the doors to swing shut behind her. She had changed since supper when she had been dressed in a pale-green jacket, her hair fastened back in a knot. Now her hair was hanging loose around her shoulders and she was wearing a skimpy pink sundress. 'Why is it I'm not surprised to find you here, I wonder, Andy?' She walked over to their table and stood over them, looking down. 'Just tell me something, Andy. Are we finished?'

Anna stood up hastily. 'Look, this is nothing to do with me –'

'Of course it is.' Charley glared at her coldly. 'Believe me, this has everything to do with you.'

'No, Charley. It hasn't.' Andy stood up too. He slammed his glass down on the table. 'Long before we came here I was sick of your clinging and whingeing, and since we've been on the boat your temper has been atrocious. I don't know what is the matter with you. I'm sorry. I don't want to hurt you, but you and I are going nowhere together. I didn't want to have to say this, but it seems I've got to. You don't seem to want a pleasant, natural relationship which is going to develop at its own rate. You want a man to provide you with a lifestyle, Charley. You want him to give you money, house, wedding ring, even designer baby, for God's sake! That man is not me. You've got to learn to make your own way, Charley, or find some other sucker who doesn't mind being sponged off. And leave Anna alone. She's right. This has nothing to do with her. We were having a peaceful drink. That's all. No more. No less. No complications.' He paused and took a deep breath. 'Listen, this is a small boat. This is the holiday of a lifetime for most of the people on it. Don't spoil it for them. No one else need know about this. I know Anna won't say anything, and neither will I. So let's keep it private, and stay friends. When we get to Aswan tomorrow let's just enjoy ourselves, OK?' He held out his hands towards her.

'Friends!' Charley almost spat the word at him. 'I don't think so. Do you know what you are, Andy? You're a smug, conceited, self-centred bastard! And you only want her because of her valuable diary and you'll do anything to get it. I know you! You'll drop her once you've got what you want, just like you went off me once you'd got my father's Hockney! Well, you deserve each other.'

The last remark was hurled at Anna as Charley whirled round and stormed out of the dining room, flinging back the doors so hard against the wall that the sound seemed to reverberate through the boat.

114

Anna looked at Andy in stunned silence. He sighed. 'I'm sorry. I wouldn't have had that happen for the world. Stupid woman. We've been working up to this for quite a while. Take no notice of anything she said. With a bit of luck this will clear the air.' He paused. 'And in case you're wondering, yes, I bought her father's Hockney. It was rather a good one. And I resold it for a profit. Legally. Above board. Everyone was happy. That is the first time she's even mentioned it!'

'I'm beginning to think this holiday is cursed.' Anna shook her head.

'What, from going into Tutankhamen's tomb? I don't think so.' He laughed. 'Come on, cheer up. I've got some more of this stuff in my cabin. Why don't we go and get a top-up –'

He was just reaching for her glass when they heard a piercing scream from somewhere in the corridor outside. They stared at each other in shock for a split second, then Andy turned and made for the door with Anna right behind him.

A crowd of people were already gathering around an open cabin door at the end of the corridor as they emerged from the dining room. It was Charley's cabin.

'What is it? What's happened? Where's Serena?' Andrew pushed to the front of the crowd.

Charley was standing in the middle of the cabin floor, tears pouring down her face. 'It was a snake! In there!' She pointed at the floor where one of the drawers from the dressing table lay, its contents spilt all around it. 'It was in there, waiting for me!' She had started to shake violently.

'Did it bite you, Charley?' Ben pushed forward through the crowd. He was clutching a first aid box.

Behind him Omar had appeared, his face a picture of anguish. 'What is this? What has happened?' Omar moved Ben out of the way bodily and stepped into the cabin. 'Please, Miss Charley, be quiet so we can hear ourselves talk.' Charley's sobs were rapidly becoming hysterical. 'Now, quietly, tell us what happened. Are you hurt?'

'A snake!' She pointed at the drawer. 'There was a snake curled up inside it.'

'Did it bite you?' Omar's face had become ashen.

She shook her head.

He took a deep breath, visibly relieved. 'I don't see how this is

115

possible.' Frowning he took a step back from the drawer. 'How could a snake get into the boat?'

Behind them Serena had suddenly appeared in the doorway. 'What is it? What's wrong?' She pushed her way into the cabin and stared round, taking in the shocked expressions of the horrified onlookers.

'Where have you been?' Charley burst into tears once more.

'I was on deck, looking at the stars.' Serena put her arm round Charley and hugged her comfortingly. 'What is it?'

'There was a snake in the drawer.' Omar shook his head mournfully. 'This is so strange. I don't see how it could happen –'

'More to the point, where has it gone?' Ben put in.

Behind him the crowd was dispersing as one by one the other passengers made their way nervously back to their own cabins, looking uncomfortably around them as they went. The corridor was well lit. There was nowhere for the snake to hide. A narrow strip of carpet ran down the middle of the floor. At the end of the corridor where it debauched into the reception area outside the dining room stood one of the brass spittoons, a relic of the boat's more stately days and the blackboard where the next day's events were posted. Otherwise the corridor was completely empty of hiding places.

'It must still be in here or we would have seen it.' Andy stared round. 'We'll have to look under the bed, in the cupboards, drawers, everywhere. It must have been quite small to have fitted into the drawer. Serena, why not take Charley into the bar while Omar and Ben and I look for it?'

Omar shook his head. 'We would not find it. Snakes can hide. They can make themselves invisible. I shall fetch Ibrahim. He is a snake catcher. He can call them and they will come.'

'Call them?' Ben echoed. He raised an eyebrow.

Omar nodded. 'His father and his father's father did this before him. They have power over snakes. He can smell them. If there is a snake here, he will smell it and he will catch it and he will take it away.'

They all stared at him. 'You're not serious?' Ben said at last. 'You mean he's a snake charmer?'

Omar shrugged. 'Not like a charmer who sits with a basket in the bazaar. Those snakes have had their poison drawn. Ibrahim will not harm the snakes and the snakes will not harm him. I will fetch him now.' He made his way out of the cabin, clearly relieved to be away from any possible close proximity to the creature.

Serena led Charley away. She glanced at Anna as they passed her. 'We'll talk tomorrow.' She smiled. 'Are you all right?'

Anna nodded. Only she and Ben and Andy were left now. She should go too, she knew, but something kept her there in the doorway. She took a small step into the cabin.

'Careful, Anna,' Ben warned. 'It might be a cobra. They are still common in the fields along the Nile.'

But her eyes were on the drawer. It contained a muddle of filmy female underwear – Charley's rather than Serena's at a guess – a few strings of beads and there, nestling in the middle ... She stepped closer.

'My scent bottle!' She bent and lifted it out. 'That is my scent bottle – stolen from my cabin!'

Andy frowned. 'You were talking to Serena about it, weren't you? Maybe she –'

'No!' Anna swung round on him. 'No, Andy. It was Charley. We both know it was Charley.' Her indignation was mitigated by relief that she need not after all contemplate the idea of some kind of ghostly interference in her cabin.

Behind them Omar had appeared. At his heels was Ibrahim, carrying a covered basket.

'Please to come away, peoples.' Omar stood back and ushered Anna out of the cabin, leaving Ibrahim standing alone in the centre of the floor. As they clustered round the doorway he turned to them, frowning, and put his finger to his lips. They froze, watching.

He stood quite still for several seconds, his head slightly to one side. Turning round he waited again, listening intently. They could see the slight flaring of his nostrils as he sniffed the air. Moving across to the window he ran his hand for a second across it. It was closed. Then he turned and surveyed the room. He was looking increasingly puzzled.

At last he shook his head. 'There is no snake here. *Pas de serpents.*'

'Are you sure?' Omar was still in the doorway.

'Ibrahim is sure. But there is something strange here.' He frowned. He was staring down at the drawer. 'If it was there it was very small. The cobra, he grows to two metres. More.' He squatted down and reached out his hand, then as though suddenly realising what the drawer contained he drew back distastefully. He stood

117

up, turned round and looked straight at Anna who was still there in the doorway with Ben and Andy. He stared at her for a moment, then he shook his head. '*Mademoiselle* has something – something the king snake guards –' His voice dropped away, puzzled. 'The snake is afraid you will give it away, to a man.'

Anna's hands tightened around the little scent bottle. 'I don't understand.' Little waves of panic rippled across her skin.

Ibrahim nodded slowly. 'He has gone now. There is no danger from him, but there is a shadow in the air.' His long thin fingers wove a pattern for a moment in front of them, and then curled into a fist. 'He is angry and that is not good.'

'We cannot have a snake on the boat, Ibrahim,' Omar put in. He frowned repressively. 'We shall have to call in someone when we get to Aswan if you cannot find it.' He added a quick quiet corollary in Arabic.

Ibrahim's face darkened imperceptibly. 'Do you not trust my words?'

'Of course I trust you,' Omar bowed. 'It is the travel company. Their representative comes aboard at Aswan to see all is well . . .' He shrugged expansively.

'And all will be well, *Inshallah*!' Ibrahim nodded. 'Now go. All go to your cabins. The king snake is not on the boat any longer.'

Andy glanced at Anna and then at Omar. 'Can you be sure of that?'

'Have I not said?' Ibrahim frowned. He was a tall man and he had, if anything, gained in stature as he was speaking to them. When he had arrived, he was no longer wearing the white *galabiyya* of a waiter; his garment was deep blue, embroidered around the edge with a rich design. Next to Omar who habitually wore black trousers and a western shirt he looked exotic and mysterious and, Anna realised, in a strange way, very powerful.

Climbing the stairs towards her own cabin, having declined the offer of an escort from both Ben and Andy, Anna turned on reaching the reception area outside the lounge, to push her way through the swing doors. She could see Serena and Charley sitting on the sofa in the corner, the two figures huddled close to each other in the near darkness, the dim light of a single lamp casting a soft glow over them. Someone had brought them cups of tea.

'It's all right,' Anna said as she headed towards them. 'The cabin is safe. It's gone.'

Charley looked up. Her cheeks were pale, streaked with mascara. 'Did they kill it?'

Anna shook her head. 'No, it disappeared. Ibrahim knows about snakes. He is certain it's gone. There's nothing to be afraid of.'

She sat down opposite them, glancing at Serena, then back at Charley. 'So, how did my scent bottle get into your drawer, Charley?'

She saw the shock register in Serena's eyes.

Charley looked down at her hands. 'It was a joke. I wasn't going to keep it.'

'No?' For a moment Anna stared at her, frowning. She reached into her pocket and drew the bottle out, laying it on the table in front of them. 'Did you realise it was valuable?'

'It's not.' Charley looked up defiantly. 'Andy says it's a bit of tat from a bazaar.'

'And so you thought it didn't matter if you took it?'

'I told you. I would have given it back.'

'And how exactly did you get into my cabin?'

'The door was wide open. Anyone could have walked in.' Charley rubbed her face with her hands. 'It was lying there on your bed, all dirty and messy and covered in earth or something, and I thought why not?'

'On my bed?' Anna frowned.

'Yes. I didn't rummage through your stuff if that's what you think. It was just lying there.'

Anna shook her head, trying to make sense of Charley's words. The bottle had been wrapped in polythene, in her make-up bag. It had been hidden. 'But you must have gone to my cabin for a reason.'

'I did. To talk to you. To tell you to butt out of my life and leave Andy alone.' Charley groped in her pocket for a tissue. Tears were streaming down her face again. 'Look, I'm sorry. I shouldn't have taken it. Of course I shouldn't. But there is no harm done. It's not damaged.' She stood up. 'I'm going to bed. Are you coming, Serena?'

'In a minute.' Serena hadn't moved.

'But I don't want to go alone. How do I know he searched properly?'

119

'He did. He was sure,' Anna said slowly. She was facing Serena across the low table. Half turning she looked up at Charley. 'It's all right. It's quite safe now.' She gave her a tight smile. 'Just tell me one thing. What did it look like? Exactly.'

'What? The snake?'

Anna nodded. She found that she was clenching her fists.

'What do all snakes look like? It was long. Brownish. Scaly.'

'Was it a cobra?'

'I suppose so. It reared up and opened its hood thing and its tongue went in and out.' Charley shuddered violently.

'Well, whatever it was it has definitely gone. There is no need to worry.'

They watched as after another second's hesitation Charley made her way across the lounge and out of the swing doors. Then Anna turned to Serena.

'Ibrahim is some kind of snake charmer. He called it the king snake, even without seeing it and he said it was guarding something which was mine, which it is afraid I will give to a man.'

They both stared at the little bottle, lying next to the ashtray on the table.

'What if it comes back?' Anna bit her lip; in spite of herself she gave a small shiver.

Serena looked thoughtful. 'What else did Ibrahim say?'

'He said there was no danger but that there was a shadow in the air. He said the snake was angry.'

Serena leant back against the cushions. She closed her eyes and shook her head. 'I'm out of my depth.'

Anna shivered. 'I'll put the bottle in the safe tomorrow, but I don't know if I dare take it back to my cabin, Serena. What if it follows me?' She gave a small mirthless chuckle. 'It makes our existentialist discussion on the subject of prayer seem a bit irrelevant, doesn't it? As you said, we're dealing with experts here.'

'Don't stop praying.' Serena spoke sharply. She raised a hand. 'I'm trying to think about the cobra. It was a very powerful symbol in Ancient Egypt. The uraeus, the symbol of kingship and the serpent goddess Wadjet who became one with Isis – they are shown as cobras.'

Anna shivered again. 'But a goddess would be a queen. Ibrahim called this the king snake. But there aren't any king cobras in Egypt, are there?'

120

Serena raised an eyebrow. 'I don't suppose he was referring to its species. Islam is a patriarchal religion so he assumed it was a male, but I think the snake's sex is academic if it's got you in its sights!'

'But was it real?'

Serena thought for a moment. 'Charley seemed to think so. Real or not, Anna, I think you should probably regard them as deadly. I don't think I would hang around to argue the toss, and neither should you if you see it!' She shook her head and ran her hand across her eyes. 'Dear God, I'm confused. My love, it's late. I think we should get some sleep. Can I make a suggestion? Why not hide the bottle somewhere safe? Out on deck, perhaps. Just until you can put it in the safe. Don't take it back to your cabin.'

Anna didn't argue. They let themselves out of the door onto the rear deck. 'The pot plants,' Anna whispered. 'Why don't I stick it in one of the pots?'

They made their way to the ladder and climbed up onto the sundeck. There, arranged around the bows, were a dozen tubs of brilliant flowers, scarlet geraniums and hibiscus and bougainvillaea. The deck was completely deserted in the darkness.

'I need something to dig a hole,' Anna said quietly. 'The earth is so hard. I don't want to break the bottle.' She glanced up. The river bank ahead of them was suddenly bright with lights.

'Hurry. I think we're nearly at Aswan.' Serena had looked up too. 'Someone told me that while we're there it's so crowded we'll be tied up alongside other boats, so this is our last chance to do anything unseen. Wait. I'll fetch something.' She disappeared in the darkness, then a few seconds later she was back. 'I noticed it earlier and it was still there. Someone left their comb on one of the tables.' It was steel and had a sharply pointed handle.

Scraping frantically, Anna dug a small pocket in the dry sandy soil and slipped the bottle into it. Pushing the soil back over it she dusted her hands together. 'That's all right as long as no one pinches the plants.'

'They won't. They take great care of them. Haven't you noticed, they water them every morning at sun up.' Serena turned to the rail for a moment.

The boat had slowed. It was turning towards the bank. They were still some distance from the town.

'You know, it's quite stunning up here, isn't it?' She paused. 'It

121

looks as though we're going to wait here till tomorrow. It's probably too crowded ahead to moor in the dark. Anna dear, you'll be all right tonight? You won't be afraid?' Her eyes strayed back to the plants for a second.

'I won't be afraid.' Anna repeated it like a mantra. She had to make herself believe it.

Even so, when she reached her cabin she hesitated. The door was still ajar, the lights on. She gazed in, looking in spite of herself for the distinctive sinuous movements of a snake.

She had searched the cabin three times from floor to ceiling before she at last turned back to the door and pushing it shut, locked it. There was no sign of either the snake or of the earth that Charley had described. She searched her bed meticulously then with another glance up at the ceiling in the shower she pulled off her clothes and turning on the tepid water she allowed it to flow over her for a long, long time. When at last she had dried herself and climbed into bed she was almost asleep.

It took only the smallest sound from the direction of the shower to shock her awake again though, adrenaline flowing. She turned on the light, rechecked the bathroom, tightened the tap against an incipient drip and climbed back into bed.

In the dark, faintly, she could smell a sickly, resinous smell. What was that stuff? And where on earth had it come from? With a shudder she reached for the diary. The urge to sleep had gone.

5

Hail thou lion god! Let not this my heart be
carried away from me!

*Three hundred years have passed. In the luminous desert the
rock face changes from silver to deeper velvet black where the
shadows hide it from the moonlight. As the three men creep
towards the cleft in the cliff they are barely more than shadows
themselves. Their sandals make no sound, so the sudden chink
of metal on rock as the pick begins its work is the more shocking
in the silence.*

*The men work without speaking, swiftly and with certainty
that this at last is the place for which they have been searching
for so long. They have looked for signs, taken bearings in the
daylight. But the exposure itself, the rape of the site, has to be
quick and secret lest pharaoh's men see them and exert
the punishment tomb robbers have courted for a thousand
years.*

*The note of the pick – metal on stone – changes. The three
men stop and hold their breath, listening as one. Then,
cautiously they step closer, hands outstretched to feel amidst the
tumbled rubble for the hidden edge of the doorway.*

Many, many years before, so legend has it, another pharaoh ordered the sealing of the tomb after the murder of the high priest . . .

Leaving the Forresters to entertain the passengers of a neighbouring dahabeeyah on their first day moored at Aswan, Louisa excused herself on the grounds of a headache induced by the intense heat or this southern latitude and persuaded them, with little difficulty, she noticed, that nothing would be better for her than for Hassan to take her over the narrow strip of water in the sandal to visit the low, blessedly green, northern tip of the Island of Elephantine.

He brought the small boat ashore on a narrow sandy beach and helped her out. She stared round in amazed delight at the trees and flowers – hibiscus, poinsettia, bougainvillaea, mimosa and acacia. After the low arid cliffs and the sandbanks of the approach to Aswan it was like heaven.

By now it was with no embarrassment at all that she took the bag from Hassan which contained her loose soft green gown and native slippers and vanished behind some bushes. They were both used to the routine now. Safely sheltered, she would strip off her dress, her petticoats, her stockings, her corset, even her drawers, feeling for a few brief moments the heaven of the sunlight and the touch of the light wind on her hot bare skin, then she would pull the featherlight gown over her head and make her way back to Hassan who would by now have unrolled the rug, set out her paints and sketchbook and the baskets which contained their food and drink.

Today she lingered longer than before over her transformation. The island was silent, save for the calls of birds in the trees and the gentle lap of water on the shore. There were Nubian villages further north, Hassan had told her, but here although boats frequently rowed or sailed across from the town, it was completely quiet.

There was no one around as the sun rose higher in the sky. If she straightened a little she could see the river; even the *Ibis* at anchor near the other boats in the distance. The dappled sunlight touched her shoulders. She smiled, lifting the hot weight of her knotted hair off her neck with her hands. It was heaven to feel her breasts free in the languid air, to experience the soft touch of leaves against her thigh.

'Sitt Louisa, there are people coming.' Hassan's voice was very close, just the other side of the bush. He sounded agitated.

With an exclamation of horror and embarrassment she grabbed her dress and pulled it on, hastily brushing back her hair as the hem settled around her bare feet. Scooping up her discarded clothes she wadded them into a pile and emerged breathless.

'Here. Please. Quickly!' Hassan took the clothes from her and put a pencil into her hand. He stooped and pulled something from the picnic basket. 'Please, Sitt Louisa, a veil for your hair.' With only the slightest hesitation he shook out its folds and laid the silk scarf over her head, draping one end across her shoulder.

As a group of some half-dozen people emerged onto the path nearby talking loudly, Hassan was once more the respectful servant, unpacking the food at the edge of the rug whilst Louisa, although somewhat unconventionally dressed, was respectably covered from head to toe. Becoming conscious of her bare feet even as the visitors approached she had drawn them quickly out of sight beneath her gown. She didn't think they had seen.

They were English, from Hampshire, on their last day in Aswan before setting out for the long voyage back to Alexandria. For a terrible moment she thought they wanted to stay, to sit down beside her, to talk, but after a pause for breath, an exchange of greetings, a polite, cursory glance at the sketchbook which Hassan had, with enormous presence of mind, folded back to show a river scene from the previous week, they were gone, the sound of their conversation dying away as swiftly as it had come.

Louisa dropped her pencil and threw back her head. The veil slipped from her hair. 'If you hadn't warned me, I should have been caught totally naked!'

Hassan dropped his eyes. 'I am sure you were careful and modest, Sitt Louisa.'

She smiled. 'Even so. I didn't hear them coming.' She slipped off the stool onto the rug and her bare toes once more peeped from beneath her hem.

125

His eyes met hers. 'You look happy here amongst the flowers.'

'I am happy.' She leant back on her elbows, staring up at the trees above their heads. 'It is beautiful here, Hassan. A paradise.' A hoopoe was flitting back and forth on the branches above their heads flirting its crest, its pretty pink and black plumage a gentle contrast to the lush green, its mellow call echoing across the water.

'The hoopoe is a bird of good fortune.' Hassan leant against the trunk of the acacia tree. He was watching her closely, an indulgent half-smile on his face. 'Would you draw a picture of the bird for me?'

She sat up and looked at him, astonished. 'Would you really like one?'

He nodded.

'Then of course I will.' Her eyes met his again. This time he did not look away. She felt a flutter of excitement deep inside her and for a moment she found she couldn't breathe.

She swallowed hard. This must not happen. She could not let it happen. She had to stop it now while it was still possible. But she was still looking at him, drowning in his gaze, feeling the strangeness of new infinite possibilities. She couldn't look away.

It was Hassan who broke the spell. In one lithe movement he was on his feet, heading down to the beach where he stood for a moment staring out across the water, clenching his fists. When he turned back to her he was in control of himself again. 'I shall serve the food, with your permission,' he said formally.

Unable for a moment to trust herself to speak she nodded.

She ate very little, her eyes on the Nile, watching feluccas swooping back and forth in the strong breeze which had arisen, funnelling down between the low cliffs. Lost in her dreams she did not even try to keep track of the time. Slowly the sun was moving across the sky.

'Sitt Louisa?' She realised suddenly that Hassan was standing at the edge of the rug. 'Shall I pack away the food? The flies . . .'

She nodded without speaking and he bowed. Silently he filled the basket with the almost untouched bread and goat's cheese and fruit. When he had finished he disappeared for a moment into the trees. When he returned he was holding a spray of scarlet flowers in his hand. He presented them to her as if they were the most precious gift on earth.

She took them without a word. Examining them closely she took in their beauty, the perfection of petals and stamens, then she glanced up. He was watching her. She smiled almost shyly, suddenly as self-conscious as a young girl, then she raised the flowers to her lips and kissed them gently.

Neither of them spoke. It wasn't necessary. Both knew that from this moment their relationship had changed for ever.

'Do you want to go back to the boat now?' She could hear the regret in his voice.

She nodded. 'There is always tomorrow, Hassan.'

'If it is the will of Allah!' He bowed almost imperceptibly. 'I will take you on an excursion to see the unfinished obelisk where it lies still in the quarry where they were cutting it from the stone thousands of years ago. We will have to go on camels!' He smiled mischievously.

'Then you can be sure that the Forresters will not want to accompany us!' She said it with some spirit. 'I should like that, Hassan. And then there are so many things to see. The cataract, Philae, the souk.' She watched as he loaded the baskets into the small boat.

When he had finished he turned to her. 'You should change your clothes now.'

For one moment she thought of refusing, of climbing back into the sandal in her cool loose-fitting gown, feeling the warm water which slopped on the bleached boards of the little boat rippling over her toes, then she realised the folly of the dream. The Forresters would be scandalised. She might alienate them so much they refused to allow her to travel any further with them. She had no money to hire her own boat. If they put her ashore she would be stranded until the steamer came and even then she would not be able to afford the ticket back to Cairo.

Taking the bundle of clothes from him she retreated once more to the bushes, and this time it was with a heavy heart that after a few moments of glorious nakedness she began to wriggle back into the stiffly boned corset, struggle with its laces, pull on her drawers and stockings and at last step into the blackdyed muslin. Then, the final act of constraint, she wound her hair into a knot and rammed her ivory hairpins into it to hold it neatly in place before putting on her black lace cap once more beneath her sun hat.

'I hate it like this,' she wailed at Hassan as she watched him pack away the soft gown, still warm from her body. 'I want to be free!'

127

It was a useless wish, for even as she said it, she knew it could never be. Not as long as she had the two boys at home waiting for her. She saw him, just for a second, hold the material against his cheek, then it was folded away and the basket had joined the others in the boat.

'My dear, we've been waiting for you.' Sir John Forrester was on deck, reaching down to hand her up onto the dahabeeyah. 'I particularly wanted you to meet our guests before they depart.' He was leading the way into the saloon when he paused as though the thought had just struck him. 'I trust your headache is now better?'

'Indeed it is – thank you.' She forced herself to smile, wondering why she had not taken the escape route his question had offered and claimed that her headache was still unendurable. Behind her Hassan had brought the food baskets up on deck. As he went back for her painting things she wondered what he did with her cool, soft clothes while they were on the boat. He could not give them to her. Jane Treece would have found them in her cabin and wondered why she took a nightgown with her on her trips ashore. As though reading her thoughts, he bowed a little in her direction and informed her that he would put the paints and sketchbooks in her cabin for her, then he was gone. For a moment she felt bereft.

She turned and followed Sir John inside and found Augusta sitting there with their guests. Two gentlemen rose and bowed as she appeared.

'Lord Carstairs, Mr and Mrs David Fielding, and Miss Fielding.' Sir John made the introductions and ushered her to a seat. 'My dear, we have a special favour to ask you.'

Louisa brushed a wisp of hair off her face, aware that she must look flushed and untidy and that her clothes were somewhat in disarray after her hasty donning of them behind the bush on the island. Even as she thought of it she saw a sprig of greenery caught in the braid on her skirt and surreptitiously she pulled it free. She could feel the critical eyes of Venetia Fielding on her. She was David Fielding's sister, rather than his daughter, she guessed. The young woman was dressed in the latest Paris fashions with her dress looped back into a slight bustle and her hair smoothed into intricate ringlets. Mrs Fielding was, in spite of her heavily draped efforts to hide the fact, as fashion demanded, clearly in an interesting condition; she looked exhausted.

It would be a portrait, of course. One of them wanted a picture of themselves or possibly an Egyptian temple, or of themselves outside an Egyptian temple, to take back to London to show their elegant companions. Lord Carstairs' words took her completely aback.

'Sir John was telling us, Mrs Shelley, about the scent bottle in your possession and the Arabic curse that accompanies it. I wondered if I could see it?'

She had been watching him while he was speaking. He had deep burnished copper hair and a narrow, sun-tanned face with prominent cheekbones and eye sockets, and a thin somewhat large nose which made him look, she thought with sudden suppressed mirth, like nothing so much as Horus, the hawk god. The effect was not entirely displeasing. He was a good-looking, imposing man.

'I'll fetch it for you, with pleasure.' She rose, thankful for the excuse to leave them for a few minutes to freshen her face and hands and make a few adjustments to her costume.

When she returned she found that tea had been served. The Fielding ladies were laughing prettily with Augusta and the three men had drawn a little apart around the saloon table. Unsure where to sit, she hesitated for a moment in the doorway. It was the gentlemen who rose and made room for her amongst them. The women continued their talk uninterrupted, but at least one pair of eyes were fixed on her back as she made her way towards the proffered chair. She glanced in their direction and found that Venetia Fielding was watching her with an expression of tight-lipped animosity.

Sitting down she produced the scent bottle, laying it in the centre of the table. The paper which accompanied it she pushed towards Lord Carstairs. 'Do you read Arabic, my lord?' She smiled at him and was surprised to see his face light up in response.

'Indeed I do, dear lady.' He lifted up the paper, but she could see his eyes had gone straight to the bottle. He was obviously anxious to touch it, but restraining himself with enormous self-control.

There was a moment's silence, then he began to read out loud. His translation was substantially the same as Sir John's and when he had finished he let the paper fall to the table.

He leant forward, staring intently at the bottle. Neither of the other men had made the slightest attempt to pick it up. There was a long pause then he looked at Louisa again. 'And have you seen the spirits that guard it?' There was no levity in the tone of the question. It appeared to be totally serious. She was about to shake her head then she hesitated.

His eyes narrowed. 'Yes?' It was the merest whisper.

She shrugged, half-embarrassed. 'I fear that I am somewhat imaginative, my lord. This country encourages one towards all kinds of fancies.'

'Just tell me.' His eyes were locked onto hers.

She moved uncomfortably in her chair. 'Once or twice I have had the feeling I was being watched. And in the temple at Edfu I thought I saw someone. I assumed it was my dragoman, Hassan.' She hesitated almost imperceptibly over his name and was disconcerted to see the other man's eyes narrow slightly.

'But it wasn't Hassan?' he echoed. His voice was smooth.

'No, it wasn't Hassan.'

'What did it look like? The figure?'

She could sense his excitement, hidden beneath an impassive face. Glancing at Sir John and David Fielding she could see both men were uncomfortable.

'It looked like a tall man in a white *galabiyya*. But it was no more than an impression, in the shadows of the temple.'

'And you checked there was no one else there?'

'Of course.'

'Yes!' This time the single word was a hiss of satisfaction. She watched, a small frown on her face, as he stretched out his hand towards the bottle. With his fingers only half an inch from it, he paused and she saw him take a deep steadying breath, then at last he picked it up. He didn't actually look at it, she noticed. He held it for a long moment, his eyes on hers, then slowly his lids dropped and he sat silently, eyes closed, totally withdrawn. There was an awkward silence, broken only on the far side of the saloon by a trill of feminine laughter.

Louisa, watching Carstairs' face, saw a sudden shudder pass through his body, before he opened his eyes and looked down at the bottle in his hands.

'Yes!' For the third time that was all he said. Just the one soft, sibilant word.

Louisa could stay silent no longer. 'You seem very interested in my bottle, Lord Carstairs.' It seemed important to emphasise her

130

ownership of it. He was holding it so gloatingly and with such proprietorial triumph.

The sound of her voice seemed to drag him back to reality with a jolt. As though remembering where he was he laid the bottle down on the table. His regret at doing so was palpable.

'Where did you say you got it?' His eyes sought hers again and held them.

'My dragoman found it for me in the bazaar in Luxor.' She hoped the inference was that she had sent him to find her something as a keepsake of her visit to the town.

'Indeed.' He was looking down at it again. 'May I ask what you gave for it?'

The question floored her. She could not admit that it had been a gift. 'I gave him money for several purchases. I am afraid I have no idea how much he beat them down to in the end. Why do you wish to know?'

'Because I wish to buy it from you. I will reimburse you and give you the full value again, so you may purchase something else.' One finger reached out to touch the bottle with an almost reverent delicacy.

'I am sorry, Lord Carstairs, but it is not for sale. Sir John, in any case, feels that it is a fake.'

'It is no fake!' Carstairs flashed a look of pure disdain at his host. 'It is genuine. From the 18th dynasty. Even so, the monetary value is not high. These are comparatively common in Luxor. Stolen, of course, from the tombs. But it pleases me.' He turned back to Louisa. 'Mrs Shelley, you would be doing me the greatest service by allowing me to have it. It is not irreplaceable. Your dragoman could probably find you several like it on your return to Luxor.'

'Then why could you not find one like it yourself, my lord?' Louisa enquired softly. 'Why must you have mine?'

Carstairs met her eyes again. His face was becoming disconcertingly florid. 'I have a personal reason for wanting this one.' As though becoming aware of the strange looks being directed at him by the other two men at the table he frowned, for the first time a little flustered. 'The legend: it pleases me. You would be doing me an inestimable favour, Mrs Shelley.' He smiled. His whole face lit up and she felt the radiance of his charm. For a moment she nearly wavered, then with a shock she realised she had almost changed her mind, almost been swayed to do what he wanted. Almost, she

131

had to force herself to put out her hand and lift up the bottle. 'I am sorry, I really am. But I intend to keep this for myself. I am sure you will find one just as intriguing, my lord.' With her other hand she reached out quickly and scooped up the sheet of paper and standing up she gave little bow. 'My lord, gentlemen, please excuse me. I am very tired after my visit to Elephantine Island. I shall retire to my cabin for a little while.' She turned to the ladies, and making a similar excuse, left them to it.

In her cabin she sat down on the bed with a sigh, looking at the bottle in her hands. Hassan's gift. Since those special moments on Elephantine Island it had become doubly important to her. Trebly so. Almost without thinking she raised it to her lips and felt the glass cool against her hot skin.

The knock on the door made her frown. Surely it could not already be time for Jane Treece to help her get ready for dinner. To her surprise it was Augusta Forrester. She pushed her way into the small cabin and closed the door behind her.

'I want you to reconsider Roger Carstairs' offer, Louisa. You would be doing a great favour to John and myself.' Both women looked down at the scent bottle which was still lying on the bed. 'I appreciate that it is an intriguing little souvenir for you, but surely you are not so attached to it as to be obdurate!' She sat down, her petite frame suddenly voluminous in her magenta silk as she perched on the small powder stool and smiled at Louisa.

'I'm sorry. I hate to upset him, but I do not want to sell.' Louisa folded her hands in her lap.

'Why? What, if I may ask, is so special about it?'

'Well, the romantic story, for one thing. And that presumably is why Lord Carstairs wants it so much. That is what makes the bottle special after all. And for me there are other reasons. It was found especially for me, exactly what I wanted. No, I'm sorry. I do not want to upset your friend, but that is an end to the matter. If he is a gentleman he will not pursue it.'

She saw Augusta's lips tighten a fraction. 'You do know who he is, my dear?'

'I don't care who he is.' Louisa's fists clenched in her lap. 'Now, if you will excuse me, I should like to get ready for dinner.'

'Roger is staying for dinner. It will be embarrassing for us all if you refuse him.'

'Then I shall not appear. I'm sorry, but I shall not change my mind.' Louisa could feel her temper rising. With an effort she curbed it, stood up, and picking up the scent bottle she proceeded to lock it in her dressing case.

Augusta sighed. 'Very well, I shall explain to him. Please do not absent yourself from the meal. That would upset John and myself exceedingly.' She stood up, allowing the folds of magenta silk to fall in place around her with an expensive rustle. She never looked anything other than cool and elegant Louisa realised, no matter how hot the temperature. Augusta smiled at her coldly. 'I am sorry this has happened. I trust it will not distress you too much. I am sure that he will drop the matter when I tell him that you are adamant. I shall send Treece to you now, so you may prepare for dinner.'

Louisa stared at the door for some time after she had gone. Then she stood up and taking the tiny key from the lock of the dressing case she slipped it onto the fine gold chain she wore around her neck. There was to be no possibility of the bottle disappearing. By the time Jane Treece arrived she had already removed her gown and was sitting at her dressing table brushing out her hair.

Anna laid down the diary and stared across her own cabin. Dragged out of Louisa's world with heartstopping suddenness she sat up.

'Who is there?' She sensed rather than heard a movement beyond the half-closed door of the bathroom.

Outside the window the night was still very black. She glanced at her watch. It was two forty-five. She had been reading for hours. The boat was totally silent. Forcing herself to get out bed, she tiptoed across the cabin and pushing open the door she switched on the light.

The room was empty, still a little steamy from the shower she had had before she went to bed. She checked it twice but there was nothing there. Slowly she pushed the door closed, clicked off

133

the light and went back to bed. She was totally exhausted, half her mind still on the dahabeeyah with Louisa, picturing the scent bottle lying safely in her dressing case, conscious of the acquisitive fingers of Lord Carstairs gently touching the glass, sensing Louisa's fear of the figure in the white robe hovering near her in the shadows. She shivered and lay back on the pillows. There was no point in trying to compose herself for sleep, and she soon gave up. There would be no rest for her that night, so why try? Turning on her side with a sigh she reached for the lightswitch again and picked up the diary once more.

It appeared that the Fieldings, who, Louisa discovered, had known the Forresters some years before in Brighton, had rented their boat in Luxor two months before. It did not take Louisa long to work out that a combination of his wife's ill health and his sister's ill temper had proved too much for David Fielding who was an easy-going, good-natured man, ill equipped to act as a referee between two singularly spiteful women. It also became obvious that the reason for their protracted stay was their meeting with Roger Carstairs whose own boat had been tied up north of Luxor at Denderah. He was wealthy, titled, and recently widowed. Any family with an unmarried lady in her late twenties or early thirties would agree that he could not be allowed to escape. When both boats turned south to cruise towards Aswan they did so in convoy, and Carstairs did not appear to have discouraged the obviously predatory plans of Venetia and Katherine Fielding.

'I don't think I should have risked staying out here in your condition,' Augusta Forrester commented a little tartly to Katherine during a moment's lull in the conversation.

Katherine blushed scarlet. Her husband came to her aid. 'It was not our intention to stay out here so long, dear Lady Forrester, I assure you. I had hoped we would have returned to London long before this. Now we shall have to remain in Egypt for Katherine's confinement.' He sent a baleful glare in his sister's direction. 'It is far too late for Kate to travel.'

'Lord Carstairs has two delightful children, Augusta,' Katherine put in amiably, in an obvious attempt to change the subject. 'Alas, now motherless, poor little dears.' She smiled archly at Venetia.

'There is nothing delightful about them,' Carstairs put in, his attention suddenly caught by the sound of his own name. 'They are a couple of small heathens. I have lost three nursemaids and a tutor already and I'm thinking of sending them off to a cage in the Zoological Gardens!'

Louisa suppressed a smile. 'Are they really so dreadful? May I ask how old they are?'

'Six and eight, Mrs Shelley. Old enough to be totally unmanageable.'

Louisa laughed. 'My two boys are the same age exactly,' she exclaimed. She shook her head sadly. 'I miss them so much. Are your boys out in Egypt with you, Lord Carstairs?'

'Indeed they are not! I left them in Scotland. I hope not to see them again until they have learnt some manners.' He leant back in his chair and suddenly he smiled at her. 'I suspect with your experience of children, Mrs Shelley, you do not see them with the naïve eye of the childless!' The remark was designed to cut and it did. She saw Katherine flinch visibly whilst the other two ladies looked crestfallen and indignant in turn.

'That is a little harsh, my lord. Some children are delightful,' she returned with some asperity. 'Mine are, for instance.'

He had been paying her particular attention since she had returned to the saloon but not once, to her relief, had he mentioned the scent bottle. Instead he had gone out of his way to entertain her. He bowed affably now. 'Your children, dear lady, could be nothing but delightful, I am sure. Perhaps I shall need to ask you for some guaranteed training methods.' To her relief he turned back to the Fieldings and with some skill proceeded to soothe Katherine's ruffled feelings. To Venetia, she noticed, he paid no particular attention at all.

It was not until the guests were on the point of leaving that Lord Carstairs dropped his bombshell. 'Mrs Shelley, may I suggest that tomorrow you might care to accompany us to the quarries to see the unfinished obelisk? It is a fascinating excursion and I have promised to escort David and Venetia.'

How could she refuse? How could she say, But I want to go there with Hassan, in my soft cool gown?

Sir John sealed her fate. 'Excellent plan,' he boomed. 'She was intending to go there anyway. I heard the dragoman giving instructions to the cook to put up a picnic. Now there will be no need for him to go. He can stay here and help me with a few errands I have to perform in Aswan.'

Anna shook her head. How unfair. Poor Louisa. That was truly sod's law. Or was she going to fall for the suave Carstairs and forget her burgeoning love for the gentle dragoman? Her head was aching with tiredness but she could not resist flipping over a few pages to see what happened next. A roughly scribbled passage under a pencil sketch of a woman veiled in black caught her eye and she frowned.

'And so, I have ridden a camel and seen the fallen obelisk and dear God! but I am so afraid. When I returned to my cabin yesterday evening the lock to my dressing case had been forced and the bottle was gone. The Forresters were furious and Roger distraught. The boat's crew have been cross-questioned – even Hassan. Then I saw him. The tall man with the white robe. He was here in my cabin, not six feet from me and he held the bottle in his hand. And he had the strangest eyes, like quick silver, without pupils. I screamed and screamed and the *reis* came and then Hassan and then Sir John and they found the bottle lying under my bed. They think it was a river pirate and are giving thanks for my safety. He would have had a knife, they say, and they think he had returned for what poor jewellery I have brought with me. But if so, why did he not take it before? What I could not tell them was that I reached out to ward him off and my hand passed through him as though he were mist.'

*　　*　　*

136

Dressed in a pair of white cotton jeans and a navy shirt, Anna let herself out of the lounge door and climbed up onto the top deck. The river was silent but it was growing slowly less dark. Leaning on the rail she put her head in her hands. Near her the flowerpot with the bottle nestled between the roots of the plants was just a darker shadow amongst the other shadows. The cool air was soothing to her face and she found herself relaxing slowly, distancing herself from the horror of Louisa's last description. She could just see the opposite bank now and high up on the hillside the silhouette of what looked like a little temple. Across the water a muezzin began to call the faithful to prayer, the dawn cry echoing in the silence.

'So, can't you sleep either?' She spun round in shock to see Toby standing near her.

'I didn't hear you coming!'

'I'm sorry. My cabin was very hot. I thought I'd get up and watch the sunrise.' He came over and leant on the rail next to her. 'It's so beautiful here.' His voice was dreamy, softened by the silence around them. 'Look!' He pointed out across the water. Three egrets were flying towards them, white shadows above the layer of mist. They watched in silence until the birds had disappeared.

'Did you hear about the snake last night?' She glanced at him. His expression was rapt. At her words however he snapped out of whatever reverie he had been in and turned towards her.

'Did you say a snake?'

'In Charley's cabin. It was hiding in a drawer.'

'Dear God! How on earth did it get there?'

She shrugged. Magic. Ancient curses. The spell of the djinn. Not suggestions she could make to this man, certainly. 'Omar thinks it must have crept on board somehow. It turns out that Ibrahim who waits on us at table is actually a snake charmer! He was completely sure the snake had gone so we all went back to bed.'

'Except that you couldn't sleep.'

She shrugged ruefully. 'No, I couldn't sleep.'

'I'm not surprised.' He continued looking out across the river in a silence which was somehow extremely companionable. They could see the ripples on the water now, close to the boat and in the distance the silhouettes of the palms were beginning to emerge against the hillside.

'I used to love snakes when I was a child. I had a grass snake

137

called Sam,' Toby said suddenly. He gave a half-smile. 'Not quite in the same league, I suspect, as an Egyptian snake, but he could still make my great-aunts scream.' There was another long silence. Anna glanced at him sideways. He seemed to have returned to his deep reverie as slowly it grew lighter. 'It won't be long before the sun disc appears.' He turned and leant on the rail to face east. 'And of course the moment it does life will return to the land.' He changed the subject adroitly. 'We're going to be moved up to a mooring alongside one of the big pleasure cruisers later and then we've got a busy three days here.' He yawned and straightened up. 'There it is. The sun.'

Almost on cue they heard the pad of feet and two of the crew appeared. They were taking in the lines to the bank as the engines began to throb gently somewhere down inside the heart of the boat. Toby glanced at his watch. He gave her a conspiratorial grin. 'Well. If I recall correctly they start breakfast early today and every-one should be getting up by now. By the time we've eaten we'll be in place and ready to go on our adventures. Do you want to come down with me?'

To her own surprise she agreed with alacrity. For once he was relaxed, unchallenging and that sudden sense of companionship had lingered.

Anna did not have the chance to talk to Serena again until they were on their way to see, in their turn, the unfinished obelisk that Louisa had dismissed in two short lines. They sat side by side at the back of the tour bus – no camels for them – as it bucketed over the potholed streets of Aswan.

Charley and Andy, she noticed, were sitting several rows apart. Toby, having collected his sketchbook and camera, had two seats to himself immediately in front of them.

'Louisa saw him again. The man in white. In her cabin! Exactly as you described in your trance,' she said as soon as the bus pulled away from the quay. 'And he tried to take the bottle. I read the passage last night. She had met someone called Lord Carstairs who wanted to buy it off her –'

'Roger Carstairs?' Serena glanced at her. 'But he's famous, or I should say infamous. He was an antiquarian, but also a rather Aleister Crowley type figure. He dabbled in black magic and things.' Her eyes widened. 'Obviously Louisa didn't give it to him?'

'No, she was adamant.'

'But he saw something in it.'

'Oh yes. He saw something, although it might have been the Arabic inscription which intrigued him. I'll read some more this afternoon.'

'Did you give the scent bottle to Omar to lock away?'

Anna shook her head. 'There were only a few minutes after breakfast and I didn't have time. And there were too many people about.' When she had been there on her own, in the dark, before Toby appeared the last thing she had wanted to do was dig up the bottle. She shivered. 'I reckoned it would be safe where it is. I am sure no one will touch the flowers.' She was silent for a moment. It would have been nearer the truth to say that she hadn't wanted to touch it.

Leaving the bus, they trooped dutifully across the quarry and climbed the path to stand looking down at the great obelisk as it lay where it had been first conceived in the heart of the pharaohs' quarry more than 3000 years before. Almost completed, it lay like a vast fallen warrior, still half embedded in the living granite, almost free when a flaw had been found in it which caused it to be abandoned. Anna brought out her camera, strangely moved by the sight.

'It's beautiful, isn't it.' Toby was suddenly beside them. He had his small sketchbook in his hand and was busy transferring the image of the obelisk onto the page with bold sure strokes of his pencil. He glanced at her. 'You can feel the anguish, can't you? The utter frustration they must have felt when they realised they had to give up on it.'

She nodded. 'So nearly finished. So perfect.' She refocused the camera. 'The sun is too high. There aren't enough shadows for the contrast which would show its imperfections.'

'Did Louisa come here?' He was concentrating on the paper. 'It is hard to convey the scale of these things. Even if I transfer it to a large canvas and put it in people to show how large everything is, it will be hard. You know this is thought to be one of the largest obelisks ever carved? It's about forty-two metres in length. Imagine that standing upright. A pointer to the heavens.' He looked up, held up his pencil for a moment then glanced back at her. 'Did she?'

'Did she what?' She tucked her camera back into her shoulder bag.

'Did she come here? Louisa. Did she paint the obelisk?'

139

Anna shook her head. 'She came here, but she didn't write much about it in her diary, other than that she came on a camel. She was distracted, I think. She came with friends – or rather acquaintances – whom she doesn't appear to have cared for much. One of them was a man called Lord Carstairs.'

She was intrigued to know what his reaction to the name would be, if indeed he had heard of Carstairs at all. It appeared that he had. He gave a low whistle. 'I remember my grandmother once telling me something about him when I was a kid. Grandfather heard her and was furious; he said she mustn't talk about him. I didn't understand why, then. But then his grandfather was a vicar, so I suppose that explains it. How on earth did she get to know an evil bastard like that?'

Anna shrugged. 'I don't think she did. They moored near his boat here in Aswan and he came to visit.' She didn't mention the scent bottle.

Squinting into the sun she realised suddenly that Andy was heading towards them. Behind him Charley and the Booths were standing with a whole group of their fellow passengers staring down at the blinding white rectangle of the obelisk as it lay below them at the foot of the quarry wall.

Andy arrived with a rattle of stones on the path near them. He glanced at Toby's sketch. 'Not bad.' The tone of his voice implied that he had reservations.

Toby ignored him. He flipped over the page and began a second drawing. His subject this time was an aged Egyptian man standing near them, arms folded, impassive as he gazed out across the city, the planes of his cheeks and nose as rugged as the hewn stone around them.

Anna glanced from Andy to Toby and back. The tension between them was palpable. She frowned. Whatever it was between these men she didn't want it spoiling her day. Turning she began to make her way hastily towards the other group, digging once more in her bag for her camera.

It proved impossible to speak to Serena again that morning. Even on the bus she found herself next to Ben – loquacious, enthusiastic and very large in the narrow seat next to her. Their return to the boat with the usual warm drink to cool them down and the hot towels for the dust was followed almost immediately by lunch and the news that they were going to have the chance to sail

140

that afternoon in a felucca to Kitchener's Island – the Island of Plants.

Andy, Charley and the Booths were aboard the first felucca. She watched with the second group as its sail filled and it drew away from them, then it was their turn to climb down into their boat where she found herself sitting once more next to Toby. He grinned at her briefly, but seemed disinclined to talk as he squinted up at the tall graceful parabola of the off-white sail against the intense blue of the sky. As they disembarked on the island to explore the botanical gardens, it was Toby who handed her ashore and Toby who fended off the swarming children begging for baksheesh with a handful of cheap biros which he produced from his bag.

As she gazed round she couldn't restrain her cry of delight. 'It's so beautiful! I hadn't realised how much I had been missing gardens and greenery.' It was as heavenly as Louisa had described on her visit to nearby Elephantine Island, and as overwhelming. Ahead stretched a network of paths, winding between trees and shrubs. Everywhere there were flowers and birds. This must have been how Louisa felt when she had landed with Hassan. She reached automatically for her camera. 'I can't take all this in, in just a couple of hours. How can they have scheduled such a short visit here!'

Toby shrugged. He was still beside her though the others had moved on. 'That applies to every site we visit, every sight we see!' He stared round thoughtfully. 'I am going to come back to Egypt on my own next time. Spend several months here.' He had brought a brand new sketchbook, she noticed, and she wondered how many he had used up already.

'Aren't you tempted to use your camera at all?' she asked suddenly. She had glimpsed one in his bag.

He grimaced. 'I use one. I have to. When there isn't time to sketch. But I have had time today. My notes mean more to me than celluloid.' He allowed her to see his page for a moment and she saw that already it was covered in small drawings, each one surrounded by notes about colour and light. 'If I have problems when we get back to England I'll get you to show me your photos.' He whisked at the page with a grubby putty rubber and sketched on at lightning speed. A tree, a peacock, a blend of spiky palms, a small enquiring semi-feral cat, one after another they flew from his pencil.

141

The assumption that they might see each other again once they returned to England filled her suddenly with strangely mixed emotions. She considered them thoughtfully. Half of her was indignant that he should presume, if only in jest, that they might remain friends; the other half was perhaps a little pleased.

'Are you a good photographer? His question was tossed over his shoulder as he drew.

She hesitated. 'I'm not sure. My husband always called it my little hobby.'

He raised an eyebrow. 'Just because your husband patronised your photography doesn't mean it was no good.'

She frowned. 'No. No, it is good.' Unconsciously she had braced her shoulders. 'I've exhibited some of my work. I've won prizes.'

Toby stopped, looking at her with renewed interest. 'Then you're good. And yet your ex-husband's view of you still matters to you?' He shook his head. 'You must have faith in yourself, Anna. It seems to me that you've been suppressed for too long!' He grinned suddenly. 'Stop hiding your camera. You keep putting it away, have you noticed? Flaunt it. You're a professional. Be proud of it.' He paused, then he shrugged. 'Sorry. End of lecture. It's none of my business.' Already he was drawing again. This time it was an old man, sweeping the path ahead of them, capturing with a few sure strokes the rhythm of the body, the dignity of age, the refusal to bow to the stiffening of the bones.

Slowly they walked on, together now by some unspoken symbiosis, drifting along the path to where, in front of them, a vista of the River Nile opened out, framed by a dead tree on the shore at the edge of a narrow sandy beach, very like the one Louisa had described. A group of egrets stood on the bare white branches, asleep in the sun.

She glanced round and realised that they were alone. The others had moved off down the main path and disappeared deep into the gardens. Toby sketched on, oblivious to anything except the rapid details he was conveying to the page he held braced against his forearm.

She squinted through the viewfinder of her camera at the river. Out on the water two feluccas had been tied together midstream, their sails lowered, and the sound of Nubian drums and singing drifted towards them across the water.

'Earlier, you said you'd heard of Lord Carstairs,' she said as she dug for a new role of film in the bottom of her bag. 'What was so evil about him?'

He gave a tight smile. 'Having been forbidden to speak his name at home I naturally looked him up as soon as I could when I got to a library. It must have been in the 1870s, he was chased out of England for what would nowadays be called Satanic practices. I think they involved little boys.' He snapped the point of his pencil and cursed. 'He ran some kind of secret society in London – a bit like the Hell Fire Club. I don't know where he ended his days. I suspect North Africa or the Middle East somewhere would have suited him rather well.'

'I wonder if Louisa realised.'

He shook his head. 'When was she out here? Late sixties, wasn't it? I don't think the scandal had broken then. I don't know much about him, to be honest, but I can imagine he would have loved Egypt with all the myth and legend and curses and *Arabian Nights'* stuff.' He produced a penknife and began to whittle at the pencil point. 'Did she only see him the once?'

Anna shrugged. 'I'm managing to read a bit of the diary each evening. Just enough to keep up with where we are on the tour. Remembering, of course,' she added with a smile, 'to keep it away from the sun and other sticky hazards!'

For a moment she didn't think he was going to rise to the remark, but snapping the penknife shut and pushing it back into his hip pocket he gave her a quick, mischievous glance. 'That still rankles, does it?'

'A bit.' She folded her arms.

'True though.'

She shrugged. 'As it happens, yes.'

'And am I going to be allowed to see it? If I don't touch it? I'll stand well back and let you turn the pages.'

'With my own fair, clean unsticky hands! Yes, I'm sure I could allow you to see it on those terms.'

For a moment their eyes met. She looked away first.

His pencil resumed its lightning stokes, conveying the scene before him onto the page. Mesmerised by the movement of his hands she saw him scribble the words: *crimson hibiscus ... green: aqua, malachite, emerald, grass ... blinding light off water/sand ... contrast deep shadow/but dry rustle ...*

'You quite fancy that chap Andy, don't you?' A quick look

143

at her under his sandy eyelashes and he was drawing again.

'I don't think that is any of your business.'

'He seems to have dumped Charley, and she is making it every-one's business. Her complaints on the bus about you were not kind.'

'The fact that he dumped her has nothing to do with me!' Anna tightened her lips crossly. 'It was much more to do with the fact that she was being a complete pain.'

'So, you don't like him.'

'I didn't say that. But I am here on holiday. I want to relax. To enjoy myself. To see Egypt. And I don't want any complications.' Stepping back onto the path she left him abruptly, ducking back between the bushes.

To her surprise he followed her. 'I'm sorry. It was none of my business.' He shut his sketchbook and tucked it into his bag.

'I think it's time we found the others.' She didn't glance back at him. The mood was spoilt.

It was early evening before she had the chance to talk to Serena again. They had taken the last two sunloungers on the top deck. The return from Kitchener's Island found the boat quiet again after a further search for the snake which had apparently taken up most of the afternoon. Serena and Anna had said nothing What was there to say? That the snake was magic? That perhaps it hadn't existed at all? If anyone needed to say something it would surely have been Ibrahim. They collected books and writing materials and went outside to relax after their exhilarating sail back. The plants had been watered, Anna noticed. The decking around each pot glistened in the evening sun; in only a short while the wood would be dry.

'I'll rescue it tonight.' Anna grimaced. 'I don't like the thought of it being soaked.'

'Of course, you could stand up now and walk over to it and dig it up. No one would notice. Probably.'

'Probably.' Anna smiled. And if they did whose business was it but hers? But she didn't move. A casual glance around the deck had revealed Andy asleep beneath his straw hat, a beer beside him on the small table between the chairs. There was no sign of Charley. And no sign of Toby.

Moored as they were now alongside another much larger cruiser in the crowded river at Aswan she had the uncomfortable feeling all the time that they were being overlooked. Two people at least were standing on its top deck looking down at them. Perhaps a dozen more might be staring from behind the shutters of their cabin windows. But it was more than that.

She shifted uncomfortably in her chair and glanced again at the scarlet, green and orange of the plants.

A tall figure was standing beside them. For a moment she could not move. She stared, taking in every detail of the long white pleated robe, the dark, aquiline features, the glittering eyes. It must be one of the crew. One of the waiters. Slowly, hardly daring to breathe she raised her hand to her dark glasses and pushed them up onto her forehead so she could see better. Immediately he disappeared.

'Serena.' Her voice sounded strangled even to her own ears.

There was no response. Serena's eyes were closed.

'Serena!'

'What is it?' Serena sat up. She had caught the urgency in Anna's tone.

'Look at the plants!'

Serena swung round to look. Then she turned back to Anna. 'What?'

'Can you see anything? Him!'

Without a word Serena turned back towards the bow of the boat. Then, slowly, she shook her head. 'What did you see?'

'A tall man. In a long white robe. He's guarding it!' She took off her sunglasses with shaking hands. 'I saw him clearly. In broad daylight! With people all around!' Her voice had risen to a high-pitched cry. 'I saw him!'

She realised suddenly that she was trembling all over.

'It's all right, Anna.' Serena hauled herself up out of her chair and perched on the edge of Anna's to put her arm round her shoulders. 'You're safe. There's no one there now.'

'What's wrong?' Andy was suddenly standing beside them. Obviously he had been watching them and heard her cry out. 'Isn't she well? Can I do anything?' His voice was sharp with concern.

Serena looked up. 'Thanks. She's fine. Just a touch of the sun and too much walking.' She glanced round and found a dozen pairs of curious eyes fixed on them. Most people looked away at once

145

when they saw she had noticed them, but Ben had levered himself upright and was coming over.

Anna rubbed her face with the palms of her hands. 'It's OK. Please, don't fuss.'

Andy squatted down beside the chair. He smelt gently but not unpleasantly of beer. 'You don't look OK. You're white as a sheet. Do you want me to help you to your cabin?'

'No. No, thank you.' She glanced down to where he had put a gentle hand over the back of hers. She didn't shake it off. 'I'm fine, Andy. Honestly.'

'It's very easy to get too much sun without realising it. Why not go down on the afterdeck under the awning? It's cooler there and I'll get you a nice cold drink.'

Suddenly it seemed easier not to argue and the offer anyway was tempting. With a furtive backward glance towards the bows she stood up and let Andy and Ben lead her towards the shade. Serena gathered up their belongings and followed.

If anyone noticed a slight shadow hovering for a moment over the display of potted plants on the deck they might have thought it came from one of the men who were ushering her towards the steps.

Once she was comfortably ensconced at one of the shaded tables Andy disappeared to find her a drink. Serena sat down opposite her. 'It could be imagination.' She shrugged.

Anna gave a small laugh. 'Perhaps they're right and I have had too much sun.' Looking up she gave a small grimace. 'I just want to be a tourist, Serena.'

'I know.'

'I could leave it there, in the earth. Or throw it in the Nile.'

'You could.'

'But it's part of my heritage! My great-aunt would never forgive me if I went home without it.'

'I'm sure she would if she knew what had happened.'

'How could I tell her? "By the way, Aunty Phyl, that lovely little scent bottle you gave me when I was a small child turned out to be cursed".' She closed her eyes and shook her head miserably. 'I don't know what to do.'

'I've told you, give it to Omar to lock up. We've got some exciting trips over the next few days. We won't be on the boat much. We don't start the return cruise until we come back from the two days in Abu Simbel. Relax. Be a tourist.' She smiled. 'And enjoy being the centre of attention!' She had glanced over Anna's head and spotted Andy approaching with a tray of drinks.

Anna followed her gaze and nodded ruefully. 'I'm not sure even that is without its complications. I can't believe your flatmate has hung up her duelling pistols yet!'

Serena snorted. 'Probably not. But at least there is something very earthy about Charley. You don't have to worry that she might dematerialise or suddenly appear as a wraith in your shower.'

When Andy put his tray down they were laughing. He smiled. 'Feeling better?'

Anna nodded. 'You were right. Too much sun. All I needed was some shade.'

It was after supper, as she was sitting with Serena in the lounge that Toby came over. Andy was sitting at the bar. She suspected he had already had several drinks.

Toby perched on the edge of a sofa near them. 'I think I owe you an apology, Anna. Sorry if I trod on any toes this afternoon.'

She shrugged. 'You didn't. Not really.'

'No, you were right. It was none of my business.'

Serena stood up.

Anna frowned. 'Are you going?'

Serena nodded. 'Forgive me. I'm so tired. I don't think I have ever been so exhausted or slept so well on a holiday before. Their policy seems to be to wear you out and then feed you until you can't move. Combine that with the heat and it works.' She chuckled. 'I'll say goodnight to you both. Don't forget we have another long day tomorrow.'

They watched her walk slowly towards the door. 'Nice woman.' Toby beckoned over one of the Nubian waiters. 'Can I get you a drink, Anna? Another peace offering.' He smiled.

She sat back on the sofa and nodded. 'Thanks. A beer would be nice.' Anna glanced at him sideways. She studied him with a quizzical smile. How could one man irritate so much one minute and intrigue her so much the next?

They sat in silence for a while, watching the others. It was she who spoke first. 'What do you do with all your sketches?' she asked curiously as Ali put down the glasses on the table. 'Do you work them up in your cabin or something, or will they all wait until you get home?'

'Most will wait.' He signed the chit and tossed it back onto the tray. 'I have been working on one or two. I need to do some of it quickly to keep the colour, the heat, the light, in my head.' He waved his arms as he spoke, drawing outlines in the air in front of him. 'One thinks one won't forget; the images are so vivid, so intense, but half an hour back in Blighty with its soft greens and mists and cloudy skies and that intensity will begin to blur.' He picked up his glass and rolled it thoughtfully between his palms. 'Painters are greedy. They want to capture ideas and keep them imprisoned on the paper or canvas. They gloat over them. They pin them down like butterflies wanting to trap the living essence of everything they see.'

Anna smiled. She suspected he did not often reveal his inner thoughts like this, even perhaps to himself, and she was flattered that he trusted her enough to reveal his enthusiasm. 'I envy you your creativity.'

'Why?' Again the acerbic tone, the sudden direct look, which she found so disconcerting. 'Anna, remember, you are a photographer. It is the same for you, your medium is different, that's all.'

'No. No, it's not the same at all. You have genuine passion. Commitment. And you do it professionally. Felix was right. I just play at it.'

'Art as a hobby can be just as passionate as you put it, just as all-encompassing as when you do it as a profession. After all, how do you know you won't want to do it professionally one day? You are good and you have proved it, and you have that depth of understanding, that sense of rapport as you focus on your subjects which I suspect could make you more than good. It could make you first class.'

He raised his eyes to hers. She could feel the colour coming to her cheeks under the intensity of his gaze.

Toby buried his face in his glass and she had the feeling that he was as embarrassed by his revelations as she was. When he looked up he was calm again. 'Louisa felt it, of course. The all-embracing intensity of this country. You can tell from her work. It must show in her diary too.' He was changing the subject and they both knew it. He put his head on one side. 'Would this be a good time to be allowed to look at it?'

148

Anna laughed. 'You're not going to give up till I show it to you, are you?'

'Nope.' Toby shook his head.

'OK.' She stood up.

She hadn't really intended him to follow her. She meant to go back to her cabin, collect the diary and bring it back to their corner of the lounge. She pictured them continuing to sit together in companionable silence over another drink or a cup of coffee while he leafed slowly through the book. But he stood up with her, draining his glass as he did so, and when she tried to stop him with deprecating gestures of hands and shoulders, he merely smiled and kept moving.

As she threaded her way past the knots of other drinkers she felt Andy's eyes on her. She didn't look at him.

She left the cabin door open. 'Let's take it and go back to the lounge,' she said as firmly as she could. She didn't feel threatened or unsafe with him, just a little overcrowded; as though she needed to hold her breath or there wouldn't be enough air for them both in the small space.

The diary was on the bedside table. He spotted it instantly and sitting down on the bed, picked it up. Immediately he opened it, holding it gently on his opened palms with a reverence she found suddenly very touching.

'Toby?'

There was no reply. She doubted if he had heard her. She stood leaning against the cupboard, watching fascinated as he slowly turned the pages, devouring the book.

Neither of them heard the step in the corridor outside. Only as the door was pushed back against the wall did Anna see Andy standing there looking at them.

'I want a word, Anna!' He sounded inexplicably angry. 'Now, if you don't mind.'

She frowned as the restrained violence in his voice finally got through to Toby, who glanced up, resting the diary on his knee, a faraway look in his eyes.

'Perhaps you could excuse us, Toby.' Andy stepped into the cabin. 'I'll put this away, I think.' Before Toby had a chance to react Andy had taken the diary off his knees. He pulled open the drawer in the bedside table and put the diary inside, then he slammed the drawer shut.

'Andy! What are you doing?' Anna said angrily. 'How dare you barge in here like this!'

Toby stood up. His face had darkened. 'What the hell is this all about?'

'A private matter.' Andy reached out as though to take his arm.

Toby flinched. 'Don't touch me, Watson. What the hell is the matter with you?'

'Nothing at all.' Andy moved back a little. 'I'm sorry to interrupt, but it is important I talk to Anna. Alone. If you'll excuse us.'

'Anna?' Toby looked at her. 'Are you happy with this?'

Anna was furious. She glared at Andy. 'No, I'm not! Get out, Andy! I don't know what this is all about! And I don't care!'

'I'll tell you what it's about as soon as we're alone.' Andy stepped back to the door and stood by it, very obviously ready to usher Toby outside.

Anna saw Toby hesitate. She could feel his rage and resentment. 'Perhaps you'd better go, Toby. We'll look at the diary another time,' she said. 'I'll deal with this.'

Toby hesitated and she saw him look at Andy through narrowed eyes. For a moment she thought they were going to hit each other. Then abruptly Toby stepped past them out of the cabin. He did not look back.

Andy shut the door. She could smell the beer on his breath. 'This is important, Anna.'

'Is something wrong? Whatever it is, it had better be good after that performance.'

Andy sighed. 'You mustn't trust him, you shouldn't be alone with him.

'Toby? This is about Toby?' She was bemused.

He sat down on the bed, almost exactly where Toby had sat only minutes before and for a moment his eyes rested on the closed drawer. 'That is a very valuable item, Anna, and you are too trusting.' He slumped back against the pillows. 'How much do you actually know about Toby Hayward?' There was a moment's silence as he scrutinised her face. 'I thought not.' He scowled. He stood up and made for the door. 'I won't say any more now. Not without checking, but don't be alone with him. Ever. And don't let that diary out of your sight.'

150

6

The doors of heaven are opened for me; the
doors of earth are opened for me.
If the dead who lie here know the words
of passage
they shall come forth by day and they shall be
in a position to journey about over the earth
among the living.

*They bring more spades and crowbars to break down the door
and penetrate the secret of the tomb, excited, always afraid, but
driven to strength by their greed. A hole is made at the corner
of the door and the dead empty air, baked hot by a hundred
thousand suns exhales like the breath of the underworld from
the darkness.*

*Behind them there are eyes; watchers in the night who draw
closer under the desert moon.*

Betrayal brings death. It is the word of the pharaoh.

*If the priests stir in the inner fastness which holds them; if the
ray of sunlight, only a pinpoint through that small chipped
hole, touches the 'ka' of either man, there is no one now to
see. The hot wind blows. In a day, a week, a month, the sand*

has heaped once more against the door and the hole has gone.
All is dark again.

After Andy had gone Anna stood unmoving for several seconds before going to the door and turning the key in the lock. Had he been drunk? She wasn't sure. He had certainly been melodramatic and was increasingly beginning to annoy her. On the other hand could he be right about Toby? She went over and took the diary out of the drawer and stood, holding it clutched against her chest, deep in thought.

Toby was an attractive man, challenging to be with. Her initial resentment had changed to one of intrigued tolerance and then even to a feeling of genuine friendship. No more than that. But his reticence and his abrupt manner meant that in fact she knew nothing at all about him or his background, other than that he was a talented painter. She frowned. There was an angry defensive side to Toby; it was what she had resented so passionately when they first met, and there was a dark side, easily sparked in the course of what seemed the most innocent remark. But that didn't make him someone to be afraid of, any more than she was afraid of Andy. The idea was ridiculous.

Sitting down, she set the diary on her knee and opened it. To Toby it was, as far as she could see, a gateway into Louisa's creative soul. He was interested in it for its content, for its pictures, for its revelations about Louisa's relationship with Egypt. To Andy it was no more than a valuable artefact. The name Louisa Shelley meant nothing to him beyond its monetary worth. Still flustered and upset, she looked down at the page of slanted writing in front of her. To her it was the gateway to another world. And a world that, just at this moment, she was finding infinitely seductive if a little frightening; certainly preferable to worrying about these men and their increasingly unpredictable behaviour. Determinedly she put them both out of her head and set about getting ready for bed.

It was very early. A transparent wisp of mist hung over the Nile unmoving in the dawn light as Louisa, wrapped in a woollen shawl climbed on deck and went to stand at the stern of the boat. She could see some of the crew swabbing down the deck in the bow, but they were concentrating on their work and seemed not to see her.

'Sitt Louisa?' Hassan appeared only moments later. His feet were bare on the cool planking and she had not heard him approach.

She turned towards him and smiled. Her heart had leapt at the sound of his voice. Behind him two egrets flew low over the water, heading downstream. On a nearby dahabeeyah the crew were making ready to raise the sail. The early night caught their colourful clothes in a patch of busy movement. At sunrise the wind would come, blowing from the north.

'You are all right? You are not afraid, after last night?' Hassan's voice was grave.

She shook her head. 'I hope the crew are not upset about being searched. That was not my idea. I know no one on the boat would have taken my scent bottle. Especially not you!'

He gave a wry smile. 'Sir John was not to know that. There was murmuring amongst the crew, but I have set it right with them, do not worry.' He held her eye for a moment. 'They say there was no river pirate. There could not have been.'

'No.' She turned away from him. 'As you know, the scent bottle was found safely. It was in my cabin as I suspect it had been all along.'

'And the man?' Hassan's voice was so quiet she barely heard it.

'Was a spirit. My hand passed through him.'

Turning to face Hassan she saw him pale visibly. '*Allah yehannin*

153

aleik! May God have mercy on thee!' He swallowed. 'It was a djinni?'

'A priest of Ancient Egypt. And that means that the story on the paper is true. You have given me a relic protected by a servant of one of the old gods of this country.' She looked back at the river. The mist had dispersed and in places the water was turning blue. 'Tell me what to do, Hassan. Do I keep it? Do I give it to Lord Carstairs as he wishes, or do I throw it into the river and allow Sobek the crocodile god to take it back into the darkness?'

'It should be at the will of God, Sitt Louisa. *Inshallah*!'

'But what is the will of God, Hassan?' She pulled her shawl around her with a shiver.

His shrug was all the answer she got. Instead he adroitly changed the subject. 'You wish to go to Philae today? To see the temple of Isis at the head of the cataract?'

She shook her head. 'Not today. The Forresters will think that I am deserting them. Let's go tomorrow. If we leave sufficiently early there will be no one to suggest otherwise and we can have the whole day there.'

He bowed. 'I will arrange it, Sitt Louisa.'

He was interrupted by a shrill voice behind her which made her jump. 'Louisa! What are you doing out here? Come in at once. The boy has brought us breakfast!' Augusta was standing at the door of the saloon.

Louisa turned to Hassan. 'Tomorrow,' she whispered.

He bowed again. *'Naharak sa'id*, Sitt Louisa. May thy day be happy.'

Augusta ushered Louisa towards the table. 'I trust Hassan is ashamed of himself. Allowing anyone to reach your cabin like that!' She seemed irritated by the incident of the night before rather than sympathetic. 'I hope he will see that it does not happen again!'

'Hassan is my dragoman,' Louisa put in gently. 'Not my keeper. But I am sure that he, like all the crew, would die to keep us safe.' She paused a moment to allow the rebuke to sink in, then she went on. 'Tomorrow I shall go out with him again. I want to make a trip to see the temple at Philae. I should like to do a series of paintings of the ruins there. I believe they are very special and truly beautiful, set as they are on an island.'

Augusta shuddered. 'I know these places are much admired. But really, they are so large and so vulgar!' She sniffed. 'Nasty heathen

154

gods!' She saw Louisa's expression and shrugged. 'I am sorry, my dear. I know you don't agree. You will have to allow me my sensitive nature.' She helped herself to a large portion of bread and cut a slice of crumbly white cheese. 'Anyway, I am glad you are not proposing to go anywhere today. Sir John has sent a message for the consul to come to the boat to hear our complaint about the thief last night.'

'But Augusta!' Louisa was horrified. 'We have no clues as to who they were, no evidence –'

'We have the evidence of your eyes, my dear. That is sufficient!' Augusta glanced up and raised an imperious eyebrow as Hassan appeared in the doorway. 'What is it?' She put a lump of bread in her mouth.

'Lord Carstairs, Sitt Forrester. He wishes to speak with you and with Sitt Louisa.'

They could see the tall figure of their visitor behind Hassan in the doorway.

Augusta swallowed her mouthful hastily and, flustered, raised her napkin to her lips. 'Oh dear! And here we are, not properly dressed to receive guests and Sir John still in bed!' She glanced at Louisa's shawl and then down at her own simple skirt and pale blouse.

There was no time to demur. Lord Carstairs was already bowing to them, dismissing Hassan with a gesture of his hand.

'So, I trust you enjoyed our trip to the obelisk yesterday,' he said at last to Louisa when Augusta finally drew breath after her lengthy description of Louisa's ordeal the night before. When told that the scent bottle had been stolen then miraculously returned Louisa had seen him frown sharply, then relax, seemingly unperturbed. He made no further mention of the matter and when, after he had received a cup of coffee from the servant he turned to her again, it was with a question. 'Are you planning any more sightseeing, Mrs Shelley?'

Louisa was about to deny any plans when Augusta jumped in. 'Indeed she is, Lord Carstairs. She is planning to go to Philae. Perhaps you're going there yourself?'

Louisa gritted her teeth against the retort she wanted to make. There was no point in being rude to her hostess who no doubt meant well. Instead she rose to her feet. 'I should certainly like to go there if there is time.' She managed what she hoped was a gracious smile. 'Maybe on our way back downriver after we have been to Abu Simbel? And I understand from the *reis* that he will take some two or three days to negotiate the cataract. Maybe I shall take the opportunity to leave the boat then and go on ahead. There is plenty of time to decide.' She nodded to them both. 'Please, Lord Carstairs, don't get up. Forgive me but there are letters I have to write this morning if they are to catch the steamer before we set off.'

Leaving the saloon with perhaps more haste than decorum she made her way to her own small cabin and threw open the door.

The knock on the door made Anna jump out of her skin. She glanced at her wristwatch. It was after midnight. Putting down the diary she climbed out of bed. 'Who is it?'

'It's Andy. I am sorry it's so late. I need to talk to you.'

She frowned, then reluctantly she turned the key and opened the door.

Andy eyed her thin cotton nightshirt and the long expanse of her tanned legs and grinned. 'I hope you weren't asleep.' He glanced at the bed where the bedside light and the discarded diary told their own story.

'No, I wasn't asleep.' Anna was still holding the door. She made no move to invite him in. 'I think you've said enough for one night, Andy. What is so important that it couldn't wait until morning?'

'It's the diary. It's worrying me. I wanted to offer to look after it for you. I am sorry, Anna, but I really don't trust Toby Hayward. I have a feeling he might try and either persuade you to give it to him, or he might just take it.'

'That is a ludicrous idea! How dare you suggest such a thing!' Anna took a deep breath. 'Andy, it's my diary and what I do with it is really none of your business.'

156

They were talking in whispers, aware that everyone else on the boat was asleep. The corridor outside her cabin was lit only by a small lamp at the end by the staircase.

She took a deep breath. 'Now please go. Leave me alone.'

He looked at her, a half-calculating expression in his eyes. In a moment it was veiled. 'I'm sorry. I didn't mean to upset you.' He stepped back and as if as an afterthought he put his hand out and gently touched her bare arm. 'Anna, I'm only worried because I care.' Before she realised what he was doing he reached out and caught her to him and almost apologetically he pressed a light kiss on her lips, then he released her. With the quick boyish smile of one who is confident he will be forgiven if he looks sufficiently contrite, he blew a second kiss and turned away.

Anna closed the door and leant against it, her eyes closed. Her heart was thumping unsteadily and without knowing she had done it she touched her lips with her fingers. She was a mass of conflicting emotions. Anger was still there, top of the list. Whatever this vendetta was that Andy was waging against Toby it made her uncomfortable not least because of her own suspicions. But then there was surprise, gratification and, she had to admit, pleasure. Andy was an attractive man and his kiss might have been nice but for the beer. At the same time she had a slight, treacherous suspicion that he knew it and that he had taken advantage of her.

Moving away from the door at last she picked up the diary again and looked at it thoughtfully. Just how valuable was this book?

Hassan had brought the felucca against the side of the larger boat in the soft, pre-dawn darkness. She could see the gleam of his white teeth in the shadows of his face as he smiled at her and put his finger to his lips conspiratorially. Silently she handed him her painting things and her bundle of clothes and shoes. Her feet like his were bare and silent on the wooden boards.

As she climbed over the side she felt his strong brown hands grip her waist and a shock of excitement knifed through her as he lifted her off the ladder and down into the boat. Then he had guided her to her seat and released her. Quietly he cast off the rope and steered the felucca out of the lee of the dahabeeyah and into the main channel. The river was totally silent.

She had lain awake most of the night. Long after dark the noise of Aswan had drifted across the water towards them and she could hear music and drums, laughter and shouting, all the noises of the eternal Arab town together with the smells of animals and the cooking from the neighbouring boats. Then as the night intensified before dawn the desert air freshened and at last it grew quiet.

Louisa found herself gazing apprehensively at the neighbouring boats, *The Scarab*, which housed Lord Carstairs and beyond it the Fieldings' *Lotus*. They lay in total darkness; there was no sound, even from the crew's quarters.

Neither of them spoke. The breeze died almost at once and they drifted to a halt as the current caught them and pushed them backwards. Quietly Hassan picked up the large oars and shipped them. With a powerful sweep he turned the boat's nose back towards the south and drove it on as the dawn call of the muezzin from a distant minaret began to echo softly across the water.

It was a long time before he turned and drove diagonally towards the bank. As the felucca nosed in at last he smiled triumphantly. A boy was waiting for them with horses, three saddled and one carrying panniers.

'We will ride five miles up the side of the cataract.' Hassan spoke normally now, well out of sound and sight of the *Ibis*. 'Then we find someone to take us across to the island.'

He watched as Louisa slipped on her shoes. Already the light was much stronger. The boy, barefoot and ragged, having stuffed all their baggage into the panniers on the pack horse had leapt onto his own mount and trotted ahead, the lead rein of the pack horse in his hand.

'You are worried, Sitt Louisa?' Hassan helped her into her saddle and stood for a moment looking up at her.

She shook her head. 'I was afraid Lord Carstairs might see us and call me back to go with him. That was not what I wanted.'

'Then it shall not be. *Inshallah!*' He smiled and turned towards his own mount. 'And the bottle, Sitt Louisa? It is well hidden?'

So he too suspected that, once it was established that she had gone, someone might be inclined to search for it.

She nodded. 'It is well hidden, Hassan. It is in my paintbox.' The smallest of gestures towards the pack horse in front of them showed where deep inside her basket of painting things the little bottle nestled inside a carefully packed small box. 'Lord Carstairs will not find it. Nor will any river pirates.'

Hassan swung into his saddle. 'And the djinni, Sitt Louisa? What of him?' She saw him make the sign against the evil eye.

She shrugged. 'We must pray that the djinn will not bother us, Hassan, and that our prayers, yours and mine, will keep us safe.'

A dozen times during the course of their ride she wanted to stop, to sketch the cataract villages, the beauty of the river hurtling over the rocks; the carvings and drawings etched into the cliffs over thousands of years by pilgrims on their way to the temple of Isis, but he would not let her. 'On our return, Sitt Louisa. We can stop then. Or while the dahabeeyah is dragged up the cataract, then there will be plenty of time for you to draw everything.' He glanced behind them nervously but there was no sign of pursuit.

Once or twice they saw glimpses of the distant pillars of the temple as they grew near, then at last they were at the top of the falls where the river widened and calmed and they could see the island of Philae in front of them. They made their way towards the landing stage where they could hire a boat to take them out to the island and Hassan began to unload the pack horse. Giving the boy a few piastres he bade him wait for their return and once more he began to row.

Louisa could not take her eyes off the island. The beauty of the temple, reflected in the still, deep-blue water was breathtaking. The contrasts were stunning. The yellow of the island where the desert came near the river; the intense blue of the water beneath the even bluer sky, the huge black rocks clumped around the island like sleeping monsters, the honey-coloured pillars and in the distance the eastern mountains which had taken on a purple hue in the heat haze.

Her transformation into the cooler, artistic lady painter had taken place this time in a secluded spot behind some rocks where the cliffs had come near the waters of the cataract. Now as Hassan rowed her towards the landing place her hand trailed in the limpid water and her feet were bare once more. Her eyes were fixed on the columns of the temple. She had forgotten Carstairs and her fear that he might follow them.

'This place is called the Holy Island.' Hassan rested on his oars for a moment. 'The heathen god Osiris was buried on the small island next to Pilak which is what we call Philae, and the priests would visit him from this great temple. People came from all over the ancient lands of Egypt and Nubia to pay homage to him and to Isis.'

'I believe it is still holy.' Louisa lifted her hand, trailing water droplets, to shade her eyes from the glare. 'Did you know that the worship of Isis spread all over the world, even to England.'

Hassan looked surprised. 'And the Christians allowed this?'

She shook her head. 'It was before the time of Christ, Hassan. I suppose it was the Romans who brought her as their goddess from Egypt.' She paused, gazing at the scene. 'Even from here I can sense how sacred a spot this must have been. You can feel it still.'

They found a place to sit in the shade in the courtyard between two of the huge carved pillars which formed the great colonnade in front of the temple and she began to draw at once whilst Hassan was still unpacking their belongings.

Hassan squatted on his haunches beside her when he had finished, content merely to watch and she became at once acutely aware of his presence near her. When she raised her eyes she found his fixed on her face. For a moment they stared at each other then Louisa looked away. Hassan reached out and very gently touched her hand. She glanced at him again. 'Hassan –' She found she couldn't speak.

He gave her his serious gentle smile and put his finger to his lips. There was nothing to say.

They stayed where they were for a long while. Slowly she became lost once more in what she was doing and it was several hours before she stopped at last and they began to eat the bread and cheese and hummus he had brought for their lunch.

Then it was time to explore. Even though Hassan said they would be safe, before leaving her paints and sketchbooks Louisa extricated the scent bottle in its small box and tucked it into her skirt pocket with a small notebook and a pencil. Hassan nodded. 'It is better always to have it with you.' He laughed. 'And my lady cannot be without her drawing book and her pencils. They too are part of her, are they not?'

160

Slowly they wandered across the island, totally covered as it was by the temple and its attendant buildings and the ruins of a Coptic village which had been built there many hundreds of years before and then been abandoned. Here and there she stopped to make a quick sketch of a palm tree or a piece of wall as they made their way towards the delicately elegant Kiosk of Trajan, perched on the eastern edge of the island. Set against the stunning blue of the water and the stark barrenness of the rocks it was astonishing in its grace and beauty after the heavy stateliness of the main temple with its square pylon. Louisa laughed in delight. 'I am going to have to paint this. As we saw it first. From the river. Or perhaps from down there, on the shore.'

Hassan smiled indulgently. He had grown to enjoy seeing her so excited.

'Perhaps both. That's it! I must paint both. But we do not have much time if we are to go back to the *Ibis* tonight.'

'We can come again, Sitt Louisa. I see no signs of hurry from Sir John. I think he enjoys the excuse to linger. The *reis* tells me that he has rented the boat until the end of the season. We have a month or more before it grows too hot and we need to return to Luxor to travel north.'

'Then we shall come again. Can you feel the magic of this place, Hassan? It is in the air all around us. More than in the other temples we have seen. This is special.'

She leant against a piece of fallen masonry and pulled off her straw hat to fan her face. As she did so her eyes fell on the dazzlingly bright sand of a small bay below them. A boat had been pulled up there and a man in European dress was standing beside it. He too had taken off his hat and he was mopping his face with a large handkerchief. He had deep-copper hair. Louisa stared at him through narrowed eyes then she let out a little cry of dismay. 'It's Carstairs!'

'No, Sitt Louisa, that is not possible.' Hassan stepped closer to her, his eyes narrowed against the glare.

'It is.' Louisa felt a rush of anger and something not unlike fear. 'I was afraid he would do this! How dare he follow me!'

'But he cannot know you are here,' Hassan protested. 'It must be chance that has brought him.'

'Don't say, *Inshallah!*' Louisa was infuriated. 'It is not the will of God that has brought him! It is his own intelligence. After all, the

161

reis knew where we were going and Augusta told him yesterday in front of me that it was what I had planned! And they would both tell him anyway where I was if he asked, of course they would. They would think it the neighbourly, friendly thing to do and they are clearly dazzled by his rank and fortune.'

Hassan raised an eyebrow. 'There is no need for us to see him, Sitt Louisa. This is a small island, but there are places to hide.'

'But he will have asked the boy who waits with the horses. He will have asked the man from whom we hired the boat, or the woman who was washing her clothes on the beach or the children over there by the ruins. They will all have told him we are here. "Yes, my lord. They are here. Give us baksheesh and we shall take you to them!"' She was almost stamping her foot in her vexation.

Hassan was staring at the shore, seemingly unworried, his face calm as usual. 'We will prove them all wrong. We will disappear into the shadows.'

She looked at him sharply. 'You're serious?'

'Of course. Come.' He held out his hand.

Without any hesitation at all she took it and they ran back the way they had come towards the great temple itself.

Hassan swept all their belongings together into a pile and threw the Persian rug over them. 'See. There is no sign that a lady artist has been here. Merely a visitor who has gone to explore the ruins. Here, boy!' He beckoned a ragged urchin over and showed him a coin. The boy's eyes grew huge. 'This is for you if you guard our belongings. If a gentleman asks, you do not know whose they are and you have seen no lady here at all. Hear me?' Louisa watched the boy's face. She did not understand the quick stream of Arabic but the meaning was clear. If the boy did his job well there would be much more. A piastre changed hands. The larger coin went back into Hassan's pocket. Louisa saw the boy watch it disappear and the emphatic way the child nodded. Moments later he was seated on top of the pile, his arms folded. Hassan smiled. 'There are several groups of visitors going round the temple now, Sitt Louisa. This could belong to any of them. I promise you, the effendi will not search long.' Once more he took her hand. 'It is best if we go inside. There are a thousand pillars to hide behind, a hundred small chapels and corners and robing rooms. There are chambers within chambers and walls within walls. There are stairs which lead to the top of the pylon. He will not find us.' His face was alight with laughter.

She couldn't help but laugh with him. Like two naughty children they ran into the shade of the colonnade and hid behind the pillars.

It was several minutes before Roger Carstairs appeared in the entranceway under the great outer pylon. He leant on his walking cane and surveyed the colonnades with enormous care, then slowly he moved forward.

It seemed to Louisa that he was making directly towards them. She caught her breath and felt the gentle pressure of Hassan's hand on her arm. He smiled down at her and beckoned. Silently they slipped back into the shadows and made their way towards the inner entrance beneath the second great gateway.

Behind them Carstairs stopped in the middle of the courtyard and stared round. Louisa felt his eyes pass over them, then come back. She was sure he had seen them but after a moment he moved on, heading as they were for the inner pylon.

A group of visitors moved into the bright sunlight for a moment and stood staring up at the huge relief of Neos Dionysos placing his sacrifices before Horus and Hathor. From behind her pillar Louisa saw Carstairs hesitate, scrutinising the women with care. After a few moments he moved on again, clearly satisfied his quarry was not amongst them. Feeling the touch of Hassan's hand she turned away to follow him into the darker shade close to the wall and tiptoed with him towards the entrance.

She wasn't sure how they did it. It was as though he had thrown a cloak of invisibility over them both and now somehow they were inside, under cover of the other party without Carstairs seeing them. They left the others immediately and flitted across this smaller open court between the vast columns with their brightly painted capitals and on towards the hypostyle hall.

'Where is he now?' Louisa breathed as they waited. 'Can you see him near the entrance?'

Hassan shrugged. 'We must wait to see what he does next. We do not want to be trapped by going further into the temple. Although it is darker, there are fewer ways out should he come after us.'

They waited, peering round the pillar, Louisa acutely aware that Hassan's arm was touching hers, that his fingers brushed her fingers. She did not move away. Her heart was hammering in her chest, half from fear, half, she had to admit, from excitement.

She felt him move slightly, heard a pebble grate beneath his sandal on the paving slab as he peered out into the court. Carstairs had appeared beneath the archway and was once more standing staring round him. She held her breath; the fear was there again. She felt he could see them, or somehow sense them near him. His expression reminded her of a dog, every sense honed, poised ready to attack its prey.

As if afraid he could feel her gaze upon him she closed her eyes. Slowly she moved her head back and turned towards the doorway to the inner vestibule at the far end of the court. Beyond it lay the sanctuary.

When she opened her eyes she saw a figure was standing there watching her. He was tall, dressed in white, his dark aquiline face a shadowy blur. As she watched he began to move towards her, drifting over the rough paving slabs. His arms were crossed over his chest, but as he moved closer he unfolded them and reached out towards her.

She didn't realise she had screamed out loud until Hassan pulled her against him, his hand across her mouth. '*Allahu Akbar; Allahu Akbar, Allahu Akbar*!' He had seen it as well. 'God is great; God is most great; God protect us.' He guided her steadily backwards towards the wall. '*Yalla*! Go away! *Imshi*! *Allahu Akbar*! God save us from both the evil spirit and from the English effendi!'

She had closed her eyes again, trembling violently, aware of the steady beating of his heart beneath her ear, and the strength of his arm around her. The box in her pocket dragged against her hip as she walked. It seemed to her that it was growing hotter and heavier with every step. Her eyes flew open as with an exclamation of horror she broke away from him and fumbled in the soft gauzy cotton of the gown. She wasn't sure what she intended to do. Take it out. Throw it away. Hurl it towards the sanctuary perhaps. The tall figure was still there when she turned. It seemed to have come no closer but it was, if anything, more solid. She could see the details of the face now, the gold embroidery on his gown with the girdle at his waist and what looked like the tail of a leopard hanging to the ground.

'Dear God save us!' Her own whisper was barely audible as she shrank back into the shadows.

'In the name of the gods which you serve and of Isis your queen, begone!'

The voice immediately beside them made Louisa gasp. She cowered back into Hassan's arms.

164

Carstairs was only a few feet from them now. His eyes were fixed on the apparition, his hand outstretched palm foremost.

For a moment no one moved. Louisa had closed her eyes again. When at last she looked up the tall figure had vanished. In its place Carstairs was standing right in front of them, his face contorted with anger.

'So. You see the danger now of playing with matters you do not understand!' he said. 'I assume that as its keeper has shown himself here, you have the ampulla with you? It would be sensible to let me have it, I think.' He held out his hand.

Neither Louisa nor Hassan moved. Carstairs' face darkened. 'Let go of your mistress, you dog!'

Hassan moved back without a word. His expression grew hard. Louisa's fright turned suddenly to blind fury. She pushed the box back into her pocket as she moved forward. 'How dare you speak to Hassan like that! How dare you! He was protecting me. He takes the greatest care of me!'

She was aware of faces watching from the shadows. The party of Europeans glanced at them as they made their way towards the next vestibule and hurried forward. From the colonnade a group of Nubian faces, blacker than the shadows, watched with rounded eyes, then melted away out of sight.

'Then he has done his duty.' Carstairs' voice was even. He took a deep breath, visibly calming himself. 'The bottle please, Mrs Shelley. For your own safety.'

'I am perfectly safe with Hassan, thank you Lord Carstairs.' Her eyes met his and held them. 'And the ampulla, as you call it, need not concern you. Nor need any superstitions and visions you may have thought you saw. Whatever it was did not harm us.' She hoped he could not see how her hands were shaking as she hid them in the folds of her skirt. 'I came here on a whim to paint the temple. I did not feel I needed your permission, nor would I have dreamt of soliciting your company. I saw when we visited the obelisk how boring for you and the Fieldings was my desire to linger over the visit in order to draw and paint the views. I do better on my own!'

'How grateful for my intervention!' he sneered. 'Do you realise, Mrs Shelley, what would have happened had I not been here? Do you realise what would have happened had the priest Hatsek appeared?'

165

There was a moment's silence. Louisa stared at him defiantly. 'The priest Hatsek?'

A tight smile illuminated his face for a moment then disappeared. 'The second djinn. The hieroglyphs are drawn on your piece of paper, Mrs Shelley. Clearly you do not recognise them.'

'No, Lord Carstairs, I did not recognise them. I read neither Arabic nor hieroglyphics, as you are well aware,' she said coldly. 'Nor do I believe in curses and evil genies!'

'Then you should. Their names are written clearly on the paper you showed me. Anhotep, high priest and servant of Isis, and Hatsek, servant of Isis, priest of Sekhmet, the lion-headed goddess. The lion-headed goddess is the goddess of war, Mrs Shelley. Wherever she went there was terror and death. The wind from the desert is the hot breath of her rage. Do you not feel it, even now? And were you not so afraid of the figure you saw just now that you threw yourself into the arms of your Egyptian servant?'

She hesitated and she saw the triumphant gleam in his eye. 'Please, Mrs Shelley, don't lie to yourself, even if you insist on lying to me. Had I not arrived at that moment, you and your servant would be dead!'

Louisa stared at him. Behind her Hassan folded his arms into the sleeves of his white *galabiyya*. His meek silence was belied by the disdain in his eyes. Nevertheless at Carstairs' words Louisa heard him mutter again under his breath the prayer for the protection of Allah.

'The ampulla, Mrs Shelley. Surely now you will allow me to take it.'

'Why should it be safer with you than with me, Lord Carstairs?' Part of her wanted to give it to him. Indeed she wanted to throw it at him and scream at him to take it, keep it, throw it in the Nile if he wanted to. Another part of her felt a healthy flash of rebellion. Somewhere in the back of her head she could hear her beloved George's voice: 'Don't let him bully you, Lou. Don't let him take it from you. How do you know he didn't conjure that fiend up just to intimidate you? What does he want it for, Lou?'

She felt herself smile at the thought of her husband and the oh so sensible advice he would have given her and she saw the surprise on Carstairs's face. He had expected her to cower in fear.

'I appreciate your help, but whatever it was we all imagined we had seen, it has gone now. So, I shall return to my sightseeing and to my painting, Lord Carstairs, and allow you to continue your own visit uninterrupted.' She turned and beckoning to Hassan began to walk swiftly away.

'You have made him very angry, Sitt Louisa.' Hassan's low voice at her elbow slowed her steps. 'He is not a good man. He will make a bad enemy.'

She pursed her lips. 'I make a bad enemy too, Hassan. I have been as decorous and polite as I know how, but I will not have him browbeat me into submission. Nor will I have him insult you.'

Hassan grinned. 'I am not insulted, Sitt Louisa. The English milord does not upset me, and he should not be permitted to upset you, but –' he paused thoughtfully. 'He has powers, this man. Powers to dismiss the djinn. But not in the name of Allah nor of your Christian God and it does not feel right. I think he has studied the evil arts.'

Louisa stared at him, shocked. 'But he is an English gentleman!'

Hassan shrugged. 'I am not a learned man, Sitt Louisa, but in my heart I feel things and in this I know I am not wrong.'

She bit her lip, scanning his face for a moment.

'He wants the bottle, Sitt Louisa, because the power of the djinn is harnessed to it.'

She shook her head. 'They are not djinn, Hassan. If he is right, they are priests of the ancient religion of your country; priests who, he suspects, are learned in magic too.' She paused. 'Do you think he was right? Do you think this Hatsek, if that is his name, would have killed us?'

They walked out of the shadow of the colonnade once more and into the sunlight and felt the heat like a hammer blow on their heads.

'I do not know. I did not feel the fear of death. Terror. Yes, I felt that. But it was of the unknown.'

If either had looked back to see whether or not Carstairs was following them they would have seen that for several seconds he stood watching them, then he turned sharply on his heel and headed towards the inner vestibule and beyond it into the darkness of the sanctuary itself.

When they reached their belongings once more Hassan gave the boy his longed for, hard-earnt coin, spread out the rug and began to lay out Louisa's painting things for her once more. 'When he walks past as he surely will you must be painting very hard,' he

167

commanded. He pulled out the little folding stool for her and set up her easel and sunshade. 'Do not look at him. Concentrate on the picture you will be making.'

Louisa smiled. 'Do you think that will be enough? He will walk away quietly?'

'I think he will, if you surround yourself with silence.'

She smiled. 'That sounds very wise.' She glanced at him but he was busy once more opening her paintbox.

She set up her sketchbook on the easel and stared regretfully at the half-finished sketch of the Kiosk of Trajan. She would have to continue painting the capitals with their bright green and blue decoration instead. There was no time to move and seat herself elsewhere. He might be coming at any time. She permitted herself a quick glance over her shoulder. There was no movement behind them in the great pillared hall. The only sound was the desultory cheeping of sparrows as the heat reflected off the courtyard and baked the island into a torpor.

Leaning forward she reached for her water pot and Hassan, ever watchful, unstoppered the container and poured some in for her. Rinsing her brush she selected an azure pigment in her box and began to transfer it to the china palette, bringing in more water and dabbing in touches of yellow until she had enough of the green she desired to begin her wash.

Hassan squatted down in the shade of the pillar she was drawing, seemingly lost in thought and as her eyes passed over him she found herself reliving the moment she had thrown herself into his arms. He had been strong, reassuring. He had smelt of a pleasing mix of sweet tobacco and spices and clean freshly laundered cotton which had been dried by the washerwomen in the baking sun.

Her tongue protruding slightly from between her teeth, she rinsed the brush again. She had sketched a man, she realised, beside one of the ornate columns in her sketch. Not Hassan. This was a tall, solemn man with a dark handsome face who stared, arms folded, out across the Nile towards the distant mountains to the west.

She became conscious suddenly of footsteps behind them on the rough paving slabs of the courtyard and she froze, her eyes fixed on the paper. She listened as they moved closer, feeling the hairs on the back of her neck prickling. They stopped, then the sound moved sharply away as though the owner had suddenly noticed them and been deflected.

Stealing another look she saw a tall fair-haired man in a brown light tweed suit and a pith helmet, carrying a bag on his shoulder. The footsteps she had heard had come from his studded walking boots. Where he had come from she wasn't sure, but as he strode away he didn't look back.

'Do not be fooled, Sitt Louisa,' Hassan said quietly. 'Lord Carstairs is still here.'

'We could go. We could go back to the boat.'

'You would let him chase you away?' Hassan raised an eyebrow. 'But you will have to face him again. He is a friend of Sir John's. Better here. Better now.'

He was right, of course. If Carstairs returned to Aswan without them, his mission would have failed and he would be less likely perhaps to talk about it to the Forresters. She turned back to the sketch in front of her, forcing herself to concentrate, aware that her hand was shaking slightly as she lifted the brush once more and began to mix her paints.

Near her Hassan sat unmoving. He appeared to be asleep but his eyes were fixed on the archway which was the only way in to the inner temple. It was a long time later that he rose silently to his feet. He watched Louisa for a moment then quietly he headed back the way they had come. She glanced after him but he gestured at her to stay and she turned back to the painting. The afternoon had grown hotter. The courtyard was airless, the bright sunlight shimmering off the stones. Even the shaded colonnade where she sat well out of the direct sunlight was without a breath of movement. Hassan had disappeared. She watched the doorway for a while then she turned back to the painting again. She was feeling sleepy. The heat folded round her like a soft blanket. Her eyes closed. She could feel the weight of the small box in her skirt pocket. It was inert. Unexceptional. Safe.

With a small sigh she slipped from her canvas stool onto the rug which Hassan had spread for her, and pulling the soft bag which contained her formal, more fashionable dress towards her, she lay down, using it as a cushion for her head. Even the sparrows were silent now. They were sitting amongst the ornate carvings at the top of the columns, their small beaks gaping as they panted in the heat.

When she awoke Hassan was sitting cross-legged on the rug beside her. He smiled as he saw her eyes open. 'You sleep like a child. I hope all your dreams were peaceful dreams.'

169

She lay still. 'The heat is exhausting.'

'Ah.' He shook his head. 'You should be here in summer! But then the Europeans flee to the north and are far away.' He chuckled softly.

'Did you see Lord Carstairs?'

'He is gone. I have searched the temple and even the roof. I do not know how, but he is not here. Sleep, Sitt Louisa. I shall watch over you.'

She smiled. 'I'm glad.' Already her eyes were closing again. She felt him gently removing her shoes, the touch of his hand on her foot. He did her much honour. It was the only thought that flitted through her head for already she was plunging in her dreams into a warm, scented silence.

She woke about an hour later. The shadows had moved and the burning sunlight on her foot was searing her skin. She drew it away sharply and sat up, staring round. The courtyard was as silent as before. There was no other sign of life. Hassan had gone.

Aware that her foot was painfully burnt, she wondered where he was. Scrambling up she moved further into the shade. 'Hassan?'

The silence was so intense she frowned. It was as though she were the only person in the world. 'Hassan, where are you?' Her voice grew sharp.

Nothing moved. The sky above was white with heat and she couldn't look at it.

Her feet still bare, she made her way down the colonnade towards the entrance, gazing this way and that between the columns. 'Hassan!' she called louder now. What if Lord Carstairs had found him and sent him away? What if he had gone without her? She must make for the landing stage, make sure the boat was still there.

At the end of the colonnade the sand was blinding in the direct sunlight. She realised suddenly that she had left her shoes and hesitated. Then she heard a voice behind her. 'Sitt Louisa?'

She spun round. 'Hassan! Oh Hassan, thank God!' She flung herself at him. 'I thought you had gone without me.'

His arms folded round her. For a moment he held her, then she felt a featherlight kiss on her hair. 'I would not go without you, Sitt Louisa. I would guard you with my life.' Slowly she raised her face to look at him. 'Hassan –'

Her reaction had been instinctive; unthinking.

'Hush. Do not be afraid, Sitt Louisa. You are safe with me.' For

170

a moment he said nothing more, gazing at her face, then he smiled. 'We have fought this; I thought it forbidden. But now I believe that it is the will of Allah.' He raised a finger and touched her mouth. 'But only if you will it.'

She stared at him. She ached to touch him; for a moment she could say nothing, then slowly she raised herself up on her toes and she kissed his lips. 'It is the will of Allah,' she whispered.

For Louisa time stood still. It was as though all she had ever dreamed, ever imagined in her wildest fantasies, had coalesced into the next moments of ecstasy in his arms. She never wanted the kiss to end. When at last it did, for a moment she stood, dazed. Was it possible to feel so happy? She glanced up at him and they remained close together staring deep into each other's eyes.

It was a long time later that he noticed her bare feet. 'You must not go without your shoes, my love. There are scorpions in the sand. Come.' He scooped her up into his arms as though she weighed no more than one of their baskets and carried her back to the rug. Before he allowed her to sit down he picked it up and shook it. Then he grinned. 'Now it is ready for my lady to sit.'

Sitting down she drew up her knees and hugged them. The real world was closing in again. 'Hassan, I am a widow. I am free. But you. You have a wife in your home village. This is not right.'

He knelt beside her and took her hand. 'A Christian may not have more than one wife. It is written in the Koran that a man can love more than one woman. I have not seen my wife, Sitt Louisa, for more than two years. I send her money. She is happy with that.'

'Is she?' Louisa frowned. 'I wouldn't be.'

'No, for you are a passionate woman. You wouldn't understand one who no longer wishes for the pleasures of the bed. We have two sons, for which Allah be praised. Since the birth of my smallest boy she has not loved me as a wife should.'

'I could not love you as a wife, Hassan. When summer comes I have to go home to my own sons.'

He looked away. There was sadness in his face. 'Does that mean we should chase away the days of happiness which lie within our grasp?' He took her hands in his. 'If heartbreak must come, let it come later. Then there are the days of happiness to remember. Otherwise there is nothing but regret.'

She smiled. 'Perhaps it is fitting that we should declare our love

171

in the temple of Isis. Is she not the goddess of love?' She reached up and kissed him again but he had suddenly grown tense. He pushed her away.

'Hassan, what is it?' She was hurt.

'*Ma feem tish*! I do not understand. Lord Carstairs. He is there!' He waved towards the distant colonnade.

She caught her breath. 'Did he see us?'

'I don't think so. I searched everywhere. I went to look for his boat, but it had gone. It is a small island. There is nowhere he could have been hiding.' He shook his head in anger. 'Wait here, my beautiful Louisa. Do not move.'

In a second he had left her, slipping like a shadow along the colonnade. Louisa held her breath. The silence had returned.

Anna put down the book and rubbed her eyes. So, Louisa had found herself a lover in Egypt. She smiled. It was the last thing she had expected of her great-great-grandmother. She pictured the face in the photograph Phyllis had shown her. Louisa had been in her sixties at a guess, when the picture was taken. The high-necked blouse, the severe hairstyle with the inevitable bun tightly drawn onto the nape of her neck, the direct dark eyes, the prim mouth. They had given no clue to this passionate exotic romance.

She glanced at her watch. It was three o'clock in the morning and she was exhausted. She shivered. The story had had the desired effect. It had for a while taken her mind off her own fears and the increasing antagonism between Andy and Toby. She stared round the cabin. There was no scent now of resin and myrrh. Nothing but the smell of cooking drifting through the open window from the busy, noisy town which did not appear to sleep and which stretched out along the bank behind them. With a sigh she stood up. There was something she had to do before she could sleep.

The piece of paper taped into the back of the diary was so flimsy it was hard to read even the clearer Arabic script. She held the book under the lamp and squinted at the flimsy sheet. Yes. There they were. She hadn't even noticed the small hieroglyphics in the corner. The Ancient Egyptian characters were so minuscule it was almost impossible to make them out at all.

So, now she knew the names of the two phantoms who guarded the tiny scent bottle. Anhotep and Hatsek. Priests of Isis and Sekhmet. Biting her lip she shook her head.

Shutting the diary she slipped it into the drawer and pushed it shut. Louisa had survived to become a famous artist and a somewhat prim-looking old lady. Whatever magic those two evil men had brought with them into the modern age it cannot have been as frightening as all that. After all, she had brought the scent bottle home with her to England.

What then didst thou do to the flame of fire
and the tablet of crystal and the water of life
after thou hadst buried them? I uttered words
over them.
I extinguished the fire and they say unto me,
what is thy name?

Hail . . . I have not done violence to any man.
Hail . . . I have not slain any man or woman.

*All memory of the entrance to the temple tomb is lost once
again; the dunes lie beneath the cliff face in a desolate corner
of the land. The spirit may roam by day and come forth by
night over the earth but the bottle is a prisoner, forgotten,
wrapped in its own silence and, without it and the secret it
contains, what reason is there to come forth?*

*One of us has gone before the gods . . . that which came
forth from his mouth was declared untrue. He hath sinned
and he hath done evil and he hath fled from Ammit the
devourer.*

* * *

When we hide from the gods all time is the same. When the gods bid us sleep they do not say for how long. A further two hundred thousand suns roll over the desert and once more robbers turn their eyes towards these dunes. The priests stir. Perhaps the time has come.

Anna woke with a start. She lay still, staring up at the ceiling of her cabin where striped shadows from the slatted shutters rippled amongst the bright reflections from the water outside the window. Her head ached and she pressed her fingers against her temples. Her exhaustion was total. She felt too tired even to sit up. It was when she glanced at her wristwatch that the adrenaline kicked in. It was almost ten o'clock.

The boat was deserted. She stood in front of the noticeboard outside the dining room, which had long ago stopped serving breakfast, wondering where they had all gone. The schedule for today had completely slipped her mind. The neatly typed sheet in front of her had the day's activities carefully listed. This morning there was an optional outing to Aswan and the bazaar followed by a short visit at midday to the Old Cataract Hotel. She frowned. She would like to have gone there. Slowly turning away she wandered up to the lounge. Ibrahim called out to her as she made for the shaded afterdeck. 'You have missed your breakfast, *mademoiselle*?'

She smiled at him, touched that he had noticed. 'I'm afraid I overslept again.'

'You like me to bring coffee and croissant?' He hastily stubbed out his cigarette. He had been polishing the bar and now he tucked the duster away on a shelf and came over to her.

'I should love it. Thank you, Ibrahim.' She smiled at him. 'Has everyone gone ashore?'

'Nearly everyone. They want to spend lots of money in the bazaar.' He grinned.

175

While he fetched her coffee she made her way to a table at the far end of the shady deck, beneath the awning of white canvas. It was the opposite end of the ship from the row of pots with their profusion of hibiscus and geraniums, bougainvillaea and the small hidden bottle. This was the perfect chance to retrieve it. It could not be left in a flowerpot on a small Nile cruiser indefinitely. But once she had it back in her possession she would have to make a decision. She stared through the rails at the water. She wanted to talk to Serena. She wasn't sure how she felt now she knew the names of the two priests who followed her bottle. And she needed to know more about the priest of Sekhmet.

Groping in the shoulder bag which she had dropped on the deck by her chair she brought out her guidebook. There was, she remembered, a brief summary of the Egyptian gods somewhere at the beginning of the book. She flipped open the pages and stared down. There she was, Sekhmet, with her huge lion's head. 'The lion goddess unleashes her anger –' the text commented. Over the figure's head was a sun disc and the picture of a cobra. She shivered.

'You are cold, *mademoiselle*?' Ibrahim was there with his tray. He put her coffee and croissant on the table with a tall glass of fruit juice.

She shook her head. 'I was thinking about something I'd read here, about the ancient gods. Sekhmet, the lion-headed goddess.'

'These are stories, *mademoiselle*. They should not make you afraid.'

'She is the goddess of anger. They show her with a cobra.' She glanced up at him. 'How do you know so much about snakes, Ibrahim?'

He smiled at her, tucking the empty tray under his arm. 'I learnt from my father and he from his father before him.'

'And they never harm you?'

He shook his head.

'When Charley found the snake in her cabin you said it was guarding something of mine. How did you know that?'

She saw him lick his lips, suddenly nervous. He gave her a quick glance as though trying to decide what to say and she thought she would help him out. 'Was it a real snake, Ibrahim? Or was it a magic snake? A phantom?'

He shuffled his feet uncomfortably. 'Sometimes they are the same, *mademoiselle*.'

'Do you think it will return?'

176

'*Inshallah.*' He shrugged.

With a slight bow and that infuriating phrase which had so irritated Louisa Ibrahim backed away. She did not call him back. What was there she could say?

It was an hour later that she finally rose to her feet and made for the steps onto the upper deck. The boat was still deserted. She had seen neither passengers nor crew since Ibrahim had left her alone but the river was busy. Tourist cruisers juggled for position along the narrow moorings, launches, feluccas, overloaded rowing boats, ferries, small fishing boats and motor boats plied up and down, some within feet of the boat's rail. She could hear the bustle of the town, the hooting of cars, the shouts from the Corniche but the deck itself was empty. She had, she realised, been trying to pluck up courage ever since she left her cabin that morning. To tell herself that she should wait for Serena was nonsense. It was an excuse. She must dig up the bottle, take it back to her cabin, put it in a sealed envelope and when Omar returned at lunchtime give it to him to put in the boat's safe.

The flowers had been watered early but already the deck was dry. She walked slowly towards them and stood at the rail, looking out across the river towards the sand-coloured hills, already half-shrouded in heat haze. It would only take a second.

She pictured the little bottle as she had known it for so many years of her life, standing innocently pretty on her dressing table, first at her parents' home, then in the house she shared with Felix. She had not been afraid of it then. She remembered suddenly the rainy afternoon when, as a child, she had taken a penknife to the stopper, working it into the seal, trying to jiggle it free. What if she had managed it? What if whatever substance was in the bottle had spilt? Why had the guardians of the bottle not appeared to stop her then? Was it the cold English climate, the distance from their native land, that had inhibited them? Or had her innocence saved her, together with the fact that, quickly bored by her lack of success she had tucked her penknife back into her shorts, put the bottle guiltily back where it belonged and run out of the house to play in the rain. It was the last time she had ever tried to open it.

A felucca swooped by, crewed by two boys. They waved and shouted and she waved back with a smile. All she had to do was turn round, put her hand under the plants and feel around in the soil with her fingers. No more than that. Then she would carry it

177

down, wrap it safely and give it to Omar. It would take five minutes at most.

She realised suddenly that there was someone watching her. She could feel eyes boring into her back. Almost certainly it was someone on the high deck of the big cruiser against which they were moored. No one else. Just an idle spectator who wouldn't be able to see what she was doing anyway. It was nothing sinister; if it were, she would know. She would feel the tiptoe of goosepimples across her skin, feel the cold and the fear as something tangible. She took a deep breath and turned, holding tightly to the rail. The deck was deserted. When she glanced up there was no one to be seen.

Gritting her teeth she moved towards the plant container and stooped over it. The inner leaves were still wet and the soil beneath them was muddy. She raked through the tangle of stems and roots and touched something cold and hard. Closing her eyes she steadied herself sternly and began to work it free of the pot. At last it came loose. Straightening, she lifted it clear of the leaves and began to dust off the clinging streaks of wet earth. It was as she did so that the deck suddenly grew cold.

She held her breath. Please God, no. Not again. Slowly she forced herself to look up.

The priest of Sekhmet, transparent, wispy as a breath of mist, was dressed in the skin of a desert lion. She could see it – the tawny pelt, the great paw hanging over his shoulder with its claws outstretched, the gold collar round the man's neck, the gold chain across his chest to hold the skin in place. She saw his long lean legs, his sandals, his sinewy arms, the single lock of hair across his shoulder and she saw, for a fraction of a second, his face, the burning fury of his eyes, the taut anger of his jaw. He had seen her even as she had seen him. He had registered her presence, she was sure of it. He knew that she was the one who had hidden the sacred bottle amongst the plants and that it was she who had brought it back to Egypt.

No!

She doubted that she had spoken the word out loud. Her mouth was dry, her throat constricted with fear. The silence around her was, she realised, total. All the extraneous sound from the river and from the town had ceased.

In one frantic movement she spun round and lifted her arm to throw the bottle into the Nile.

As she did so a hand closed round her wrist, and the bottle fell harmlessly onto the bleached calico of the cushions on one of the deckchairs. Suddenly she could hear again: the boats, the cars, the shouts, all the noise of the modern day and with them a familiar voice.

'What on earth are you doing?' It was Andy. He stood staring at Anna, puzzled. 'Whatever it's done it doesn't deserve that.' He grinned at her and bent to pick it up.

There was a moment's silence as she stared at him, then turned to look at the empty deck behind her. She was hallucinating. Of course she was. Her tiredness, her obsession with the story, even her conversation with Ibrahim. They had all conspired to make her imagine she had seen something.

Andy squinted carefully at the bottle in his hand. 'It's not genuine. But obviously you know that. I wasn't wrong. These are always fakes. All the genuine stuff is in museums by now.' He was rubbing off the soil. He took out a handkerchief and gave it a quick polish, seemingly incurious about why it should be covered in wet earth. 'Do you see this?' He held it out to her, pointing at the stopper. 'The glass here has been machined. It's not even a particularly old fake.'

She did not put out her hand for it. 'It has to be over a hundred years old if it belonged to Louisa Shelley.' She swallowed hard. To her surprise her voice sounded quite normal, even defensive. If he were right, there could be no ghost. How could there be a ghost?

He looked taken aback at her comment. 'Of course. I had forgotten it was hers. But are you sure it is the same one? Family legends and stories are famous for getting it wrong. I know about provenance. It's my job, remember. People swear their grandmother or great grandfather did this or that and often it's a complete fabrication. They are not deliberately lying, it's just that memories and stories get confused over the years. Maybe Louisa sold it or lost it. Maybe a son or daughter found this in one of her drawers and thought, this is it. This is the bottle she writes about in her diary. Did she write about it?'

'Oh yes, she writes about it.'

'And does it fit the description?' He was picking at the seal with his fingernail.

'Yes it does.'

He looked up at her and frowned. 'Then why were you going to

179

throw it away? Even if it's Victorian and not Pharaonic it has a certain curiosity value, you know.'

'It's not Victorian, Andy. It's genuine.'

He glanced at her thoughtfully and then brought the bottle up close to his face, squinting at it with one eye closed. 'And you were going to throw it in the Nile?'

She grimaced. 'I had my reasons, believe me.'

'Perhaps I had better look after it for you?'

She hesitated. It would be so easy to give it to him, to forget the whole business. To abrogate responsibility.

Watching her face he frowned. 'What is it about this wretched little bottle? First Charley nicks it; now you want to get rid of it.'

'It's haunted, Andy. There is a curse attached to it. It has a guardian spirit –' She broke off abruptly as she caught sight of his face.

'Oh, come on! I don't think so. Serena's behind this, isn't she!' He suddenly roared with laughter. 'Oh my poor Anna. Listen, lovie. You mustn't be led on by her. Serena is as mad as a hatter. All her psychic stuff and her Ancient Egyptian mystic magic. It's tosh! She got into all that when her husband died. You mustn't let her scare you.'

'It's not like that, Andy.'

'No? Well, I'm glad to hear it. They almost certified her at one point. That's why Charley went to live with her. Charley's mum and Serena's sister are close friends. In fact I think they went to school together or something. I think everyone reckoned it was better Serena didn't go on living alone.'

'I don't believe you!' She stared at him again. 'Serena is knowledgeable. Reliable. I like her.'

'We all like her, Anna. That's why we've taken so much trouble to help her. That is why if we're honest we've all come on this trip. To keep an eye on her in case she gets carried away by all the mumbo jumbo.' He sat down abruptly on the deckchair. 'I'm sorry. This is obviously a shock for you. Perhaps I shouldn't have said anything. But all this occult stuff is worrying and if she's got you believing it . . .'

'She hasn't got me believing it, Andy.' She paused. 'I believe it because I have seen things happen with my own eyes.'

There was a moment's silence. She studied his face. He was watching her, head a little to one side, a quizzical twinkle in his

180

eyes. 'So you said. So what exactly have you seen? Remind me.'

'A man. Two men. A man with a lion's skin; a man with a long robe.'

'Practically every Egyptian you see is wearing a *galabiyya*, Anna,' he said gently. 'We are on a boat where there are more crew to wait on us than there are passengers. You must have noticed, they change our sheets and towels about a dozen times a day. They hover around, waiting for our every whim –'

'Andy!' She raised her hand. 'Stop right there. I am not a fool. Please, don't patronise me. I know what I saw.'

He shrugged. His smile was as ever charming. 'In that case I apologise.'

'I saw the second priest just now,' she went on. 'Here. Almost where you were standing. He wasn't dressed in a *galabiyya*, he was dressed in a lion's skin. That was why I wanted to throw the bottle away. I was afraid.'

He shook his head. 'The whole thing sounds very strange, and perhaps I see why you were tempted to throw the bottle away. But there must be some other solution, surely.'

'I thought Serena had the answer.'

He shook his head forcefully. 'Please, don't get involved with her over this stuff. I suggest you put that away,' he glanced at the bottle, 'and forget it. Concentrate on enjoying your holiday. Why didn't you go with the others this morning? Serena and Charley were all revved up to learn how to haggle in the bazaar and spend lots of money on exotic things.'

She smiled faintly. What was the use of trying to explain her feelings? 'I overslept.'

'Ah. Too much reading into the small hours!' His grin broadened. Neither of them had mentioned the previous night's activities, but suddenly the memory of his kiss hung in the air between them. He leant forward and patted the chair next to him. 'Listen, you look so poised for flight, standing there. Why don't you sit down for a bit and I'll go down and get us both a drink. The others will be back before long and after lunch there is a coach coming to take us to see the high dam. That will be worth visiting. And your genie of the bottle won't be able to get you there.' His tone was conciliatory.

She frowned. 'You still don't believe me, do you?'

'Anna, my dear –'

Her irritation was mounting. 'No. Excuse me, Andy, but I have things to do in my cabin. I'll see you at lunch.' Picking up her bag she tucked the bottle into it and began to walk away.

'Anna! Don't be cross. I'm sorry, I really am. I'm sure you do think you've seen something. Perhaps you have.' His voice followed her across the deck. Then its tone changed. 'Anna, listen to me. Before you go there is something important I must tell you. I was thinking last night. About Toby —'

She stopped. Slowly she turned round. He had levered himself out of the chair and was following her. When he saw her pause he halted in his tracks. 'There is something in his past. I was right. It's something serious. I don't gossip, but this is a small boat and you have clearly caught his attention and I think you should know, I'm fairly sure where I remember seeing his name now. And his face. It was in the papers. He was indicted for something very serious.' He paused. Anna waited, her bag on her shoulder, half of her wanting to leave, half wanting to stay and hear what he had to say.

'I think he was accused of killing his wife, Anna.'

Her eyes widened in shock. 'I don't believe you!'

'I hope I'm wrong. But I had to tell you. Just to make sure you're careful.'

'I will be.' She was stunned. And very angry. Angry at Toby and angry at Andy. 'That is gossip, Andy. You don't know for sure and anyway whatever it was it is clearly in the past or he would not be here now!' She spun on her heel and made for the steps. She didn't wait to see if he followed.

Letting herself into her cabin she threw the bag on the bed. All thoughts of the bottle had vanished. She was thinking about Toby.

'Shit!' She stared at herself in the dressing table mirror for a moment. Her cheeks were flushed but whether with anger or from standing on deck in the sun she wasn't sure. Her eyes filled with tears. It was all too much. The sleepless night, the bottle, the ghostly apparition on deck and now this. She was, she realised suddenly, desperately hoping that Andy was wrong. That Toby was not the man he thought. And she was also certain that she had had enough of them both and their insatiable desire to get their hands on her scent bottle or the diary.

Turning furiously towards the bed she took the bottle out of her bag. Glancing round the cabin she held it out. 'OK, Anhotep or Hatsek, whoever you are! Where are you? If you're there, why

182

don't you take the damn thing?' Her voice was shaking. 'If it's so special and precious, why didn't you take it a long time ago? Why wait till now?' She paused. 'Or did you have to wait for me to bring it back to Egypt? Is that it? Nothing happened as long as we were in cold old England! But now we're here you want it for yourself. Fine. Take it. Have it!' She held it out, turning slowly round in a circle. 'No? No takers? Well then, leave me alone! If I so much as glimpse you once more it's going over the side and it will never be seen again. Never!' Pulling open the drawer in the dressing table she tossed the bottle in and slammed it shut.

At almost the same second there was a knock on the door. She swung round to face it, her heart hammering with fright. 'Who is it?' she swallowed nervously.

'It's me, Andy. I want to apologise.'

'There's no need.' She made no move to open the door.

'Please, Anna, let me in.' The handle turned. She hadn't locked the door and it swung open. 'I am truly sorry I upset you. I didn't mean to. I just thought you should know.'

'You didn't upset me, and I wish you wouldn't keep barging into my cabin uninvited! For your information, I couldn't care less about Toby or his past, and I don't care whether or not you believe me about the bottle, either!'

'Are you sure?' He gave a rueful little grimace. 'You could try convincing me.'

She hesitated, glaring at him. Then she shrugged. 'All right. Let me show you something.' She stepped over to the bedside table. 'You think I'm imagining Anhotep? Look at what Louisa says about him. See if you believe her.'

'It's not that I disbelieve you, Anna –'

'Yes, it is. You think I'm a neurotic fool. After all, that's what you think of Serena and if we believe the same things you must think it of me too.' She pulled the diary out of the drawer and sitting on the bed flipped it open.

Andy came over and sat down on the bed beside her. His eyes were fixed greedily on the book. 'Show me,' he said quietly. 'Show me what Louisa says about all this.'

She glanced up at him, then quickly looking away again she began to leaf through the pages. 'OK. Look. Here: "I reached out to ward him off and my hand passed through him as though he were mist." And here: "The figure was watching me . . . he began to move towards me, drifting over the rough paving slabs. His arms were crossed over his chest but as he moved closer he unfolded them and reached out towards me. I screamed . . ." And look at this. And this. And look how keen Lord Carstairs was to get his hands on the bottle. Why would he be interested if it were not genuine?'

Andy made as though to take the book from her. Changing his mind at the last moment he let his hand fall between them on the coverlet. His eyes were riveted to the open page lying on her knee. Between the blocks of close-written, slanted writing there was a small watercolour sketch some two or three inches high. It showed a handsome Egyptian, staring into the middle ground against a background of desert dunes. 'Is that your ghost, Anhotep?' he asked meekly.

She shook her head. 'It doesn't say, but I think it must be Hassan, her lover.'

'Her lover!' He tore his eyes away from the diary to look at her.

She nodded. 'Her dragoman. She fell in love with him as they visited the sites together. It was he who gave her the bottle as a gift.'

'Good God! That was a bit daring, wasn't it? That crossed every sort of Victorian taboo. Class, race and religion all in one go! Good for Louisa!'

Anna nodded. 'It strikes me she was a very brave woman. There, look. There's another description of the spirits.' Her finger traced the words across the page. 'Do you believe me now?' She glanced up at him.

He rubbed his chin. 'I really am not into spirits and things, Anna. Whatever it says here. I'm sorry. I always look for a more down-to-earth explanation when unusual things happen. After all, there must have been as many good-looking Egyptians floating around in white robes behaving shiftily in her day as there are in ours!' He paused, obviously aching to see what happened next. 'So, leaving aside these spirits for a minute, and assuming they didn't actually do anything beyond drifting about at Philae in the shadows, what happened when she got back to the boat? Did Carstairs pursue the bottle?'

She turned over the page. There were two sketches there, one of a felucca swooping across the Nile as the sun set behind a sand cliff and the other of a woman in Nubian costume, a veil draped over her head and part of her face, a jar balanced on her head. Beneath them the writing flew across the page, growing more and more cramped as it approached the bottom.

' "It was nearly dark when we drew alongside the dahabeeyah and Hassan threw a rope up to the *reis* who was waiting for us. As I climbed aboard once more, uncomfortable in my respectable shoes and gown the *reis* shook his head in some perturbation. 'Sitt Louisa, there is big trouble! You must go at once to the saloon.' This was followed by a tirade of Arabic directed at my poor Hassan." '

Anna looked up. 'Are you sure you want to hear all this?'

Andy nodded vehemently. 'I certainly do. Go on. What happened next?'

Louisa saw at once that Lord Carstairs was sitting at the table in the saloon. Near him were the two Fielding ladies and Augusta. Sir John was waiting for her by the door.

'Thank God you are safe, Louisa, my dear. Thank God!' He grabbed her by the shoulders and planted a kiss on her cheek. 'We have been sick with worry!'

She frowned. 'You knew where I was, surely?'

'Oh, I knew where you were, but when Roger told us some of what has happened to you we were distraught, my dear. What a disaster! What a scandal!'

Louisa stared first at him, then at Carstairs. 'What disaster, what scandal? I don't understand.' She was suddenly suspicious. Carstairs, having stood up briefly to acknowledge her entry into the saloon had sat down again at once and was now studying his hands, clasped on the table in front of him. He did not look up.

'Please, Lord Carstairs, what scandal is this you feel you have to report to my friends?' A sudden wave of anger gave strength to her voice and he looked up at last to meet her eyes. She quailed slightly. The extraordinary depth of his gaze was without expression. For a moment her mind went completely blank. Desperately she grabbed at her composure and as she did so he smiled. It was a smile of extraordinary warmth and radiance.

'Mrs Shelley, forgive me. I am so sorry. It was my desperate and sincere concern for your safety which made me speak to the Forresters in the way I have. I had no intention of breaching confidences; I would never knowingly have spoken of anything which might in any way harm your good name.'

'Nor could you, my lord!' She persisted in holding his gaze and was relieved when finally he looked away. 'I have done nothing which could possibly incur such an accusation. How dare you imply that I have!'

She was aware suddenly of the eyes of the others in the saloon all fixed on her face. Katherine had placed one hand gently over the swell of her stomach as though to protect her unborn child from the unspoken horrors which surrounded it. On Venetia's face there was an expression of strange, excited, awe. Augusta looked merely embarrassed, Sir John angry and David Fielding obviously wished himself heartily anywhere else on earth.

It was the latter who broke the silence. He had remained standing after Louisa's arrival in the saloon and now stood, his hands clasped behind him, as though addressing a meeting. 'I think, my dears, it is time we returned to our vessel. It has been a tiring day for all of us and I am sure Mrs Shelley would like a little time to rest and compose herself without us all here, too. Katherine?' He held out his hand to his wife who stared at him for a moment, her face registering naked disappointment at being denied the spectacle of the first-class quarrel which seemed in the offing. Venetia, clearly also aggrieved, turned on her brother in fury. 'We cannot go without Roger! We were all to spend the evening together, surely?'

David pursed his lips. 'I am sure Roger will forgive us on this occasion. We can always meet once more tomorrow.'

His mild-mannered politeness belied the determined note which had entered his voice. In seconds Katherine had levered herself to her feet and shortly after that Venetia found herself with no option but to stand up as well.

Watching them make their farewells and troop up on deck to call their boatman Louisa at last sat down. With Sir John and Lord Carstairs gone after their guests to bid them farewell, she found herself alone with Augusta.

186

'What is this nonsense?' she asked briskly. 'What has he accused me of? That man is a perfect nuisance. He followed me uninvited, interrupted my visit, and generally spoilt the day for me entirely. And now I return to find he has been making some kind of accusations behind my back? What exactly has it pleased him to say about me?'

Augusta settled herself into one of the chairs and clasped her hands in her lap. 'He told us about Hassan, my dear, and his totally inappropriate behaviour. I cannot tell you how sorry I am. He was so highly recommended.' She shook her head. 'But alas, I suppose you are an attractive woman,' she made it clear by her tone that this was a criticism, 'and you and he have spent so much time alone together. He could not restrain himself. And there was something else.' She frowned, not taking her eyes from Louisa's face. 'Roger informed me, discretely, of course, that you were,' she hesitated for the first time, looking suddenly very uncomfortable, 'that you were not properly dressed! In fact you were wearing some kind of native attire which was both provocative and totally unacceptable in a decent woman!' Her face had begun to glow quite pink and she reached into her sleeve for a lace handkerchief to dab her upper lip.

'And was Lord Carstairs spying on me, to make these accusations?' Louisa asked hotly. 'I don't remember inviting him to join me at any point. The dress to which he refers I brought with me from England,' she went on furiously. A small moment of guilt had vanished as quickly as it had arrived. 'It is most certainly not native attire, as he puts it. It is both cool and sensible wear for the climate and is totally decent, I assure you.' Her anger was almost choking her suddenly. 'As for Hassan, he has never ever been anything other than respectful to me. How dare Lord Carstairs imply anything else! He insults me, Augusta!'

Augusta stood up, agitated, and took one or two small steps up and down the saloon. 'No, my dear. He does not mean any such thing. He was right to speak to John and me, he really was. He was enormously concerned for your reputation. He admires you, Louisa. He has a tremendous respect for your talent which he tells us is considerable.' She picked up one of the letters from a pile which had been left lying on the side table and she fanned her face with it. 'He meant it for the best, my dear, he really did.'

'In which case I have now set your mind at rest in all particulars.'

Louisa could feel her face flaming. 'Forgive me, Augusta. I need to go and change before dinner.' She paused at the door. Augusta was standing still, staring at the floor and Louisa felt suddenly very sorry for her. 'I will show you some of my sketches later, Augusta, if you wish. You may see for yourself what it is I do all day on my trips to the temples.' The woman had not up to now shown any interest in her drawings. 'And once we have passed the cataract you will also see how beautiful the island is,' she added gently.

Augusta gave a small smile but she did not look up.

It was not until after dinner when Augusta had gone to bed and Sir John and Louisa were sitting together in the saloon over cups of scented tea by the light of a single shaded lamp that Sir John dropped his bombshell.

'I have sent a message to the consul to ask him to recommend a dragoman for you for the rest of the trip.'

Louisa put down her cup. 'I have no need of another dragoman. Hassan suits me perfectly.'

He shook his head. 'I have let Hassan go.' He was concentrating on his cigar, turning it round and round between his fingers.

'You have done what?' Louisa sat without moving. She did not look up. A wave of blackness seemed to have settled over her.

'I have dismissed him. He was a nice enough fellow, but not of the standard one requires, don't you think?' He stuck the cigar in his mouth. 'Don't fret. We'll find someone new for you, my dear. It won't effect your little drawing trips at all.' He hesitated. 'You won't want to wander off anyway while we're going up the cataract. Everyone tells me it's very exciting. There will be lots for you to draw from the boat . . .'

Anna looked up angrily. 'Poor Louisa. How could she put up with it? Sir John was so patronising! And what a complete bastard Carstairs was!'

188

Andy was sitting beside her, staring down at the book on her knee. His arm was pressed against her arm, she noticed suddenly, his thigh against hers. It was not an unpleasant sensation sitting so close to him. Almost unconsciously her fingers strayed to her lips as though she could still feel last night's brief kiss. Embarrassed, she closed the book. 'Andy, it's nearly time for lunch. I can hear the others. They must have come back from their shopping trip. Perhaps we can read some more another time.'

He nodded reluctantly. 'Sure. I enjoyed that.' Standing up he made for the door. 'I can't wait to find out what happened next.' He turned and winked. 'I'll leave you to get ready. See you in a minute.'

She stared at the closed door. The room was suddenly larger, emptier, somehow more lonely. Shaking her head she stood up and opening the drawer in the bedside table tucked the diary away.

When she reached the dining room the others were already seated. A chair had been left for her beside Andy, she noticed. She slipped into it, glancing towards Toby as she did so. He was sitting with his back to her and did not appear to have noticed her entry. For a moment she gazed at him thoughtfully, then she turned back to her own table. Charley was sitting on Andy's left and beyond her Ben and then Serena. Anna leant forward and grinned across at Serena. 'I'm sorry I missed this morning's trip. I would have liked to see the bazaar. Did you buy anything nice?'

Serena nodded. 'I'll show you later.'

'I trust you had a nice morning too.' Charley put her elbows on the table and peered round Andy. 'You wouldn't have been lonely. Not with Andy to keep you company.'

Ali appeared with a pile of hot plates and began distributing them around the table. Behind him Ibrahim followed with a tureen of steaming lentil soup. Relieved at the distraction Anna turned away but Charley was not to be deflected.

'Strange that you should both oversleep, isn't it.' She flicked her hair back over her shoulders, ignoring Ibrahim's efforts to serve her.

'Did you buy anything nice in the bazaar, Charley dear?' Ben put in mildly.

She ignored him. 'I suppose the bazaar was too common for

189

Anna. After all, she's the descendant of a famous painter. She's just going to lounge around and wait for everyone else to dance attendance on her. I'm surprised she didn't have her own private boat. But then she wouldn't have had the chance to meet any nice eligible men.' She sat back triumphantly. 'Ali? Where is my wine?' Her call made the young waiter jump nervously. He bowed and hurried to the central table to find the bottle which had her name on it. She poured herself a glass and drank it straight down.

'Charley, go easy.' Andy leant towards her. 'There's no need for any of this.'

'No?' She helped herself again. 'This Egyptian wine is crap. It's not strong enough!'

'It's fine.' Andy took the bottle out of her hand and put it on the table out of reach. 'Come on, we don't need this. We can all be friends, surely.'

The dining room was very silent, Anna noticed suddenly. People were embarrassed, concentrating on their soup which was thick and spicy and garnished with fresh mint. She was conscious of Ibrahim, hovering behind her, passing round a basket of warm rolls. She glanced up at him, but his eyes were fixed on the basket, his face completely without expression.

Omar, seated with the others at the next table stood up at last, clearly reluctant to become involved. He wandered over. 'Is everything all right, people?'

'It's fine.' Andy glanced up at him. 'We can manage.'

Omar paused for a moment, then he nodded and turned away. Toby, she noticed, was sitting sideways in his chair, his arm across the back, openly watching the situation. He caught her eye and gave her a wry wink. She smiled uncomfortably back.

Plates were collected, replaced. Huge heaped platters of steaming rice and *kebeiya* meatballs were carried in.

Anna glanced round the table. Charley had poured herself another glass of wine. She sipped it in moody silence whilst Serena watched.

'It certainly is a bit different from an elegant lunch on a private dahabeeyah,' Andy commented quietly. 'It must have been wonderful, travelling as they did, with all that leisure and time and money.'

Anna nodded.

'Don't forget, you're going to let me read the next instalment,'

190

he went on. 'I want to know what happens next.' He smiled at her.

'I'm sure you do.'

Beyond him Charley was sitting, her fingers linked around her glass, staring into space. As though feeling Anna's glance she suddenly sat up. Swigging down the contents of her glass she leant forward to look at Anna again.

'I'm not going to let you have him, you know. You're mine, aren't you, sweetie.' Her hand came down on Andy's as it lay next to his empty plate and she raked a nail up the skin of his wrist.

He jumped. 'Charley!'

She smiled sweetly. 'Yes, Charley. And if sweet little Anna comes between us, I shall do more than steal her silly little Egyptian bottle to teach her a lesson, believe me –' She broke off with a squeal as a hand came down on her shoulder.

'That's enough threats, young lady!'

Toby had stood up without them noticing and was standing immediately behind her. 'Come on. You're not eating and you're causing a lot of grief. I suggest you go and sleep it off.' He grabbed her arm and pulled her up out of her chair. Her glass of wine flew out of her hand, depositing its contents over Andy's shirt.

With a scream of rage Charley whirled round and hit Toby in the face.

'Take your hands off her!' Andy was frantically wiping himself down with his napkin.

'Please, Mr Toby, let me deal with it!' Omar tried to pull Toby off as Ibrahim and Ali appeared anxiously on either side of him brandishing cloths.

'Leave it. I can cope.' Toby had the screaming Charley by the shoulders. 'I'll dump her in her cabin. Come on, no more of this nonsense.' He pushed her off balance and she collapsed against him. In seconds he had dragged her out of the room and the doors had swung shut behind him.

Serena stood up. 'I'd better go and look after her.' Andy leapt to his feet. 'No, you stay here. I'll go and see that she's all right.' He threw down his wine-stained napkin and ran after them. But not before he had turned to Anna. 'I told you he was violent!' he murmured, then he had gone.

Serena sat down with a shrug and turned back to the table. It seemed only seconds before Ibrahim and Ali had replaced the cloth, re-ordered the table and finally began to serve the food. As they did so, the conversation in the dining room resumed – at a slightly louder pitch than before.

It was ten minutes before Andy reappeared. He had changed his shirt and trousers. 'She's asleep.' He slid into his chair.

'And Toby?' Anna studied his face. 'I hope you didn't hit him.'

Andy laughed. 'No, I didn't hit him. I helped him carry Charley to her cabin and put her on the bed. We took off her shoes and left her to it.'

'So, where is Toby?'

'I don't know. Perhaps he wanted to rush off and draw the scene as Louisa would have done. Who knows?' There was an angry tick in his cheek and he had suddenly become very pale. He sat down and reaching for Charley's wine poured himself a glass.

Anna frowned. 'I'm sorry I asked.'

The meal continued in silence for several minutes, then Serena looked up. 'So, when do we leave to visit the high dam?'

'Soon.' Omar had heard her question. He stood up. 'People, please be quick with your coffee. We leave very soon.' He smiled round the room. 'Very soon, English time, please, which is today. Not very soon Egyptian time which is next week.'

Anna caught Serena's eye as they all laughed. Egyptian indifference to time was one of Omar's favourite jokes – one he no doubt repeated to each succeeding group of passengers. She had already decided to sit beside Serena on the bus on the way to the dam. There were urgent matters to be discussed.

Her decision was thwarted immediately by Andy who inserted himself into the seat next to her as soon as she had made herself comfortable. 'You don't mind, do you?'

She hid her impatience, although she desperately needed to speak to Serena. 'Of course not.'

'Have you brought your haunted bottle with you?' His eyes were sparkling.

She glanced down at the guidebook on her knee. 'No, I've left it in my cabin.'

'And the diary?'

'And the diary. I'm sure they'll be perfectly safe.'

'I hope so.' He glanced round the bus as the doors closed and the driver pulled away from the quayside. 'Toby doesn't appear to be with us. I knew Charley wouldn't come – she's out for the count

'– but why hasn't he? I'd have thought he'd be interested to see the high dam.'

'Well, whatever the reason, it is not so that he can go through my cabin,' Anna put in firmly. Serena, she could see, was sitting by herself towards the front of the small coach.

'I hope you're right.' He folded his arms and grinned.

When the coach stopped for them to see what remained of the cataract after the first dam was built at the beginning of the twentieth century and again when it reached the high dam itself, Andy stayed close by her side. She was beginning to think he was deliberately coming between her and Serena and she was becoming increasingly irritated as they left the coach and walked out onto the top of the vast concrete edifice to stand staring over the far side at Lake Nasser, the inland sea created by the building of the dam.

'It's amazing, isn't it.' Serena had followed them. 'But sad to think that there are so many temples and things lost under all that water.'

'They moved the important ones.' Andy stepped between them.

Serena nodded. 'But they lost many more. The dam has not been all good news.'

'No?' Andy was impatient. 'How do you work that out?'

'Well, for one thing, the lower reaches of the Nile are becoming poisoned with salt from the sea, because the current is no longer strong enough to hold it back, and the lake is filling up with all the silt the annual floods would have deposited on the fields to fertilise them.' She caught sight of Andy's face and shook her head. 'Yes, I know it has done wonders and everyone has electricity.'

Andy smiled. 'Which has been overwhelmingly good for Egyptian prosperity. Economics was never your strong point, my dear.'

Anna saw the colour flame in Serena's cheeks. 'There are more things in life than having a TV in every house.'

Andy scowled. 'Of course. And there are all the unhappy little birdies too, no doubt,' he scoffed. 'And miserable thwarted crocodiles, and all the lovely sensitive magical things that the nasty electric fields interfere with!'

Serena closed her eyes for a second and took a deep breath. 'Buzz off, Andy. Go and annoy someone else, there's a dear.'

Anna glanced from one to the other impatiently and changed the subject. 'There's a dog down there on the dam wall and she's got puppies. I want to photograph her. Have you noticed the sand-coloured dogs everywhere we go? I don't know if they're wild or stray but they don't seem to belong to anyone.' She led Serena away from Andy, and fumbling in her bag she took out her camera and began to snap the animals as they played at the edge of the water.

'He's really taken you in tow!' Serena watched as Andy wandered away from them, looking back towards the river. 'I take it you don't mind?'

Anna gave a wry smile. 'The jury is still out. He is a bit over-whelming sometimes.' She glanced at Serena. The other woman was staring out across Lake Nasser. Anna could not see her expression behind her dark glasses. 'I can't make up my mind about some of the things he says. He's fun. He's attractive –'

'Don't trust him, Anna. Not completely.' To her surprise Serena suddenly caught her arm. 'Be careful, my dear. Please. You've enough problems and he is just the kind of person who could exacerbate the energies that are whirling round you at the moment.' She paused. 'As you have probably gathered, we don't get on too well. Ever since he's been seeing Charley he's taken it upon himself to try and interfere in my life too. I expect he's told you that he thinks I'm batty.' She studied Anna's face. 'Yes, I can see he has by your expression. Well, perhaps I am. But at least I do things for the best. Andy is single-minded, greedy and cruel and for some reason ever since we arrived in Egypt he seems to have been getting more aggressive and predatory by the minute! So watch yourself, please.' She turned and walked away.

Anna stared after her. 'Serena?'

Serena shook her head without turning round. She was moving swiftly away from the rest of the party along the dam, her shoulders hunched.

'Let her go.'

Anna jumped. She hadn't heard Andy come back. He put his hand on her arm. 'She'll come round. She always does. Very sunny person, our Serena.'

She glanced up at him. 'Did you hear what she said?'

He shook his head 'If you've been telling her what I said about her I expect she was very rude!'

She frowned. 'You don't give me any credit for tact then.'

'Sorry.' His arm moved casually around her shoulders. 'Come and stand over here. I want to take a photo of you.' He guided her towards the wall. 'If you stand here, I can get the length of the dam in the picture.' He paused and frowned. 'What is it, Anna? What's wrong?'

She hadn't heard him. She was staring into the middle distance, her mouth open, her body taut with shock, oblivious suddenly to her surroundings.

Only thirty feet away from her the priest Anhotep was watching her, his hand upraised, his finger pointing at her heart.

8

That which was shut fast hath been opened . . .
Hail ye who carry away hearts.
Hail ye who steal and crush hearts . . .

The legend has been enduring. The sands shift and a shadow betrays what once was there. Memories are stirred. Was this the tomb of the priests? Was this the tomb which history recalled but then forgot? The robbers this time are better equipped. They are stronger. The guards of the pharaohs are long gone. When the door cracks asunder and is levered from its place there is no one there to protect the contents of the grave.

Where is the gold? Where are the precious gems which would adorn the men who served the gods? The mummies are carried out onto the sand. They are broken, desecrated, turned back to dust. The canopic jars are smashed.

There is no treasure. No provision for the after life. These were men whom the gods had turned away.

In the corner, hidden, they find the bottle. They carry it outside into the desert, glance at it and toss it away. Glass by now is common. It has no value to the seeker after gold.

When they leave the tomb lies open. The spirits of the dead feed on the sunlight and the silver blessing of the desert moon and grow stronger.

But in the night the men who laid sacrilegious hands upon forbidden places encounter the servants of Anubis and of Sobek. The gods will always protect the sacred phial of Isis's tears and the robbers die as all who touch it will die. Their bodies are eaten by jackal and crocodile as the judgement of the gods demands.

'It's a mirage, Anna. A trick of the light.' Andy pulled her against him as she stammered out what she had seen. 'Come on. Let's get out of the sun. It's too darned exposed up here.' He began to guide her back towards the end of the dam where a few trees provided a patch of dense shade.

'Andy! Anna! Wait!' Serena, glancing back at last had realised that something was wrong. 'What is it? What's happened?' She hurried back towards them.

'It's nothing to concern you, Serena,' Andy threw over his shoulder.

Anna frowned. She did not need his interference, however well-meaning it might be, especially now. 'It was Anhotep,' she said shakily. She stood still. 'Serena, he was here, just for a second, on the dam. But I left the bottle on the boat. Surely he should stay close to it? He wouldn't follow me? Why would he follow me?'

Serena's eyes were on Anna's face. 'You are sure you saw him?'

'She didn't see anything.' Andy put his arm round Anna's shoulder again. 'The sun is so bright it's easy to imagine things – after all, whole cities show up in mirages.'

'I saw something!' Anna stepped away from him sharply. 'It was not a mirage, Andy. And I've seen him enough times to recognise him.' She shuddered. 'He was looking at me! Watching me!'

197

Feeding on me. The words came to mind unbidden. He's using my anger. My fear. She gave a violent shudder.

Omar, who had been talking to Ben and a group of others, regaling them with a lively account of the building of the dam by the Russians, turned, attracted by Anna's raised voice. He frowned. 'There is a problem, people?' He strode quickly towards them. 'Anna is not well?'

'I'm fine.' Anna forced herself to smile. She could hardly confide in Omar. Between him and Andy they would have her locked up.

'Too much sun, perhaps,' Andy said. 'I'll take care of her. Nothing a cool drink in the shade won't put right.'

He began guiding Anna back towards their bus, but she stopped. 'Thanks Andy, I'm fine. I think I'd like to talk to Serena, if you don't mind.'

He laughed. 'Ah, but I do mind. I can't bear to be parted from you and Serena wants to go and hear Omar's history of the dam, don't you Serena?' His voice became hard suddenly.

'I don't think so.' Serena folded her arms. 'I think we need some girl talk, Andy. Something you can't help with.'

Anna suppressed a smile. 'Please, Andy. Serena and I can get a drink in the bus. You go and listen to Omar. Then you can tell us all about it later.'

The two women turned and made their way back along the dam. Behind them Andy stood watching as they headed towards the bus, then with a shrug he turned away.

Anna clutched Serena's hand. 'He was here, looking at me. Pointing at me! Oh God! I can't believe it. Why? Why should he come here? This place is modern. No Ancient Egyptian set foot here, on the dam. And the scent bottle isn't here.'

Sitting side by side on the grass in the shade of a dusty tree she and Serena drank from their water bottles. Anna lay back, her arm across her eyes. 'Am I imagining all this? Is he right? Is it too much sun and imagination?'

There was a pause. Serena was looking up through the sparse silvery leaves at the intense blue of the sky. 'What do you think?'

'I'm beginning to think I believe it.'

'And I think you're right. Anna, I'm not sure I know very much about all this. In some ways, as I said before, I'm out of my depth. But I feel I'm all you've got, so you must let me help you if I can. Don't let Andy stop you trusting me. Please.'

A shadow fell across her face and she looked up towards its source, startled. Andy had changed his mind and followed them. 'Why should I try and stop her trusting you?' He stood looking down. 'She has enough common sense of her own, Serena. I don't have to point out the obvious.'

Both women sat up.

'Andy, can you please give us some space?' Anna was beginning to feel really irritated.

He sat down beside her. 'Surely you don't mean that?' He gave her a roguish grin. 'How are you feeling? Has the drink done you good? I've got some beer in my bag on the bus if you'd like some.'

Serena drew up her knees and wrapped her arms around them. 'You won't give up, will you Andy?'

He shrugged. 'I'm only saying it as it is. Your Ancient Egyptian stuff is all very fascinating, my love, but that's what it is. Ancient. History. It's not supposed to be practised today. Your altar to Isis in the corner of your bedroom, and all the incense and stuff. It's weird. Dangerous. You shouldn't be believing in it yourself and you certainly shouldn't be trying to indoctrinate Anna. She's too sensitive. This country is a touchpaper to anyone with imagination and a bit of a romantic soul. You've got to stand back.'

'Like good old solid Andy with his down-to-earth views and steady masculine brain?' Anna responded gently. 'Does it ever occur to you, Andy, that Serena might be in touch with ancient truths? That what she says and believes might be totally valid?'

'It's crap, darling.' He scrambled to his feet. 'I can see I'm not going to convert you instantly, so I'll go back to the others. You've only got fifteen minutes then we're heading back to the boat.'

There was a long silence after he had gone. Serena rested her chin on her knees thoughtfully. 'Thank you for standing up for me.'

'Why don't you do it yourself?' Anna was still cross. 'Andy is a bit of a bully. He'll keep on at you if you cave in. What you should do is turn round and give him a good blast of Ancient Egyptian invective.' She gave a sudden giggle. 'I'm obviously feeling better.'

'Good.' Serena looked up and smiled. She drew in a deep breath. 'The reason I don't blast him, as you put it, is because he gets to me quite badly and sometimes he makes me so angry with his cheap jibes and sarcasm and bullying that I'm terrified I might just snap and say something I'll regret for the rest of my life.' She paused. 'And I could do him some serious damage, Anna. Believe me. I know enough what you call invective to do that!'

There was a long silence. 'This is all real, isn't it.' Anna rubbed her face with her hands. 'Just because most people can't see or understand, it doesn't mean it's not there.' She sighed. 'And one can't make it go away by saying it doesn't exist. Not in the end.' She looked at Serena. 'I'm afraid.'

Serena leant across and took her hand. 'I'll be there for you. Whenever you want me.' She glanced up and shook her head wearily. 'Look, the others are coming back. It must be time to go. We'll talk about this later.'

On the bus Anna sat next to Ben. Andy seated himself at the very front and bombarded Omar with questions. Serena across from Anna said very little. She appeared to be deep in thought and when they returned to the boat she disappeared at once towards her cabin. Anna stared after her thoughtfully then making her way towards her own cabin, she picked up the phone. It was several seconds before Serena answered. 'I wanted to talk to you some more,' Anna said quickly. 'Can you come here, to my cabin? That way we won't be interrupted again.'

Serena gave a quiet laugh. 'By dear, oh so attentive Andy? All right, my dear. Give me twenty minutes and I'll be with you.'

Anna did not check to see if the scent bottle was there. Nor did she allow herself to look over her shoulder or into the mirror. If the priests were real then she had to decide quickly if Serena could help or if her interference would merely exacerbate the situation. There was, she reminded herself, one final remedy for the situation which would end things once and for all: the river. And next time she would make sure there was no one there to see her throw the bottle in. She bit her lip suddenly. Suppose she did throw it in? And suppose that merely made the priests angry?

She took a deep breath. Don't think about it. From now on, her mind was closed. All she had to do was to keep it that way and if she was strong enough and made a tremendous effort and refused to give in to her imagination there would be no more visitations; she would allow herself to imagine nothing; anticipate nothing; fear nothing. And there was another thought to cling to. The possibility that Andy was right and she and Serena were wrong. That the shadowy visions which had invaded her mind were no more than the febrile imaginings of an overheated brain.

Sitting down on the bed she pulled open her bedside drawer. There was no harm in glancing at the diary until Serena appeared. Even if Louisa were writing about the priests and her own visions, it would still distract her. She pulled it out and sat for a moment looking at the worn cover. Had Phyllis had any idea, she wondered suddenly, what a time bomb she had unleashed on her great-niece when she had passed over the diary, and years earlier, the little scent bottle, a romantic present for a small acquisitive child?

She sighed. Refusing to so much as look up and glance round the cabin she opened the diary and began to turn the pages slowly, looking for the marker she had left between them, the postcard she had bought which showed the temple of Edfu against a blazing sunset.

Louisa spoke to the *reis* in private, begging him to give a message to Hassan but he merely shrugged and shook his head. The friendly smile, the twinkling eyes of their captain had gone. He looked at her with cold reproach and his politeness was formal and curtailed as he turned away about his duties. Louisa climbed onto the upper deck and leant against the rail, her parasol shading her from the heat of the morning sun. She stared across the Nile at the moorings on the far side. The Fieldings' dahabeeyah was deserted. That of Lord Carstairs just beyond it showed only one man, sitting cross-legged on the afterdeck, stitching a sail. Miserably she crumpled the note she had written to Hassan in her hand then she let it drop into the water. It floated for a while then grew water-logged and slowly sank out of sight.

Some time later the squeak of oars nearby made her glance up and she saw with a sinking heart that Lord Carstairs was being rowed over towards them. She watched unsmiling as he raised his hand in salute. Feigning not to notice she turned away and walked across to the other side to look instead towards the town. Augusta had gone ashore with the Fielding ladies earlier that morning to visit the bazaar. Louisa had declined to go with them. She had no heart for shopping.

It was only a short time later that she heard a step on the deck behind her.

'Mrs Shelley. I feel I owe you a deep and heartfelt apology.'

She did not turn round. 'You do, Lord Carstairs. And you owe an even greater one to my dragoman who has been dismissed thanks to your interference.'

There was a moment's silence. Seeing that she did not intend to turn and speak to him Carstairs moved over to the rail and leant on it beside her. 'My motives were entirely honourable, I assure you,' he said softly. 'Will you allow me to try and make amends? I understand they will start to take us up the cataract this afternoon. The *Ibis* is to go first, I believe. Will you allow me to escort you on a picnic on the rocks so you can watch her as she starts her journey upriver from here? It would make a wonderful subject for your painting. I have heard that the Nubians take to the water like fish as they pull on the ropes. Their children join in. It will be a wonderful spectacle.'

They were staring out across the water, side by side. In the distance she could see the horse-drawn garis on the Corniche, the donkeys with their assorted riders, several boats pulled up on the sand near the quay. He watched beside her in silence, content to have planted the idea, perhaps aware of the struggle she was having with her conscience. Half of her wanted desperately to accept his invitation; the chance to draw the boat from the rocks was too tempting to ignore. On the other hand she was still furious with him, still intensely aware of the disloyalty it would show to Hassan.

'Think of your paintings, Mrs Shelley. It would be a shame not to show the cataract in all its aspects.' The soft voice beside her was persuasive. 'It is the least I could do to try and make up for your loss.'

She looked at him sharply. He was still staring into the distance. He did not turn.

She gave in, in the end. It was, as he said, foolish to throw away the chance of watching at least for part of the time from the rocks and getting the chance to record the event. And going with him did not mean that she had forgiven him, or ever would.

Gathering up her painting equipment later that afternoon she followed Carstairs down into his sandal, intensely aware that on this occasion she would not be able to change into her comfortable dress

202

and would remain fully and formally clothed even in the river spray.

It was only as they rowed away from the *Ibis* that she noticed Venetia Fielding on the deck of her brother's boat, watching them. Even from that distance she could feel the woman's anger and jealousy.

They landed on an outcrop of rock above one of the narrower gorges between the islands and Carstairs nimbly leapt ashore. The boatman passed over the picnic, her painting things and an array of soft tapestry cushions wrapped for dryness in oiled cloth, Carstairs slipped the man a handful of coins in return and then he waved him away. 'This will give us a splendid view as they pull the boat up against the current.' He smiled at her. Holding out his hand he helped her towards the cushions with effortless courtesy and handed her the parasol. She sat down, wondering how he expected her to paint and hold the thing at the same time.

The rush of water precluded much speech. Leaving her to unpack her paints alone Carstairs went and stood on the edge of the rock, staring downriver towards the place where the boat would first appear. He stood for a long time seemingly lost in thought, then at last he turned back towards her. Propping her parasol behind her she had opened a sketchbook and was pencilling in a rough outline of the canyon. The spray from the falls had soaked a corner of her skirt but she had not noticed.

She glanced up. 'Would you be very kind, my lord, and bring me a little water?' She held out her water pot to him and smiled. He took it and for a moment their eyes met. In the bright sunlight his irises were colourless as glass, his expression fathomless. She couldn't tear her eyes away from his. She felt for a moment as if she were falling, then abruptly, she tore her gaze away. As she glanced down at the water swirling round the rock she caught sight of an enigmatic smile, there only for a second, then it was gone – so swiftly that she wondered if she had imagined it.

She watched as he squatted at the edge of a rock pool constantly filled by spray and quickly swished her little paint pot round, then he stood up again and brought it to her.

She took it with a nod. 'I'm afraid you will be bored, my lord.'

He shook his head. 'Indeed not. You are quite wrong about my boredom levels. I have infinite patience.' To her surprise he lowered himself onto a cushion next to her and crossed his legs. She shrugged. Dipping her brush into the water he had brought her

203

she selected colours from her box, mixed them, and began to brush the resulting shade swiftly onto the paper.

When next she looked at him the sun had moved slightly. The shadows just beyond her were deeper than before. There was still no sign of the dahabeeyah and its escort. He was sitting in exactly the same position as he had been when she had last looked up, his eyes focused on her sketch but, she was certain, not actually seeing it. She stopped painting and laid down the brush softly. He made no move. Pushing the sketchpad off her knees she rose silently to her feet and stood looking down at him. He still gave no sign that he had noticed her at all.

'My lord?' She spoke quietly in his ear. 'My lord? Roger? Are you all right?' His eyes were open, his pupils tiny points of black in the strange clear irises. His back was absolutely straight, his hands resting loosely on his knees. He was, as far as she could see, in some kind of reverie.

With a shiver she straightened. After watching him for a few more seconds she turned away. She went to stand by the water's edge, staring at the rocks, wondering if she should try to wake him. At that precise moment she saw the first figures appearing at the mouth of the gorge, the ropes over their shoulders. Within a few seconds the river was a turmoil of shouting, laughing men, as, with a dozen or so on each of the four lines she saw them dragging the heavy boat up against the torrents of water towards her.

'It's a splendid sight, is it not?'

She jumped at the voice right beside her. Carstairs was standing close to her, his eyes on the activity before them.

'It is indeed.' She glanced at him sideways. His face was shaded beneath the brim of his white pith helmet and she could not see his eyes at all.

'Do you wish to make a few quick sketches? I shall unpack our food and I must find some baksheesh for the boys. The moment they spot us they will want to dive for us.' Suddenly he was all efficiency as she sat down once again with her sketches, unpacking the picnic hamper, laying out the small cloth, pouring the wine.

With a roar of triumph the men dragged the boat closer and Louisa could see Augusta and Sir John now, on the roof of the forecabin. As she looked up they began to wave.

'We'll rejoin them once they are through the first rapid.' Carstairs passed her a glass of wine. 'Then you'll be able to experience it from the other end of the tow rope, so to speak. Shall we drink a toast?' He held out his glass and she felt obliged to respond. For a second their hands touched then he raised his wine and put it to his lips. '*Saluté*, beautiful lady.'

However hard she tried to resist she could not stop herself from glancing up to meet his eyes. This time it was more than she could do to look away. She was too tired. She felt herself relaxing back onto the cushions. He had moved closer to her now, bending over her. 'Louisa, my dear, shall I take your glass? We do not want to spill it, do we.' His mouth was close to her face, his eyes, holding hers, so huge they were like great whirlpools, threatening to draw her in and drown her. 'Shall I move your parasol, my dear, to shade you better? There.'

Her eyes were closing. She couldn't help it. She could feel his mouth on hers. It was firm, commanding. A thrill of excitement coursed through her veins and then suddenly he was sitting up.

'*Yalla*,' he roared. '*Imshi*! Go away!'

A small boy, dressed only in a loincloth was standing dripping on the rock beside them.

As she dragged herself drowsily upright she saw the boy turn. He leapt off the rock back into the boiling foaming waters. 'Oh my God, he'll drown.' She heard her own voice, shrill and frightened.

'Of course he won't drown. How do you think he got here? He's only after baksheesh!' Carstairs plunged his hand into his pocket and brought out a handful of coins. Throwing them high in the air he watched them splash into the water round the small bobbing head. In a second the cheeky smile had been replaced by a pair of small brown feet.

'Your wine, my dear.' He was handing her the glass once more. 'And let me pass you some food.'

It was as though it had never happened. She brushed her hand against her lips, confused. He was kneeling now, in front of the hamper, producing bread and hard boiled eggs and fresh white cheese and fruit.

She shook her head in confusion. 'How will we get back onto the *Ibis*?' Suddenly that seemed important to her. She wanted to go back to the others.

'You'll see. As she comes past it will be easy.' He heaped her plate with food for her as if she were a child and sat down a few feet away. He had not looked directly at her again.

She glanced at the parasol. It had been moved, so that it was between the river and the spot where she had been lying. No one on the boat would have been able to see what had happened, if it had happened at all. Confused, she looked down at her plate. What appetite she had, had gone.

Carstairs looked at her at last. 'What is it? Don't you like it?'

She shrugged. 'I'm sorry. I'm not hungry any more.'

Setting down the bottle with which he had been topping up his own glass he moved closer to her again. 'I hope the sun has not been too much for you?'

'No.' She shook her head. 'No, I thrive on the sun.'

Had she dreamt it? If she accused him of taking advantage of her, would he call her a liar?

He was smiling again now, beside her, reaching for her hand. She tried to look away.

'Louisa?' His voice was clear above the roar of water. 'Don't fight it. Look at me. You know you want to.'

She took a deep breath, staring hard at the dappling of sunlight on the water, trying to resist. 'Roger, please –'

'Look at me, Louisa. Why fight it? Look at me. Now.' His hand over hers was ice cold. She shivered. Unable to stop herself she felt her face lifting towards his.

'That's right.' His eyes were intensely overwhelming. She could feel herself being drawn in by them once more, her thoughts wiped from her mind, her body that of a limp, obedient doll.

'That's right. It's so easy this way.' He trailed his fingers lightly up her arm and took her chin between them, raising her face a little more.

This time her lips parted obediently beneath his, even though her body did not respond. She was totally without defences. She knew he had moved the parasol again; then she felt him unbutton her high-necked blouse, felt him insert his hand, pushing aside the soft damp lace of her chemise as his ice-cold fingers groped for her breast. She gasped but she did not push him away.

'The scent bottle, Louisa. You are going to give it to me. You are going to make me a gift of it, my darling.' His lips were by her ear now. The words echoed in her mind. The scent bottle. A gift. The scent bottle. A gift.

Hassan's gift!

Her eyes flew open. 'No!' She pushed him away violently. 'No! What are you doing?'

Scrambling up she ran a few steps on the slippery rock and felt her feet going from under her. With a gasp of fear she threw out her arm to save herself, somehow recovered her balance and stood swaying on the edge of the water.

It was at that moment that she saw the tall figure standing between her and Carstairs.

It remained there for a moment between them, hands outstretched, the face a mask of fury, then it was gone.

Carstairs seemed frozen to the spot. He was as white as the foam on the water around them, trembling violently, his eyes alight, but whether with excitement or fear she could not tell . . .

'Ahoy, Louisa! Ready to come aboard?' A voice reached her suddenly over the roar of the rapids and she turned to see the dahabeeyah within fifteen yards of her rock. All around it suddenly were dozens of men, pulling at the ropes with which they were dragging and levering the boat up against the roaring water. Sir John raised both hands and waved. In a moment one of the crew was there on the rock with them. In seconds their belongings were being packed. In another ten the boat was close enough for her to grab the handrail of the ladder and pulled herself aboard. Behind her Carstairs handed the last of the cushions up to the *reis* and scrambled up himself.

'So, did you sketch us? Let's see.' Sir John held out his hand for her book. She gave it to him mutely.

Behind her Carstairs leant forward and put his hand on her elbow. His fingers on her bare skin were like cold India-rubber.

With a start Anna looked up. She frowned and glanced at her watch. Nearly an hour had gone by and there was no sign of Serena. Reaching for the phone she picked it up and dialled the other cabin.

Charley answered. 'Who is it?' She sounded as though she had been asleep.

'It's Anna, Charley. I want to speak to Serena.'

There was a pause, then a hollow laugh. 'Tough. She's not here.'

'I see. When did she go out, do you know?'

'I've no idea.' The voice was suddenly very bored. 'I'm not her keeper.' And the phone was slammed down.

Anna pursed her lips.

Closing the diary she pushed it back into the drawer. She was making her way towards the door when there was a knock.

Serena was standing there. One glance told Anna she had been crying.

'What's the matter? Oh, Serena!' She caught her hand and pulled her into the room. Pushing her down to sit on the bed she stared at her for a moment then she sat down beside her. 'Please tell me it's not Andy. Has he been having a go at you because of me?'

Serena shrugged, then reluctantly she gave a slight nod. 'It's not your fault, Anna. He's been on the point of saying all this ever since I met him.' She sniffed and groped in her skirt pocket for a tissue. 'It's just that he was so cruel.' She looked straight ahead, her face crumpled and bewildered. 'I'm no use to you like this, Anna.'

Anna stared at her, aghast. Standing up she went over to the dressing table and poured a glass of water. Handing it to Serena she shrugged helplessly. 'What did he say? Would you like to tell me?'

'I doubt it. I'm sure your imagination is good enough to fill in the gaps. Basically I'm to keep my menopausal madness to myself and not come near you any more.'

'Or what? Exactly what does he intend to do about it?' Anna could feel her fury mounting.

'Nothing to you, obviously.' Serena drank the water quickly, her eyes closed, both hands clamped round the glass. 'But he'll make my life hell. And he can do it, believe me. He's done it before. He comes round. He phones. He implies that I'm going round the bend. He threatens me with psychiatrists and exorcists and God knows what! It's not worth it, Anna.' Sighing, she put the glass down and shook her head. 'Even if I wanted to I can't be there for you. He's drained every particle of confidence from me. In this state I'd be mincemeat for your priests. My only consolation I suppose is that I don't even have enough energy now to make it worth their while trying to possess me.'

Anna closed her eyes. The temperature in the cabin seemed to have dropped several degrees. She was thinking of Louisa and her fear. 'What makes you think they would try to possess you?'

'I'm an initiate. I probably have the kind of energy they want. If I was strong, centred, I'd be able to stand up to them. I'd be able to fight them on their own ground and maybe I'd be of some use to you.' Serena shook her head. 'But according to Andy I only have my self-obsessed paranoia left now. I begged him to try and see it from our angle. To try and imagine the threat to be real. To try and think what would happen if those two priests get stronger. There is no one to fight them except me.'

'I can still throw the bottle away, Serena,' Anna interrupted.

'That won't do any good! You said yourself they followed you to the dam. They're not tied to the bottle, Anna. They are real independent beings! I don't know why they didn't show themselves before. Maybe they knew you would bring it back to Egypt one day. Maybe they couldn't find enough of the right kind of energies in London. But now they have found the means to gain enough strength they are not going to jump in the river after the bottle and disappear in a plop of steam!'

Anna smiled involuntarily, inspite of her fear. The description conjured up a wonderful image. 'Then you must help me, Serena. You have to. I need you. I keep thinking of Louisa; of how frightened she was.' She stood up again, suddenly resolute. 'I'm going to have this out with Andy right now, and get him to lay off you.'

'No, please!' Serena caught her hand.

'Don't try and stop me. I've had enough of his interference, I really have. We've both said he is a bully and you're right, this is none of his business.'

'He's made you his business, Anna. He fancies you, and to be honest,' she hesitated, 'I think he fancies that diary of yours even more. At heart Andy is always the dealer first; friend or lover second. It sounds awful but he's probably got a buyer and a price in the back of his mind already. If I'm in danger of coming between him and his turn on a swift buck I'm dead meat!'

Anna stared at her in silence for a moment, then without another word she spun on her heel and stormed out of the cabin.

Andy wasn't hard to find. He was sitting on a stool at the bar, watching Ali with his cocktail shaker.

'I want a word. Now.' Anna stopped in front of him, her hands on her hips, her eyes blazing. 'Your interference has gone far enough! It has to stop.'

She was aware of various other people in the lounge glancing at her quickly then looking away. She took no notice of them.

'So, Serena went straight to you did she?' He scribbled his name on a chit and took the glass from Ali. He raised it to her in mock salute. 'I just wanted to save you from getting dragged into her drama sessions. You would have thanked me, you know. But,' he shrugged, 'if that's what you want. So be it.' He took a deep swig from his glass.

'It is. And I don't want to hear that you've been intimidating her. For God's sake, stop sticking your nose in! What makes you think you've got the right to have any say whatsoever in what I do or who I have as friends? I've only known you a few days!' She was over-reacting, she knew it, but suddenly she had seen Felix in front of her, choosing her friends, dictating her life. No more. The new Anna was free and a far more powerful person than the old one.

'You've only known Serena a few days, too,' Andy retorted. He shook his head.

'So, I'm going with my gut feelings,' she flashed back. 'I like her and I trust her.'

'Ouch! Do I infer from that that you neither like nor trust me? I'm sorry. I'd somehow got completely the opposite impression.'

She looked him in the eye. 'I like you, Andy, and I'm sure I can trust you. But that does not mean I have to give my whole being into your hands; nor does it mean you can pick and choose my friends for me.'

Andy held her gaze. 'Similarly,' he said softly, 'may I remind you that I have known Serena for years. You have known her for only a very few days. My relationship with her is none of your business.'

There was a moment's silence.

She stepped back and gave a small nod. 'Touché! As long as your relationship with her doesn't interfere with my relationship with her!' She turned sharply away from him to find Toby standing behind her. Beside him was Charley. Toby had, Anna realised suddenly, been holding Charley's arm.

'Is this a private war?' Toby gave her a wry grin. 'If not, we'd like to join in –'

He broke off as Charley lunged past him, breaking free of his restraining grip.

210

'Andy, you bastard!' Her words were slurred. Her eyes were unfocused, wandering past him across the room and back as though she couldn't quite locate him. As Anna moved away she lurched forward, putting her hands out towards the bar. 'Andy? I have to do this for the goddess Sekhmet. She needs me, Andy. She wants me.' In the shocked silence that followed her words she stared round. 'Andy, what's happening?' Her voice was suddenly quite pathetic. 'Andy, what's happening to me?'

Anna turned at a slight pressure on her shoulder. It was Toby. He beckoned her away and with a hasty glance first at Charley then towards Andy, she followed him.

'Andy? What's wrong with me?' She could still hear the pathetic high-pitched voice as they got to the door.

'You're drunk.' Andy's harsh rejoinder could probably be heard by everyone in the room.

'No!' She burst into tears. 'No, I'm not. I haven't had anything . . .' Her voice trailed away. She stood for a moment, swaying slightly, then she crumpled slowly at his feet.

'Leave Andy to deal with her.' Toby ushered Anna towards the door. 'Let's go outside.'

'She doesn't look well.'

Sekhmet. Had Charley really mentioned Sekhmet? She shivered. As she followed Toby out onto the shaded afterdeck she was frowning. 'She didn't look drunk to me.'

'I don't know that she was necessarily drunk when she kicked up all that fuss at lunchtime.' Toby sounded thoughtful as they leant against the rail, looking out across the river. 'There was no smell of booze. I'd say she was ill. I suppose it could be the heat.' He shrugged. 'Perhaps someone should have a word with Omar.'

He turned round. 'Andy seems to have quite a few problems at the moment one way and another. And one of them seems to be with me.' His voice was light, casual as he changed the subject.

She was gazing down into the water. 'As you say, Andy has problems with a lot of people.' She glanced up at him suddenly. 'She did say Sekhmet, didn't she?'

He looked blank for a moment. 'Who?'

'Charley. Charley was talking about the goddess, Sekhmet.'

'Was she? She was ranting and raving like a mad woman. It was all I could do to hold her off long enough for you to have a go at

211

him first.' He gave a mischievous grin. 'Don't read too much into anything she said. She really wasn't with us.'

Anna bit her lip. She was silent for a moment or two and Toby took the opportunity to study her face. 'Can I buy you a drink before dinner?' He stood away from the rail and glanced back towards the door. 'I suspect they have gone by now.'

She shook her head. 'Thank you, but I think I'm going to go and have a quick word with Serena. I want her to know that that bastard is not going to keep me away from her.' She paused, scrutinising Toby's face, suddenly realising that this was the first time she'd been alone with him since Andy's revelation. How could she have forgotten it? But so much had happened, she had ignored it, pretended she hadn't heard. Certainly she hadn't believed it. Had she? She frowned, her eyes on his, then she shook her head. That was not the face of a murderer. If it was, she was the worst judge of character in the entire world.

Serena was nowhere to be found. Her cabin was in darkness, occupied solely by a quietly snoring Charley. She wasn't in Anna's cabin, or on the upper deck, nor was she in the still-empty dining room. Puzzled, Anna went back to her own cabin and sat down on the bed.

Where was she? She frowned. Surely she couldn't have gone ashore alone. The boat was not so big that someone could disappear on it. She must be in someone else's cabin. Ben's perhaps, or the Booths or one of the others.

With a weary sigh she sat down on the bed. There was half an hour till dinner. She could go back in the bar and have that drink with Toby, or she could lie down and perhaps have another look at the diary, to see what happened when Louisa got back onto the boat.

Changing out of her spray-soaked dress Louisa went back on deck to find the Forresters talking to Roger Carstairs as they looked down at the straining teams of men pulling the vessel up the rapids. Her face coloured as she saw him. She had hoped he would have gone back to his own boat which would be following them up the next day.

He turned to look at her and she was astonished at the expression of triumphant amusement he directed at her. She could, she suddenly realised, read him like a book. He was confident, completely secure that she remembered nothing of the incident on the rocks this afternoon, and faintly mocking. She shivered and felt as she had before, like a rabbit cowering before a weasel, unable to move or run. With an effort she tore her eyes away and stepped closer to Sir John, very aware of the comfort of his burly good-humoured solidity.

'So, Lord Carstairs,' she said from this position of security. 'You are presumably going back to your own vessel this evening? I should thank you for arranging the picnic for me.'

He bowed very slightly. His smile was a little lopsided she noticed for the first time. It gave him a vulpine look which was extremely unsettling. She felt herself shiver once again.

Sir John noticed. He put an arm round her shoulders and gave her a brief squeeze. 'Cold m'dear? It's all this spray.'

She smiled at him. 'I am a little.'

The night wind from the desert had not yet come and the sun, though about to disappear below the cliffs, was still radiating warmth. Only between the rocks and the low cliff faces was the air chill. The boat was calm suddenly. The men who had been manning the ropes to pull them up the rapids in the course of the day were vanishing one by one back in the direction of their villages and the splendid Nubian pilot, who had sat all day at the helm directing matters with almost regal dignity, had saluted first the *reis* then Sir John and finally he too had gone home. Tomorrow they would all be back for the last leg of the journey before returning to the foot of the cataract for the next vessel.

'Roger has agreed to accept our invitation to dinner, m'dear.' Sir John was beaming. 'He will go back to his boat later. We are here for the night. We will be pulled up the last rapids tomorrow, I understand, then we'll lie at Philae for a day or so and wait for the Fieldings to come up as well. It will be fun to go on in convoy as far as the second cataract.'

Louisa forced herself to smile; she forced herself to say the right things and then she excused herself to go once more below. In

213

her cabin she stretched out on the bed, exhausted and depressed, thinking about Hassan as outside the sun went down in a blaze of gold.

The knock on the door made her sit up with a start. She must have fallen asleep. The cabin was in total darkness and as she groped for the candlestick she could see nothing around her at all. Another knock rang round the small space as the flame caught and she realised it must be Treece already, coming to help her dress for dinner. She had forgotten she had locked the cabin door. The shadows flared over the deep russets and golds of the rugs and hangings which decorated the small area as she groped her way to the door and unfastened it.

Roger Carstairs stood there, his head bowed beneath the low ceiling. With one swift movement he pushed her back into the cabin and stepped in after her, bolting the door behind him.

'How dare you!'

He pushed her sharply so that she collapsed backwards onto the bed and was forced to watch as he picked up the candlestick and swept it around, scrutinising her belongings.

'Where is it?' he hissed.

'Where is what?' She was at a disadvantage, sitting down, forced to look up at him but there was no room to stand without actually pushing him away. She shuddered. 'How dare you come in here?' she repeated. 'Get out! I'll call for help! There will be terrible trouble if you are found in here with me.'

'I don't think so.' He laughed. 'The Forresters wouldn't dare cross me, my oh so proper little Mrs Shelley. Especially when I tell them how eagerly you received my attentions this afternoon.' He reached down and caught her chin between iron fingers just as he had before, forcing her to look at him. 'Yes, you do remember. I shall have to be careful. You are wilful. You think you can resist me.' He breathed out heavily through his nose. 'So, Mrs Shelley. Where is it?'

'The scent bottle?' There was no point in pretending she didn't know what he meant. 'I've hidden it ashore.'

His eyes blazed. 'Not today. It was not possible today. Yesterday, then. You left it at Philae? Where?' He pushed her head back against the cabin wall. 'Tell me,' he whispered through gritted teeth.

The cabin had suddenly grown very cold. The candleflame flickered and streamed black threads of smoke. His eyes were dark

214

pits, close to hers. She couldn't look away. Desperately she shut her eyes, trying not to breathe the unpleasant sweet scent of his breath.

'I'll never tell you.' She pushed her fist against his face and was rewarded with a quiet laugh.

'Oh, you'll tell me, sweetheart. Believe me, you'll tell me.' He caught her wrist.

With a little gasp of pain she felt the small delicate bones crushed between his fingers. 'Help me!' Her cry was no more than a whisper. 'Anhotep, if you exist, help me now!'

The candle flared.

Carstairs laughed once more. 'So, our little widow invokes the high priest, but she doesn't know how.' He pushed her back so violently against the cabin wall that all the breath was knocked out of her body. 'Where is the bottle –' He broke off in mid-sentence. The boat was rocking violently. Above, on deck the *reis* looked over the side. A mooring rope had come loose and the *Ibis* had swung with the strong current. They heard the shouts and the thud of urgently running feet.

'Why?' she gasped. 'Why do you want it so badly?'

He stared down at her. 'I have to have it. It is imperative I have it. It is not a bauble for you to play with. It is a sacred chrismatory. It contains power. Power only I know how to use!' His eyes glittered feverishly as his hand tightened round her wrist.

'Anhotep!' Louisa struggled ferociously. 'Don't let him hurt me –'

As the candleflame flickered and streamed sideways in the tiny airless cabin she opened her eyes to peer past him towards the window. A figure stood there – misty, indistinct. Through him she could see the wall, the shutters, the shawl she had thrown down across the stool.

'Anhotep! Help me!' Her voice was stronger this time. Her fear of the man half-sprawled across her was greater by far than her fear of a shadow from the distant past.

Carstairs moved back slightly, aware of the change in the atmosphere in the small space, aware of the strange behaviour of the candleflame. Noticing her gaze focused somewhere over his shoulder he glanced round towards the window and gasped. In a second he had pushed himself off the bed.

'Servant of Isis, greeting!' He bowed low, ignoring Louisa who cowered back on the bunk, making herself as small as possible.

215

The cabin had become totally airless; the candleflame, a moment before flaring wildly and streaming smoke, had died to a tiny glow. In a second it would be out altogether. The figure was fading.

Louisa launched herself off the bed towards the door, groping for the bolt. Frantically she scrabbled for it as the light died altogether. As the figure vanished totally Carstairs turned back towards her. She felt his hands groping for her shoulders just as her flailing fingers found the bolt. Desperately she pulled at it and felt it slide back but it was too late. He was dragging her away from the door, thrusting her back onto the bed. She drew breath to scream and felt his hand clamp over her mouth. Once again she heard him laugh. There was excitement in the sound now, and triumph.

At the very moment he began to rip open her blouse there was a loud knock at the cabin door.

9

Homage to thee, Amen-Ra who passest over
the heaven,
every face seeth thee. Men praise thee in
thy name.
Millions of years have gone over the world.
Thou dost pass over and dost travel through
untold spaces. . .

Once more the sands drift here and there. The open abandoned tomb is buried yet again. The mummies are gone for ever to the dust of oblivion; only their names survive, safe on walls of rock. Centuries pass and the priests are shadows without substance, nothing in the sunlight, nothing beneath the moon, dying vows forgotten, spent anger no more than a sigh in the wind across the dunes.

God has come to the Land of Kemet under a new name. The old gods of Egypt sleep. Their servants have lost their glory. It is 3000 years since the tomb was first sealed on the bodies of the two priests.

The hand that digs the small forgotten bottle from the dune,

*as his father seeks for greater treasures in the night, is that of
a child. The boy scrabbles it free with eager fingers and holds
it aloft in delight, seeing the colours of the glass against the
rising rays of the new-born sun.*

*Coalescing from the breath of the dawn like so much moisture
on the leaf of a papyrus, first one shadow then another looks
down at the boy and smiles. Only the donkey senses the danger.
Its ears lie back and it cries its fear into the empty desert wind.*

The knock was repeated. Anna looked up, frowning. It was dark
outside the open window and the only light came from the small
bedside lamp. Confused, she put down the diary, her mind full of
Louisa's terror. Standing up she went over to the cabin door and
pulled it open, her thoughts still half in the dark smoky cabin of
the dahabeeyah.

Ibrahim stood there, his empty tray under his arm. He gave her
a look of grave anxiety. 'You are not well, *mademoiselle*? I was
concerned that you were not at supper.' Behind him the corridor
was empty.

She dragged herself back to the present with difficulty. 'I'm all
right, Ibrahim. I'm sorry. I was reading and I didn't realise what
time it was. I didn't hear the gong.' She rubbed her face wearily
with the palms of her hands.

He was studying her closely and after a moment he seemed
satisfied with what he saw. Slowly he nodded his head. 'I will bring
you something to eat in your cabin.' He didn't wait for her to reply.
He turned and walked away. She watched his slow stately gait. In
his white *galabiyya*, his turban and his leather sandals he was a
timeless figure, almost biblical. She turned back into the cabin,
leaving the door ajar and stood staring thoughtfully out at the
night. Poor Louisa. She must have been so afraid. And so angry.
The words in the diary conveyed a mass of conflicting emotions as

the small neat writing in faded brown ink moved steadily down the page, the only sign of her perturbation the way the lines drew closer together, the words more slanted, here and there, a careless stroke joining word to word as the writing speeded up, once or twice a fine spray of ink droplets from a nib pressed too hard too often.

'*Mademoiselle*?' A gentle knock and Ibrahim was in the doorway again. He had a tray with a glass of hibiscus juice and a plate of bread with a hard boiled egg and some cheese. He slid it onto the dressing table and gave her a grave smile. 'There is one other thing, *mademoiselle*.' He reached into his pocket and brought out something attached to a fine gold chain. She could see it as the links slid between his fingers.

'I would like you to wear this, *mademoiselle*.' He held it out to her. 'As long as you are on the boat. Please give it back to me the day you go home to England.'

She stared down at his hand, then slowly she reached out her own. 'Ibrahim, what is it?'

He dropped a gold charm into her palm. It was small and intricately worked. 'It is the Eye of Horus. *Allah yisallimak*. May God protect thee. It will help to keep you safe.'

She found her mouth had gone dry. 'Safe from what?' She looked up and met his deep brown eyes. He held her gaze for several seconds before giving a small shrug. He looked down at the floor in silence.

'Ibrahim? Is this to do with the old gods? And with the cobra?' She swallowed.

'*Inshallah*!' There was no shrug this time. Instead, the ghost of a nod.

'Then thank you. Thank you very much. It is gold, Ibrahim. You are very generous to trust me with it.' She smiled suddenly. 'I wish I knew the right thing to say in Arabic.'

'You say: *kattar kheirak*.' His eyes twinkled.

'*Kattar kheirak*, Ibrahim.'

He bowed. '*Ukheeirak, mademoiselle*.' He gave her a huge smile. 'Now I must go and work in the bar. *Bon appetit, mademoiselle. U'i. Leilt ik saideh*. That means take care, and may thy night be happy.'

After he had gone she stared down at the charm in her hand. It was an eye surmounted by an arched brow with below it a tiny swirl of gold. The Eye of Horus was, she knew, a symbol of protection and

219

healing used for thousands of years all over the world to ward off danger and illness and bad luck. She held it for a moment tightly in her hand then felt for the clasp and carefully hung it around her neck. It touched her enormously that Ibrahim should have trusted her with something so precious. It also terrified her. What did he know that had made him so afraid for her? She glanced down at the dressing table drawer, but she did not open it. Some time today she would see that the bottle was put away in the safe. She shivered.

Picking up the glass of scented fruit juice she sat down on the bed and reached for the diary. In the morning she would decide whether to go on the sailing trip which was scheduled on the blackboard outside the dining room or whether to take the chance to track down Serena whilst Andy was well and truly out of sight and talk to her at leisure and without a chance of being interrupted. But first, tonight, she must find out what happened to poor Louisa at the hands of the villainous Roger Carstairs. Pulling the pillows up around her she put her hand for a moment to the small gold charm and she smiled. It had made her feel safe and cared for, something, she realised, she hadn't felt for a very long time. She sat for several minutes lost in thought, savouring the feeling, then she opened the diary again.

The candle held high in her hand, Jane Treece surveyed the scene. It was clear what had been going on. Louisa Shelley had been behaving like the trollop she had always suspected she was, entertaining Lord Carstairs in her darkened cabin. With one disdainful look she took in Louisa's flushed face and bruised mouth, her torn blouse and the handsome angry man hastily climbing off the bed. He was still fully dressed, so she had arrived in time to thwart their lust. With a self-satisfied smile Jane Treece cleared her throat.

'Would you like me to help you get ready for dinner, Mrs Shelley, or shall I come back later?' Her voice was at its most repressive.

'Thank you, Jane. Yes. Please stay. I should like to change.' Louisa's voice was shaking. She turned to Lord Carstairs and pointed at the door. 'Go.'

For a moment he hesitated, then with a smile he ducked outside. In the narrow passage he turned and raised his hand. '*A bientôt*, sweetheart. We'll continue our delightful discourse very soon.'

Louisa closed her eyes. She was shaking as she watched Treece light her bedside candle and the others on the table. In a very short time the cabin was full of gently flickering light.

Without a word Treece gathered Louisa's discarded clothes from earlier that afternoon and folded them. Then she picked up the ewer and withdrew to fetch hot water and towels. Louisa glanced at her dressing case. It was still locked, the tiny ornate key safely hidden beneath the thimble in her small sewing box.

With shaking hands she reached up to her pins and combs and allowing her long chestnut hair to fall round her shoulders she picked up her hairbrush and began to brush it with slow rhythmic strokes, trying to brush away the feel of Carstairs' hands, the smell of his breath, the cold fascination of his glance.

She looked up as Treece reappeared. 'Thank you, Jane.' She bit her lip, trying to steady her voice. 'Has Lord Carstairs left the boat?'

'I'm sure I don't know, Mrs Shelley.' Treece put down the heavy jug with a resentful bang which slopped the water onto the dressing table. 'Did you wish me to run and fetch him back for you?'

Louisa stared at her. 'You know I don't! The man is a vicious brute.' She found herself suddenly fighting back tears. 'I only wished to be sure he had safely gone.'

There was a long pause as the woman considered her words and Louisa saw a slight softening of the grim expression on her face.

'I had thought to hear them say he was staying for dinner,' she commented as she took Louisa's ruined blouse and stared at it distastefully. 'This will have to go to the *ghasala* woman to be washed and mended.' She looked up. 'The Forresters are thrilled to have made such friends with another member of the aristocracy and one of so high a rank. They would be very put out if they thought one of their guests had upset him.'

'Would they indeed.' With pursed lips Louisa reached for the soap. 'Please pour out some water.' She shivered, though the cabin was still very hot. 'I'll wear my silk for dinner, thank you, if you could find it for me, then you can go and help Lady Forrester.' She straightened suddenly and looked the woman in the eye. 'Please do not speak about this to the Forresters. As you rightly said, it would upset them.'

She intended to speak to Sir John herself, and soon. But she had no wish for the sour-faced Jane Treece to spread the word first. Although she had detected a slight thaw in the woman's attitude, she was, she suspected, quite capable of relaying the story in some no doubt biased and unpleasant way. She watched with a deep sigh as Treece closed the cabin door, then she sat down on the stool and wearily surveyed her image in the mirror, taking in her full rounded bosom, shown off by the ribboned corset with its low neckline, her narrow waist and the long luxuriant hair hanging round her shoulders. Her face, for all her care with sun hat and parasol had caught the sun a little and the unaccustomed colour in her cheeks had made her dark eyes sparkle. Had she in some unknowing way led him on? Not deliberately, certainly. Never that. She shivered, and plunged her hands into the basin, splashing her face and neck, feeling her hair trail in the water.

When she looked up once more she could see nothing, blinded by the water. Shaking the droplets from her eyes she stared at the mirror and she gasped. In the steamy glass she could see that there was a figure standing immediately behind her.

With a cry of terror she spun round, but there was no one there. All she had seen were shadows from the masthead lamps of a boat, edging close beside them in the narrow mooring, blending with the criss-cross of shadows from the candles. Clutching the towel she stared round. The cabin was empty but for her. It glowed warmly as the light fell on the luxuriant colours of the hangings which decorated it. Steadying her breath with an effort she reached for her comb. It was her imagination. Nothing more. There would be no further ghostly visitations tonight. When she was dressed she would have a few minutes to soothe herself by catching up with the entries in her journal, then she would go to the saloon and if she must, brave the cruel hard eyes of Roger Carstairs for the rest of the evening.

222

EGYPT

Getting up Anna wandered over to her own dressing table and broke a piece of bread in half. Cutting up the egg and selecting a slice of cheese she made herself a sandwich and moved back to the bed. The Eye of Horus nestled between her breasts, the gold warm against her skin. She paused for a moment, listening, and glanced at her watch. It was nearly eleven o'clock. The others would by now have finished listening to the talk by Omar on the modern history of Egypt which had been scheduled for this evening. They would be quietly chatting and drinking amongst themselves in the lounge before finally going off to bed.

Sir John was in the saloon on his own when Louisa walked in. He stood up hastily. 'My dear, you look beautiful!' He eyed the midnight silk, and as though unable to stop himself, took her hand and kissed her fingertips. 'Louisa, m'dear. I fear I have some disappointing news. Roger has had to leave us. He had a message that there was a problem with one of the crew on his own boat, and he has had to go back. He asked me to beg your forgiveness for leaving so abruptly.'

'I don't think it was leaving he was begging forgiveness for!' Louisa said tartly. She sat down on the cushioned seat near him. 'Is Augusta joining us soon?'

He shook his head. 'Alas, the excitements of the day have proved too much for her. She has retired early. So I have asked Abdul to serve dinner early for us.' He reached for the decanter. 'Allow me to pass you a drink, m'dear. And let us toast our ascent of the cataract and its happy completion tomorrow.'

She sipped from the glass he gave her and then put it down. 'John, I'm afraid I must ask you not to allow Lord Carstairs to set foot on this boat again. He came to my cabin this evening and behaved with shocking impropriety.'

Sir John stared at her, his pale blue eyes huge above his moustache. She saw him drum his fingers on the table.

'Louisa, I find this hard to believe. My dear, he is a respected man. A gentleman in every way.'

'No, not a gentleman.' Louisa clenched her fists. 'Had Jane Treece not interrupted, he would have ravished me! He has some strange power, some ability to use mesmerism on me, which rendered me incapable of fighting him off. And he is trying to persuade me by underhand means and by threats to part with my little scent bottle. No, I cannot allow you to let him come back! I didn't want to mention it in front of Augusta. I know she likes him, but this is outrageous behaviour, you must agree!' She fell silent as she reached with a shaking hand for her glass once more.

Sir John was staring at her. 'You say he tried to ravish you?'

She nodded.

He licked his lips. 'He forced his way into your cabin?'

She nodded again.

'And touched you improperly?' His eyes left her face and dropped to the neckline of her gown. Suddenly he was breathing very heavily. 'My dear Louisa, you must remember that you are a very attractive woman. And in this heat, even the most august person might feel his blood race in your company.' He half stood suddenly, and moved closer to her. 'I myself have felt strongly attracted to you. Strongly!' He put out his hand and touched her wrist with hot fingers.

'John! What are you doing?' Augusta's voice interrupted him as she sailed into the saloon.

He leapt back as though he had been scalded. 'My dear! I didn't hear you! How fortunate you are here. Louisa has told me such terrible things. Terrible.' He was babbling with terror. 'My dear, Carstairs has proved to be the most awful painted sepulchre. A cad. A dreadful disgrace to our sex.'

Augusta had seated herself at the table. With commendable calm she reached for the decanter.

'I thought it was exceedingly foolish of you to go out with the man unchaperoned, Louisa,' she commented. 'Did you appear for him, too, *en déshabille?*'

Louisa found herself blushing slightly in spite of her anger. 'I did not, I assure you. I have found Lord Carstairs' behaviour totally unspeakable. I hope very much you will forbid him to set foot on the *Ibis* again.'

Augusta leant back in her seat and sipped thoughtfully from her glass. 'I don't think we can do that. The man is a peer of the realm. I have to admit that he has made me too feel uneasy, but I had thought his ambitions fixed on Venetia Fielding, so I have to say I am surprised he should jump on you.'

Louisa raised an eyebrow. 'You make it sound as though I am unworthy of his attentions.' She was indignant in spite of herself.

Augusta gave a dry smile. 'Not so much unworthy, my dear, as probably not rich enough. David Fielding has a large fortune and he has let it be known Venetia's dowry will be considerable.'

She glanced at her husband. 'Is there a reason for his interest in Louisa?'

Sir John was sitting meekly with his hands on the table in front of him. 'He wants her little perfume jar.' He shrugged. 'God knows why, but I think it has to do with his study of Ancient Egypt. I wish you would give it to him, Louisa, and have done. It can mean very little to you in real terms and you can name your price. The man will pay whatever you ask.'

Louisa glanced at him. 'It is not for sale. I have told him that. And for me it is also now a memento of Hassan who bought it for me and whom you so unjustly dismissed –' She caught herself in mid-sentence about to say more and bit her lip. 'He was my friend, and that makes it doubly precious to me. I assure you, I will never part with it. Not as long as I live.'

Anna put down the diary. She frowned. Was that a sound outside the door? She stared at the handle nervously, straining her ears and nearly jumped out of her skin as she heard a quiet knock.

'Who is it?' She cleared her throat anxiously.

'It's me, Toby. I didn't want to wake you if you were asleep. I was just checking you were OK.'

She climbed to her feet and went to open the door. 'I am fine. Thank you.' He was standing, leaning against the wall, one arm casually raised behind his head. He grinned at her, making no move to come in. 'I was just a bit worried when I saw you weren't at supper. I rather hoped Andy hadn't dragged you off to his lair.'

She smiled. 'Not a chance.'

'I have to say, I'm glad. OK. Goodnight. Sleep well.'

She stood in the doorway as he walked back along the corridor and watched as he turned the corner. Then thoughtfully she went back into the cabin.

She refused to allow herself to read any more that night. Exhausted, she had a quick shower and climbed into bed. Her last thought was of the charm around her neck. With it there she still felt strangely safe.

And she slept well until the early hours. Then she half awoke, thinking of Louisa. She dozed again, woke again and slept. When she awoke the next time almost before her eyes were open she found herself reaching for the diary again. To know what had happened to Louisa was becoming an obsession.

Louisa had slept late after her uncomfortable conversation with the Forresters and Augusta was alone in the saloon the next morning, when she left her cabin, dressed in a cool blouse and skirt. Augusta led the way on deck, where they sat sipping lemonade in the shade of the draped sail. 'Sir John and I have been talking, Louisa,' she began. She gave the younger woman a quick glance. 'We believe we may have been too hasty in dismissing Hassan. I think perhaps we were misled by Roger. Unintentionally, of course,' she added hastily. 'The *reis* thinks Hassan has not yet gone downriver. He and Sir John have gone ashore to try and locate him. The men will be back soon to pull us up the rapids but it will be easy for Hassan to find us should he wish to, when we are lying at Philae.'

Louisa held her breath. She closed her eyes, trying hard to keep her expression composed. Her heart was beating very fast.

'That would please you, my dear?'

She became aware suddenly that Augusta was studying her face. She nodded. 'That would please me very much.'

'John is a good man, you know, my dear.' Augusta bit her lip. 'He sometimes gets a little excitable. But he means no harm.'

Louisa smiled. 'I know that.' She was touched. Augusta must have found it hard both to ask forgiveness for her husband and to warn her off. She had managed both with infinite tact.

There was only one bone of contention left. 'And Lord Carstairs?'

'If Hassan is here there is no need for you to be alone with him, my dear. I believe Roger was probably a spoilt child and has continued to behave as one now he is an adult. If he wants something he believes he should have it and nothing must be allowed to thwart his desires. We will have to show him that, though he is still welcome on the *Ibis*, in this case he is not going to get what he wants.'

*   *   *

Louisa spent the rest of the morning sketching the cliffs and rocks. It was midday before the men began to return, ready to drag the boat up the last part of the cataract. With them came Sir John and Lord Carstairs.

Louisa had withdrawn to the far rail so that she could watch the proceedings from the boat. She didn't greet the two new arrivals, staring instead at the men forming up on the rocks, getting ready to heft the great ropes like tug of war teams preparing themselves to do battle against the elements. After a few moments, out of the corner of her eye, she saw Sir John and Carstairs go below into the saloon where Augusta was sheltering from the sun.

It was a while before any of them emerged, then at last Augusta appeared. Her eyes were sparkling as she hurried aft and sat down beside Louisa.

'Such wonderful news! You are not going to believe it!'

'Sir John has found Hassan?' Louisa felt her heart lift in excitement.

'Hassan?' Augusta looked vague for a moment. 'Oh no. I believe John has left word for him to follow the *Ibis* if he wishes to have the job back. No, no, far better than that. My dear, Roger Carstairs has asked John if he might call on you. My dear, he wishes to ask for your hand!'

Louisa stared at her. For a moment she was too stunned to react. An icy clamp seemed to have fastened itself over her lungs so that she could not breathe. Her mouth had gone dry.

Augusta clapped her hands. 'Of course Sir John said yes. He knew you would be thrilled! Roger was so apologetic about frightening you yesterday. He said that his love for you completely overrode his sanity. He has brought you the most beautiful gift, Louisa –'

At last Louisa managed to move. As stiff as a wooden doll she rose to her feet. Pencils and brushes cascaded to the deck and rolled away as she stared at Augusta. 'How dare he!' Her voice was so dry it rasped in her throat. 'How dare he come and try to inveigle his way onto the boat? Why should he ask Sir John? He is not my father! How dare anyone presume I should be pleased?'

Augusta looked stunned. For a moment she didn't appear to know what to say. She raised her hands and let them fall to her sides in a gesture of total bewilderment. 'He asked John because he is your host. This is his boat. We are caring for you, my dear.'

She sounded near to tears. 'We thought you would be so pleased. Think of it. His title –'

'I do not want his title, Augusta!' Louisa snapped back. 'And I most certainly do not want him or his gift. I shall not receive him. Please tell him to go.' She turned and leant against the rail, staring down into the water.

'Louisa –'

'No.' She did not look round. 'Please. Get rid of him.'

'I can't do that, Louisa.' Augusta paused for a moment, looking at her, then, with a sigh she turned away. As with a shout the mooring ropes were loosened and the boat swung into the channel Louisa found herself alone on deck.

It was perhaps an hour later that she made her way somewhat cautiously back to her cabin. As she passed the door she glanced into the saloon. Augusta and Sir John were there alone. Of Carstairs there was no sign. With a sigh of relief she turned towards her door and pushed it open. He was sitting on the bed. On the counterpane beside him was her journal and her dressing case.

At her gasp of surprise and fear he smiled. 'Please don't scream, Louisa. It would be so embarrassing to have to tell Sir John and Augusta that what they heard was merely the voice of your passion. Give me the key to this silly little box and we'll have done.'

'You've been reading my private diary!' She was overwhelmed with anger.

'Indeed I have. And what interesting reading. You don't appear to like my company, my dear. Your penchant is for natives, I see.' He sneered at her. 'Luckily I'm not particularly worried by your views, either way. The key, please, or I'll be forced to break the lock.'

'Get out of my cabin!' Louisa could feel her anger mounting. Heat was flooding through her body. 'Get out now!' She moved towards him and snatched the diary out of his hand. 'Do you want me to summon the high priest once more to my aid? He came when I called him. Remember? Who knows what he might do to protect me.'

Carstairs laughed. 'Summoning spirits, my dear, is what I do, not you. I have trained for years in the occult practices which will bring forth the guardians of your little bottle. Is that really what you

229

want?' He stood up suddenly and she fell back, frightened. He seemed very tall in the small cabin. Although she was trying very hard to disguise the fact, her courage was draining away as fast as it had come, leaving her numb with fear.

Carstairs looked down at her, not hiding his disdain, then he raised his face and took a deep breath.

'Anhotep, priest of Isis, I call you forth here. Now. Anhotep, priest of Isis show yourself before me now. Anhotep, priest of Isis come forth into the daylight!' He flung up his arms, his voice echoing into silence.

Louisa gave a small whimper.

She could see the figure already, transparent in front of the window, the thin arrogant face, the square shoulders, the strange, pale eyes, so like the eyes of Carstairs himself with his frightening, penetrating gaze. The silence in the cabin was suddenly intense, the atmosphere electric. Louisa closed her eyes.

'Did you call, Mrs Shelley?' Jane Treece's voice, immediately behind her, made her gasp.

For a moment she couldn't move, then she turned towards the new arrival. 'Yes, please!' She clutched at the woman's arm. 'Would you show Lord Carstairs the way out? He was just leaving.' She had begun to tremble violently.

She closed her eyes again as Treece led Carstairs away and sank onto the bed, unable to move. When she opened them again the figure in the window was still there . . .

'Oh God!' Anna spoke out loud. She shut the book and took a deep breath. Her hands were shaking. She glanced across the cabin at the closed drawer of the dressing table. Forcing herself to stand up she was about to cross to it when a cough outside her door made her jump.

It was Toby.

He took in her short nightshirt and dishevelled appearance when she opened the door. Then he focused on her face. 'I was worried when you didn't come to breakfast, having missed supper last night. Are you sure you're OK? You look awful.'

She gave a brittle laugh. 'Is that your usual chat up line?'

'No. As chat up lines go, I can do better.' He smiled again. 'What is it, Anna? Your hands are shaking.'

She wrapped her arms around herself self-consciously. 'I'm all right.'

'No. You're not all right. Is it the sight of me, or is it that damn diary again?' He had spotted it lying on the bed. 'Anna, forgive me for saying so, but if it upsets you, and it's taking up so much of your time that you are missing the excursions you have paid thousands of pounds to come and see, is it wise to go on doing it?' He held her gaze for a moment, his expression fierce. 'Why not junk it? No, I didn't mean that, it's too valuable. Put it away. Read it when you get home, sitting in the garden.'

'I can't. I need to know what happens.' It came out as a wail.

'Need to?' His voice was marginally softer suddenly. 'Why? What's so important?'

'It's about the scent bottle. Someone was trying to steal it from her. She thought it was cursed in some way.' She pulled herself up short. She was rambling.

Toby was still looking down at the diary. 'And you too think that the bottle might be cursed?'

She glanced up, expecting him to be laughing at her, but his face was perfectly serious.

'Will you show it to me, Anna? Watson thinks it's a fake, doesn't he? He's made no secret of the fact. I'm not an expert but I do have a feel for things.'

She hesitated, then suddenly making up her mind she went over to the dressing table and pulled out the drawer. She handed him the bottle, wrapped as it was in her scarf. He unwound the piece of silk and dropped it on the bed, then he brought the bottle up close to his face and squinted at it with one eye closed. She watched as he ran his fingers gently over the surface, finding herself strangely fascinated by the way he stroked the glass and ran his thumb over the seal, then held it out at arm's length, with it lying on his palm, as though guessing its weight.

'It feels right to me.' He glanced up at her. 'Hand blown. Rough

231

surface with a lot of imperfections, crude in some ways, but more than that.' He frowned, running his finger over it again. 'I can feel its age. Don't ask me how, but I can.'

'Andy said the top was machined,' she put in quietly.

'Crap. He doesn't know anything about glass if he says that. And he calls himself a dealer! No,' he ran his forefinger over the seal, 'no, it's not machine made. I couldn't date it for you. A museum would have to do that.'

'But it is Egyptian?' She looked up at him.

'Does Louisa Shelley say it is?'

'Oh yes.' She bit her lip.

'Then it's Egyptian.' He gave her a reassuring smile. 'Anna, why not find a nice bit of diary to read?' he suggested suddenly. 'Something cheerful. There must be nice bits in it. Then put it away for now and come sailing. Can I try and find you a cheerful bit to read?'

She hesitated.

'I won't damage it, I promise. I'll just glance through and look at the writing. You can tell a lot from writing, you know.' He paused and when she didn't say anything else he sat down on the bed and began to leaf carefully through the diary beyond the place she had marked.

She stood watching him without a word, wondering why she had let him, why she had invited him in, why she had shown him the bottle. Why she felt more comfortable with him than she did, she now realised, with Andy. In spite of Andy's accusations, accusations which, she acknowledged thoughtfully, she never had for one moment believed!

He looked up suddenly. 'Here. Look. This seems to be a good bit. See, the writing is springy and even and the picture is cheerful. Can I read it to you?'

Shrugging, she sat down on the stool.

Hassan had returned the day they moored at Philae. *The Scarab* had moored a stone's throw from them and the Fieldings' dahabeeyah a few yards beyond that.

With quiet dignity Hassan had accepted Sir John's explanation that it had all been a misunderstanding and he had slipped quietly back into the life of the boat as though he had never been away, except that now, Louisa knew, the Forresters must have guessed that her relationship with him was more friendly than any of them chose publicly to admit.

It was dark when Louisa crept out on deck to find Hassan waiting to row her ashore. 'I have told the Forresters that I wish to paint the river in the moonlight,' she said quietly. 'They no longer try to stop me, and I believe Lord Carstairs is aboard the *Lotus*, discussing the taking of photographs with Mr Fielding who has brought a camera with him, so we should be undisturbed.'

'Save for the baksheesh boys.' Hassan smiled. 'They are here day and night.'

'And can be bought off?'

'Oh indeed. They can be bought off.' He nodded.

A huge moon shone across the water, throwing black shadows across the sand. They walked slowly, taking in the intense beauty of the night. All around them the temple pillars, the distant hills, the dunes, the sand, had turned from gold to glittering silver.

'We will go up on the wall,' Hassan whispered. 'I'll show you.'

Carefully they climbed the worn steps, pitch-black inside the darkness of the stone to emerge once more into the moonlight. It was cooler up there and Louisa pulled a shawl round her shoulders. They could see the whole island beneath them with the three moored boats like small toys in the distance. To the north they could see the islands of the cataracts with the rapids and spray, all silver in the moonlight. To the south the broad, slowly flowing river curved away out of sight. Immediately beneath them the huge temple lay silent and mysterious, great pools of blackness interspersed with the silvered columns.

'You wish to paint up here, Sitt Louisa?' Hassan's whisper was somehow shocking in the silence.

She nodded. 'Are we safe here, Hassan?'

He was unsure whether she had meant from Carstairs, or from the spirits. Perhaps from both. 'We are safe. I shall unpack.' He began to spread out the rug.

The river was totally silent beneath them. On the *Ibis* the Forresters were already in their cabin. On the *Lotus*, the Fieldings and their guest, having exhausted the intricacies of the new camera, were sitting on deck, enjoying a sherbet as Venetia read to them from one of the novels of Jane Austen.

Louisa sketched the scene for a long time, every now and then so overwhelmed by the surrounding beauty that she sat spellbound, her pencil at a standstill on the paper. Hassan sat cross-legged a few feet from her. He had seemed reserved since he had returned. Quieter. More thoughtful.

'You think much, my friend?' she said at last.

'I watch the night. And I watch you.' He smiled.

'And I you. Look.' She held out the sketchbook to him. There was a small picture of him; thoughtful, handsome, the wry smile playing round his eyes unmistakable.

'You do me much honour, Sitt Louisa.'

'I show only the truth.'

She leant forward. 'I told Sitt Augusta that we would sleep in the temple if we grew tired of the moon.'

He nodded gravely. 'I have cushions and rugs. Then you may watch the sunrise.'

'We will watch it together.' She reached across and touched his hand – just the gentlest of movements.

He moved closer to her. 'When they sent me away I thought my heart would cease to beat for unhappiness,' he said at last. 'You have been my sun and my moon and the stars of my heaven, Sitt Louisa.'

Slowly he leant across and touched her lips with his own. She closed her eyes. The rush of warmth and happiness which enfolded her drove everything out of her mind but the gentle handsome man who had put his arms around her.

'Keep us safe, great Isis, and hidden from prying eyes, I beg you.'

Her murmured prayer rose into the darkness and spun out towards the moon as, far below them on the river, Lord Carstairs stood up and stretched, made his farewells to the Fieldings in their saloon, and emerged on deck to stand for a moment staring through the palm trees on the river bank, towards the temple standing so serenely on its island in the moonlight.

There was a long silence. Toby closed the diary and laid it on the bedside table.

'So, Louisa Shelley found love in Egypt,' he said at last. 'Does that please you? Can you put away the book and relax and enjoy yourself now? There was no mention of curses there. Or evil sprits.'

She smiled. 'You're right. Yes, I'll put it away.'

'And you'll come sailing?'

She glanced at her watch. 'If it's not too late.'

'It's not too late.' He stood up. 'You get dressed and I'll check there's a boat left for us and see if I can persuade Ali or Ibrahim to give us some sandwiches. I can't promise Persian rugs and moon-lit trysts, but we'll do our best.' He was just turning to the door when he stopped. 'Anna, forgive me, asking a personal question, but what is that charm you are wearing round your neck? I haven't seen it before, have I?'

She put her hand to it quickly. 'It's to keep me safe.' She gave him a wry smile. 'It's called the Eye of Horus.'

He nodded. 'Well, I'm sure it's doing its job. See you in a few minutes.'

She met him on deck and found that there had indeed been a felucca left from the cluster around the stern of the boat which earlier had taken the rest of the passengers off on a morning of individual excursions.

Helping her to make herself comfortable in the boat Toby scrambled back onto *The White Egret* twice, once to fetch his own sketchbook and once to ask Ali for a couple of extra cans of juice, before at last he climbed in beside her and allowed their boatman to sail slowly away, swooping gently towards the further bank where the reeds reflected in the still water. It was heaven to settle onto the worn cushions, glancing up at the huge triangular sail, with its darker patches, white against the intense blue of the sky. With a sigh of deepest pleasure Anna rummaged in her bag for her camera.

'Happy?' Toby glanced at her in amusement as she leant back to photograph the sail.

'Very. Thank you for digging me out of my cabin.'

He was sitting arm outstretched along the side of the boat, his hand close to her shoulder. His bag lay on the boards by their feet. He had kicked off his shoes, she noticed, and his feet on the warm planking were as brown as those of their steersman. He smiled. 'You needed rescuing. Like Rapunzel.'

'You think I've let down my hair?' She laughed.

'I think you're on the way.'

There was a gentle ripple of water under the bow as the boat turned and caught the wind. The sail flapped once and then filled, a white wing against the blue. She reached for her camera again. The boatman, standing effortlessly on the bow near the mast, was staring across the water towards the far bank, his hand shielding his eyes. His profile, against the sail, was, she realised straight off a temple relief – the high forehead, the huge almond-shaped eyes, the planes of the cheeks, the angle of lips and chin. She aimed the camera at him, wondering if he would mind her taking the photo but already he had seen what she was doing. His face had split into a huge grin and he struck a pose for her, balancing, one arm looped around the mast.

'Do it again when he's not looking.' Toby's quiet advice in her ear made her smile. He was partly right. The unselfconscious grace had been good, but this pose was part of the scene as well. The constant interaction with the tourists, the game played by both parties: the people of the Nile pandering to the expectations of the visitors; the visitors bringing much-needed currency and very seldom any very stretching demands. On the whole the relationship seemed to work very well. The good nature and the humour of the Egyptians allowed them to keep a balance. If there was resentment there, or a sense of exploitation, it was well hidden.

Anna closed her eyes and let her head fall back, allowing the

236

sun under the brim of her hat. The heat on her face was sudden and intense and she could see the violent scarlet of her eyelids. She drew back hastily and as she did so the steersman put his tiller across, his companion stepped away from the mast and sat down opposite her to adjust the sheet, the boat swung round and the shadow of the sail fell across her face. The new figure on the prow of the boat, balancing easily on the planking in his gilded sandals, was staring out across the water, his arms outstretched, his head raised as he looked up directly at the sun. She gasped and the three men with her in the body of the boat glanced at her.

'Anna?' Toby touched her arm. 'Are you O K?'

She swallowed. The figure had gone. Of course it had gone. It had never been there. It was the shadow of the boatman, or a fleeting mirage in the transparency of the hot air above the boat.

She shook her head. 'Sorry. I got the sun in my eyes.'

'That is not good, missee.' The boatman shook his finger at her. 'Very dangerous.'

She shrugged and nodded and looked repentant, pulling down the brim of her hat. She didn't see Toby's frown or notice the way he leant forward to stare past her at the front of the boat.

Pre-lunch drinks were being served in the bar when they returned and it appeared that Andy had already bought her one. 'Specially for you!' He presented it to her with a flourish. 'To say sorry. I won't interfere any more and I won't be bossy.' The boyish charm was firmly in place.

Anna glanced over her shoulder at Toby and saw the swiftly hidden sardonic grin. He winked at her. Then he raised his hands in surrender. '*Inshallah*,' he whispered. He put his hands together in mock salute. 'You drink with the *effendi*.' Turning away he made his own way to the bar and she saw Ali reaching for a bottle of Egyptian beer.

Anna turned to Andy. 'It's not a question of forgiveness, Andy. It's just that I want to be able to speak to Serena whenever I like without your interruption. Where is she now?'

He shrugged. 'I don't know. I genuinely don't know. Perhaps the felucca she was on hasn't come back yet, but when it does, I shall buy her a drink, kiss her feet, pat her hand, anything you like.'

Anna smiled. 'Just being nice would be enough.'

237

'Then I shall be nice.' He grinned hugely. 'I am nice. I am always nice to everyone.' He slapped Ben on the back as the latter walked past him. 'Aren't I, Ben?'

'You sound as though you're high on something, my friend,' Ben responded jovially. 'But if it means that you're going to buy me a drink as well, then I'm all for it, whatever it is.'

Andy gave him a knowing smile. 'It's sunshine, Ben old chap. That's all.' He swung round suddenly. 'And here's Serena. And Charley with her.'

The two women had appeared in the doorway side by side.

'Andy's buying, girls. I should order something exotic and expensive,' Ben put in mischievously.

'Cocktails for the two ladies?' Ali had been following the conversation with great care and now smiled hopefully. 'Ali make very good cocktails. Lots of things. Very expensive.'

Serena shook her head. 'No thank you. Some fruit juice would be lovely.'

'I'll have one.' Charley climbed onto a bar stool. 'A cocktail with as many things as you can think of, Ali.' Her eyes were feverishly bright and the sun had caught her skin, dusting it with a fine scattering of freckles. She was wearing a low-cut sundress and around her neck there were some turquoise beads.

Serena took her guava juice and retreated to a sofa. After a minute Anna followed, leaving the others clustered around the bar.

'We need to talk soon.' Anna sat down next to her. She had realised as she moved away from the bar that Toby was nowhere to be seen.

'So, where did you get to?' Serena looked gloomily into her glass.

'I went sailing too with Toby.' Anna glanced at her, conscious that she was blushing slightly. Serena did not notice. 'I saw the priest Anhotep again today,' she went on. 'At least –' She hesitated. 'I think I did. On the felucca.'

Serena looked up, surprised. 'Did you take the bottle with you, then?'

'No. It's still in my cabin. It doesn't seem to make any difference what I do. I keep seeing him.'

Serena pulled a face. She shrugged. 'I hope that he hasn't attached himself to you.'

'Attached himself to me?' Anna forced herself to lower her voice again. 'You are joking I hope. Dear God! You mean I'm possessed!'

'No!' Serena sat forward sharply. 'No, that's exactly what I don't mean!' Her eyes were fixed on Charley at the bar and she frowned as she watched her. Shrugging, she turned back to Anna. 'No, you mustn't get the wrong idea. In no way are you possessed, but he might have formed an energetic attachment to you. That means he has –' she looked around with a helpless wave of her hand – 'it's as if he's using you as a petrol tank. He's low on gas because he doesn't have a body of his own so he's got to borrow someone else's to give himself the energy to move around and show himself. He's put a sort of suction pipe into your energy field so he can use your energy and that means he's staying near you all the time.'

Anna shuddered. 'I do hope you are wrong.' She took a sip from her glass and in spite of herself shivered violently once more. 'How can I get rid of him?'

'If you are strong-willed, your intention might be enough.'

'I am strong-willed.'

'Then next time you see him, tell him to go.'

'I tried that! I screamed at him, told him to take the bottle and leave me alone. He didn't appear. Nothing happened.'

'Wait until you see him, Anna. Then speak to him. Don't be afraid or angry, that will weaken you. Just be strong and loving.'

'Loving!' Anna stared at her. 'I don't think so! How could I love him?' She was indignant.

'Love conquers all, Anna.' Serena gave a wistful smile. 'Especially hate and fear.'

'No. No, I'm sorry. I don't happen to believe that. Sadly.' Anna took another sip from her glass. 'And I think our friend would see it as a weakness.' She stared down at her sandalled feet. 'There were two priests, weren't there,' she went on thoughtfully. 'What happened to the other one?' She glanced up.

Serena was staring over at the bar again as Charley threw back her head with a loud giggle. She frowned. 'I don't know,' she said at last. 'I don't know what happened to the other one.' She sat back and stared at Anna. 'No, you are right. It wouldn't be easy to love Anhotep. But I don't think he means you harm. I think you should go out of your way to confront him. Challenge him. Show him you are strong. Once you are in a dialogue with him you can ask him why he wants the bottle so badly and maybe what you should do with it and how you can help him and then you can ask him to leave.'

'By then we'll be on first name terms and I'll be asking him to dinner!' Anna retorted. She paused. Louisa had done it. She had invoked Anhotep to protect her from Lord Carstairs. Perhaps Serena was right. Perhaps she could make contact. On the other hand . . . she shuddered. 'You are expecting too much, I'm afraid. I see even the haziest shadow of the guy and my knees turn to water.' She paused. 'I can't believe I'm having this conversation!' She leant forward and put her head in her hands. 'I want to get rid of the bottle, Serena. I can't cope with it. This was supposed to be a happy holiday. And instead it's turning into a nightmare!'

There was a pause then Serena leant forward and touched her arm. 'Do you want me to look after it for you?'

'You?' Anna looked up wearily.

Serena nodded. 'I'll take it to my cabin. I can say some prayers over it. Perform an invocation and a dismissal. Burn some incense.'

'Not with Charley there I take it!'

'No, not with Charley there. Let me do it, Anna. I do know what I'm talking about.' A note of urgency had crept into her voice.

Anna sat back and closed her eyes wearily. 'Why did I do it? Why did I bring it here? It was so needless. Just a stupid romantic gesture.'

'You weren't to know. Besides, you probably couldn't help it. Anhotep might have put the idea in your head.'

Anna shuddered. 'Thanks. So now he's not only sucking my energy, he's inside my skull as well!' She pummelled her temples with her fists.

Serena stood up. 'Let's do it now. While Charley and the others are here. Then we can move it quietly, take it to my cabin and say the first prayers before anyone knows anything about it.' They both knew that by anyone she meant Andy. 'I'll do the rest later when Charley is sleeping it off on deck.' She cast a look over her shoulder at Charley, whose giggles were growing increasingly shrill.

Anna nodded. Climbing to her feet she followed Serena from the room.

Andy glanced at them as they disappeared through the swing door and frowned.

Fishing out her key Anna opened the cabin door. Then she paused. 'Someone has been in here.'

She moved cautiously into the small room and looked round. The bed had been made and clean towels left on the counterpane, but that happened every morning. This was different. She looked round, feeling the hairs on her forearms stir. 'Is it Anhotep?' she whispered.

She moved over to the bathroom and pushed open the door. It was empty.

Serena had followed her in. She looked round too and then shook her head. 'I can't sense Anhotep. I don't think he's here.'

'Then what is it?' Anna stepped over to the dressing table and pulled open the drawer. The bottle lay where she had left it, wrapped in the scarf. She lifted it out with reluctant fingers and handed it to Serena. 'All yours.'

Serena nodded. 'Come with me to my cabin. We want to make sure that Anhotep follows.' She paused. 'What is it?'

Anna was staring at her bedside table. With a little gasp of dismay she lunged forward and pulled open the drawer. It was empty. The diary was gone.

10

I have made myself whole and complete; I have
renewed my youth;
I am Osiris, the lord of eternity . . .

*In the mud-brick house at the edge of the village a woman
sweeps the floor keeping the sand always at bay. Under her
son's sleeping mat she finds a cloth and in it, still encrusted
with the desert sand from which it came, a little bottle. She
holds it for a moment, curious, angry at him for his deceit in
hiding it for himself. In her hands she feels it tingle and grow
hot and she shivers suddenly, rewraps it and hides it beneath
the mat once more.*

*When he returns to the hut from the fields he is happy. He has
made a decision. The bottle is worthless – so his father says –
so he will give it as a gift to his mother and win blessings from
her for his generosity. He unwraps it and takes it to the river
where he washes it in the muddy waters at the edge of the
fields. The glass is shiny now and bright and clean but its age
is written in the imperfections of its surface.*

His mother takes the gift and smiles. She hides the new shiver

*of revulsion as it lies in her hands and she tucks it into a corner
out of sight. Now each time she passes that spot she will shudder
and make the sign against the evil eye. She senses the shadows
which guard it and she is afraid.*

*The boy is young and strong, as is his brother. The priests
can gorge on their life force and, at each morning's rebirth of
the sun god, they grow more powerful.*

The children grow weaker.

'What's happened?' Serena was clutching the bottle against her
chest.

'The diary. Someone has taken it!'

'Oh, Anna! Surely not. I know it's valuable, but no one on
the boat would take it, not even Charley. Are you sure you
haven't put it somewhere else? In your bag? You were carrying
it everywhere with you. Or in another drawer, or a suitcase or
something.'

'No. It's gone.' Anna tightened her lips grimly. Her hands were
shaking as she began systematically to search the small cabin. It
wasn't the value of the diary she was thinking about, it was the
story. How could she bear not to know what had happened to
Louisa and Hassan!

She knew it was pointless taking down the suitcase from the top
of the cupboard, undoing it, searching through discarded tissue
paper, but she did it just the same. It was as she was relocking it
and swinging it back into place that there was a knock at the door
and it was pushed open.

Andy peered into the room. 'Everything all right, ladies?'

'No, it isn't.' Anna faced him, distraught. 'The diary has gone!'

'Louisa Shelley's diary?' he frowned.

'What other diary is there?'

'Anna, I did tell you to take care of it! You knew how valuable

243

it was.' He stepped into the room. 'Are you quite sure it hasn't fallen behind the cupboard or under the bed or something?'

'I'm quite sure.' She stood stock still in the centre of the cabin. 'Someone has taken it.'

'In which case I think we can all guess who that someone is.' Andy shrugged. 'I did warn you, Anna.'

'If you mean Toby, it can't have been him. I went sailing with him this morning.'

Andy raised an eyebrow. 'And were you with him every second of the time?'

'Yes.' She hesitated. 'Well, I suppose not every second.'

He had left her sitting in the boat before they set sail. What had been his excuse? To fetch his sketchbook. She frowned bleakly. As if he was ever without it. And then he had gone off again, to fetch some cans of juice from the dining room. And again, on their return, he had left her in the bar. Where had he gone so quickly? At the time she had thought nothing of it, given his antipathy to Andy, but now . . .

Seeing her frown, Andy smiled. 'Exactly. Would you like me to speak to him?'

'No!' Her response was instantaneous. 'No, don't say anything. If anyone does, it'll be me.'

She didn't believe it was Toby. How could it be? And yet, she had to admit, he had certainly had the opportunity to take the diary several times over.

'Anna,' Serena put in quietly. 'You don't know it was Toby. It could easily have been one of the crew. Or a stranger – someone who came on board while we were all sailing this morning.'

'But how would they know about the diary?' Anna said bleakly. 'If it was a thief, they would have taken my lapis beads and my silver bangle. I left them lying on the dressing table. They must be worth something.' She shook her head. 'No, it was someone who wanted just that one thing. Thank God he didn't take the bottle. What an irony that would have been!'

Andy, following her gaze, looked at the silk-wrapped bundle in Serena's hands. 'Is that it?' he asked sharply. 'Why has Serena got it?'

'Because I have given it to her to look after,' Anna replied firmly.

'I don't think so.' Andy stepped forward and with calm authority took it out of Serena's hand.' I think I'll look after this, if you don't

244

mind. It's not genuine, but it has a certain curiosity value and it will be safer with me under the circumstances. Besides, I'm not having Serena getting involved in any more of her mumbo jumbo and unsettling Charley. This whole boat is heaving with superstition and hysteria already as far as I can see.'

Wrapping the bottle even more firmly in the scarf he tucked it into his pocket, then he turned towards the door. 'Don't worry about it. I'll keep it safe.'

'Andy! Bring that back!' Anna found her voice at last. 'Bring it back this instant!'

But he had gone, striding down the corridor and round the corner, out of sight.

'I don't believe he did that!' Anna turned back to Serena, who had slumped on the bed. 'Did you see what he did? He just took it!'

'I saw. I'm sorry, Anna.'

'He's a complete bastard!' Anna actually found that she had stamped her foot in her anger. 'And he's so pleased with himself. Did you see? Because Toby turned out to be a thief.' She paused. 'Or at least . . .'

'Exactly.' Serena looked up at her. 'Don't jump to conclusions on Andy's say so, Anna, please. Use your own judgement about the diary. Or speak to Omar and ask him what you should do.' She hesitated. 'I suppose the police ought to be called really if it's as valuable as all that.'

Anna sat down beside her. 'I'll go and talk to Toby and I'll ask him outright. If he's taken it, it's to read, that's all. He was looking at it and we both got very involved with the story. He would never steal it. Never.'

'And the bottle?' Serena's eyes were suspiciously bright.

'Oh, don't you worry about the bottle. I'll get that back.' Anna folded her arms. 'If Andy really thought that by buying me the odd drink he'd lull me into quiet acquiescence he's got another think coming. How dare he speak to you – to us – like that!'

'That's Andy for you.' Serena gave a rueful smile. 'He'd do any-thing to spite me. You're getting to know him at last.'

Anna stood up. 'Why does he do it?'

Serena shrugged. 'I think he's afraid of me, or perhaps more accurately what I represent. A woman with power.' She shook her head self-deprecatingly. 'I see through him. I'm not won over by his charm. I have – or had – influence over Charley. Ergo I'm an enemy, to be put down and humiliated.'

'That's horrible.'

Serena nodded. 'But he was right about one thing. Word is getting round the boat that something odd is going on and we do have to be careful not to let superstition and hysteria as he calls it, cloud our judgement.'

With a rueful nod Anna headed for the door. 'Point taken. Listen, I'm going to go and see Toby now, before lunch. Don't worry about the bottle.' She smiled. 'Let's see what Anhotep does about it. I'm more than happy not to have it for the time being and it may be that Andy is a good person to leave it with!'

Serena levered herself off the bed and shook her head. 'I doubt it. I'll leave you to go and see Toby – unless you want me to come?' She paused. 'No. Then I'll see you later. I do hope he's not a thief. To tell you the truth I rather like him.'

So do I. Anna pushed away the thought as she made her way to Toby's cabin. She clenched her fists. Who else could have taken the diary? Who else knew about it? Who else would have any interest at all?

She knew which was his cabin; she had seen him coming out of it when she had visited Serena's. Standing outside his door she took a deep breath. The boat was totally silent save for the subdued wave of conversation from the bar in the distance. Lifting her hand she knocked quietly. There was no reply. She knocked more loudly. There was still no response so, glancing left and right along the deserted corridor, she gently tried the handle. The door opened; he hadn't locked it.

She peered inside and caught her breath. The cabin itself was identical to hers in layout; the only other single cabin on the boat and like hers, which must be directly above it, tucked into a forward corner of the boat. But the resemblance ended with the basic furniture. He had turned his into a studio. In the middle of the floor was a folding easel, on it a large sketchbook, clipped back to reveal a sketch of the waterfront outside the window. On every wall he had stuck sketches and paintings. On the dressing table and bedside cabinet were paintboxes and charcoal and pencils. The open door of the bathroom showed a wet sketch apparently pinned up to drip into the shower. She stared round in astonishment and took a step inside. The room was an Aladdin's cave of colour. For a moment she forgot why she had come. When had he done all these? How had he had time? He must have been painting all night and every free second between their trips ashore.

She took another step inside and the door swung shut behind her.

The paintings were beautiful. Vibrant. She stood in front of the easel and stared at the busy waterfront with its array of huge cruisers, their own little paddle steamer moored alongside a vast gin palace of a floating hotel.

It was several minutes before she remembered what she was looking for and turned her attention from his paintings to his personal belongings. The drawers under the dressing table were filled with a jumble of shirts, a couple of sweaters and some underwear. The bag nearby held more pencils. She pulled open the wardrobe. A couple of pairs of trousers and some jeans and a jacket. The drawer of the bedside table held a torch, some notepaper and postcards and a fountain pen. That was all. A couple of paperback books, both unopened as far as she could see, completed his belongings with a thumbed guidebook to Egypt, and his shaving gear and toiletries on the glass shelf in the shower room.

She pulled back the counterpane and looked under his pillows then she bent and ran her hand along beneath the mattress. Nothing. With a sigh she stood up again, pushing her hair back from her face.

Where else could he have hidden it? She was turning to survey the cabin again when a slight sound from the door made her swing round to face it. Toby was standing in the doorway, one arm propped against the doorjamb, the other in the pocket of his jeans, watching her. He looked as though he had been there for some time. His face was hard, his eyes cold.

'Have you quite finished your inspection?'

'Toby!' Any further words died in her throat as he took a step into the cabin and, closing the door behind him, drew the bolt.

'Why have you done that?' Her mouth had gone dry.

'Because I want the chance to speak to you without Andrew Watson poking his nose in. You have a reason presumably, for being here?'

She hesitated. A wave of real panic had swept over her. 'I was looking for you. I wanted to thank you for the trip. I wondered where you were.'

'And you thought I might be hiding in a drawer inside the dressing table.' He raised a sarcastic eyebrow. 'Or under the mattress, perhaps.'

With an effort she steadied herself. 'Toby, I'm sorry. I came to find you. I knocked. The door opened. I saw the pictures and –' She paused with a shrug. 'I came in to see them.'

'And thought you'd have a quick pry while you were in here.' His voice was still hard.

'I wasn't prying!' She was stung. 'If you want to know, I was looking for my diary.'

'Your diary?' he echoed.

'My diary has disappeared from the drawer in my bedside table. You were the only person who knew it was there.'

'So you thought you'd look in the drawer beside *my* bed! In other words you thought I'd stolen it!' There was disbelief in his voice.

'No.' She had answered too quickly and she knew it. 'No, I didn't think that.'

'Then who did?' he asked softly. 'Don't tell me. It was Watson.' She shrugged.

'And you believed him.' He folded his arms.

'It was a possibility,' she flared. 'You might have borrowed it. You might have wanted to study it.'

'Without asking you?' She could hear indignation as well as anger in his voice now.

'Yes! What else was I supposed to think? You and I were looking at it. We were discussing it. You helped me into the felucca then you left me there, remember? And you came back to the cabins. How do I know you didn't do that so you could go to my cabin, tell me that!'

'You tell me something first,' he put in sharply. 'Why on earth didn't you lock your cabin door if you mistrust everyone so much?'

'That's the point, isn't it?' she flashed back. 'I did trust everyone!'

'Everyone except me.' His voice dropped. 'So, tell me, why do you not trust me any more? Why does Andrew Watson not trust me? What have I done to deserve all this suspicion?'

He looked her in the eye suddenly and she found herself colouring. 'I don't know.'

'You don't know.' He took a deep breath. 'Or you don't intend to say. My guess is Watson has been poking his nose in where it's not wanted and poisoning the well.' He rubbed his chin, still scrutinising her face. 'I see I'm right. You didn't think to ask me the truth? You didn't doubt him, just a little bit? I thought we had a friendship of sorts. I was obviously wrong.'

He sat down heavily on the bed after grabbing an armful of his belongings and hurling them to the floor to make room.

Anna bit her lip. Her fear had evaporated. 'All right, I'll tell you what happened! I didn't believe him, I didn't believe him for a single second! Until this happened. And then . . . I'm sorry.' She hung her head. 'I was so frantic about the diary that I wasn't thinking clearly.' She straightened her shoulders. 'If I'm honest, I was hoping you did have it. If you haven't, who has?'

He considered for a moment. 'Do you really want my opinion?'

She nodded, but her wry smile was wasted on him. He was staring at the picture on his easel. 'I'm prepared to bet fairly large odds on Watson himself.'

Anna shook her head. 'He wouldn't. Besides, he was there –' She broke off.

'He was there. He sympathised and he pointed the finger at me. I can see the scenario, Anna. I can see it clearly.' He sat forward suddenly. 'Why would I want the diary, tell me that? He's the wheeler dealer. He's the man who has the contacts.' He looked up at her. 'Well? I asked you a question. Why would I want it?'

She shrugged. 'It's desirable. It's a historical artefact. It has Louisa's sketches. It's worth a lot . . .' Her voice trailed away.

'It's worth a lot of money!' He echoed. 'I don't need money, Anna. And I don't want Louisa's diary. Is that clear?' He glanced at the cabin window. 'Now, you'd better go.'

'Toby, I'm sorry.'

'Go!' The implacable coldness was back in his eyes.

She grimaced and turned towards the door. As she opened it she turned back to him. 'I am sorry,' she repeated.

'So am I.'

'Can we still be friends?'

There was a moment's silence then he shook his head. 'I don't think so, Anna.'

Outside in the passage she stopped and took a deep breath; to her chagrin she was near to tears. Turning, she fled down the corridor.

Behind her Toby's cabin door reopened. He stepped out and looked after her. 'Anna!' he called.

249

Ignoring the shout she ran up the stairs and headed back towards her own cabin.

Throwing open the door she ran in, hurling it back on its hinges so that it slammed against the wall, rebounded and closed behind her. With a sudden frantic gasp, she stopped dead.

The cabin wasn't empty. The air was heavy with the sickly smell of resin and myrrh.

Standing in the middle of the floor was a shadowy figure, tall, insubstantial, but unmistakable in its bearing. Anhotep half turned towards her and she felt his eyes searching for hers as slowly he began to raise a thin wispy hand towards her.

Anna screamed. Her whole body had gone cold. She couldn't breathe. Desperately she tried to turn back to the door, to move, to tear her eyes away from his, but she couldn't. Something held her where she was. She could feel her legs beginning to buckle, strange red lights beginning to flicker behind her eyes.

As she started to fall the door was pushed open as Toby flung himself into the cabin behind her. 'What is it? What's wrong? I heard you scream.' He stared round frantically as he caught her hand and swung her towards him. 'Anna, what is it? Was there someone here?'

Behind her the cabin was empty.

'Is it Watson?' He pushed her away, more gently now and, stepping across the cabin, pushed open the shower room door. There was no one there and nowhere that anyone else could be hiding.

'No, it's not Andy. It's Anhotep the priest.' She was trembling violently. 'You read about him in the diary. The priest who haunts my little scent bottle. He was in here. Standing here!' She indicated a spot on the floor about two feet in front of her. 'But the bottle has gone. Andy took it away with him.'

She was shaking so violently that her teeth were chattering. Slowly she collapsed onto the bed and sat looking up at him.

There was a long pause and she wondered suddenly if he was going to laugh; to ridicule her every word.

He pursed his lips. 'Andy Watson's name seems to crop up rather a lot in our conversations, doesn't it?' He stared round the small room again. 'Have you seen this apparition before? Didn't you see something on the boat this morning? Is that what you saw? The priest?'

Relief flooded through her. He believed her! He didn't think she was insane. She nodded.

'You told me the bottle was cursed. But you never told me how or why. Why didn't you mention all this when we read about it in the diary?'

'And have you think I'm mad? What do you think would happen if a story like this got round the boat? "Woman passenger sees Ancient Egyptian priest!" Either everyone would panic and go home or they'd have me sectioned or at the very least I'd become a laughing stock.' She put her head in her hands. 'I can't take much more of this.'

'Does anyone else know about it?'

She nodded. 'Serena.'

'And what does she think?'

'She believes it. She knows quite a bit about Ancient Egypt. She's studied its religion and rituals. She knows what to do. She was going to take the bottle and bless it or something, but then Andy took it away.'

'Why on earth did you let him?'

She shrugged. 'He just walked off with it. I suppose I was taken by surprise. I could hardly wrestle him for it. He said he was going to keep it safely for me.'

Toby sat down beside her. 'I think it's more likely he plans to flog it,' he said cynically.

'He'd have to buy it off me first.' Anna shook her head and gave a watery smile. 'And as he thinks it's a fake, he wouldn't offer very much!'

'Unless he sold it as genuine.' Toby sighed. 'And in the meantime we haven't solved the problem of the whereabouts of the diary.' He glanced at his watch. 'It is almost lunchtime. Can I suggest that a meal in a crowded dining room would be a good thing for both of us? Very grounding. And no ghost would show himself there. We can cool off and rethink the situation and study Watson's behaviour. No harm is going to come to your scent bottle or to the diary wherever they are. Not as long as they are potential money earners. My guess is he has them both and he'll take care of them.' He paused, waiting for her nod. 'And then we have an afternoon free before we all go to Abu Simbel tomorrow. So during the afternoon I suggest we talk to Serena. If your ghost is genuine and I have no reason to suspect otherwise, we need to consult her obviously about what steps can be taken to keep you safe from any paranormal repercussions. Perhaps at the same time we could have a council of war about recovering the diary and thereby –' he paused and gave her a wry grin – 'clear my name, once and for all.'

Anna and Toby and Serena held their council of war at the Old Cataract Hotel, sitting on the terrace over a pot of Earl Grey tea. Only when they were settled in their chairs, facing out across the Nile, did anyone mention the reason they had left the boat.

'Did you see Andy's face when the three of us went ashore together?' Serena was absent-mindedly stirring her tea. 'He lost his famous sang-froid. To me he looked distinctly worried.'

'As well he might.' Toby sat forward and studied Serena's face for a few moments, then he nodded. 'Anna tells me you know about the old Egyptian ritual. By that I take it you have studied modern spiritual techniques and magic based on Egyptian texts?'

Serena met his eye steadily. 'I've studied with Anna Maria Kelim, if you've heard of her.'

Toby shrugged. 'I took a bit of an interest in these things when I was younger. I'm not an expert, but the name certainly rings a bell. The important thing is that you know what you are doing. I suspect Anna's ghost or ghosts are not going to be deflected by a bit of New Age chanting.' He leant back in the chair. 'Anna says you're good. Do you think so too?'

Serena didn't say anything for a moment, clearly taken aback by his direct approach. Her instant initial indignation subsided as swiftly as it had come. After a few seconds thought she nodded slowly. 'As long as Andy's not around. He is very good at disem-powering me. I've never worked in Egypt before. Never even been here. All I can say is that I have a little experience of rescue work back home – you know what rescue work is, don't you?' She glanced up at Toby as he picked up his cup and was in time to see him give a curt nod.

'He may, but I don't,' Anna put in quietly.

'It means someone who works with earthbound spirits and helps them move on. Most "ghosts" if you like to use that word are lost. Trapped. Unhappy. They don't want to be here. Some of them, if they died violently, suddenly, don't even realise they are dead.

Nobody came to collect them or look after them. I have worked with one or two cases like that and helped them move on.' Serena sounded more confident now she saw she had an audience who respected what she had to say. 'I have never worked with a spirit, however, who has chosen to remain earth-bound because it has unresolved business here. They are the scary ones. Out for revenge. Out to do mischief. Still involved with the world they have left. Unable to let go. Anhotep and his colleague are like that. And they are not just ordinary ghosts. They were trained priests, with knowledge of one of the most powerful occult systems ever known. They probably chose not to die.'

There was a short silence. Anna shivered. The warmth of the terrace, the cheerful groups of people languidly chatting over their tea cups, the waiters, the stunning picture-book view of the Nile, all seemed suddenly to distance themselves, acquiring a strange feeling of unreality.

'And what has happened to the colleague? The second priest?' Toby put in after a moment. 'You haven't mentioned him.'

Anna shuddered as she recalled Louisa's terror and her own at the apparition of Hatsek, the priest of the lion-headed goddess. 'I've seen him. And so did Louisa, at the temple. He seemed the more powerful, the more evil of the two.'

Toby grimaced.

'You still believe us?' Anna looked at him. 'You don't think we're mad?'

'No, I don't think you're mad. I've seen ghosts.' Toby did not smile. 'Our culture is very foolish to dismiss out of hand anything it can't prove with an algebraic formula or a test tube. Luckily most other cultures of the past and many today are far wiser than us in the West. The trick is to ignore the materialists in our world and go with our gut feelings and our intuition. And those of us who have the courage of our convictions because we have that intuition or because we have seen something with our own eyes must for the time being risk ridicule and carry the rest.'

Serena put down her cup with a small clatter and shook her head in disbelief. 'I can't tell you how it cheers me up to hear you say that!'

'And me.' Anna gave a small hopeful smile.

'Good. Well, having rallied the troops we'd better decide what we are going to do.' Toby sat forward, concentrating. 'We only have a few hours before we leave for our trip to Abu Simbel. As you know the coach leaves in the early hours so we can travel through the desert before the worst of the heat. We have several days to cruise back to Luxor when we come back, but my guess is that Anna would like this resolved now, before we go to Abu Simbel, rather than later. And don't forget, there are two things on the agenda. Besides Anhotep we have the all too material problem of the missing diary.'

'You don't think they are related? You don't think that Anhotep has somehow taken the diary?' Serena asked thoughtfully. She was still stirring her tea.

'No, I don't. Why should he? I think Andy Watson has taken it. Perhaps we could raid his cabin rather as you raided mine.' He glanced across at Anna.

She blushed. 'He shares a cabin with Ben. It wouldn't be easy.'

'Not as easy as searching mine, you mean?' He grinned mischievously. 'Agreed. But with three of us we could arrange some kind of distraction, I'm sure. It would be very unpleasant for everyone on the boat, to have to tell Omar and perhaps get the police involved, so if it's possible I think it would be best to resolve the matter ourselves.' Pausing, he looked at Serena. 'If you are prepared to do an exorcism or whatever you choose to call it, when do you think that should happen and what would we need?'

Serena thought for a moment. 'We really do need the scent bottle itself to act as a focus. Other than that I need some time to prepare myself. I brought the things I need with me for my own spiritual practice. Incense. Candles. A bell.' She shook her head. 'I haven't been able to use them, of course, sharing with Charley. I'll do it in Anna's cabin and I suggest we do it tonight. If we have to leave so early in the morning, everyone will go to bed early and we won't be disturbed. And Toby, don't be angry but I don't think you should be there. I think this is just for Anna and me.' She looked at him apologetically. 'I may be wrong, but I have a feeling that we would be safer, just the two of us. Just women. Women are de facto servants of Isis. Women are less likely to come to harm.'

Toby nodded. 'I'm not going to argue. As long as you think you'll be safe.'

Serena shrugged. 'I hope we'll be safe.' She sighed. 'I'm hoping a lot of things here.'

There was a moment's silence.

'So, the next step is the raid on Andy's cabin to rescue the book and the bottle.' Toby drained his cup. 'One of us can search. The others can make sure Andy or Ben don't come back and catch them.' He looked across at Anna. 'I suggest you search. You have had practise at it.'

'I have apologised, Toby!' Anna flashed back at him, suddenly impatient. 'How long are these digs going to go on? I am sorry. I was wrong to listen to Andy. I was in such a panic about the diary. I had no reason to think for a single second he might have taken it –'

'But you were happy to suspect me.'

'No. I wasn't happy. Not at all happy. Just as I wasn't happy even considering that Andy's accusations about you might be true!' She had obviously touched a raw nerve. 'I just couldn't think of any other possibility. You were the only person who knew about it.'

'Apart from Andy himself.'

'Apart from Andy.'

'And Charley and Serena and probably every other person on this boat.'

Anna shut her eyes with a deep sigh. 'OK. I'm doubly sorry. I grovel. Please, Toby, we need your help. Don't give me such a hard time.'

No doubt one day he would feel able to tell her what it was all about. Until then she would just have to trust him and wait.

He looked at her for a long moment, then he dropped his gaze.

'No, you're right. I'm the one who should be sorry. I'm a bit over-sensitive on some matters. OK. Let's go. We may as well start right now. If Andy has gone ashore we can search his cabin straightaway without any hassle.'

The door was locked.

'Damn!' Toby shook the handle.

'Try your key.' Anna glanced nervously over her shoulder. Andy and Ben were, it turned out, sailing.

Toby fished in his pockets and eventually retrieved it. It didn't fit.

'Yours?' He looked at her.

She already had it in her hand when Ali appeared at the end of the passage. He came towards them. 'Problem?' He flashed them a brilliant smile.

'We need to get into this cabin.' Anna knew it was no use pretending. He had obviously seen them.

'OK.' Ali dived into the deep pocket of his *galabiyya* and came out with several keys on a ring. 'This one opens all. Very useful. Mustn't lose your key.' He unlocked the cabin door and pushed it open then turned and shuffled away down the corridor in his flat loose sandals.

'Phew!' Toby looked at her and grinned. 'He didn't want to know why we needed to go in!'

'Probably thought it was ours.' Anna stepped inside and looked round. The cabin was cheerfully untidy, littered with discarded clothes and shoes. A camera stood on one of the bedside tables, a bottle of water and various toiletry articles on the other. On one bed lay two guidebooks and some postcards, on the other an inside-out sweater and a crumpled damp towel.

'It will be hidden. Drawers. Suitcases. Down the back of something.' She was pulling open the dressing table drawer and didn't notice the quizzical look Toby threw in her direction. Methodically they went through all the obvious places, searched under the mattresses, in the wardrobe, in the bathroom, even behind the framed David Roberts prints hanging on the walls.

'No sign anywhere.' Anna shook her head.

'They have to be here. He wouldn't take them sailing. It's too much of a risk.'

'Then there must be somewhere we haven't thought of.' She turned round slowly, trying to think of some last place, somewhere subtle – somewhere obvious. 'It's not here. Neither of them is in here.' Miserably she shook her head. 'We've searched every square inch.'

'Have you indeed!'

The voice in the doorway brought her up with a jerk. She and Toby spun round.

Andy was standing in the doorway, staring at them. 'May I ask what exactly you are searching for?'

'I hardly think you need to ask!' Toby had straightened from looking through the contents of one of the bedside table drawers, this time inserting his fingers right down the back. 'Anna wants her diary back, and her scent bottle.'

'And you think I have them?' Andy was looking very flushed. They could smell beer on his breath.

'I know you have the bottle, Andy and I want it back. And I suspect you've got the diary as well.' Anna fought to keep her voice calm. 'I think you accused Toby this morning to put me off and it worked for a while. But not now. Give them back to me, please.'

'I've put the bottle somewhere safe, which is what you should have done in the first place! But to dare to come here and accuse me of taking your diary! That is outrageous!' Andy was working himself up into a self-righteous rage. 'Get out! Get out now!' He caught Anna by the arm and swung her towards the door. 'Go on. Get out!'

'Leave her alone, you bastard!' Behind him Toby stepped forward.

Letting go of Anna, Andy reeled back.

As he turned away Toby caught him by the shoulder and spun him round to face him again. 'Don't you touch her!' The aggression in the cabin was palpable.

'Toby!' Anna screamed. 'No!' She snatched at his arm. 'Don't! Leave it! What's the matter with you all? Why is there so much anger on this boat?

Toby's expression was furious. He shook Anna off, his fists clenched

'Toby!' Anna shouted again. 'Toby! Don't! Please!'

Toby paused. For several seconds the three of them remained unmoving, as if frozen in a tableau on a stage, then slowly the fire went out of Toby's eyes and he dropped his fist. He pushed Andy away.

Andy sat down on the bed. His face was white.

Anna glanced at Toby. 'I think we'd better go.'

He nodded. With a final furious glance at Andy he walked out of the cabin.

'Will you be all right?' Anna followed Toby but in the doorway she paused, looking back.

Andy nodded.

'It was your fault. You shouldn't have touched me. And you shouldn't have taken my things.'

Andy looked up. 'I'm sorry, Anna. I'm not sure what came over me. This isn't like me, it really isn't. But you do believe me now, don't you? He's a killer! Be careful, Anna. Whatever you do, be careful.'

Anna turned and leaving the cabin pulled the door shut behind her. Toby had gone.

Shakily she turned away from the stairs towards Serena's cabin and knocked on the door.

Serena pulled it open. 'Did you find it –' She stopped in mid-sentence. 'Anna, what is it? What's happened? Not Anhotep?'

'No, not Anhotep. Andy came back and caught us in the cabin. He and Toby nearly had a fight.'

'A real fight?' Serena's eyes rounded.

'A real fight. With fists.'

Serena bit her lip. 'Well, I suppose I can't honestly say I'm surprised. Come in.' She pulled Anna inside and closed the door behind her. 'Is Andy all right?' she asked suddenly, almost as an afterthought.

'He'll live.'

'And Toby?'

Anna shrugged. 'He was terrifying, Serena. He almost lost control for a moment. I could see it in his eyes. If I hadn't been there, I think he might have hit Andy.' She bit her lip anxiously, shaking her head. She didn't believe Toby was a killer, of course she didn't! But she had seen a side of him now which had frightened her and suddenly she was full of doubt.

Serena studied her face. 'Did you find the bottle?' she asked quietly.

'No.'

'That's a pity.' She was thoughtful for a moment, then she shook her head. 'I have got a theory, Anna. I hope it is wrong.' She hesitated. 'I desperately hope it is wrong.' There was another long pause. 'The thing is, the other priest, Hatsek, the priest of Sekhmet. He is here. On the boat. I have had my suspicions for some time that when Charley stole the bottle she was in some way affected by him; that maybe he is using her energy and that is why she is growing weaker. There is no question that she is becoming slightly unhinged. She never used to drink the way she does now. And she's mentioned Sekhmet once or twice at night in her sleep, crying out the name.' She shuddered. 'Charley is not a student of Ancient Egypt, Anna. She had never heard of Sekhmet. She is not interested in any of the stuff I do. In fact she hates it.'

258

Anna nodded. '*And* Charley talked of Sekhmet in the bar the other day.'

'Yes, and now there's something else,' Serena continued. 'Toby and Andy. I think he could be feeding on their anger too. There's this atmosphere on the boat. I can feel it intensifying. It's affecting us all. Did Toby touch that bottle of yours?' Anna nodded again.

'And Andy did, of course.' Serena moved thoughtfully over to the window and stood staring out. Moored as they were against a much larger cruiser all she could see was the glossy white paint of its hull about four feet from her window. 'And then there is you. Anhotep follows you around. He must be using your energies.' She sighed. 'Andy wouldn't give you the bottle back, I take it?

'No, and we couldn't prove that he had it.' Anna sat down on the bed.

'Even though he took it openly and we know he has it. That's not actually like him. Not like him at all. As you've gathered, I don't get on with him. I don't really like him, but he is not a thief, Anna.'

'Can you do the ceremony without the bottle?' Anna looked up hopefully. 'Could we do it quickly?'

Serena nodded slowly. She did not look convinced. 'We can try.' She reached into a canvas holdall by her bed and pulled out a spiral-backed notebook. It was full of closely packed writing interspersed here and there with diagrams. 'I've been trying to think of an appropriate form of words and ritual to use. We have to conjure them up, summon them both then dismiss them in such a way that they do not come back.'

'And you know how to do this?' Anna's eyes were on the notebook.

Serena looked up at her doubtfully. 'In theory, yes.'

'What's the option if we fail?'

Serena shrugged. 'I'll have made matters worse. By paying them all this attention we make them stronger.'

'But if we get it right we can help Charley?'

Serena grimaced. 'If we get rid of them it must help you both. That's if I can get it right.'

'Let's do it now. In my cabin.'

'Now? Anna, I don't know if I'm ready.'

'You have to be ready.' Anna grabbed her hand. 'It'll be all right. It has to be. Please.'

259

Serena took a deep breath. 'All right. I'll do my best. It'll be a bit like what we did at Kom Ombo only better. More powerful. We'll have time and privacy and we can set it up right.' She glanced round the cabin as though checking she had all she needed, then tucking the notebook under her arm, she picked up her holdall. 'Come on.'

Anna followed her. 'Do we need Charley to be there?'

Serena paused. 'I've been wondering about that. I think probably not at this stage. We couldn't do the ceremony if she was there, she'd be too disruptive and besides, the energies are everywhere. What I am hoping is that I shall be so thorough that the various attachments to you, to Charley, perhaps to Andy and Toby – even me – are destroyed and we are all freed at the same moment.' She licked her lips nervously. 'Oh God, Anna, I hope I'm right about all this.'

They closed the shutters and, pulling the bedside table into the centre of the room, covered it with one of Anna's silk scarves. On the makeshift altar Serena put candles held in small coloured-glass candleholders, a brass incense burner and a tiny carved statue of Isis. She looked round and shook her head. 'It's not dark enough. The curtains are thin and there's too much light coming through the slats. We have to pin something over the shutters.' They wedged a bath towel across the window and over that, Anna's pashmina. At last the cabin was dark. Serena switched on the light and then delved into her bag. She pulled out an ankh – the looped cross which is the Egyptian symbol of eternal life – which she laid next to the statue and finally she produced an intricate red amulet on a black leather thong which she hung around her own neck.

'What is that?' Anna, who had sat silent through the preparations so far, leant forward and squinted at it.

'It's called the tyet. It represents the knot of Isis's girdle. Or her sacred blood, which is why it's carved in red jasper. It is a very powerful symbol.'

Unconsciously Anna groped for the amulet which hung around her own neck. Serena saw the action and gave a quick nod of approval.

She reached into her bag and produced a box of matches. 'I'm going to invoke the protection of Isis before I start. Then I'm going to summon the two priests before her altar. I made this incense before I left London. It's the nearest I could get to something called *kyphi* which was sacred to Isis. They used it in the temples during her rituals.' She gave a quick deprecating laugh. 'I did it for fun. It's got so many ingredients. Raisins. Myrrh. Honey. Wine. Resin. Spikenard. Juniper berries. Lots of other things. I never imagined I'd be using it like this.'

Anna bit her lip. 'Are you sure this is safe?'

Serena nodded. 'The worst that can happen is that it has no effect or that they hear, but refuse to come. It may be that we do need the scent bottle here on the altar, but I'm going to try.' She lit the candles then she moved to switch off the light. She stood for a moment in silence, her eyes closed, then she reached into her bag for the last time and produced a small bundle wrapped in a square of white silk. Unwrapping it she held up a metal object about twelve inches high, shaped rather like the ankh with four pieces of wire stretched across the looped head. On the wires were strung small finger cymbals. 'This is a sistrum, the sacred instrument of the gods,' she said as she laid it on the altar and carefully folded away the white silk. 'It is shaken to invoke, to purify, to protect.'

'And do we need some wine?' Anna sat down on the bed as far away from Serena's centre of activities as humanly possible.

'Not this time. If . . .' She paused imperceptibly. 'When. When we succeed I'll make an offering to give thanks.' She picked the little incense cone out of the burner and held it to the candleflame. 'I'll bless and protect you, Anna. If you could just stay there and stay quiet, whatever happens. If you feel afraid, visualise yourself surrounded by an impenetrable circle of blue fire.'

Anna nodded. Her mouth had gone dry.

As the rich spicy smell of the incense began to curl out of the burner the candles flickered.

Serena began to intone under her breath. Then she picked up the sistrum and started to shake it towards the four corners of the room after which she spun to face Anna and shook it in her direction. 'Hail, Isis, protector of thy daughters. Be with us here. Hail Isis, watch over us. Hail Isis, keep us safe. Hail Isis, surround us with thy protective fire so that your servants Anna and Serena may serve you and speak with thy priests, Anhotep and Hatsek!'

Anna could feel the palms of her hands sweating in the darkened cabin. The candleflames didn't stir; the fine spiral of blue smoke

261

from the incense straightened and rose towards the ceiling. She recognised the incense with a shiver of nausea. It was similar to the strange, cloying smell which sometimes permeated her cabin.

Serena was speaking again, her voice rising and falling in a rhythmic chant. In the light of the candles Anna could see the perspiration standing out on her forehead. Her eyes were wide and staring, her fingers clamped round the handle of the sistrum like taut whitened claws.

'Hail to thee, Anhotep and greeting. Come that we might speak with thee . . .'

The litany was repeated again and again, rising in the airless cabin, trapped by the ceiling, building like a tangible presence, inexorably winding up the tension in the room. Anna found she was holding her breath, every muscle in her body tensed, her eyes darting backwards and forwards seeking in every corner for the shadowy figure of Anhotep until between one breath and the next, with an almost imperceptible sigh, the candles went out.

Anna swallowed hard, biting down the urge to scream. The rattle of the sistrum stopped and the silence intensified. Anna became conscious suddenly of the drumming of her own pulse in her ears, then a strange gurgling noise from the centre of the room. She strained her eyes to see Serena in the shadowy darkness standing still, staring at the altar. The sistrum dropped from her hand with a rattle, then she fell slowly to her knees. For several seconds she swayed groggily backwards and forwards then she slid to the floor.

Anna had frozen where she was. She was too frightened to move, but the sound of Serena's breath rattling in her throat galvanised her into action. Leaping off the bed she ran to the window and tore down the blackout, wrenching back the shutters, then she turned and flung herself down beside Serena, reaching for her wrist.

'Serena! Serena, speak to me!' She shook her hand, then she gently slapped Serena's face. 'Wake up! Come on, wake up! You've got to speak to me!' Serena's face was suffused with a dark, livid red, her eyelids fluttering uncontrollably, her pupils beneath them dilated.

'Serena!' Anna shouted in her ear, then letting Serena's head fall back on the floor she scrambled to her feet and ran into the bathroom. Filling the glass with the tepid water from the cold tap she brought it back and threw it in Serena's face.

262

Serena gasped. For a moment her whole body seemed to gather itself into one great spasm, then she fell back on the floor and her eyes closed. As Anna watched, the colour drained from her face and all the tension seemed to leave her.

'Serena?' Anna stared at her in terror. 'Serena?' She grabbed Serena's wrist again and felt for her pulse. It was there, irregular, light, but growing increasingly steady. Serena took a deep shuddering breath and then another and her eyes opened. She lay looking up at Anna blankly.

'Are you all right?' Anna reached for the towel she had thrown on the bed and used a corner of it to wipe Serena's face and hair. 'Come on. Let me help you sit up. What happened?' She braced her arm round the other woman's shoulders and helped her into a sitting position.

'Can I have a drink?' Serena's husky whisper was barely audible. She leant back against the bed and closed her eyes again. Her hands had begun to shake.

Anna rose to her feet and reached for the bottle of water she kept on the dressing table. Pouring out a glass she handed it to Serena, steadying the shaking hands around it and helping her bring it to her lips. Serena took a sip and then another, then she took another deep shuddering breath. 'What happened?' Her eyes were focusing better now as she looked up at Anna.

'I don't know. I was hoping you'd tell me.' Anna sat down on the floor beside her. 'You were chanting in the candlelight and the cabin suddenly got very hot and airless, then the candles went out and you started making funny gurgling noises. I thought you were being strangled. I was terrified.'

Serena reached for the glass and took another deep drink. 'Can you open the window? I can't breathe properly.'

Anna glanced up. 'It is open, Serena. Do you want to go on deck?'

Serena shook her head. 'Not yet. Did something go wrong?' She rubbed her eyes. 'I can't catch it . . . In my head . . . It's like a dream. It's there, but just out of reach. Something happened.' She finished the glass and held it out.

Without a word Anna brought the bottle and refilled it. 'Anhotep didn't come.'

Serena frowned. 'Anhotep,' she repeated.

'Anhotep. That name . . .' She shook her head again. 'The sunrise. I saw the sunrise. And the sunset.'

263

Anna frowned. She was studying Serena's face.

'Eons of sand, drifting.' She fell silent for a minute, then she closed her eyes. 'I died yesterday, but I come forth today. The mighty Lady who is the guardian of the door hath made way for me. I come forth by day against mine enemy and I have gained mastery over him.' She fell silent again as Anna stared at her. It was several seconds before she spoke. 'That's from the *Book of the Dead.*'

Anna raised an eyebrow and grimaced. 'What's that?'

'It's instructions, really. Written on the walls of the tombs. Ancient texts. Hymns. Prayers. Invocations. I didn't know I knew any by heart.' She shivered suddenly. 'I protected myself, Anna. I did all the right things.'

'He didn't come, Serena. I didn't see him.'

'Then who did?' Serena rested her head back against the bed. Her face was white and strained and she looked totally exhausted.

'I don't know.' Anna stood up. She pushed her hair back from her face. 'I think I probably chased him away. I was so afraid. I thought you were dying.'

'Dying?' Serena's eyes rounded.

'You were gasping for breath. Your eyes were all funny. You collapsed and your pulse was almost nothing. It happened when the candles went out. It was weird. They didn't seem to blow out. They were just extinguished. Suddenly.'

Serena shook her head. 'And the incense?'

Anna turned to the little altar. The small brass incense burner still stood between the candles. It was cold.

'I don't understand what made that happen. I suppose the energies in the cabin were fluctuating in some way. You probably did stop it happening. Whatever it was.' Shakily Serena climbed to her feet.

'I think he was trying to possess you,' Anna blurted out suddenly. 'I think that, just for a moment, he was inside you. Your face changed. It looked so unlike you. Oh, Serena, what we did was dangerous! I think something awful nearly happened there. Supposing he had succeeded! Supposing he had possessed you?'

There was a long silence as Serena stood deep in thought, then at last she shrugged. 'I suppose it is possible my protection wasn't strong enough.' She sighed, then gave a small uncomfortable laugh. 'Presumably he knows far more about all this than I do!' She bent

264

and picking the sistrum up off the floor she laid it gently on the makeshift altar. Then she stretched her arms over her head.

'Anna, I think I am going to go up on deck for a little while. Do you mind if I go alone? I need to get my head straight.'

Anna stared round the cabin after she had gone, then slowly she began to tidy it. Serena had left everything just as it was, the altar still in place with candles and statue and ankh. Carefully Anna put them one by one into the holdall, rewrapping the sistrum in the white silk square. Then she folded the pashmina and pushed her bedside table back into place. The semblance of order made her feel better but she was still uncomfortable in the cabin – jumpy, looking over her shoulder at the slightest noise. And there was noise, all around. Noise from the deck of the boat next door; noise from the town; music drifting in the window from somewhere on the quayside, a sudden shout of laughter and conversation outside in the corridor. So where had the silence come from? That extraordinary silence which had preceded the extinguishing of the candles? The profound silence Louisa had heard in the temple of Isis? She shuddered and went to the door.

Ben was at the bar thoughtfully drinking some fruit juice when she made her way into the lounge. Outside she could see several people sitting at the shaded tables in the afternoon sun, reading, writing postcards, or just quietly chatting amongst themselves, watching those who had taken to the water for another sail.

'Ready for the early start?' Ben smiled at her. 'Four in the morning is a bit of a challenge for most of us, I think!'

Anna nodded. She had forgotten the trip to Abu Simbel.

'I gather there's been a bit of a barney between Andy and your friend, Toby?' Ben raised an eyebrow. 'Do I suspect a touch of the green eye, there?'

Anna frowned. 'I'm not sure I follow you.'

'Oh, come on. They both fancy you rotten!' Ben grinned. 'What power you ladies have!'

Anna shook her head. 'I think my diary was more of a temptation than me.' She sighed. 'Did you know it was missing? Someone has taken it from my cabin. Andy and Toby were both accusing each other.'

Ben looked shocked. 'That's bad. Have you told Omar?'

She shrugged. 'I don't want to make a great fuss. As long as it is returned. That's the important thing.'

265

'I'll do a bit of subtle sleuthing.' Ben winked. 'If Andy has it, he'll tell me in the end.'

She smiled. 'Thanks. It's valuable, but there's far more to it than that. Far more.' Like knowing what happened to Louisa and Hassan.

Serena was on the top deck leaning on the rail staring down into the river when Anna eventually joined her. She stood a little way away, hesitating, but Serena glanced at her and smiled. 'I'm OK now. Sorry about all that.'

'You're sure?'

Serena nodded. 'Whatever it was, it's gone. I'm fine.' She glanced across at Anna. 'I've decided to go to Abu Simbel tomorrow. I don't want to leave this unfinished, but I need to get off the boat for a bit. Put some space round me; distance myself from all this. Are you going to go? You should.'

Anna shrugged. 'I suppose so. It's the high point of the trip, isn't it? Driving through the desert, seeing the temple of Rameses.'

Serena grinned. 'Good. No more ghosts. Two days away. Some hard sightseeing to distract us.'

Anna frowned. 'I'm sorry. It's my fault you got into all this.'

'No. It's no one's fault. After all I am interested in Egyptian magic and religion and besides, I offered.' Serena smiled again. 'It's just got a bit heavy and I want to stand back for a day or two. I am sorry. I don't want you to feel I don't care. It's just that I feel so drained. I've never felt like this before. I'll be there if anything happens on the coach or in the desert or at Abu Simbel. But I hope it won't. Then I thought perhaps when we come back – we have one day to see Philae before the cruise back to Luxor – at Philae maybe we can try something again. Philae is, after all, the temple of Isis.'

'You've been wonderful.' Anna put in. 'You've taught me a lot.' She put her hand on the amulet on the chain around her neck. 'You think he won't follow us to Abu Simbel then?'

There was a short silence. Serena was watching a felucca drifting with the current past them, the steersman sitting dreamily in the stern, his arm over the tiller. The boat was full of large boxes and it occurred to her suddenly what a contrast he made to the equivalent delivery man with his van in a crowded London street. She smiled, then she glanced back at Anna. 'No, I don't think he'll come to Abu Simbel. I hope not,' she said at last. 'I wish we knew what had happened to Louisa Shelley. She came through it. She coped.'

Anna nodded sadly. 'I don't think I can bear not knowing what happened. I keep thinking about her. But as you say, she coped. She went home and got on with her life.'

But what happened to Hassan? The question increasingly echoed in her head. And what about the priests Anhotep and Hatsek? They haunted Louisa, as they haunted her great-great-granddaughter. How had she made them leave her alone? A new wave of frustration and fury shot through her as she thought about the diary. Andy had said he wanted to know what happened next when he had heard the story. It was obvious now that he hadn't meant a word of it. She sighed. They stood in silence, for several minutes lost in thought and it was only as Serena turned to go and look for a chair that Anna realised she had made a decision. She wouldn't go on the coach tomorrow. At the last minute she was going to change her mind and stay alone on the boat. That would give her two days to search with no one there to interfere.

She could always go to Abu Simbel another time.

Just for a moment she forgot that the priests of Isis and Sekhmet would probably stay with her.

11

Hail to you, O ye divine beings, ye divine lords of
things who exist
and who lived for ever and whose double periods of
an illimitable number of years is eternity . . .
O grant thou unto me a path whereon I may pass
in peace.

The children grow sick. Their strength has ebbed away into the desert wind. They have no inclination now to dig for ancient worlds and seek the treasure of long-dead tombs. Their mother watches and keeps her sorrow hidden in her heart.

The bottle is forgotten – in the dark corner of the peasant hut it reflects no light. Its keepers are invisible without time or space to define them, without flesh or bone, without tomb or burial goods or names.

The younger boy dies first, his soul sucked dry. His body is buried in the sand and watered by tears. Then the elder falls sick for the last time. As he lies on his bed of fever he sees the priests hover over him, feels them gorge on the breath of his life and he knows it was he who brought them to his house.

He tries to whisper a warning, but the words are sucked from him by the dry lips of death.

Soon his mother will feel the night-time kiss of the servants of the gods and she too will give her life to grant them eternity, leaving a sorrowing man in an empty house, who, soon, takes up his belongings and leaves the place to the shadows and the sand. He does not see the bottle on the back of the shelf and it remains behind.

The telephone by Anna's bed rang at a few minutes after three-thirty a.m. She sat up with a start, wondering where she was. Her dream hovered for a second, insubstantial and floating. Then it was gone. She didn't even recall the sound of a sandal or the whisper of a linen robe. Disoriented, she stared round, then she remembered. They were getting up to drive across the desert some 280 kilometres southwards from Aswan, to Abu Simbel. The wake up call on the phone was followed by a knock at her door and a cup of tea. She dressed quickly in jeans and a tee-shirt and pulled on a sweater against the cold of the night, then she set out to find Omar. He merely shrugged when she explained she didn't want to go with them. *Inshallah!* It was up to her. Tell Ibrahim she would require meals, and enjoy her rest.

Andy was standing near the reception desk where the passengers were gathering in sleepy groups ready to go ashore. He scowled when he saw her and turned away. Well, it was good that he had seen her. He would assume she was getting on the coach with the others. When he found she hadn't after all climbed on board with the rest of them it would be too late for him to change his mind and stay behind too.

Finding Serena wearily lifting her overnight bag onto her shoulder she whispered her decision. Serena nodded. Was she, Anna

269

wondered, even a little relieved? She couldn't see Toby, but already the passengers were streaming across the gangplank onto the silent ship alongside them, where they would creep through the deserted lounges and passages smelling eerily of cold cigarette smoke and stale beer, towards the second gangplank which would lead to the shore. There, a small charabanc was waiting to take them out to the assembly point where a convoy of coaches and taxis gathered every morning to leave under escort for the drive south across a desert which was also a military zone.

When they had all gone Anna stood still for a moment, listening to the silence, wondering a trifle wistfully if she had done the right thing. It was too late to change her mind. With a shrug she turned back to her cabin.

At the door she hesitated for a moment, afraid of what she might see when she opened it. Taking a deep breath and with one hand clamped firmly on the gold charm around her neck, she gave it a tentative push. The cabin was empty.

When she woke she was lying on her bed, fully dressed. She frowned, disoriented for a moment, aware that something on the boat had changed. Then she realised. She could sense the emptiness around her, the deserted cabins, the lack of distant bustle. Omar had told her that only two or three of the crew would be staying on the boat, the others were taking the opportunity to go ashore for a couple of days before the return voyage to Luxor. As far as she knew she was the only passenger who had made the decision to skip the overland trip to Abu Simbel and stay aboard.

Slowly she climbed out of bed. She wasn't sure where she was going to start her search for the diary, but Andy's cabin seemed the obvious place. Either she had missed it the first time, or perhaps, even if it hadn't been there before, it would be there now.

To get in, she would need the help of a key. As she expected the boat was completely deserted. It was a simple matter to run down to the reception desk, duck behind it and lift Andy's key off the hook where Omar had placed them all before they left. Slipping it into her pocket she made her way, for the second time, towards Andy's cabin.

When she reached the door she stopped suddenly. Supposing she was wrong. Supposing for some reason he had changed his

270

mind and turned back, as she had done, and he was there? She closed her eyes and took a deep breath to steady her nerves. Then quietly she inserted the key in the lock and pushed open the door.

It was neater this time. Presumably both he and Ben had realised that the packing of an overnight bag was easier if some kind of order prevailed in the cabin.

Bolting the door behind her to make sure that on this occasion she was not interrupted, she went through the place systematically and ruthlessly, checking and double-checking every square inch until at last she had to give up.

Standing still she looked round with an overwhelming sense of defeat. There was no sign of the diary or the bottle and there was nothing for it but to let herself out of the cabin, checking before she left that there was no evidence of her intensive search, and return the key to its hook. Then she wandered back up the stairs, deep in thought. It hadn't occurred to her that he might have taken the diary and scent bottle with him. All she could do was hope that he had hidden them somewhere else on the boat.

Pushing open the door to the lounge she wandered in. Ibrahim was behind the bar, polishing glasses. He greeted her with a big smile. '*Misr il khir*. Good morning, *mademoiselle*.'

She saw him stare at her closely, and she guessed it was to check that she was wearing the amulet when she saw him nod to himself, obviously pleased that he had glimpsed the gold chain at her throat.

'Good morning, Ibrahim. It looks as though I'm all alone for a while.'

He shook his head. 'Omar says three people for meals, *mademoiselle*. I cook for you all myself.'

'Three people?' She frowned. 'Do you know who the other two are?'

He shrugged. 'Nobody is awake yet. I cook lunch soon and leave in dining room on hotplate. Soup. Rice. I am going to grill chicken with roast banana. You like that?'

She smiled. 'It sounds wonderful. I didn't know you were a cook, Ibrahim.'

'The real cook, he's a Nubian, and he goes to see his mother in Sehel. But Ibrahim is a wonderful cook too. *Inshallah*!' He roared with laughter. 'Would you like a drink now?'

She ordered a beer and wandered out on deck. It was already hot, the air shimmering over the scrubbed planking as she stood watching yet another huge cruiser manoeuvre its way in towards the bank, its upper deck lined with interested spectators in brightly coloured shorts and shirts. The hill on the far side of the river with its rounded Fatimid chapel was almost hidden in a heat haze and the few feluccas she could see plying their trade on the broad stretch of water were drifting, sails slack, without a breath of wind. Behind her the pot plants blazed with colour, the deck around them long ago dry after their early morning watering.

It was too hot to stay on the top deck. She turned and made her way back downstairs to sit beneath the awning, her glass on the table in front of her. Whilst Ibrahim was cooking she would take the chance to make a perfunctory search of the lounge area. It was just possible, she supposed, that Andy had tucked the diary away in there somewhere. She sighed. It was also possible of course that it wasn't him at all and that someone else entirely had taken it, that she would never see it again.

'Anna!'

The quiet voice behind her took her completely by surprise. She swung round. Toby was standing in the shade, his sketchbook under his arm.

They stared at each other awkwardly for a moment then he said, 'I thought you would have gone to Abu Simbel with Serena.'

'I couldn't go without knowing what has happened to the diary.' Anna squinted up at him. 'Are you all right? I was worried after the scene in Andy's cabin.'

He shrugged. 'I went on deck to cool off. I might have killed the bastard otherwise.'

She frowned. 'You were standing up for me and I didn't get the chance to thank you.'

Raising his hands he shook his head. 'No need.'

She gave an uncertain smile. 'So, why did you stay? I'd have thought you'd want to see the temple of Rameses.'

He shrugged again. 'I thought it better not to be anywhere around Watson for a bit. I can always see the temple another time. I'm coming to Egypt again, don't forget.' He pulled out the chair next to her. 'May I?'

She nodded. 'Ibrahim said we could help ourselves from the bar. Just write it on the pad. He's cooking lunch.'

Toby grinned. 'Great.' He headed towards the door into the lounge, then he stopped. 'I take it you have searched his cabin again?'

272

She nodded. 'I have indeed.'

'No luck?'

She shook her head. 'It would be an irony if he had taken it with him after all, wouldn't it?'

'It certainly would.' He ducked through the door, to reappear a moment later with two beers, one for himself, the other for her. As he sat down he was frowning. 'We'll have to be systematic, of course. Each possible place to be searched in turn and we'll tick them off as we do it. He won't have taken it with him. That would be too risky. He'll have left it somewhere safe on the boat.'

She realised after a moment's thought that she liked the way he assumed he would be helping her.

He glanced at her over his glass. 'Of course, the safe! What about the safe? Have you thought of that? It's the obvious place.'

They found Ibrahim laying three covers at one of the tables in the dining room. From the open door into the kitchen came a wonderful smell of garlic and onions.

'Is it possible to look in the safe?' Anna sat down at the table and looked up at him pleadingly. 'I lent my grandmother's diary to Andrew Watson and I think he may have put it there for safety, not realising I wasn't going with them all this morning. I need it urgently.'

'Your book with the little pictures?' Ibrahim straightened with a frown.

'You remember? You saw it in my cabin?'

He nodded. 'I have the key. I will come and look for you.'

They followed him down to the reception desk and waited whilst he fiddled with the lock, muttered quietly to himself, fiddled again and at last swung the small safe door open. It was full of envelopes and packets.

'Passports. Money. Jewels.' He shrugged. 'So much. I shall find it. *Inshallah!*'

He rummaged through the packages, glancing at the larger envelopes, apparently reading the scribbled names on them with ease. 'Andrew Watson!' He pulled one out.

'It's too small.' Anna looked at it in dismay and shook her head. 'The diary wouldn't fit in there.'

Ibrahim felt the envelope carefully. 'Passport and traveller's cheques.' He grinned. 'I look again.'

A few minutes later he triumphantly produced a second envelope. This one was much more bulky.

'That's it! That's the right size and shape,' Anna cried in delight. Ibrahim passed it to her. 'You look.'

She ran her thumb under the sealed flap of the envelope and pulled out the diary.

'Good! Good!' Ibrahim beamed in delight. 'Now we go to eat lunch.'

'Wait.' Anna stretched out her hand. 'My scent bottle. He was looking after that as well. If it's here it can stay, but I'd like to check.'

'Bottle?' Ibrahim frowned.

'The little bottle.' She met his gaze. 'The bottle which was guarded by the cobra.'

Ibrahim shook his head. 'That is not here,' he said firmly.

'But you haven't looked?'

'No. Not here. Ibrahim is sure.' He slammed the door of the safe shut and turned the key.

She glanced at Toby, who raised an eyebrow. 'At least you have the diary. And the envelope with Andrew Watson written on it presumably in his own hand.' He grinned. 'Proof enough for you? Am I totally exonerated for ever?'

She nodded, hugging the diary to her chest. 'Proof enough. If you wish I shall grovel to you for the rest of my days.'

His smile deepened. 'A day or two will be sufficient.'

They waited until after lunch to look at the diary again. The third guest had not appeared, and eventually they left the dining room without seeing who it was, having decided with alacrity to follow Ibrahim's suggestion that they take a felucca to Kitchener's Island with a picnic tea and it was there, amongst the trees and the hibiscus and the bougainvillaea that they sat down with the diary and Anna began at last to read out loud.

In the afternoon Hassan had taken the tiller himself as they sailed away from the *Ibis* towards the south. They beached the boat on the sand just out of sight of the shouting, laughing villagers, far enough away to avoid the crowd of Nubians who had waved at them as they passed and they stumbled up the bank onto the dunes. It was intensely hot. Louisa stared round, holding her parasol over her head. In one direction she could see an arid mountain range, in another on the far horizon a vast magical lake of water shimmered complete with palm trees. She gazed at it longingly and shook her head. 'It's too hot to paint. The paint would dry on my brush.'

'And is it too hot to make love?' Hassan smiled.

She reached out to touch his hand. 'It's too hot to breathe.'

They slid down the burning sand and Louisa climbed once more into the small boat. In the distance on a sandbank two crocodiles were basking, their mouths open. A heron stood near them, completely unafraid.

'We could stop near those palms.' Louisa pointed to a distant group of trees. Hassan nodded and put the tiller over, edging the boat towards the opposite shore. There were no crocodiles here. The sand was deserted as Hassan leapt over the side and pulled the boat up. He helped Louisa ashore and they made their way over to the palms. She painted for an hour or so before the heat drove them back to the water and to a new plan. Now they would return to the *Ibis*, but in the evening, when it grew cooler they would go ashore again and ride into the desert to camp under the vast open sky.

Hassan had sent away the donkey boy. He would return just after sunrise so they could ride back to the *Ibis* before the sun had gained its full strength. Now, as the sun was setting they could feel the first cold breaths of the desert wind.

'You are sure he will find us again?' Louisa gazed around her.

The vast distances were unbroken in any direction as far as she could see. There was a line of golden hills on the far horizon, still touched by the sunlight, and on the other side of the river the soft black haze which was the coming night. In front of them there was a raised hill, surmounted by a rocky plateau, scattered with soft sand-filled ravines and crevasses.

Hassan smiled. 'He will come. There is nothing to fear. We are within sight of the river. It is here all the time. We have only come a few miles upstream from where the *Ibis* is moored. Come,' he held out his hand and began to pull her up the narrow valley between the dunes. 'We follow this wadi, then I will show you my surprise.'

They began to scramble upwards at last, their feet slipping in the sand as it constantly shifted and rearranged itself into curves and swathes and undulating parabolas of light and shade until they had gained the rocky heights of the small hill.

'There! The top!' At last he triumphantly hauled her up the last couple of yards and he stood back so that she could see what it was they had come to visit.

On the summit of the plateau stood a small, exquisite temple, similar to the kiosk they had seen at Philae. Louisa stared in delight at the delicate leafy carvings on the capitals, and the heads of the goddess. The temple was badly ruined, but it was a beautiful red-gold in the light of the dying sun with behind it the deep, nearly dark waters of the river, already in the shadow of the night.

Louisa stared at it, speechless with delight. 'Where is this?' She asked at last.

'It is the temple of Kertassi.' He gestured around with his hand. 'This temple too is sacred to Isis. It is very beautiful, is it not? I knew you would like it.' He smiled.

Louisa stared up at the pillars with their long black shadows running down to the water, where the gleaming reflections were already deep in darkness as the great sleeping river wound steadily back towards its distant source in the heart of Africa, then she turned to look beyond them across the desert where she could see the huge crimson sun rapidly sinking out of sight. She turned again, breathless at the beauty of the view, stepped back, slipped in the soft, constantly moving sand which encroached on every side and nearly fell, grabbed Hassan's arm and laughed with delight. She could see the donkey boy now in the distance, the animals' shadows thrown, elongated in front of them as he retraced his steps towards his village. The figures were no bigger than tiny toys in the distance and as she watched they vanished out of sight into the darkness of the river valley.

'Soon the sun will go down.' Hassan put his arm around her shoulders. 'Look, it slips into the world of the gods as we watch.' The segment above the skyline was growing steadily smaller, its crimson darkening imperceptibly.

Louisa watched. She found she was holding her breath as the inverted crescent grew smaller and smaller until there was barely a sliver left. Then it was gone.

There were tears in her eyes as they watched the afterglow disappear, then at last it was fully dark and the stars appeared. Louisa had pulled off her sun hat. She shook out her hair, staring up in delight. 'I can see every star in the firmament! If I stood on tiptoe I could touch them! The sky is like a black velvet cloak, sewn with diamonds!'

Hassan didn't speak. He too was staring up, lost in thought. They stood there together for a long time until her sudden shiver reminded them that the air was growing sharply colder.

Hassan had carried one of their bags up on his shoulders. Now he let her start unpacking it whilst he went down to the spot where the donkey boy had left them and brought up the other two with all they needed for their camp. The rug, the tent, food and drink. He had even brought her paints in their woven bag, but she made no move to unpack them and he left the bag at the foot of one of the pillars.

'I am afraid that I will fall asleep and miss the sunrise.' Louisa had pulled a rug around her as she sat in the centre of the temple watching him unpack the food by the light of a small lamp.

Hassan smiled. He had erected the tent and leaving the baskets, he came and sat beside her. 'Do not be afraid. I will watch for you.'

'All night?' She could feel the warmth of his body close to her and almost hesitantly she put out her hand to touch his arm. Nearby the flame of the lamp flickered and smoked beneath the pillars of the temple.

'All night, my Louisa.' He caught her hand and brought it inside the neck of the shirt he was wearing under his red woollen burnous, pressing it against his chest. Then he drew her against him. 'You are cold?'

She nodded. Her heart was beating very fast.

'The desert is very cold when the sun has gone. Then in the daytime it is more and more hot. And soon the wind from the south, the khamsin, will come with sandstorms. You do not want to be in the desert when that happens.' He was gently stroking her hair. Nestling against him she raised her face to his and felt the touch of his lips in the dark.

Dreamily she let him guide her inside the shelter and down onto the pile of cushions he had put there. She felt him drawing a rug around them, then gently, every move a caress, he eased her dress back from her shoulders and pushed it away until she was lying naked in his arms. Closing her eyes she felt her body relax until she was drifting in a dream. His hands, his lips, moved delicately across her skin and she felt herself an instrument touched into wild music at his command.

Far away across the desert a jackal howled. She tensed but his hands held her and soothed her and as his mouth came down over hers she abandoned herself to the ecstasy which was building in every part of her body.

Afterwards she slept, secure in the crook of his arm. Faithful to his promise, he lay awake, staring out from under the shelter and up at the stars.

Sometime before dawn he dozed, then he woke suddenly. The sand near them sighed and hissed under the soft touch of the wind. His eyes opened and he stared into the darkness. Already there was a grey loom in the east from where the dawn would come.

There was another sigh of movement in the sand and he tensed sharply. There was someone, or something, near their belongings. A jackal, attracted by the smell of food, though he had wrapped it well, or a boy from the village intent on mischief.

Carefully he drew his arm out from beneath her shoulders. She stirred and her eyelids fluttered.

'Is it dawn?' Her voice was soft and husky, her naked body warm and relaxed beneath the rug.

'Nearly dawn, my love.' He spoke in a whisper. 'Be still. Do not stir.'

He slid out from the rug and stood up, staring round in the darkness as he pulled his clothes around him with a shiver. The air smelt sharp and cold.

Nothing moved now. The desert was silent. In the east the patch of grey was lighter. Out of the corner of his eye he saw Louisa sit up and crawl to the mouth of the shelter. She was no more than a shadowy outline as she rubbed her eyes like a child, her hair tumbled on her shoulders. The stars were suddenly less bright.

He took two steps towards the baskets and he stopped again. Some sixth sense told him there was someone, or something there, behind the pillar. He glanced round for a weapon. Piles of stone lay all over the place amongst the ruins and cautiously he bent and picked up a couple of pieces, feeling them reassuringly heavy in the palms of his hands.

Louisa strained her eyes. It had grown marginally lighter but she couldn't see him any more. Where, an instant before, she had pinpointed his indistinct silhouette now there was nothing. She wanted to call out but something warned her to be quiet. Cautiously she groped for her gown and carefully, trying to make no sound, she pulled it over her head and, easing herself into a kneeling position, let it fall over her hips.

Something moved suddenly over towards the food basket and she held her breath, not stirring in the silence.

Hassan's sudden shout brought her to her feet as she saw a violent movement near the far pillar, and heard a gasp and then the grunt of men fighting.

After only a second's hesitation Louisa bent in her turn to pick up a piece of fallen sandstone as a weapon and ran towards the sound.

Hassan was wrestling with another man, a man dressed in European clothing. As she drew closer she gasped. It was hard to see in the strange pre-dawn twilight, but she knew who it was. She recognised his shape, his hair and now as he groaned his fury, his voice. It was Carstairs.

Almost at the same second that she recognised him there was a sharp cry from Hassan and he reeled to the ground and lay still. Louisa froze then she threw herself towards him. 'What have you done? Hassan, my love, are you all right?' Dropping to her knees she touched his head, her eyes fixed on Carstairs as he stood over them. The wound on Hassan's head was wet and sticky. Without looking she knew it was blood.

Carstairs was holding a knife. 'The sacred ampulla. Or I kill him.' His eyes glittered as he stepped towards her.

'You're mad!' She was trying to protect Hassan with her hands.

'Quite possibly.' Carstairs was regaining his breath rapidly. 'My sanity need not concern you, Mrs Shelley. Give me the bottle and I'll leave you in peace, otherwise I'll be forced to kill him. Are you insane coming out into the desert alone with only a peasant to guard you? Have you not heard of the bandits who rob travellers out here?'

'There are no bandits here, but you!' she shouted at him desperately. 'And you will answer before the law.'

Hassan was trying to move. He groaned and she pushed him back gently. 'Don't move, my love.'

'No, don't move.' Carstairs smiled. It had grown lighter, she realised suddenly. She could see his face quite clearly now. 'And as for the law, who would believe you, crazed as you would be with horror and thirst and the ravages of the men who had captured you and taken you out into the desert and left you to the noonday sun?' He slowly tucked the knife into his belt. He was wearing, she realised, a broad embroidered sash over his English trousers. 'In a minute the sun will come up, and with it will come the heat.' He put his hands on his hips. 'The ampulla, Mrs Shelley.'

'I don't have it.'

'Oh, come.'

'Of course I don't. Would I bring it into the desert?'

He smiled. 'I can see I am going to have to persuade you to take me seriously.' He took two steps away from her. 'Have you seen the temple decorations, Mrs Shelley? Have you seen the carvings of the *uraei* along the wall, the sacred cobras of Egypt? Have you seen the asps up there on the altars above the goddess? This is a desert temple, Mrs Shelley. A temple where the lioness follows the wadi out of the desert to come to drink at the river and where the king snake waits to protect her!' He turned to face the east, his arms upraised. 'Great Sekhmet, hear me! Sister of Isis and of Hathor, Eye of Ra, mighty one, goddess of war, breath of the desert wind, ruler of the serpent Apophis who fights the sun god at his rising, send me the *uraeus*, your flame-spitting servant, that it may protect your priests and the container of their magic! Send it to me now!' His voice was echoing amongst the pillars, making them ring. Louisa stared at him unable to look away, Hassan's head in her lap, his blood seeping onto her skirt.

Behind them, on the far side of the river the first thin, blood-coloured segment of the sun, mirror image of its setting self the night before, appeared, sending horizontal rays of red and gold shooting towards them across the sand, turning the shadows of its undulations black, reflecting crimson and gold in the water at their feet.

'Dear God, please save us,' Louisa heard the whispered words from her own lips as though they came from someone else.

At Carstairs' feet she saw a shadow move. A shape was appearing on the sand. She could see it clearly now, the long brownish body, the gleaming scales, the small beady eyes. It moved towards him with one or two sinuous movements then it stopped. It seemed to be watching him and as he gestured towards them it reared up and spread its hood, swaying gently from side to side, its eyes fixed on his.

She heard Hassan groan. 'Move back, slowly. Move very slowly, my Louisa. Leave me.'

Carstairs smiled. 'Mrs Shelley is not in danger, you dog. The servant of Isis would never harm a woman. But men. Men are different. No man but a priest may touch that bottle. If they do, the servant of Isis and of Ra will kill them. That means you, you worthless son of a dog. It is you who is going to die.'

Hassan was struggling to sit up, but Louisa pushed him back. She took a step forward, refusing to look at the snake as it swayed at Carstairs' feet. 'If you kill Hassan, you will never see the bottle again. He has hidden it somewhere in the fields along the Nile. No one else knows where it is, not even I! Don't let it touch him my lord, or you will be very, very sorry.'

Carstairs smiled, but she saw a trace of uncertainty in his eyes. 'Why should I believe you?'

'Because it is the truth.' Her shoulders back, her fists clenched, she held his gaze for several seconds.

He looked away first.

'So be it. But what has been called forth, cannot be sent away!' he said softly. 'Wherever you go my servant will follow.' He gestured down at the snake. 'Until I have the sacred tears of Isis in my possession, it will guard them. Do not think this dog will escape me. I shall be watching him.' He smiled grimly. 'For all eternity, if necessary.'

The book fell from Anna's hands and she stared blankly ahead of her.

'The cobra in Charley's cabin. Carstairs conjured it up, not the priests!'

Toby reached across and taking the diary from her lap he closed it and put it to one side. 'Possibly. On the other hand, there are still cobras in Egypt.'

'But in the cabin of a pleasure cruiser? In a drawer in the cabin of a pleasure cruiser?'

He shook his head. 'I concede it does seem to be more than a coincidence.'

They sat in silence for a while, staring at the river. It was Anna who spoke at last. 'The tears of Isis. It sounds romantic, doesn't it? That's the first time I think there has been a specific clue as to what is actually in the bottle. I've held it up to the light, of course, but the glass is completely opaque. It's impossible to see if there is anything in it.'

'How scientific-minded are you?' Toby lay back and put his arm over his eyes. The shadows of the palm fronds over their heads played across his face. 'You could take it to the British Museum when you get back to London, tell them the whole story and ask them to unseal it. They could do it under sterile conditions and find out what, if anything, is in there.'

Anna was staring dreamily into the distance. 'Science versus romance. That seems somehow a very modern solution to the problem. Shall we read some more?'

Toby glanced at his watch and shook his head. 'We promised Ibrahim we'd be back before sunset so he can cook for us and then go off duty. We could read it later.' He frowned. 'Ibrahim knows the cobra is magic, doesn't he? Look how he reacted when we asked him if the bottle was in the safe. Shall we tell him the story of how it got here?'

Anna nodded. 'He is very wise. I think he knows quite a bit

about this sort of thing; a lot more than he lets on.' She shivered. 'I don't know whether it's better or worse to find the cobra was put there by a nineteenth-century occultist or by the priests themselves thousands of years before that.'

'I think that's a technicality which is relatively unimportant at this stage.' Toby grinned. He sat up. 'Egypt is a magic place. Its past is so much around all the time. Someone who knows what they are doing can probably summon things from the past very easily, be it priest or serpent. You said Serena nearly succeeded last night.'

Anna nodded. She drew her knees up to her chin, hugging them thoughtfully, her eyes on the distant, coffee-coloured hills.

'Come on.' Toby stood up and reached down for her hand. 'Let's go call a cab to take us back.'

She laughed. The ease with which they could summon a boat enchanted her. She watched as Toby gathered up their belongings and put them in his pack. 'You do think Serena is genuine then?'

'Yes.' He paused, and then frowned. 'Don't you?'

She nodded. 'She's going to do another ceremony. At Philae. In the temple of Isis.' She shivered. 'But she's almost afraid of Andy.'

'Aren't we all!' He looked grim suddenly. 'In her case it's because Andy bullies her. If you ask me there's some Freudian thing going on there because Charley lives with her and clearly respects and likes her and I suspect Serena has told Charley on more than one occasion what a prat she thinks he is! Anna, what are you going to do about the diary? When he comes back?'

She took off her sun hat and fanned her face for a moment or two. 'I don't know. It would be awkward to make too much fuss. I don't want the police involved. Heaven knows what would happen, and I have a feeling it wouldn't be wise to make an issue of it. He would only deny it and say I had lent it to him or something, and it would be very difficult to prove that I hadn't. I'll keep it locked up or with me at all times, and probably leave it at that.'

He stared at her. 'Anna, he tried to steal something which could be worth thousands of pounds.'

'I've got it back,' she said firmly. 'And he's got to live with the fact that you and I and Serena know he's a thief. He won't know who else we've told. He'll be sweating.'

'And that's all you are going to do? Watch him sweat?'

She nodded. 'As long as we're in Egypt, yes.'

283

He exhaled loudly and shook his head. 'O K. If that's what you've decided. It's your diary.'

They had walked down the path towards the landing stage. When they reached it several small boats were already clustered there, just off shore and on the landing stage dozens of men and boys milled around selling every shape and size of souvenir and tourist bric-a-brac. Somehow Anna and Toby pushed their way through the crowd and beckoned one of the boats. Toby, after a swift good-humoured exchange of figures and a lot of gesticulations managed to clinch a deal on the price back to *The White Egret* and they scrambled aboard, fighting off the plastic gods and heads of Rameses and the tin Bast cats until the last possible moment, when the vendors, holding them out enticingly, were wading thigh deep in the water.

'I hated this when we first arrived, but I'm getting used to them now.' She shrugged, turning her back on the island and the men who had abandoned their efforts to follow them and withdrawn to besiege another group of tourists. 'I'm sure people would buy more if they were allowed to look quietly. As it is one has to run away. Even a second glance is a disaster!'

Toby leant back on his seat, staring up at the sail. There seemed to be some kind of wind, as they were making good speed towards *The White Egret*, although the tall sail was hardly bellied as it hung at the masthead. 'It's all good-humoured, though. I like the people here.' He glanced at the man at the helm who having captured them from the competition had settled calmly and seemingly indifferently to his job without giving them a second glance. 'I suspect it is only this bad around the tourist honey pots. In the rest of Egypt it's probably possible to move around without being followed. After all no one followed us on the island itself, did they?'

They dined alone in state by candlelight on Ibrahim's speciality, something he called *mulukhiyya*, which turned out to be a herb soup poured over white rice, followed by fried perch and vegetables. For dessert they were given dates and soft cheese and then Egyptian coffee. Only when they assured him they could eat no more did Ibrahim bid them goodnight and leave.

'And so,' Toby turned to Anna and smiled. 'We have a boat to ourselves.'

She nodded. 'Don't forget the captain is still on board.'

'But we don't see him. He is the *éminence grise*.' Toby smiled. 'Perhaps he doesn't exist. Or perhaps he is Ibrahim too, with

284

another hat on!' He glanced at her and slowly his face became thoughtful. He led the way out on deck and went to lean on the rail. There was a long silence after Anna joined him and she found herself wondering if he was trying to make up his mind whether or not to tell her something. Leaning on the rail beside him, she waited quietly, content to watch the evening drawing in.

It was several minutes before he spoke at last. 'What did Andy tell you about me?' He didn't look at her.

She bit her lip. For a moment she didn't answer, then she turned towards him. 'He seemed to think you had some kind of a scandal hanging over you.' She shrugged. 'Under the circumstances I didn't take much notice. I think I could accuse him of what is known as the pot calling the kettle black!'

He grimaced. 'Why haven't you asked me if it's true?'

She hesitated, scanning his profile. 'Because I believed – hoped – it wasn't.'

He still hadn't looked at her. There was another long silence, then at last he glanced towards her. 'It is true. Anna, I don't want there to be any secrets between us.'

She waited, aware that there was a sudden knot of anxiety somewhere in her stomach. Her mouth was dry with fear when at last she managed to ask, 'What happened?'

'I killed someone.'

There was a long silence. She bit her lip. 'Why?'

His jaw tightened. 'He raped my wife.'

Anna closed her eyes. Her hands had gripped the rail until her knuckles were white.

Beside her, Toby straightened, staring out beyond the lights clustering along the edge of the river, towards the darkness of the hills. 'I don't regret it. If I hadn't done it he would have got away with it. It was a justice the gods of Egypt would have approved of.'

There was a long silence. 'Did you go to prison?' she asked at last.

'For manslaughter, yes.'

'And your wife?'

She studied his profile in the dark.

'My wife is dead.'

'Dead!' Anna stared at him.

'She killed herself while I was in prison. The state took it upon itself to punish me. It did nothing about the man who attacked her and tormented her. It chose not to believe her story. While I was in prison it did not help her; it left her alone to cope with her unhappiness and her shame. She was pregnant when she died, apparently by him. She had no one. No family. My father was dead. My mother was abroad. She couldn't get there in time.' He took a deep breath and turning walked away from her. He climbed up onto the upper deck and she saw him disappear into the darkness. For a long time she stayed where she was, then at last she turned and followed him.

'Thank you for telling me.'

'If I hadn't, Watson would have done so in the end, no doubt. People always remember these things even though it happened years ago now.' He turned to her at last. 'Do you want a drink?' To her embarrassment she could see the emotion raw on his face. It was masked instantly. 'If you want to drink with a murderer.'

'You weren't a murderer; not if they said it was manslaughter. And yes, please, I think I'd like one very much.' She wanted to touch him, to reassure him and comfort him, but she sensed that would be wrong. Now wasn't the time. Instead she forced herself to smile and it was she who turned and led the way down to the bar.

Toby poured two slugs of whisky, signed a chit from the pad by the locked till and pushed one of the glasses towards her. '*Slainte*!'

She raised an eyebrow.

He shrugged. 'Cheers, then. Here's to you and me and the mysteries of Egypt, *Inshallah*!'

She clinked glasses with him. 'Toby –' She hesitated. How could she put into words the strange mixture of feelings she was experiencing? Rage at the injustice of life. Sympathy. Pain for him, for his wife, for the unborn child who was the innocent victim of so much unhappiness. Anger at the man who had ruined so many lives. It was impossible and looking up, she realised suddenly as he met her eye that he understood.

'Shall we read some more about Louisa?' he said quietly. It was a signal to change the subject.

She nodded.

The diary was in her cabin, left there, locked in the suitcase, when she had showered and changed for supper. She stood up. 'Shall I bring it here, or shall we read it in my cabin?'

He studied her face. 'Which would you like?' He sounded hesitant.

She hadn't intended her words to sound like an invitation, but suddenly she realised that that was what they were. She smiled and reached out her hand.

In the cabin she turned on the bedside light. 'The diary is locked up. A classic case of bolting the stable door.' She laughed. There was a sudden tight knot of excitement in her stomach as she felt him standing very close behind her. Reaching into her shoulder bag for the key on its ring she turned towards the suitcase.

Toby stretched out his hand and caught her wrist. 'Anna?'

She stood stock still. Then she turned and looked up at him.

They remained wrapped in each other's arms for a long time before Anna gently disengaged herself. 'Are you sure this is what you want?' She was amazed that it was she who was taking the lead, she who had initiated this move, overwhelmed as she was by a desire for him so great it almost paralysed her. She had never felt like this before. If anything proved to her that whatever she had felt for Felix, it was not love, it was this incredible, undeniable longing which had swept over her.

Toby smiled. 'It's very much what I want.' He reached out and caught her by the shoulders. As he drew her close once again she could feel him searching for the zip of her dress. It slipped to the floor and she felt his hands on her burning skin, cool and firm as he stroked her shoulders and ran a finger down her throat towards her breasts. She gasped, raising her mouth to his again as he reached for the hooks on her bra, letting it fall to the floor, then he pulled her towards the bed.

It was much later, asleep in the crook of his arm that Anna was awakened by a violent knocking on the door.

She lay still, holding her breath, feeling him stir beside her.

They looked at each other for a moment. 'It must be Ibrahim?' Anna sat up. She grabbed her cotton dressing gown and pulling it tightly round her she knotted the tie and then headed for the door as a fresh fusillade of knocking echoed round the cabin. Unbolting it, she pulled it open.

Charley almost fell into the room. 'Anna! You've got to help me!' Tears were pouring down her face. 'Oh God!' She glanced behind her down the passage, then stumbling into the cabin she slammed the door and shot the bolt across. She didn't appear to have seen Toby, who had reached over the edge of the bed for his trousers and was surreptitiously pulling them on. Charley was shaking

287

violently as Anna put her arm around her shoulders and guided her to the stool in front of the dressing table. 'What is it? What's happened? I thought you had gone with the others.'

Charley shook her head. She had grabbed Anna's hands and was clinging to them as though her life depended on it. 'Don't let him in. Keep him away from me!'

Toby was pulling on his shirt. He frowned. 'Who? Who is it, Charley? What's happened?'

'I was asleep. In my cabin.' She shook her head. 'I thought I was dreaming. I was dreaming.' Her breath was coming in short gasps, her hand in Anna's shook violently. 'Then I woke up. I'd locked the door. I know I locked the door. But he was there.' She broke into fresh sobs.

Toby came and knelt in front of her. He took one of her hands. 'Charley, listen to me. You are safe. We are not going to let anything happen to you.' He paused.

Her sobbing had subsided. She glanced at him, her face white as a sheet, streaked with mascara, her eyes puffy and red. 'You're sure?' She was pathetically like a child suddenly, clinging to both of his hands.

'I'm sure. Now tell us quietly what happened. Who was in your cabin?'

'It was a man. In a green *galabiyya*.'

'An Egyptian?'

'Yes, of course an Egyptian!'

'Did he hurt you? What did he do?'

She shook her head. 'No. He didn't hurt me. I don't think so. But he was reaching out towards me.'

'Describe him. Was he one of the waiters?'

'No. No. He was very tall. He was wearing an animal skin round his shoulders –'

'A lion skin?' Anna had gone to sit on the bed.

Charley glanced up and shrugged. 'I don't know. I suppose so. It could have been.'

Toby glanced at Anna. 'We need Serena, don't we.'

Anna grimaced. She nodded silently.

'Charley?' Toby tried another tack. 'Why didn't you go with the others?'

'I was going to. I wanted to.' She shook her head 'I remember waking up early and Serena and I were getting dressed. Ali brought

288

us some tea. Then she was ready, but I didn't feel well. I went to the loo . . .' She shook her head again, pressing her fingertips against her temples. 'I said I'd follow her. I was feeling so cold. So tired. I sat down on the bed for a minute. Serena came back, and I think she asked me how I was, and I suppose I said I wanted to go to sleep.'

Anna stood up. Finding her box of tissues she pulled some out and pressed them into Charley's hands. 'That must explain the third person on the boat. Serena must have told Omar and he told Ibrahim you were staying. What happened next?'

'I don't remember anything till I woke up and saw him standing there.' Charley began to sob again, the tears running down her cheeks and falling into her lap.

'Then what?'

'Then I screamed. I sat up and screamed and he sort of stepped towards me. Then he began to shake.' She shook her head, confused. 'He was shaking quite violently, then he –' She stopped and shrugged. 'He sort of wasn't there any more.'

'You mean he left the cabin, or he disappeared?'

She shrugged again. 'He didn't open the door. I did. I didn't wait to see. I ran outside and I couldn't see anyone. It was so quiet. They haven't gone, have they?'

'Who?' Anna shook her head. 'You mean the others? They left yesterday.' She glanced at her watch. 'That was twenty-four hours ago, Charley.'

Charley's eyes focused on Anna's face. 'No.' Her face resumed the child-like pout. 'I only dozed off for a minute.'

'If you've been asleep since they left, Charley, Anna's right.' Toby looked up at her with concern.

'No,' she shook her head. 'No. I can't have. No.' She began rocking backwards and forwards suddenly. 'No.'

'Charley!' Toby stood up and put his hands on her shoulders. 'Listen.' He paused. 'Are you listening? Good. You were asleep. But it doesn't matter. You must have been exhausted. You needed that sleep.'

'I wasn't drinking.' She didn't appear to have heard what he said. 'I wasn't drinking. I know I have been silly and spiteful and childish. I know I have. But I wasn't drinking. Andy said I mustn't drink any more. I wasn't. I promise.' She was shaking her head again, back and forth, back and forth, like an automaton.

'When did you last eat, Charley?' Toby had taken her hands again. He glanced at Anna. 'Do you see how thin she's got?' he said under her breath. 'I can't believe it. In a week.'

Anna nodded. She had been studying Charley's face whilst Toby was talking to her. 'Charley, are you quite sure this man didn't touch you?'

The question seemed to throw Charley. She stopped rocking and frowned.

'Are you sure he didn't touch you while you were asleep?'

Charley shuddered. 'I had my clothes on. These.' She gestured down at her jeans and black tee-shirt. 'I had got dressed to go on the coach. I never took them off. I had packed my overnight bag. I was ready to go.'

'And you sat down for a moment and when you woke up it was twenty-four hours later.' Anna was wishing fervently that Serena had stayed behind. 'Charley, you said you were dreaming when this man woke you. Can you remember what you were dreaming about?'

Charley shrugged and shook her head.

'Do you think anyone touched you in your dream?'

'You mean –? No! Oh ugh, no!'

'I don't mean sex.' Anna glanced suddenly at Toby and was relieved to see him wink. Their awakening had been so sudden and so traumatic she hadn't thought for one second about him or the touch of his body since Charley's knock on the door. She could feel herself colouring slightly now, and she shook her head quickly. 'I mean did you feel him touch you here.' She put her hand to her own stomach. 'Or on the mouth, or the throat or on your head?'

Charley shrugged. 'I don't know. I feel sore here.' She put her hand to her stomach. 'I thought I'd eaten something bad.'

'Pharaoh's curse.' Toby grimaced. 'It's possible. But Anna is thinking about something else.' He looked across at her. 'Am I right? The incubus? Taking her energy?'

Anna nodded. 'That's what Serena thought.'

'What? What did she think?' Charley's eyes were round again and Anna noticed she had begun to tremble once more.

'Andy will be so angry. He was going to sit next to me. And now you're with him,' she nodded at Toby, 'and not after my Andy at all. Or do you want them both?' She shot a pathetically defiant look at Anna. 'Did you know he had your stupid little bottle with him? So if you've lost it again, you know it wasn't me.'

There was a moment's silence in the cabin. Then, 'He's taken it with him?' Anna stared at her. 'Are you sure?'

Charley nodded. 'Popular, isn't it.'

Anna's face had frozen. She was staring at the suitcase in front of the cupboard. Locked inside was the diary where only hours before she and Toby had read about the snake. The king snake, programmed to kill any man who touched the sacred ampulla.

She glanced at Toby. 'The cobra,' she whispered. 'The guardian of the scent bottle. Only women have owned that bottle. Louisa. My great-great-grandmother. My great-aunt. Me.'

'Oh shit!' Toby rubbed his chin. 'What do we do? Don't tell me you want us to follow him?'

'We have to. It might not be too late. If we can warn him. Get it back.'

'What is it? What's wrong?' Charley grabbed at Toby's arm.

'The snake you found in your cabin,' Anna said sharply. 'It didn't hurt you because you're a woman. If you had been a man it would have killed you.'

Charley stared at her. 'Why? What do you mean?'

'It guards the bottle. Look, don't ask, Charley. Just believe it! Find Ibrahim,' Anna said to Toby urgently. 'He knew about the snake. He'll know what to do. Perhaps we can phone Omar and get him to warn Andy.'

'No! Don't leave me!' Charley clung to Toby as he turned towards the door. 'What about the man in my cabin!'

'We won't leave you, Charley.' Toby sighed. He pushed her towards Anna. 'Stay here both of you. I'll see if I can find Ibrahim.'

As he disappeared Anna closed her eyes. She took a deep breath. 'If we can't contact Omar, we're going to have to find the others ourselves. Andy is a bastard, but he doesn't deserve to die. We are going to have to find a way of warning him. Take a bus or a taxi or something. How much money have you got, Charley? We'll need cash.'

She scrabbled under the bed for her shoes and grabbed her bag. Unlocking the suitcase she took out the diary and pushed it into her holdall. 'Do you want your stuff? We'll collect it as we go by. Where's Toby got to?'

'You sent him to look for Ibrahim,' Charley objected. Then she clutched her stomach. 'I think I'm going to be sick.'

'Loo!' Anna pointed.

Trying to ignore the noises coming from the shower room she automatically dug out her sun hat and glasses and her guidebook and threw them in the holdall with a bottle of water. By the time Toby returned Charley had reappeared looking whiter than ever and Anna was ready.

'I spoke to the captain. He knows nothing. Not where they are or where Ibrahim might be, though he thinks he has gone to visit friends in one of the villages. But he did have a contact who can find us a taxi. It'll be by the gangplank in ten minutes.'

'Don't leave me!' Charley was clinging to them both. 'I won't go back to my cabin. You can't make me. He'll kill me!'

'We're not leaving you, Charley,' Toby said gently. He was trying to disengage her hands from his sleeve. 'You can come with us, or we can drop you off at a hotel before we go. You'd be safe there.'

Charley shook her head. 'I hate all this. I want to go home.'

'A hotel can arrange that for you, if that's what you really want.' Toby glanced over her head at Anna. 'I think it's the right decision. She can't stay on the boat and she can't come with us. It's about two hundred and fifty kilometres. It's going to take hours.'

It was Anna who went into Charley's cabin whilst Charley clung to Toby in the corridor outside. It was empty. She stood for a moment looking round, listening. As though her senses were in some way newly honed by everything that had happened, she found herself paying attention to her intuition in a way she never had before. It told her there was nothing there; nothing to fear at least for now. Grabbing Charley's overnight bag she turned out the light and closed the door behind her with a fervent prayer that the priest of Sekhmet would stay wherever it was he lived and would not follow them.

A black car was waiting for them at the water's edge. The young man at the wheel was wearing western clothes and greeted Toby with some deference as they climbed in. In seconds he had spun the wheel and pulled away from the gangplank, heading south along the Corniche.

He pulled up outside the Old Cataract Hotel.

'Wait here,' Toby said to Anna. He took Charley's arm and bundled her out. 'I'll be five minutes.'

As they disappeared into the hotel entrance Anna frowned. Then she shrugged. She was too tired to think. If Toby could get Charley looked after here, and at this hour, well and good. She'd wonder how he was going to manage it later.

It was fifteen minutes before he returned and she had dozed off. She woke up as he pulled the car door open and climbed in, giving the driver some quick instructions. He seemed pleased with himself as they set off. 'She'll be fine. They'll take care of her and I've made a couple of phone calls. Someone is going to check up on her in the morning and see if she is OK. She can either stay there till we cruise back to Luxor or they'll get her a ticket to fly back home early. And I've sorted us out, too. South of Aswan it's a military zone. I just thought I'd check in case we need passes and things to go through the desert.' He leant back beside her.

'And do we?'

'All organised. No problem.'

She glanced at him sideways. 'You're sure?'

'Positive. Now, get some sleep. I'll wake you when we get there.'

'Toby?' With a shiver she pulled her sweater more tightly round her shoulders. The car had grown very cold while they were waiting. 'What happens if the priest of Sekhmet has got hold of her? What if he comes back when she's on her own?'

'The hotel staff will keep an eye on her. If anything happens they'll call a doctor.'

'And what could a doctor do?'

He shrugged. 'We'll be back in Aswan very soon, Anna. Probably tonight. And we can phone from Abu Simbel. It's not as though it's the ends of the earth. Once we've found Andy and relieved him of the bottle the urgency is over.' There was a moment's silence. 'As long as you don't expect me to touch it!'

Anna smiled grimly. 'No, I don't expect you to touch it.' She gasped as the car lurched into a pothole, throwing her against him. 'I'd hate you to get swallowed by a snake.'

He put his arm around her and pulled her close to him. 'So would I, believe me.'

There was a long silence as the taxi rattled through the streets, turning this way and that towards the southern edge of town. The main roads were brightly lit, the side roads dark, houses shuttered against the cold night air.

'Toby?' Anna was wide awake now.

'What is it?' he asked. He groped for her hand.

'Supposing we're too late?'

293

'We won't be.' He squeezed her fingers tightly. 'Assuming anything at all is going to happen, we'll get there in time. I'm sure we will.'

12

Hymns of praise to thee O thou god who makest
the moment to advance,
thou dweller among the mysteries of every kind,
thou guardian of the word which speaks . . .

The house was left empty. Everyone knew of its curse: all who lived there died. But time passes. Villages themselves disappear. In the desert air the mud bricks lie scattered. The few possessions left behind are abandoned and lost and succumb to the sand.

The priests grow weak, insubstantial wraiths without the life blood of man's energy. They look to the sun and the moon for their existence and the strength of the desert wind and they hover, fuelled only by their mutual hate.

Once again men and boys pass that way, always watchful, always aware that the detritus of millennia may spell riches and fame for the lucky few. A man stoops, picks up a shard here, a pot there. He sees the glint of glass and kicks at the sand to free the tiny bottle lying there. It is attractive. It is interesting. Who knows, perhaps it is old. He picks it up and rubs it on the skirt of his galabiyya and tucks it away. Only

*once as he moves around does he stop and look over his shoulder
and shiver.*

*The gods watch over thee, man of the desert, lest thy hour be
come upon thee soon . . .*

They were awakened some time later when the taxi lurched to a
standstill in the middle of the road. The driver turned and leant
over the back of his seat to prod Toby's knee.

'You want to see birth of sun god, Ra?'

Toby glanced out of the window with a grim smile. Every tourist
since the beginning of time had obviously requested this stop. It
was probably obligatory. 'Dawn! Come on, Anna. Five minutes
won't make much difference now and this is worth seeing. Sunrise
in the desert.'

Opening the doors they climbed out. The air was fresh and
sharply cold as they stood in the middle of the deserted highway
and stared round. In the bleak dawn the tarmac stretched across
the desert, straight as a die in front and behind them, here and
there masked by drifting sand and shingle and a scattering of boulders. The light was cold and colourless and very still. The only
sound was the ticking of the car engine as it cooled. The driver had
not bothered to get out of the car. He sat behind the wheel and
within seconds his eyes had closed.

The loom of light in the east was very bright, increasing every
second. Above them the stars, which earlier had seemed close
enough to touch, had all but disappeared. Two or three small flat
clouds reflected a touch of red for a moment, hanging motionless
over them, then first the colour and then the clouds themselves
vanished.

Anna reached for Toby's hand. She was shivering. 'It's as though
the whole world is holding its breath.'

He nodded. 'Watch. Any minute now.'

They stood in silence, their eyes fixed on the increasing brightness as around them more and more features of the desert came into focus and the light grew stronger. There was something inexorable, almost menacing in the inevitability of it all as suddenly the rim of the sun erupted blindingly over the horizon.

Anna caught her breath, inexplicably moved near to tears by the beauty of the moment as it rose visibly higher. Within seconds she could no longer look and she turned instead to stare around as the light flooded towards them and on across the desert towards the far horizon.

'OK. That's it. Come on.' Toby took her hand. 'We must go on. It's going to start getting hot soon and we've still got a long way to go.'

When they arrived at Abu Simbel Anna was once more asleep. She woke as they rattled into the car park and the driver cut the engine.

'Good speed, yes?' He leant across his seat again and beamed at them.

Toby nodded. He reached for his wallet. 'Good speed. Good bonus.' As he pulled out a wad of dirty notes and began counting them out into the man's hand Anna was already climbing out of the car. The heat hit her like a hammer blow as she stared round at the ranks of cars and coaches. 'How will we find the others?'

Toby raised a hand to the driver and watched as the taxi backed away.

'Is he leaving?' Anna stared after it.

'Not if he knows what's good for him. I've only given him the fare here. If he wants the rest he'll wait for us.' Toby smiled. 'No, he's gone to find a parking space. Then he'll snooze until we're ready to go. Now, my guess is the others will already be at one of the temples or perhaps down on the shore. We'll try the great temple first. There is so much to see there.'

Joining the already considerable queue to enter the gates Anna and Toby began to scan the crowds around them for faces they knew, surrounded as they were by snatches of every language under the sun as they shuffled forward.

Toby frowned, concentrating, trying to make sense of the words and laughter and shouts around him.

'I think we'd hear about it if anyone had been threatened by a snake. I suspect a cobra would be quite rare up here and it is the sort of gossip which would get people talking very quickly.' He gave her an encouraging smile. 'Keep your chin up. We're in time, I'm sure we are.'

She was so tired she could barely keep her eyes open as they moved slowly towards the entrance, bought their tickets and made their way in. They followed the path around the side of a low hill and found themselves suddenly in front of what must possibly be one of the most famous sights in the world, the four colossal statues of Rameses II, set into the cliff face, staring towards the brilliant blue waters of Lake Nasser and beyond.

In front of the temple the sea of swirling humanity threatened to overwhelm the facade, for all the enormous height of the statues, and Anna found herself gasping at the sight of the crowds. 'We'll never find them!'

'Of course we will.' Toby stared round. 'I hope Andy comes to realise how much effort you are going to, to protect his hide. He doesn't deserve it.'

They were threading their way through the groups of tourists. Each group seemed to have their own guide standing bellowing out a potted history of the great sun temple and its smaller neighbour, erected by Rameses for his favourite wife, Nefertari, before heading into the temple itself. 'For all we know the villainous Carstairs might have taken off the curse.'

Anna shook her head. 'You've forgotten. Charley saw the snake.' She was forging ahead towards the temple facade, desperately looking left and right as she moved through the crowds.

Toby hurried to catch up with her. 'We mustn't lose each other! My God, I never realised it would be so crowded. When Omar told us the trip was optional I imagined only a few people were intrepid enough to come here and we would be a select few!'

'The others might be inside.' She was looking towards the doorway.

'It is the most likely place.'

Still scanning the faces all around them at every step they made their way into the darkness through the entrance to what the guidebook had called the *pronaos*, a vast rock-cut hall with two lines of four lofty columns. They stood close together, staring into the dark, aware of the vast crowds of people milling around the pillars. Only

298

close to the doorway was it possible to see much. Everywhere the walls were covered in relief carvings of Rameses' victories. Further in all was almost dark.

'We'll never see them!' Too tired and worried to take in the scale of the scenes around her, Anna was near to tears.

Suddenly there was a touch on her shoulder. 'Anna?'

It was Serena. She gave Anna a hug. 'What on earth are you doing here? Why did you change your mind? How did you get here?'

Anna returned her embrace with relief. 'It's a long, long story. Where is Andy?' She was looking round frantically.

Serena shrugged. 'I've no idea, as he's my least favourite person at the moment I'm hardly likely to be watching out for him!'

'But he's all right?'

'As far as I know. I saw him at breakfast in the hotel. He seemed OK then. Why?'

'And he's here?'

'Somewhere, yes. We're all supposed to be here. Yesterday we went for a sail on Lake Nasser and last night we saw the temples floodlit and had one of Omar's lectures. This one was rather good actually, with a film about how they moved the temples when the valley flooded and how they chopped them up and built an artificial hill to put them in and everything. Today we see the two temples themselves and then we're supposed to be leaving to go back to the boat.' She paused for a second. 'So what is all the panic about Andy?'

'He left the diary in the safe on *The White Egret*, but he has brought the bottle here with him. And probably the cobra too. And it will kill him.'

'Why should it kill him?' Serena dodged out of the way as a determined Italian woman elbowed her in the ribs and shoved a camera in her face, ignoring the guard who was shouting at her for taking photographs with a flash.

'It'll kill him because Carstairs summoned it to kill Hassan! That's its job; it's there to protect the ampulla. We have to get it back before the wretched creature bites him! It was nothing to do with the priests. It was conjured up to kill Hassan and any man who touches the bottle! And I mean man, not woman. That's why Charley and I – and you – were safe.'

Serena raised an eyebrow. 'In that case I'd be inclined to let it

299

get on with it.' She grimaced. 'No, OK, I didn't mean it. Of course you've got to take it seriously. So, you want me to help find him and warn him?'

Toby nodded. He tapped his watch. 'We'll do better if we separate, then we can search a bigger area. Let's all meet in half an hour outside the main door and hope one of us has located him.'

'He'll never believe us,' Serena said as she turned away. 'God knows how you'll persuade him even to admit he's got it with him, never mind that he's in danger of being poisoned by a magic snake if he doesn't give it back!' She was still shaking her head as she and Anna separated and turned to push their way one on either side of the huge *pronaos* towards the entrances leading further into the darkness of the interior.

The crowds were less dense once they had passed from the huge pillared hall into the smaller chambers at the back. Anna, who had walked slowly down behind the righthand column of pillars stepped into the first and squinted at the few people looking at the reliefs in there. In the dark they were just silhouettes, but none had the height and breadth of shoulders of Andy. She moved on to the next entrance and was glancing into the second, smaller chamber when a voice at her elbow made her jump.

'Anna, my dear. I thought it was you. How on earth did you get here?' Ben smiled at her. His hat still in place, his old canvas bag on his shoulder, his eyes were shining. 'Isn't it an extraordinary place? What a feat of engineering! When you think this has all been cut into blocks and moved and reassembled like a huge lego model.' He hesitated. 'Is something wrong, my dear?'

'Ben, I need to find Andy. I can't concentrate on looking at anything until I see him. Do you know where he is?'

Ben shook his head. 'To be honest I don't think I've seen him since last night. I don't remember noticing him at breakfast.' He closed his guidebook, leaving his forefinger inserted between the pages to mark the place. 'If I see him shall I tell him you're looking for him?'

Anna grimaced. 'That might make him head off in the opposite direction. Could you bring him to the entrance? We're all meeting just outside at half past. It's really important. A matter of life and death!'

Ben nodded, a trifle absent-mindedly. Already he was reopening his book. 'I'll keep my eyes open. I promise.'

The next small chamber she looked into was empty. For a moment she stood in the doorway peering in, struck by the strangeness of the sudden stillness. In so few of the places she had visited in Egypt had there been somewhere one could stand lost in one's own thoughts and absorb the atmosphere, but in this temple, more than any, the noise and bustle had been overwhelming and that was hardly surprising. Rebuilt to save it from the rising waters after the building of the high dam it had been mobbed by crowds ever since. And yet now, in this small side room, she found herself suddenly shivering. The silence was intense. Perhaps the ancient gods or their attendants were here after all. She found the palms of her hands sweating as the stillness of the chamber reached out towards her, and for a moment enfolded her in silence.

Then suddenly a group of people appeared behind her. Talking loudly and excitedly in French they pushed past her into the chamber and almost at once a forbidden flash lit the cave-like room for a fraction of a second in harsh white light. There was a shout of laughter, an excited exchange of comments and a throaty giggle. Anna turned away.

There were four other people in the sanctuary, deep in the heart of the temple. It was here, twice a year, that the sun's ray pierced all the way through from the entrance, into the depths of the rock to fall on the altar, illuminating three of the four seated statues which guarded it. The temple had been carefully aligned exactly as it had been in its original setting so that this miracle could take place in such a way that the fourth statue, that of the god Ptah, the creator god, god of the mortuary, lord of darkness, remained for ever in the dark, untouched ever by the sun.

Ptah, of course, was the husband of Sekhmet . . .

Anna stopped. The words floating out of the darkness towards her had come, she realised, from the group of people standing near the statues.

Sekhmet.

She felt her stomach turn over with sudden fear. Would Hatsek come here? Would he recognise this temple, rebuilt and swarming with unbelievers from a different age though it was?

Almost as the thought crossed her mind she knew that he would, that between one second and the next, as though summoned by the processes of her mind, he was there. She stepped sideways into the corner of the sanctuary, staring round.

301

'Andy?' She didn't realise she had called out loud until one of the group around the statue turned and stared at her.

Andy wasn't there. The visitors who shuffled out, still gazing around them in awe, one or two of them glancing at her as they passed, were strangers. Two other people were in the chamber, examining the seated statues. Near them the air shimmered for a moment and grew cold.

Anna tried to turn back, but her feet were rooted to the spot. She couldn't tear her eyes away. The sanctuary was growing darker and in the strange chill that surrounded her, she could hear voices somewhere in the distance, chanting.

Light flickered to one side of the statues. It came from a lamp, she realised, set in a niche in the wall. In the foreground, on what she had thought was an altar, she could see the dark shape of a model boat.

And then she saw him, a tall man, very dark of complexion, his face drawn into harsh lines, his bare arms corded with muscle. He was naked but for a short skirt around his hips and the tawny pelt of a desert lion hung around his shoulders. On his feet she could see gilded sandals and in his hand was a long staff. At its top there was a carving – the formal, angry, snarling head of a lioness.

He was staring past her, not seeming to see her as, slowly, he turned towards the entrance to the sanctuary. The chanting was growing louder. She was aware of the pentatonic cadences of the tune, of the rising and falling of the sound as though it were coming from an inestimable distance, carried on the desert wind. She could smell the strange sweet spicy smell of incense. He was standing in front of the statue of Ptah, bowing, placing something before it, bowing in turn to the other statues.

Frozen with fear, Anna became aware of someone standing beside her in the doorway. The figure advanced past her and moved towards the centre of the sanctuary. She could see shadows moving across the chamber, two people were talking softly. The two scenes, two eras, seemed for a moment to co-exist within the same place. They seemed not to see the priest standing near them. They gave no sign of hearing anything untoward. It was they who seemed transparent; wraiths out of time. It was the priest of Sekhmet about his sacred ritual who was real in this strange reconstructed place which still had the power to call back ancient echoes.

'Are you all right?' It was the touch on her arm which shocked

302

Anna back to the present. She recognised one of the women from their boat – her husband was the retired vicar, she seemed to remember, and they had ten grandchildren who had clubbed together to send them on this, the holiday of a lifetime.

Anna staggered slightly, her hand to her head and the woman moved closer, putting a supportive arm round her shoulders. 'Shall I help you outside, my dear?' she said. 'It's close in here, isn't it, and that strange smell doesn't help.'

'Smell?' Anna stared at her, still dizzy and confused.

'It's like the inside of an Italian cathedral. Incense.' The woman smiled. Celia Greyshot. That was her name. It came to Anna suddenly.

'Incense? How can there be incense in here?' The statue of Ptah was alone again. No offerings about its feet. There was no priest.

'Well, no.' Celia looked puzzled. She sniffed loudly. 'You're right. It's gone. It must have been someone's perfume. Or perhaps I imagined it.' She shivered. 'This is such a powerful, weird place, isn't it?'

Anna did her best to smile. 'I think I would like to go outside. I am feeling a bit odd.' She glanced at her watch, squinting in the dim light at her wrist. It was already past the time she and Serena and Toby had agreed to meet.

Serena was sitting on a bench outside. She jumped up in consternation as Anna and her companion appeared. 'Anna, what is it? What's wrong?'

Anna shook her head. 'Too much heat and no sleep, I think. Celia was kind enough to look after me.' She flopped onto the bench. 'No sign of Andy? Or of Toby or Ben?'

Serena shook her head. 'None.' They watched as Celia with a pleasant word and a wave disappeared into the crowds in search of her husband.

'I saw Hatsek! In the temple.' Anna turned to Serena as soon as her companion was out of earshot. 'He was beside the statue of Ptah in the sanctuary. Someone said that Ptah was Sekhmet's husband!'

Serena thought for a moment. 'Did you feel your energy depleted?'

Anna shrugged. 'I suppose so. I nearly fainted; that's why Celia helped me. But it was fear, Serena. Cold hard total fear!'

Serena nodded again. 'I've made a decision while I've been here, Anna. I want to try and call up the priests again. But on my terms.

303

I think I can do it this time, and I'm sure it is the right thing to do. We'll try it if you like at Philae, this evening as I suggested. And it'll be all right, I promise.' She gripped Anna's hands. 'So, do we go on looking for Andy?'

Anna closed her eyes wearily. 'Toby and I have driven about a hundred and fifty miles through the night to save Andy! We'll have to look for him. We have to. Supposing he is bitten by the snake?'

'You are positive the snake will try and kill him?'

'That's why Carstairs called it up: to kill Hassan.'

'And did it kill him?'

Anna shrugged. 'I don't know. I haven't read that far yet. I don't think so.'

'Did you bring the diary with you?'

Anna nodded. 'I'm not letting it out of my sight again!'

'Then can I suggest we find somewhere shady and have a drink and look at it? It may be that Louisa found a way of dealing with it. This whole panic might be without any foundation.'

Anna nodded slowly. 'I suppose that does make sense.'

'It does, Anna. And then, if he hasn't already turned up with Toby or Ben or someone we'll have another shot at finding Andy. Come on.' Serena stood up and held out her hand. 'Let's get out of the sun.'

'I hid it under the planking.' Hassan showed Louisa a loose panel on the side of the cabin superstructure. 'You see? Here.' He glanced round to make sure that they weren't being observed, then he pulled out the small package and handed it to her. 'What do we do with it?' The bruise on his head had subsided and the wound had nearly healed.

That morning the *Ibis* had anchored amongst several other boats off the shore opposite the temple of Abu Simbel. Amongst their neighbours she had recognised Carstairs' *Scarab*.

After the rescue party had brought Hassan back to the *Ibis* from the kiosk at Kartassi, Louisa, alone and shaking with anger, had demanded that one of their crew row her over to Carstairs' boat, but when she got there she found he had gone. His *reis* shrugged when she asked for him. 'He say he go for three, maybe four days. No say where.' The black Nubian face was full of concern. 'May I help the Sitt?'

Louisa shook her head. 'Thank you, no. I'm sure I shall see him soon.'

She instructed the boatman to take her next to the *Lotus* on which she could see David Fielding and his two ladies with their parasols. Venetia greeted her with a scowl. Neither David nor his wife moved.

'Katherine is resting. I don't believe she has the strength for visitors,' Venetia called down frostily.

Louisa inclined her head slightly. It was hard to remain dignified, floating in the small dinghy looking up at the other woman above her head. 'Then I shan't incommode her. It was you or your brother I wanted to speak to. Do you know where Roger Carstairs has gone?'

Venetia's face reddened perceptibly. 'I have no idea. You are the one I had thought privy to all his movements.'

'As I think you know by now, he attacked my dragoman, Hassan, and beat him fearfully.' Louisa stared up into the other woman's face, her words echoing across the water and, presumably, clearly audible to David and his wife. 'If you see him I want you to emphasise that he is no longer welcome for any reason aboard the *Ibis*. I never wish to see him again and Sir John has forbidden him to set foot on the boat.' She smiled coldly. 'I have no doubt you find such news pleasing as it leaves the field clear for you, Venetia, but do beware. The man is a fiend.'

As they rowed back towards the *Ibis* Louisa could feel the other woman's eyes on her back for every stroke of her boatman's oars. When she climbed back on board Venetia was still standing at the rail looking after her.

'Sitt Louisa?' Hassan, bandaged and much restored, had been waiting on deck. 'You should not have gone to see him.' He was looking furiously angry.

Louisa shrugged. 'You expect me to leave it at that? He tried to kill you! He is a dangerous man . . .' She shook her head slowly.

'Anyway, he wasn't there. He won't be back for several days. No one knows where he has gone.' She reached over and touched his arm. 'We do not need to think about him for a while. We can be happy.' She smiled at him pleadingly. 'We are going to stay here for a few days so I can paint the Sun Temple, and then we can go for lots more painting trips as we sail up towards the second cataract. I hope we never see him again.'

He nodded. 'Of course, my Louisa. We will do whatever you want.'

It was then he had shown her the hiding place of the bottle and now he was staring at her, holding it in his hand. 'What shall we do with it?'

Louisa shrugged. 'Is there nowhere safe?' She took it from him. 'While Carstairs is away I shall keep it with my painting things.' She sighed. 'So precious a gift, my love, and so dangerous. I intend to treasure this for the rest of my life. He will not have it.'

'For the rest of your life?' Hassan repeated quietly. He glanced at her. 'You will take it back to England with you then?'

Louisa bit her lip. The future was something she did not want to contemplate but she knew soon there would be no escape from it.

He went on with a shake of his head as though he too could not countenance the content of the words he was making himself speak. 'Soon it will be too hot to stay in Upper Egypt. Sir John will follow all the other visitors and turn north again. What will you do when you return to Cairo and Alexandria?'

Louisa turned away from him. She walked to the end of the deck, then she turned back. 'I have to go back to England, Hassan.' She hesitated. 'To my children. But how can I leave you? I don't know what to do!' Her voice suddenly trembled. 'I have never felt such love for any man before!' She closed her eyes aware of the treachery of her words, aware that she was near to tears.

There was a movement behind her and she realised suddenly that Augusta had appeared at the door of the saloon. Desperately she tried to compose herself as Hassan moved a discreet pace or two away from her.

'My Louisa, you must not cry,' he murmured. 'You and I will be together in our hearts, if it is God's will. This afternoon I shall take you to the great Sun Temple over there. We can walk in the hills behind it.' He smiled sadly. 'We will be happy while we can. I can

306

stay with you all the way to Alexandria if it is your wish and if Sir John permits it. Then next year you will come again to Egypt and your Hassan will be waiting for you.'

She was staring out across the river and the desert. '*Inshallah*!' she whispered.

'Louisa, my dear. You cannot stay out here without shade!' Augusta's voice boomed out as her hostess sailed towards her. In her hand she carried Louisa's fringed parasol. Hassan bowed and moved away as Louisa hastily dabbed at the traces of her tears.

'I saw you coming back from the Fielding boat earlier. You didn't say you were visiting them. I would have come with you, had I known.'

Louisa managed a tired smile. 'I had a message to deliver to Lord Carstairs. I hadn't realised he had gone.'

'Gone?' Augusta frowned. 'How could he have gone? Where has he gone?'

'I don't know the answer to either of those questions. I had the boy row me over to the Fieldings' to see if they knew, but Venetia said not.'

Something in the set of her lips made Augusta raise an eyebrow. 'She is not too happy about Lord Carstairs' interest in you. I'm afraid she still hopes for him herself.'

'Does she indeed? Well, she is welcome to him.'

'You are still implacable, my dear? He would be such a catch. Title. Money. And such a handsome man.'

'And a loathsome one.'

Augusta sighed. She glanced towards the stern of the boat where Hassan had settled with the *reis* in conversation over a hookah in the shade of the sail.

'Once you are back in England you will feel differently about things, my dear,' she said gently. 'And it will be time to return very soon.' She was fanning her face as she spoke. 'Sir John has decided not to go any further south. The heat is becoming unbearable and David Fielding tells us he has made the same decision. He is anxious to reach Alexandria before Katherine's confinement. She too is finding the heat intolerable. Whatever Roger is going to do, our two boats will travel together and make as good speed as we can. We are to start back north this very afternoon.'

Louisa followed her into the saloon. 'But Hassan is taking me ashore this afternoon to sketch the great temple of Rameses.' She

307

gestured across the water towards the four giant figures, still half obscured by sand, carved from the living cliff face which dominated the shoreline.

Augusta sighed. 'My dear, you have seen so many temples already. Enough for most people for a lifetime,' she said firmly. 'Surely you can draw it from here, if you must take a likeness of those ugly great brutes? You do not have to go ashore.'

'But I do!' Louisa felt a wave of panic sweep over her. Her longing to be alone with Hassan was overwhelming her.

'What's this, what's this?' Sir John strode into the saloon and stared round. 'What is it you must do, Louisa my dear?'

'She wants to go and see that temple this afternoon,' Augusta answered for her. 'I told her she couldn't. We are turning for home.'

'No, no. We must see the temple before we go. This is one of the wonders of the world, Augusta, or if it isn't, it should be, I shall go ashore with Louisa. Why don't you come too, my dear?'

Augusta shuddered. 'Indeed not. I have not been to visit any of these heathen places and I do not intend to start now. I shall remain on the *Ibis*.'

'Well and good.' He nodded. 'It will not take us long. I understand that in spite of there being so much sand heaped around it, one can go inside and see the great hall of pillars and the inner sanctuary of the gods. After we've done that we'll return and we'll get the *reis* to make ready to sail as soon as we set foot on the boat. I understand it will take us a long time to travel north, even if we don't stop along the way. The wind is likely to be against us much of the time but at least we shall have the current in our favour.' He smiled at Louisa. 'My dear, you are looking very serious. Does my plan not please you?'

Louisa shook her head. 'I am sorry,' she blurted out. 'I imagined I would have time to paint this afternoon. I had no idea you would want to come with us.'

He frowned. 'Can you not make quick sketches, my dear? You have done so in the past. Then you will have as much time as you need to paint on board on our way back down the river.'

'I know that John will want to come back to me very soon, Louisa,' Augusta commented. She raised an eyebrow. 'Should you wish to stay longer on the shore I am sure that would be possible. Even if the *Ibis* sets off downriver I feel certain you would have no trouble catching us up. These little feluccas seem to travel so much faster on the light winds than does a larger boat. You may have your few extra hours with –' She hesitated. 'With your paintbrush and your muse.'

Louisa glanced at her gratefully but Augusta was not looking at her. She had seated herself on a chair near the open door and was fanning herself vigorously.

They spent an hour inside the temple looking at the carvings and peering over the piles of sand towards its as yet unexcavated corners, then Hassan rowed Sir John back to the *Ibis*, leaving Louisa alone sketching the four great heads of Rameses, peering from their sandy pall. When Hassan returned he was alone, carrying a bag over his shoulder. 'I have permission to escort you wherever you wish as long as we join the boat by dusk. They will be leaving soon, but the wind, all that there is, is against them. We shall catch them easily.' He smiled. Then he held out his hand. 'Come. Pack up your painting. I want to show you the hills behind the temple.'

They soon lost sight of the river and the other boats moored along its bank. Here, in the fierce heat they were totally alone. Hassan smiled at her. 'I was talking to a dragoman from another dahabeeya. He told me of a secret entrance into the hill on the far side of the temple where we can find shelter from the sun and be alone.'

She stopped. They were both panting, and she could feel her skin sticky from the cooking heat. 'This may be the last time.'

He shook his head. 'No, there will be others. They cannot keep you a prisoner on the boat. When it is becalmed, then you and I can go on excursions once more.'

'But there is no chance to be alone at the temple sites.'

'There is always a chance, my Louisa. Always. We will make a chance.' He smiled at her and reached for her hand.

They found the dark entrance in the sandstone cliff without difficulty and stood peering in. 'It's like the Valley of the Tombs,' Louisa whispered. The sandy hills behind them were empty, save for a lone vulture circling high over-head.

He grinned at her and held out his hand. 'Shall we explore?'

They stepped into the shadows and Hassan dropped their belongings. He rummaged in the bag for a candle. 'Do you want to see inside?'

She frowned uneasily and shook her head. 'We don't need to go any further in, do we? Let us stay here, near the light.'

He laughed. 'Don't tell me that my Louisa has had enough of the dark?'

She nodded. 'Just for now. Let's spread out the rug and sit down here. No one will see us unless they come right up to the rockface and there is no one for miles.'

He shrugged and did as she bid, laying out the rug and reaching for the bag which contained fruit juice and water and leather travelling cups. Then he frowned. 'What is this, my Louisa?'

'The scent bottle. I didn't know where to hide it. Even your place on the boat seemed too obvious and I could not get near it without being seen.'

Hassan shuddered. 'It is accursed three times over, my Louisa. You should not touch it any more.'

'I know.' The little bottle was wrapped in silk, tied with a length of ribbon. She stared down at it as it lay in the palm of his hand. 'So small a thing to have caused so much trouble.'

Behind them, in the darkness something stirred. Neither noticed. They were both looking down at the small beribboned parcel. 'It was your present to me,' Louisa said with a shake of her head. 'Right at the beginning.'

He nodded. 'I loved you, my Louisa, the first moment I saw you. But you were an English lady and I a lowly guide.'

'Not lowly, Hassan. Why lowly?'

He shrugged. 'That is the way your people see mine, my Louisa.' He smiled. 'And perhaps, if we are honest, the way my people see yours. *Inshallah*!'

The shadows in the cave were very dark. Behind them a passage led out of sight, deep into the heart of the hill.

'Whatever our peoples feel, you were my friend and now you are my love.' She moved towards him and their lips touched. Slowly they sank down onto the rug. With eyes only for each other they did not see the sinuous movement on the rock-strewn sandy floor of the cave, nor hear the dry rustle of scales.

The snake was young, perhaps only four feet long and capable of great speed. Ignoring Louisa it went for the man who still held the scent bottle in his hand.

As he felt the sudden agonising pain of the venom-filled fangs Hassan leapt to his feet and spun round. The scent bottle flew into the air and rolled to the edge of the rug. For a moment he stared down at the wound on his arm near his shoulder then he let out a cry of anguish, his face contorted with pain and grief as he stared at Louisa.

'Hassan!' She had seen the snake for only a second. Already it had slithered away out of sight amongst the rocks. 'Hassan, what shall I do?' She clung to him. 'Tell me quickly! What shall I do?'

His face had gone grey. A sheen of clammy sweat broke out on his skin. He was staring at her, his expression suddenly concentrated, his eyes fixed on hers as he gasped for breath, clutching at his chest.

'Louisa! My Louisa!' The words were slurred as the muscles at the side of his mouth tightened and froze. He slumped to his knees and then he doubled over. Around his mouth the skin was turning blue as he toppled sideways onto the floor of the cave.

'Hassan!' She stared down at him in disbelief. 'Hassan, speak to me!' She touched his shoulder lightly with one finger, hardly daring to breathe. 'Hassan, my love. Speak to me . . .' Her voice trailed away into silence, as she knelt beside him. He was gasping for breath, as he collapsed back onto the rug where he lay, unable to move. A slow paralysis seemed to be creeping over him as he looked up at her through dimming eyes, then between one anguished breath and the next his heart stopped beating.

'Hassan!' Her whispered cry of agony was so quiet it barely stirred the hot shadows of the cave.

She didn't know how long she sat there with his body. The sun moved round so it no longer shone into the mouth of the cave. The heat remained intense. She cried a little, then she sat, staring into space. She had no fear the snake would return. The servant of the gods had done its work and vanished back to the kingdoms from which it came.

At last she moved. She bent and kissed the poor tortured features and the wound which was already going black and rotten, then she folded the rug over his face and whispered a quiet prayer. Climbing stiffly to her feet she stood for a moment, overwhelmed by grief, before she turned away and staggered out into the pitiless sunlight.

She barely remembered the walk back through the hills to the front of the great temple, or her tearful plea to the other visitors she saw there and to the tall blue-robed dragoman from another yacht who took charge, sending men for Hassan's body, calling for a boat to take her to the *Ibis*, summoning women from the village to weep and cry for the man they did not know. She would not be allowed to see him again, to attend his funeral which would be before dark, to know even the place of his grave.

She was dimly aware of Augusta's arms around her, of Jane Treece helping her off with her dusty, stained dress and of lying in her darkened cabin. She heard the anchor being pulled up, the creak of the rigging, and the gentle slap of the river water, then lulled by a drink heavily laced with Augusta's laudanum she slept at last.

Anna stared at Serena. Both women had tears in their eyes. 'Poor Louisa. She loved him so much!' Anna was clutching the diary to her chest.

'Do you think the Forresters knew they were lovers?' Serena reached for her can of juice, then pushed it away untouched.

Anna shrugged. 'I get the feeling that Augusta guessed. I don't suppose it crossed Sir John's mind that such a thing could happen. If only they hadn't gone off alone. If only she had drawn the temple from the boat!'

They sat for a moment, lost in thought, then Serena turned back to her. 'I think we'd better go on looking for Andy, don't you?'

Anna nodded. Then she shook her head violently. 'I want this all to be a legend!' she cried suddenly. 'A story! I don't want it to have been true.'

'It is true. And Hassan died somewhere out there.' Serena nodded towards the shining blue waters of the lake. 'Those low hills around the temple site are all drowned now under that great inland sea. His grave, wherever it was, has gone.'

A shadow fell over them for a moment and they looked up. Toby and Omar were standing looking down at them.

312

'Are you all right?' Toby touched Anna's shoulder gently. He had seen the tears in her eyes.

'We were reading about Hassan's death,' Serena replied for her.

Toby sighed. 'So, the bastard killed him, did he? Poor Hassan. I've told Omar why we feel we have to find Andy urgently.' He glanced at the other man. 'He's prepared to give history the benefit of the doubt even though he doesn't believe it himself, isn't that right?'

Omar nodded. 'It is only necessary to believe one is cursed for the curse to begin to work its way in one's head,' he said. 'I have told Toby that I think Andy has gone round to see the back of the temple. One can walk in to see how the artificial hill was constructed. It is very interesting. I show you?'

They followed him back towards the great temple statues where the crowds were as thick as ever. Beside them a small entrance led into the face of the cliff. Omar gestured towards it. 'If you go in here I think you will find him. I will search elsewhere in case he changed his mind and went somewhere else. I will follow you soon.' He bowed and disappeared back into the crowd.

'He doesn't believe there's any danger, does he?' Anna was following Toby towards the entrance.

He shook his head. 'Of course he doesn't. He thinks we're mad. He says there are no snakes here. They are shy creatures. No way would they come to a place like this, that's crawling with humanity. But he's a good tour guide. He's prepared to indulge us. And he doesn't want any of us to be unhappy so he'll do his best and that's all that matters.'

They plunged out of the sunlight into darkness as they found themselves penetrating the huge hollow area beneath the artificial hill which had been constructed to hold the reassembled temple. Anna gazed round at the vast dome over their heads, for a moment too astonished by this strange juxtaposition of space age technology with the ancient temple thousands of years old which had been slotted into its heart to do anything other than stand and stare.

As they climbed the stairs their eyes grew used to the dimmer light after the bright sunlight outside. Here too there were crowds of people, displays, a soft-drink stall and at the top of the stairs a huge walkway. 'We're not going to find him.' Anna was staring round frantically. 'I can see faces in here, but there are too many.'

'We'll find him.' Serena was emphatic. 'I promise you we will.'

313

Toby was in front of them, narrowing his eyes as he peered round the viewing platforms. He shook his head. 'I don't think he's here, you know. He's probably ducked out again. Omar says they're all due to meet anyway in about an hour to get back on the coach.'

'It'll happen here. In Abu Simbel. I know it will.' Anna was frantic suddenly. 'We've got to find him.' She turned and began to push her way back towards the entrance. 'We've got to find him. We've got to! Andy!' Her cry was lost in the huge spaces around them.

'Let her go!' Toby called to Serena. 'I don't think he's here, but we'd better be systematic.'

But Serena had already turned to follow Anna. He stayed where he was, frowning. Then he turned to scan the faces of the crowds once again.

Anna was pushing her way out of the entrance, staring more and more anxiously around her. She could not rid herself of the image of Hassan lying on the ground, his body contorted by the swift passage of the venom; the cobra, if cobra it was, sliding silently towards the lovers as they kissed in the shadow of the cave; the desperation and sorrow of Louisa as she walked away from the body of her love, never to set eyes on him again.

However angry she was with Andy she would not wish that on him. Her anger itself was serving to make her feel guilty. If anything happened to him it would be because he had taken her bottle; if she had not brought it to Egypt, if she had not talked about it, if she had not shown him the diary, let him read the extracts, if she had not in some way led him on he would not be in this position now.

She turned blindly towards the one place she hadn't looked – the smaller temple which Rameses had built for his wife, Nefertari. It was far less crowded than the great Sun Temple itself.

A frieze guarded the door to the temple. A frieze of cobras. Anna stopped and stared. There was a lump in her throat. For a moment she hesitated, trying to steady herself, then she plunged into the darkness beyond the square entrance.

As her eyes grew accustomed to the dim lighting inside, the first person she saw was Andy standing studying one of the pillar capitals, at the near end of the *pronaos*. She stared at him, unable to believe her eyes, then almost hesitantly she walked up to him and

314

touched his arm. Serena, some ten paces behind her, stopped and watched.

'Andy?'

He jumped. 'Anna! What are you doing here? You weren't on the bus!'

She shook her head. 'I wasn't feeling well. I came on later with Toby in a taxi.' Suddenly she wasn't sure what to say. She realised that Serena had stepped up beside her and she glanced at her helplessly. 'I need the scent bottle, Andy,' she burst out at last. 'You must give it back to me. Now.'

He inclined his head slightly. 'What scent bottle?'

'Oh please, Andy. Don't play games with me.' She held out her hand.

He shrugged. His face was cold. 'I put it somewhere safe. On the boat. You don't think I brought it with me, do you?'

She was overwhelmed with a feeling of relief. 'Where on the boat did you leave it?'

'I gave it to Omar to put somewhere safe.'

She shook her head. 'Well, it's not in the boat's safe. I looked.'

His eyes narrowed and she saw the angle of his jaw harden. 'Did you indeed? So, you stayed behind to snoop.'

'Andy, I had to.' She couldn't believe she was trying to justify herself to him. 'You had taken two things that belonged to me. Two things you had no right to.' She held his gaze resolutely. 'I found the diary.' She paused.

His expression did not change.

'That was in the safe, in an envelope under your name, but the bottle wasn't there and I want it back.'

'OK. So I didn't leave it in the safe.'

'So, where is it?'

'Somewhere else. In my cabin. It's perfectly all right.'

'It's not in your cabin. I looked there too.'

His face darkened. 'You had no right to do that.'

'You had no right to steal my belongings.' She took a step forward and was surprised that he stepped back defensively. 'It was *stealing*, Andy.' She pressed home her advantage. 'I asked you if you had my diary and you denied it. It is worth a great deal of money, as you yourself pointed out.'

'Hang on a minute!' he interrupted. 'I took it to make sure it was safe. I wasn't going to keep it. You be careful about your

315

accusations.' A patch of red had appeared above each cheekbone.

'Then you should have told me what you had done with it and not accused Toby.' She could feel her own anger rising to match his.

'Ah, Toby! The hero of the taxi trip across the desert!' He folded his arms. 'Well, I was right about him!'

There was a moment's silence. A group of Italian tourists filed past them and disappeared into the depths of the temple. There was a flood of excited conversation and a howl of laughter as they made their way into the depths of the great hall and stopped, clustered round a far pillar.

'What Toby did is in the past. He paid for it.'

'Oh, he paid for it, did he, Anna? Is that what he told you?' Andy glanced at Serena. 'Well, he doesn't seem to have learnt from his past. As you were not there, on the bus, I sat next to a chap called Donald Denton. He's a retired doctor who used to live near Toby. He remembered the whole story. Toby killed a man who he claimed in court had raped his wife, but in fact the wife and this chap were having an affair and she was about to run away with him! And Toby murdered his wife as well.' His face softened. 'I'm sorry, Anna. I know how disappointed you'll be –'

'It's not true! She committed suicide.'

'Is that what he told you?'

'He told me all about it, yes.'

'And you believed him, of course.' He sighed. 'I don't suppose I can change your mind then.' He pushed his hands into his pockets and stared up at the great cow-head of the goddess Hathor above their heads. 'You really like him, don't you?' He glanced at Serena. 'And I suppose you do too? I can never understand women!' He grinned. He had relaxed, obviously confident that the diary and bottle were forgotten.

'Why don't you speak to Toby yourself? He's here somewhere.' Anna gestured towards the doorway. 'I'd like to hear what he has to say about your accusations.'

'Oh no! You're not setting us up for another sparring match, sweetheart.' He looked at his watch suddenly. 'Anyway, the coach is leaving before long. I suspect it's time we were heading in that direction.' He strode past her towards the entrance.

Anna looked towards Serena. 'I don't think he has got the bottle with him. After all that, he was safe!'

Serena nodded. 'So, Andy lives to fight another day,' she said succinctly. 'And in more ways than one.'

Anna shrugged. 'I don't believe him. Not about Toby.'

'Good. He's a complete, congenital liar.' Serena tucked her hand through Anna's arm. 'Come on. Come back with us on the bus.'

Anna hesitated. 'We came in a car. Toby told the driver to wait.'

Serena wrinkled her nose. 'How very rich this ex-con must be!'

'I don't think so.' It was Anna's turn to colour. 'He did it for me. He cares, Serena. You saw how much he cares.'

They emerged from the temple and looked round. There was no sign of Andy.

Omar was standing some fifty yards away, a cluster of people around him. He saw them emerge into the sunlight and he raised his hand to beckon them over. 'We must go soon, people. The bus is waiting.' He grinned at Anna. 'I saw Andy. He says you found him.'

Anna nodded. 'I did indeed.'

'And there was no cobra?'

She shook her head.

'Jolly good!' Omar smiled even more widely. 'Now please, we collect everyone and go.'

Anna was looking round. 'Serena? Where did Toby go?'

'He stayed in the hill when we left to look in Nefertari's temple.' Serena gave a small grimace. 'I'm sure he will find us.'

'I don't know what to do. He'll expect me to go back with him. I'll have to find the car.'

'Well, that won't be a problem. Presumably it will be in the car park, near the bus.' Serena sighed. 'OK, we'll find it and then you'll have to choose. Anna, I like Toby too. I trust him and I would never trust Andy, but be careful. When all is said and done we don't know anything about him do we, any more than we really know anything about each other.'

The two women looked at one another for a moment; Anna grinned and with a helpless shrug she turned to follow Omar.

Andy met them in the car park. He was smiling broadly. 'Well, you'll never guess what's been happening here!'

Anna frowned. He was looking at her. Almost, she suspected, he was gloating. Her heart sank without knowing why. 'So? What's been happening?'

'Your friend, Toby. The police came. They've taken him away,

317

and your car has gone. I'm afraid you'll have to make do with the hoi polloi on the bus.' He gave a small bow.

'Toby's been arrested!' Anna echoed. She stared at him. 'You're lying!'

'You wish! No, I'm not lying.' He stopped and his face sobered. 'Oh dear, I can see it's been a shock. He had you fooled, didn't he? He had us all fooled. The painting he was doing must have been a cover for something. To make him look respectable.'

'But what's he supposed to have done? I don't understand. Has he left me a message?'

Andy shrugged. 'No doubt we'll hear all about it soon enough!'

Serena touched Anna's arm. 'Let's get on the bus,' she said softly. 'There's nothing you can do here.'

Andy was watching Anna's face intently. 'Don't think about him any more, Anna. Just be thankful you didn't get wound into his net.' He lifted a hand in greeting as he saw Joe approaching and turning, climbed into the bus past Omar who was standing by the door counting heads.

Anna sat with Serena at the back, too shocked and miserable to speak as the doors shut and the coach swung out of the car park and back onto the dusty road. In minutes they were out of the shabby breeze-block town of Abu Simbel and into the desert, insulated from the broiling desert heat by air conditioning and window blinds and the gentle crooning of an Egyptian singer on the bus stereo.

Twice they stopped on the way back. Once to see a particularly spectacular mirage which everyone but Anna, who was without her camera, duly photographed, gasping in the dry oven-heat of the early afternoon, and once to see a camel train coming in off the desert. She stayed in the coach this time, watching the poor creatures being loaded onto lorries and beaten to their knees beneath the heavy rope nets which would hold them in place, wondering bleakly whether the few shots of the young blades cavorting round on their racing camels really made up for the despair in the eyes of those proud creatures on their way to the meat markets in Aswan.

'You OK?' Serena climbed back into the bus and lowered herself into the seat beside her.

She nodded. 'I think I've had enough of Egypt. As a holiday meant to cheer me up and restore my sense of self-worth and security it has failed totally.'

Serena sat back, staring up at the ceiling. 'Toby means a great deal to you, doesn't he?'

'Yes.'

'I'm so sorry. Andy's a bastard. I bet he's got the whole thing wrong. I'm going to double-check everything he's told you.'

Behind her sunglasses there were tears in Anna's eyes. 'I don't understand any of it.' She gave a deep sigh. 'But there must be something we can do to help him.'

It was like coming home. The crew with their friendly smiles were all back after their two-day break, with scented towels to wipe away the heat and dust of the desert and warm freshly made lemonade.

Standing in the crowded reception area sipping her drink before making her way to her cabin, Anna was suddenly confronted by Andy. He came up to her and put his hands lightly on her shoulders.

'Anna, I am truly so very sorry. It was crass, the way I broke the news to you. And will you forgive me for taking the diary? I never meant you to be worried. It was thoughtless beyond belief. Meet me in the bar when you're freshened up and we'll have a drink. Please.' His eyes on hers were sincere and very kind.

'Andy, I'm so tired. I just want to rest . . .'

'And so you shall. After the meal. We're having a late lunch, then we can rest so that after dark we're restored enough to go to Philac to see the son-et-lumière. Please, Anna. I want us to stay friends.' He paused and grinned enquiringly at Omar who had stopped beside them.

'Your bag, Andy. You left it on the bus.' Omar slapped him on the back. 'Luckily the driver spotted it.' He handed over the bag and moved on, searching for the owner of some other piece of left luggage.

Andy automatically swung the bag onto his shoulder. 'Say in half an hour? In the bar?' he said to Anna. 'Please.'

She was looking at the bag. As he had lifted it up the side pocket had gaped open and she had spotted the flash of scarlet silk. Banging down her lemonade glass on the reception desk counter she reached out and caught at the broad canvas strap as it hung over his shoulder, pulling the bag towards her.

'Strange, this scarf looks so much like mine.' Before he could move back she had pulled the small bundle out of the pocket and unrolled it in her hand to reveal the scent bottle. 'You had it with you all the time?' She spat the words at him. 'You had the bottle on the bus! Don't you realise what that could have meant? Why did you lie, Andy?' She shook the bottle under his nose. 'Why do men always have to lie?'

13

My place of hiding is opened, my place of hiding
is revealed.

*There is a trade in all things old. People come from far away
and buy anything and everything from the days of the tombs.
The bottle travels in a box of shards and beads and amulets
across the waters of the Nile and is taken to a merchant in
Luxor. Coins change hands.*

*For months the box lies untouched in a store room; when it is
unpacked the merchant picks out the bottle at once. He had not
noticed it before and now he feels a catch of excitement in his
throat. Early New Kingdom glass is rare. He brings it to his
work table and picks up his magnifying glass.*

*The stopper is wedged in tightly and sealed. He finds a knife
to uncork it, hesitates and changes his mind. Instead he sends
a message to a friend. His house has grown cold; the air flickers
with desert lightning and an unearthly shimmer runs across
the shelves and over the table.*

*The newcomer, head and shoulders wrapped in a white
shawl, touches breast, mouth and forehead in greeting and
comes forward to the table. He is venerable and learned and*

has studied the magical arts. He stands in silence looking down at the small glass container.

The silence lengthens. Outside, the sun moves across the sky and gains entrance at the latticed windows, throwing fretted shadows on the floor.

The man looks up, his face white.

'There is power in this sacred vial. Power beyond measure. And it is guarded by priests of old who have never left it.' He shakes his head. 'Bring me paper and ink that I may write their wishes down. Those who have touched this object with sacrilegious hands have paid the price with their life's blood.'

Anna was sitting on the bed in her cabin when Serena knocked and pushed open the door. 'You OK?'

Anna nodded. The bottle was lying beside her on the covers.

'I've spoken to Omar.' Serena sat down and picking it up she turned it gently over and over in her hands. 'He was a bit taken aback by your outburst just now and I sort of tried to explain.' She shrugged. 'He doesn't know anything about Toby being arrested. He was astonished when I told him. He spoke to the captain immediately because he had been in charge of the boat while Omar was away and he said no one had come asking for Toby. And Toby's passport is still in the safe.'

'What does that mean?'

Serena raised an eyebrow. 'It means there's a strong possibility Andy's lying, as I suspected.' She held out the bottle. 'It's strange that Louisa kept this after Hassan died. I'd have thought she'd want to get rid of it.'

Anna shook her head. She picked up the bottle and stroked it gently with her little finger. 'It's so small and it's brought so much unhappiness. She kept it, I suppose because Hassan gave it to her. I wonder if she saw Carstairs again?'

Serena gestured towards Anna's bag. 'I think I'm as hooked on this story as you are. Haven't we got time to read a little before our meal?' she asked hopefully. 'And it would take your mind off Toby . . .'

Sir John knocked on Louisa's cabin door and pushed it open. 'How are you feeling, my dear?' She was lying on the divan, wrapped in a silk bed-robe. Her head was aching and her skin as hot as fire. 'Can we not persuade you to eat a little? Mohammed is concocting more and more wonderful titbits for you.' He was looking at the untouched plate beside her.

She turned towards him and forced a tired smile. 'I'm sorry. I'm not hungry.'

'No. Well, I'll tell him to keep trying.' He nodded. 'A party of Nubians came to the boat this morning, Louisa. They brought your paints; the things which were left in the cave.' He looked down at his feet suddenly. 'They are very honest, these people. I rewarded them well.' He glanced back at her. 'I thought you'd want your things.' He went to the door and fumbled outside for a moment, turning back with her woven bag. 'Shall I leave it here?' He waited for an indication of what she wanted. When she gave no sign, he shrugged and placed the bag against the wall, under the small table.

Some time later he left, closing the door quietly behind him. When he returned it was dark. They had moored above the cataract near Philae. Outside the river was bright with moonlight.

'Louisa, Lord Carstairs is in the saloon. I understand he came up to Aswan on the steamer. Are you well enough to receive him?'

She sat up slowly, pushing her hair out of her eyes. 'He's here? On this boat? I thought you had forbidden him to set foot on it!'

Sir John shrugged uncomfortably. 'He heard what happened. He wants to see you.'

For a moment she sat still, as if gathering her strength, then she pulled herself to her feet. 'I'll see him in the saloon.'

'Shall I call Treece to help you dress, my dear?'

'No, there's no need.' She pushed past him. 'What I have to say to Roger Carstairs requires no formal dressing.'

He was sitting in the saloon sipping sherbet with Augusta when Louisa burst in. They both turned to face her and she saw Carstairs' eyes widen. In her deep-blue robe with her hair wild, her face white and tear-stained she must have looked strange indeed.

'Please leave us, Augusta!' Her request was so peremptory Augusta rose to her feet without comment and disappeared out on deck. The saloon was silent.

Louisa stood in front of Carstairs, her eyes fixed on his face. 'So, my lord, are you content?'

He eyed her coldly. 'What happened is unfortunate. You had the means to prevent it.'

'So it was my fault?' Her voice was very quiet.

'Indeed it was.' He folded his arms. 'I do not permit people to cross me, madam. And now to prevent further tragedy I suggest you give me the sacred vial.'

'Never!' Her eyes blazed. 'You will never have it. All the gods of Egypt saw what you did, Roger Carstairs, and they revile you for it. The priest who guards that bottle, the priest of Isis despises you!' Her voice had risen at last to a wail.

Carstairs sneered. He had not stepped back an inch. 'Isis is no goddess of love. You misjudge her, my dear Louisa. She is goddess of magic and her servant, my servant, is the cobra.' He smiled. 'Where is the bottle?'

'I no longer have it. It is lost in the cave where Hassan died and there it will stay, buried in the sand and guarded by your snake!' She laughed suddenly, a quiet, bitter sound which gave him pause as nothing she had said before had done. 'If you search for it, I hope the snake of Isis kills you with all the certainty of purpose with which it killed Hassan!'

He unfolded his arms and gave a quick bow. 'It had not occurred to me that you would leave it at Abu Simbel. I trust for your sake that it is safe!'

He made for the door but she was standing in his way. 'Don't ever set foot on this boat again. Not ever. The Forresters support me in this; and don't show your face anywhere decent people go.

324

I shall spread word of your evil. In Luxor. In Cairo. In Alexandria. In Paris. In London. I shall make sure that the name of Carstairs is reviled throughout the world!'

For a moment he frowned, taken aback by the force of her words, then he smiled. 'No one will believe you.'

'Oh, they will. I'll make sure of it.' She turned and moved away from him, and stood still, her back to him. For a moment he hesitated, then she heard him leave the saloon, ducking out on deck into the sunshine. In the silence that followed she heard Augusta's voice carrying clearly across the deck. She had obviously heard every word Louisa had said. 'Please don't come back, my lord. Louisa is right. You are no longer welcome in decent society!'

He did not reply. She walked to the door of the saloon and she was in time to see him jumping down into the sandal in which one of his Nubian servants had rowed him to the *Ibis*. His own boat was moored on the far side of the river near the Fieldings'. She gave a wry smile. There was one family who would still make him welcome.

She walked out into the sunshine aware of the sympathetic glances from the *reis* and the other members of the crew. Augusta was standing looking across the river at the departing back of their visitor. 'Loathsome man!' she said.

Louisa nodded. She was grateful to Augusta for understanding; for at last giving her the benefit of the doubt. The story she had told her was after all beyond all normal credibility.

'Sir John will support us in forbidding him aboard the boat,' Augusta said softly.

'Thank you.'

Augusta glanced at her. 'He has gone across to see David Fielding. I have no doubt he will let our feelings be known.'

'They like him.'

'They like his title, my dear. When they poke the toes of their shoes beneath it and find the loathsome creature who hides there I feel sure they will agree with us.' She screwed up her eyes against the glare. 'Look! He's changed his mind; he's going directly to his own boat and they are already making sail.'

Louisa smiled. 'He is going back to scrabble in the sands at Abu Simbel, to look for the scent bottle which I left there.'

Augusta raised an eyebrow. 'Ridiculous man! He really believes in all this magic, doesn't he!'

'Oh yes.' Louisa nodded sadly. 'He really believes in it.'

She turned away and walked slowly back towards her cabin. Picking up her hairbrush she was brushing out her long tangled hair when her eye fell on the woven bag lying on the floor under the table where Sir John had left it. She paused, and frowning she put down her brush. Stooping, she picked up the bag and tipped it up over the bed, taking the corners and shaking it so that a cascade of pencils and sketchpads fell onto the bedcovers. There was her small painbox, the water pot and water bottle, though why she had taken them with her to a spot where the paints dried on the tip of her brush before she could bring it to the paper she wasn't sure. There was a packet of charcoal strips for sketching, wrapped in tissue, an indiarubber, a small knife for sharpening her pencils and, under it all, the silk-wrapped bundle tied with ribbon which was the scent bottle of the priests. She picked it up and held it in her hands for a few long moments, then quietly she began to cry.

'So, that's how it came back.' Serena shook her head. 'And Carstairs had already sailed. He was reviled, of course. His name is still known for his carryings on. I don't think he ever went back to England.'

'And he never got the sacred bottle.' Anna was staring at it. 'I think I should throw it into the Nile.'

Serena grimaced. 'No! No, don't do that. I want to do another ritual. To talk to the priests.' She stood up and went to stand at the window, staring out across the river. 'The bottle belonged to them, Anna. Or at least to one of them. Until this is all resolved they can't rest. We have to find out what they want us to do. Please, let me have one more go.'

'And the snake?'

'The snake will not harm us.'

'How do you know? How do we know Carstairs wasn't so furious he gave it orders to kill anyone who went near it?'

'We don't. But on the evidence we've got it looks as though he didn't. After all, no one else has died. Can we do it, Anna? After lunch, while people are having a siesta. Can we call up the priests again? I want to talk to Anhotep.'

Anna's mouth fell open. 'I thought we were going to wait until tonight, on Philae.' She shivered.

Serena nodded. 'I was, but there is no reason to wait. Please, Anna. It almost worked last time. And I have a feeling it will now.' She nodded excitedly. 'But first we must find out about Charley. Can we ask Omar to see what's happened to her?'

Omar called the hotel on his mobile phone. He listened and nodded, spoke rapidly and at last cut the connection. 'She is coming back to the boat. They say she is rested and fine and they are putting her in a taxi.' He glanced at them. 'They said the bill has been paid by Toby Hayward, and he was there this afternoon.'

'He was there?' Anna looked at him, stunned. 'He was at the Old Cataract Hotel?'

Omar nodded.

'And he saw Charley?'

'He spoke to her and settled all her expenses.'

'Then where is he?'

Omar shrugged.

Two minutes later Anna and Serena were outside Toby's cabin. Anna knocked. There was no answer so she reached for the handle. The door swung open and they peered in. The cabin looked totally normal, if tidier than when Anna had last seen it. The pictures, the paints were neatly organised, the luggage still there.

Serena stepped into the cabin behind her. 'He hasn't moved out then.'

'Why should he have? Where would he have gone? We were planning to come back together.' Anna bit her lip miserably. 'If he was at the hotel, then he can't have been under arrest.' She stared round her at the dressing table, the neatly made bed, the rails in the bathroom with their fresh white towels. 'Omar said his passport was still here,' she said wistfully, sitting down on the bed.

'Perhaps Charley will know where he is,' Serena suggested.

There was a sound outside in the corridor and they both looked up as Andy appeared at the open door. He stared round. 'Lunch-time, ladies.'

'I don't suppose you've heard where Toby is, have you?' Anna

327

tried to restrain the hostility she could feel welling up inside her.

He shook his head. 'Presumably the police still have him.'

'He's not under arrest, Andy, he is in Aswan. Or at least he was a little while ago.'

Andy looked taken aback for a moment, then he rapidly recovered. He shifted from one foot to another. 'It's all beyond me. Why don't we have lunch and stop fussing about Toby Hayward?' He walked off briskly towards the dining room.

The meal was subdued and Ibrahim and Ali, as though sensing everyone's exhaustion after their long drive through the desert served it with the minimum of delay. Only some forty minutes later Anna and Serena, after surreptitiously making sure that Andy had retired with much yawning and stretching to his own cabin, made their way to Anna's on the deck above.

The preparations were much quicker this time. Anna pinned the shawl over the window shutters whilst Serena laid out her altar. The candles, incense, statuette were all put in place, then Anna reached for the scent bottle, unwrapped it, and laid it reverently next to Serena's sistrum.

'Ready?' she breathed. Her hands were shaking.

Serena nodded. She reached into her bag for a box of matches and lit first the small incense cone and then the candles.

Behind her Anna retreated once more to the bed and drawing her legs up under her sat as far away from Serena as she could in the cramped space of the small cabin, watching breathlessly as Serena glanced at her. 'Whatever happens, don't try to interfere. Don't try to stop it and don't wake me if I go into a trance. It could be dangerous for me. Just keep yourself safe and watch.'

As the first low chanting began to fill the room, rising and falling to the accompaniment of the rattle of the sistrum Anna felt the atmosphere tighten perceptibly. Her eyes were fixed on the bottle. A pale wavering light was falling on it from the candles, interlaced in flickering, intersecting arcs. From the incense a spiral of smoke rose towards the ceiling, curling lazily upwards and dispersing in the gloom. The bottle sat before the statue of Isis, its bright colours muted and iridescent in the candlelight. As the reflection of the flame played on the glass it looked as though whatever was inside the bottle moved.

Anna clenched her fists. She could feel perspiration running down her temples and between her breasts. Serena's voice was growing stronger, either she was less self-conscious now or she had forgotten Anna completely and had lost herself in the phrases of her invocation. When she stopped the cabin seemed to echo for a moment with the words of power then the candleflames began to stream sideways as though in a strong draught. Anna swallowed. She brought her hand to her breast and fumbling for the amulet, clutched it tightly between her fingers.

She could see him – the tall figure – so transparent he was barely more than a shimmer in the air near the window.

Serena flung back her head and rattled the sistrum in front of her. 'Come! Oh Anhotep, servant of Isis, come! Show yourself before me and before this vial of sacred tears!'

He was easier to see now, his features more distinct, the outline of his shape clear in the shadows of the candlelight.

Serena, her hands on the altar, dropped to her knees. Her head back, her eyes closed she gave the sistrum a final rattle and laid it down. Anhotep was suddenly closer to her. He was towering over her. His body, a transparent shadow, was so close he was touching her, and slowly as she stood up their two outlined shapes seemed to coalesce and become one.

She convulsed forward shaking, then slowly she straightened again and opened her eyes. 'Greetings.' Her voice was completely unlike anything Anna had heard before. Deep and bell-like it contained the echoes of three thousand desert suns. 'I am Anhotep, servant of the servants of the gods. I come to take possession of that which is mine.'

Anna's mouth had gone dry. Terrified, she stared at the figure before her as slowly she realised that she was alone in the room with him. The body that was Serena's was somehow inert, vacant. It was as though Serena herself had stood aside and lent him the flesh, the muscles, the organs he needed to function once more on the earth.

She cleared her throat nervously and was alarmed to see that the figure standing before the altar had clearly heard her. The face turned towards hers.

'Who approaches the altar of the goddess?' The words seemed to fill the air around her.

'I am Anna.' She forced herself to speak out loud. 'It is I who brought the sacred vial back to Egypt. I . . . we need to know what you want done with it?'

329

She could see a hand stretching out in the candlelight. It hovered over the little bottle and Anna noticed with a shudder that as it passed between the bottle and the candleflame it cast no shadow though it was Serena's hand.

When the cabin door flew open, for a moment nothing changed. The light flooding in from the corridor missed the altar and the figure standing before it, and the shadows for a moment grew darker.

'Help me!' Charley's voice was unmistakable. 'Help me! It's happening again. I don't know what to do –' She staggered slightly, then slowly she fell forwards into the cabin.

With a hiss of rage the figure at the altar turned. 'Hatsek!'

Charley scrambled unsteadily to her feet and stood where she was, shaking violently. Anna looked from one to the other, paralysed with fear.

Whatever happens don't try and interfere!

Serena's words seemed to hang in the air for a moment.

'Hatsek! I curse thee for thy vile betrayal!' As the words filled the cabin Anna became aware of a second figure in the doorway.

She dragged her eyes away from Charley and Serena and saw that it was Toby.

'Curse thee for the mothers thou hast caused to weep for their sons! Curse thee for the deceit and slaughter, curse thee for the evil words thou hast uttered!'

Charley took a step back then she seemed to rally. She drew herself to her full height. 'Thou wert ever a fool, Anhotep!' She moved forward and reached out towards the altar where the candles streamed sideways, dripping coloured wax. As her hand moved through the smoke of the incense towards the little bottle Anhotep let out a great cry of rage and lunged at her.

As the two women collided Charley let out a scream and flung herself back towards the door. Behind her Serena slumped to the floor.

The two priests were gone.

'Turn on the lights, Anna, for God's sake!' Toby had caught Charley by the wrists. She was struggling frantically as he pushed her back into the room and down onto the bed beside Anna.

Anna leapt to her feet and reaching for the shawl pulled it away from the windows, then she dragged open the shutters. 'Serena!'

She dropped to her knees beside the lifeless form lying huddled on the floor. 'Serena, are you all right?'

On the bed behind her Charley was sobbing hysterically. She grabbed at the bedcover and pulled it up over her head, rocking back and forth.

'Is Serena OK?' Toby snuffed the candles, then he sat down on the bed beside Charley and put his arm round her.

'She's breathing. She's unconscious. Oh God!'

'She'll be all right. Put a pillow under her head. Here.' He pulled one off the bed. 'Fetch some water for her to sip.'

'What's wrong with her?'

'Don't you know? You heard her. She's what they call a trance medium. A channeller. She allowed the priest to talk through her, but without allowing him to possess her. She was just a vehicle and she obviously knows how to protect herself. She must, if she's done rescue work. You've got to wait for her to come back. She'll be all right.'

'And Charley? What is she?' Anna looked up.

'The same perhaps. No, it didn't happen voluntarily. Perhaps she is possessed. Hatsck used her energy and now he's used her body as well. I shouldn't have brought her back to the boat.'

'No, you shouldn't!' Suddenly she was shaking with fright and anger. 'Where have you been? What happened to you? Why did you disappear like that? We needed you!'

He was gathering Charley into his arms, rocking her like a baby. 'Later, Anna. I'm sorry I had to leave you. I couldn't help it. I'll explain it all later. Let's get this mess sorted out first.'

There was a groan from Serena and Anna turned back to her. She caught her hand and stroked it gently. 'Serena? Can you speak to me? Are you all right?' She climbed to her feet and as Toby had suggested fetched a glass of water. With an effort she helped the other woman sit up and with her arm round her shoulders she held the glass to her lips.

'What happened?' Serena's voice was hoarse. She frowned and rubbed her eyes, moving her head from side to side.

At the sound of her voice Charley moaned and clung to Toby more tightly still.

'Did Anhotep come?' Serena grabbed the glass from Anna and began to gulp down the water.

'Yes. He came.'

331

'Did he say what he wanted done?'

'He didn't get the chance.'

Serena let the empty glass fall from her hands and allowed her head to hang down for a moment. Her skin was pale and damp, her eyes unfocused and strangely bloodshot. 'Why not?'

'Hatsek came.'

'How?' She didn't seem to have noticed the two other people in the room.

'Charley came in. He appeared to have taken her over. It was terrifying.'

At last Serena turned her head towards the bed. She registered the sight of Toby with Charley in his arms and frowned. 'You? You brought Charley back?'

He nodded. 'I am sorry. I chose a bad moment.'

'I thought you were supposed to be in prison.' Serena struggled to her feet. She stood for a moment swaying slightly, then she sat down stiffly on the stool in front of the dressing table.

Toby grimaced. 'Not lately, I'm glad to say.'

'Then where were you?'

'I was with a friend. I'll tell you the whole story, but not now. OK? Let's get all this sorted out. What do we do with Charley here?' He pushed her gently into a sitting position.

Charley raised a tear-stained face. 'I want to go home.'

'Then that's what you shall do.' Toby eased himself away from her and stood up. 'I've got a friend at the consulate in Cairo. I've already been on the phone to him once today. I'll get him to arrange a flight back and ask if there's someone to travel with her. Poor Charley. You'll be fine. Do you want to go back to the hotel for the night?'

Charley nodded. 'I liked the hotel.' She was rocking again.

'How in God's name did you get her in there?' Serena asked wearily. 'I thought the Old Cataract was booked up months in advance.'

Toby grinned. He tapped his nose. 'You worry about Ancient Egypt. Let me deal with the modern version.'

They watched as he guided Charley out of the cabin and up the corridor. Anna closed the door behind him and leant against it. In the bright cabin only the slight smell of incense hinted at the scene which had taken place there so short a time before.

Serena shrugged. 'So was that a success or another miss?'

Anna gave a wry shake of the head. 'I think it was a success. Maybe without Charley there it would have worked. He came. He was actually here in the cabin. He was in –' She hesitated suddenly. 'I was going to say inside you, but he wasn't. He kind of slipped over you like a glove.' She shuddered. 'Oh, Serena, are you sure this kind of thing is safe? Yes, he was communicating, but supposing you couldn't get rid of him?' She sat down suddenly, overwhelmed with exhaustion.

'I wasn't possessed, Anna.' Serena was folding the sistrum into its piece of silk. 'I was allowing him to use me.'

'Isn't that possession?'

'No. Possession is like rape. It is uninvited. A violation. A theft.'

'That's what happened to Charley?'

Serena bit her lip. 'I think that's what has happened to Charley, yes. Hatsek has been using her energy, sucking it like a leech. And he found it easy, when he needed to invade her personality, to walk straight in.'

'And is she free of him now?'

'I don't know.' Packing the last candle Serena turned away from her bag and went to stand in front of the dressing table mirror. She studied her face for a few moments. 'I really don't know. I ought to speak to her before she leaves, but will that make it worse?'

'Surely he won't go back to England with her?'

'I don't know that either. I just don't know anything at the moment.' The face Anna could see reflected in the mirror looked suddenly old. 'I feel dreadful about all this. If I hadn't interfered . . .'

'If you hadn't interfered I would probably have been carried off screaming to a mental hospital by now.'

Serena sat down on the stool. 'Some of the things Andy said about me are true, you know. I played at all this. It was fun. Romantic. Wild. It felt a bit wicked for me as an old woman – well, oldish.' She smiled. 'A widow, respectable, very, daughter of a clergyman for goodness sake.' She gave a mirthless laugh. 'Meditation. Prayers to Isis. Rituals by candlelight. Not in the nude or anything, but it was a secret. Something to gloat over. It wasn't real, but it led on to other things that were: the rescue work, being a trance medium, channelling. But the Egyptian stuff . . . that started as a game.'

'Until you came to Egypt.'

'Until I came to Egypt.'

'When you found out that it was all real, including your powers as some sort of a priestess.'

Serena chewed her lip for a moment. 'A priestess,' she echoed. 'It sounds so exotic. So powerful. I revelled in the idea of being a priestess of Isis.'

'Good.' Anna stood up. 'Because you are the only ace I've got.'

'So, what do you want to do?'

They looked at each other glumly, then Anna shrugged. 'Have you the strength to try again? We don't know for sure if Hatsek will follow Charley back to London. What if he follows you or me? What if the cobra comes too? Somehow my coming here has activated this whole, stupid charade. Do you know, when I was asleep in the car, driving across the desert, I dreamt that this whole thing was part of the holiday, laid on by the travel company to keep us amused on the boat – like a murder weekend at a hotel in the Cotswolds – and that the denouement will happen the night before we reach Luxor or at the Pasha's party they're giving for us, or, I don't know, perhaps it will happen at the airport before we fly home!'

'I wish it was a dream.' Serena shook her head. 'But it isn't and we have to do something. I suppose we should try again tonight. On Philae, as I originally planned. In Isis's temple.'

Anna's mouth dropped open. 'So soon?'

'Yes.' Serena nodded. 'It would be perfect. We're going to the sound and light show, right? It might be difficult, but we'll have to try to slip out of the audience into the dark areas while everyone is distracted. I'm sure there will be hundreds of people there, but they'll all be watching the show. We'll have to hope that no one notices us.'

'But Philae is like Abu Simbel. It's not the real place. It's been moved to higher ground.'

'I know. The sacred soil of Isis is under water now, but I don't think it matters. After all, the priests came here and they were at Abu Simbel. It would help me to focus if we were near the temple and of course, if they want you to give up your bottle to them, it would be the perfect place. You will part with it, Anna, if they demand it?'

'Of course I will.' Anna looked down at the little bottle, the only thing remaining on the small table that had served as an altar. She picked it up and turned it over in her hands. 'I wonder what would happen if it broke?'

Serena closed her eyes and shook her head. 'I don't think we want to know.' She stood up and picked up her bag. 'I'm going to go and have a sleep. I'm completely exhausted. I'll meet you later, OK?'

Anna nodded.

She stayed where she was for a long time after Serena had gone, then at last she lay down on the bed and closed her eyes.

Twenty minutes later she gave up trying to sleep. She reached for the diary and held it for a few minutes, thinking. The marker was nearly at the end now. There were only a few more pages left to read.

Louisa had dozed off at last. When she awoke she lay still, looking as she had so often at the darkened ceiling of her small cabin. The boat was silent, but she could smell cooking from the crew's quarters and from far away, somewhere on the shore in the distance she could hear the thin wail of a musical instrument, eerie above the faint rustle of the palms.

Moving her head slightly she could see her paints and sketchbooks piled on the table where Jane Treece had left them when she removed them from Louisa's bed. In front of them lay the small silk-wrapped parcel tied with ribbon. Louisa closed her eyes as a tear slid down her cheek.

The knock on the door was hesitant. For a moment she ignored it, then with a sigh she called out to come in. Augusta peered round it, a candle in her hand.

'Please join us for supper, Louisa. It would make the men so happy. The *reis* says Mohammed is distraught that you cannot be comforted. You will fall ill if you don't eat, my dear.'

Louisa sat up. Her head was swimming. Augusta was right. There was no point in starving herself to death. After all, she had to return to England, to her sons.

'Shall I ask Treece to come and help you dress?' Augusta stooped and picked up the blue bedrobe which had slipped to the floor.

Louisa nodded. 'Yes, I'd like that. Please. I'll come and join you.' She managed a watery smile as Augusta set down the candle and disappeared to summon Treece.

In the still, shadowy cabin Louisa sat motionless, her head in her hands. She could still hear the music, but it seemed further away now.

The deeply coloured woods of the cabin and the hangings which lined the walls were a rich mixture of colour and shade in the light of the single candleflame and as she looked up at last, the shadowy figure by the table was just that, a shadow, bending over the table, reaching out its hand.

'Hassan?' For a moment she was confused. She didn't react. It was several seconds before she leapt to her feet, flinging out her arms, but the figure had gone.

Behind her the door opened and Treece appeared, carrying a basin and a steaming jug of water. It smelt of attar of roses and Louisa could see the thin film of the rose oil floating on its surface.

Miserably she allowed Treece to sponge her face and hands, then her neck. She let her help her on with her dark-green loose gown and then gather up her hair into a knot on her neck. It was as she was leaving the cabin that she heard the other woman sniff in exasperation. She had pushed open the shutters and tossed the water out into the darkness. 'Such a fuss!' The words were deliberately loud enough for her to hear. 'And all for a native!'

Her anger carried her out through the saloon onto the deck where the others were waiting for her, sipping their drinks. It was as she took the proffered seat from Sir John that she turned and looked out across the river. It was broad just here, a wide sweep on a bend where the palm trees grew down to the water's edge on both sides, their fronds waving gracefully against the starlit sky. Against the far bank she could see two boats moored side by side. Even in the dark she recognised them.

The Fieldings' boat and that of Lord Carstairs were brightly lit with lamps and the music, she realised suddenly, was coming from a group of musicians on the deck of *The Scarab*.

She pushed past Sir John and walked over to the rail, staring

336

out across the water. He followed her. 'Ignore them, my dear. Come on, have a drink and then we'll eat together.'

'Are they having a party? A soirée?' Her hands closed over the rail, her knuckles white.

'Nothing like that, I'm sure. They've just asked a band of musicians to play for them. They have every right, Louisa –'

'They are on Roger Carstairs' boat!'

'Indeed they are.' He was uncomfortable. She saw him run his finger around the inside of his collar.

'But I thought he had sailed back to Abu Simbel!'

Sir John shook his head gloomily. 'Apparently not.'

'Why not?'

'My dear, I don't know why he should have wanted to go back there in the first place. His boat has accompanied ours all the way down the cataract and through Aswan. As has the Fieldings'.'

'I told him to go!' Her voice was deep and angry. 'I told him and he took no notice.'

'Louisa, he knows he will not be welcome on this boat. He has made no attempt to come on board. But I cannot prevent him from sailing near us!'

'No, but I can!' She swept round and ran forward towards the crew's quarters. 'Mohammed! Call the boy. I want the sandal now. I want to be taken across the river.'

'Louisa, no!' Sir John hurried after her.

'You cannot stop me!' She turned on him. 'Don't even try. I shall not require you to come with me. I just need the boy to row me over.'

Behind them the crew had all leapt to their feet from their seats around the brazier where the meal was being prepared. Mohammed stepped forward, his face a picture of concern. 'If the lady Louisa wishes to go on the river I shall row her myself.'

'Thank you, Mohammed. I should like that. I want to go now.'

Her face was as white as a sheet as she watched him pull the little dinghy alongside after she had fetched her shawl from her cabin. He held the small boat steady as she climbed in and spinning it expertly with an oar began to paddle across the dark water.

It was David Fielding who helped her up on deck. Behind him she could see Venetia and Katherine ensconced on huge silken cushions, sleepily watching the entertainment before them as they sipped their Persian tea. Roger Carstairs had been sitting near them.

As Louisa appeared he rose to his feet. He was dressed in a white turban and black robe, with around his waist a multi-coloured fringed sash from which hung his long curved hunting knife.

Katherine smiled and held out her arms in sympathetic welcome but Louisa did not see the gesture. Her eyes were on Carstairs' face. Katherine hesitated. Her smile died and she put her hands anxiously on her stomach.

'Good evening, Mrs Shelley!' Carstairs bowed. Behind him the musicians had fallen silent.

'Good evening, my lord.' She was conscious that Mohammed had climbed over the rail after her and was standing close behind her. When she stepped forward he did the same. His presence was comforting.

Carstairs nodded. 'You still have a native at your side, I see, Mrs Shelley. He is welcome to join the other servants if you would care to sit down and watch the entertainment.'

'I have not come to be entertained,' Louisa retorted. 'And Mohammed will stay here at my side if he so wishes. He is the friend of my friend.' She narrowed her eyes. 'Why did you decide not to go back to the cave?'

He smiled. 'Because I was informed that the vial was no longer there. You tried to trick me, Mrs Shelley.'

'The thing you wanted so badly you were prepared to kill a man to get it!' Her voice was very even.

There was a slight moan from Katherine.

'Oh yes, Mrs Shelley. I was prepared to kill a man.' He smiled. 'Though in the event I didn't have to. The snake did it for me.'

She laughed. 'The snake did it for you!' she echoed. 'Have you told your friends here just how badly you wanted my little scent bottle? And have you told them what you have done to get hold of it? Have you told them how evil you are?'

'Oh Louisa!' Katherine's groan was anguished. 'Please, my dear, don't.'

'Don't try and stop me telling you what happened!' Louisa turned on her for only a second, but the force of her words made Katherine shrink back on her cushions. 'This man, who entertains you as a friend, is an evil fiend, a practitioner of the black arts. You are not safe on this boat. No one is!'

She could see the faces of the musicians and Carstairs' crew all turned towards her. She didn't know how many of them spoke

338

English but they all looked afraid. 'You are in danger!' she shouted at them. 'Don't you understand?'

'Louisa, my dear.' David Fielding put his hand on her arm. 'We all know you are upset. With good cause. But this will not help. What happened out there in the desert was no one's fault. It was a tragic accident. People are being killed by snakes and scorpions all the time out here.'

'No!' Louisa shook her head. 'This was no accident. Hassan knew about snakes and scorpions. That was his job! To escort me and keep me safe.' Her eyes filled with tears. 'Don't you see? He did it. As surely as if he had plunged that knife into Hassan's heart a second time!' She flung out her arm towards Carstairs.

Carstairs shook his head slowly. 'These are the imaginings of an overheated brain.'

'Are they?' She dashed the tears out of her eyes. 'So, you don't want the bottle?'

He tensed suddenly. She saw his eyes grow watchful. 'You know I am very anxious to acquire your scent bottle, Mrs Shelley. I have offered to buy it from you. I told you that you could name your price.'

'All right. My price is Hassan! If your magic is so powerful, you can bring him back to life!' She took another step towards him and felt Mohammed shadowing her once more. 'So, is your magic that powerful, Lord Carstairs?' She was smiling at him wildly.

He narrowed his eyes. 'You know it is not. No one can bring someone back from the dead.'

'What, not the priests that guard the bottle?' She folded her arms. 'I have seen them. They have power. And were they not dead themselves?'

His eyes were heavily lidded and she couldn't tell whether or not he was looking at her from under his lashes. He was so still he appeared to have stopped breathing. 'The priests are not living beings. They are still dead, even when they walk this earth.'

There was a sharp intake of breath behind him and Louisa saw eyes rounding amongst the cluster of men on the deck near them. Some of them at least were following the conversation.

'So, you cannot pay my price?'

'I have offered you money, Louisa. Any amount you would like to name.' His voice was growing impatient.

She shook her head. 'Money is of no use to me.'

'Then anything else that it is in my power to give. Jewels. Land.' He frowned. 'I have already offered you my title and my own hand!'

There was a small cry from Venetia behind him. 'Roger! You promised me!'

He ignored her; his eyes were fixed directly on Louisa's face. 'Well, what is it you want?'

She shook her head. 'I don't think there is anything you can give me that I want, my lord.' Her voice dropped suddenly to a whisper. 'Except revenge.'

Venetia had thrown herself sobbing towards Katherine, who leant across to take her sister-in-law in her arms. At Louisa's last words, which had somehow cut through Venetia's tears, they both turned towards her and fell suddenly silent.

The boat was completely quiet. The only sound was the gentle rustle of reeds along the bank. Louisa held his gaze. Then at last she nodded. 'I have the bottle here,' she said quietly. She slipped her hand into the pocket of her dress and drew out the silk-wrapped parcel.

His eyes widened hungrily. 'And you are going to give it to me!' He smiled in triumph.

She looked down at her hand thoughtfully. 'No,' she said at last. She glanced up at him again. 'No, I'm not going to give it to you. I am going to give it to the gods you claim to serve. You will never set eyes on this again, my Lord Carstairs. Never!'

With one quick movement she hurled the bottle as hard as she could out into the darkness. There was a pause as every person on the boat held their breath, then a small splash far out in the river.

'No!' Carstairs threw himself towards the rail. He hung over it, staring frantically at the water. 'Do you realise what you have done?' He turned suddenly and his eyes were blazing with rage. 'Do you? Do you realise what you've done?' He caught her by the shoulders and shook her hard.

'Hey! Wait! Take your hands off her!' David Fielding grabbed his arm as Mohammed stepped forward, his face set. He had his own knife in his hand.

'No!' Katherine let out a scream. 'No! Someone is going to get hurt! David, be careful! Let her go, Roger. What's the use? It's gone!' She pulled herself to her feet. 'For pity's sake! This has all

340

gone on long enough. Louisa, I think you should go. You've made your point!' She broke off suddenly and clutched at her stomach with a groan.

'Kate?' David Fielding's cry was anguished. 'My love, what is it?'

She straightened up, her face white, and staggered back to the cushions. 'I'm all right.' She was breathing heavily. 'Louisa, you should go.'

Louisa had stepped back towards the rail, tearing herself away from Carstairs' restraining hands. 'I'm going.' She threw the words over her shoulders as she turned to her escort. 'Mohammed, will you help me into the boat –'

Her words were interrupted by a piercing scream. Katherine had doubled up once more. 'My baby! It's my baby!' She tried to stand, reaching frantically towards her husband.

Louisa stopped at the top of the ladder and turning round she saw with horror a red stain spreading on Katherine's skirt. For a moment nobody moved. Then Venetia put her hand to her head and fainted back onto the silken cushions. No one took any notice of her. Louisa stared round the assembled men in horror. They were paralysed, staring at the agonised woman and at the pool of blood appearing on the deck of the boat below her skirts.

'Carry her below into a cabin!' She stepped forward, pushing Carstairs aside. 'Now! Quickly!'

'We'll go back to the *Lotus*!' David Fielding looked round wildly for his own servants. 'She should be there.'

'There's no time. Take her below, David. My lord,' she turned to Carstairs with a contemptuous stare. 'See that the other men leave the boat. Presumably they can go across to the *Lotus*. Mohammed, will you go and fetch Lady Forrester to help me? Venetia, pull yourself together. You will have to stay to help, too. Do it!' She shouted at the stunned faces around her as Katherine let out another scream. The sound sent the men scurrying in all directions and eventually it was Carstairs himself who pushed aside David, who seemed paralysed with shock, picked Katherine up and carried her towards the saloon where he laid her on the cushioned divan.

Coming face to face with Louisa who had followed them as he turned away from the sobbing moaning woman, he gave her one quick cold glance then he pushed past her and went back out onto the deck.

Venetia, white as a sheet and tearful was standing in the doorway, clearly terrified of entering the cabin. 'Tell someone to heat water for us,' Louisa called, 'and find some clean sheets.'

Katherine let out another groan as David appeared in the doorway, his face as white as paper. 'What can I do?'

Louisa glanced up at him. 'Go and help Venetia bring water.'

She turned back to Katherine and with soothing words began to try and make her more comfortable. Somehow she managed to help her sit up so she could undo the impossibly tight gown and draw it up over the woman's head before settling her back on the pillows. Katherine's fear was contagious. Louisa could feel herself fighting down waves of panic as gently she pushed back the woman's hair and then bundled her bloodstained clothing out of sight. 'You'll be all right, Katherine. You'll be fine.' She took her hands and held them firmly.

'And the baby? What about the baby? It's not due for two months!' Katherine burst into tears again. 'It's David's fault. He wouldn't listen. He would insist on coming to this God-forsaken country. I begged him not to, but he wanted to bring Venetia. He wanted to try and find a man for her.' She broke off with a catch in her breath before she could say any more, wailing with pain.

Louisa was still holding her hands tightly. As the next contraction started to build she could feel the clutch of Katherine's fingers tighter and tighter until her own bones were screaming in agony. There was a movement in the doorway. 'Here are the sheets.' Venetia stepped into the cabin and pushed them at her, averting her face from the woman on the divan.

'Keep them for later. Fetch a bowl of warm water and a wash cloth so we can sponge her.' Louisa glanced up at her. She was sorry for Venetia suddenly. No unmarried woman should see such a sight, especially if the baby was going to die. She bit her lip. Katherine was panting, quiet now between contractions, her face tear-stained and white. Louisa leant forward to sponge her forehead but already another pain was coming. 'It's your fault!' Suddenly Katherine was screaming in her face. 'If you hadn't come over and picked a fight with Carstairs this wouldn't have happened!' She clutched Louisa's hands more tightly. 'You shouldn't have come! Why did you?' She was panting frantically, sweat pouring down her face and body.

When the pain had passed Louisa heard a noise at the door. She glanced round to see Mohammed hovering on the threshold. He had turned his head away to avoid looking directly into the saloon. 'Lady Forrester will not come, Sitt Louisa. She says she knows nothing of childbirth. *Maleesh*! No matter! I have brought a woman from the village who is wise in these things.'

Behind him a heavily veiled woman peered anxiously into the cabin. She had huge dark eyes which glanced shyly round above the veil and rested on Katherine with a frown of concern.

Louisa smiled at her, remembering Hassan telling her that the wise women of the villages often had great knowledge of simple medicine and midwifery.

Mohammed whispered to the woman quickly and she slipped into the cabin past him and approached Louisa with a bow.

'Do you speak English?' Louisa asked.

The woman shrugged. She was carrying a small basket which she put on the table near them.

Katherine grabbed Louisa's hand. 'Don't let her come near me!' She screamed. 'Dear God, I'm going to die and you bring me a native! Where is David? Oh God!'

With the door closed behind her the woman removed her cloak and veil. She was older than had first appeared and as she looked at Katherine she took stock of the situation at once. She nodded and moving forward placed a cool hand on Katherine's belly.

Katherine shrank back but the woman nodded and smiled.

'Good. Good,' she said. 'Baby good. *Inshallah*!'

'Send her away!' Katherine pushed at the woman's hand, but already the pains were coming again.

When the cabin door opened a few minutes later the three women standing around Katherine looked up. At first they could not see who stood there. Silhouetted against the night sky the figure was tall and dark and indistinguishable from the night around it. It was the village woman who recognised him first and she turned away with a moan, trying to hide her face.

'Roger? Is that you? What is it?' Venetia stood away from her sister-in-law with obvious relief as the village woman reached for her scarf and pulled it over her head and around her face.

'I have brought help.' He stooped and peered into the cabin. 'I have invoked the priest of Sekhmet. She is goddess of healing and with his help she will grant this woman succour!' His voice rang round the cabin.

Katherine groaned. 'Get him away from me! Don't let him near me!' Her voice was hoarse from screaming. She clung to Louisa. 'Don't let him come in!'

'You heard her! Don't come in. Keep your foul magic away from us!' Louisa looked up at him. 'You are not wanted in here!'

'Not even to save her life?' The sneering voice echoed round the room. 'Believe me, madam, only magic can save her!'

'Your kind of magic can do nothing for her! It is destructive, murderous magic!' Louisa shouted.

'Do you dare take the chance?' The voice was becoming more and more mocking. 'I think you had better let me come in.'

'No!' Katherine's sobs became ever more hysterical. 'No, please, make him go away! David!' Her final scream was so shrill that the village woman forgot her fear of Carstairs. She placed her hand on Katherine's stomach and uttered a couple of incomprehensible instructions to Louisa, followed by a sequence of far more easily understood gestures as she tried to pull Katherine to her feet and indicated that she should squat, ready for the birth.

It was left to Venetia to push Carstairs out of the room and onto the deserted deck of the boat to join David who had been standing by himself in the stern. A few minutes later both heard clearly the feeble cry of a baby. At the sound David turned. 'Was that it? Was that my baby?' He was shaking.

Carstairs shrugged. Standing away from him he made his way across the roof of the cabin to the bows. There he stood and raised his arms to the sky.

By the time David was allowed into the cabin it had been tidied, the woman's basket with the ointments of fenugreek and honey, acacia, birthwort and tamarisk had been repacked and Katherine was lying on the divan propped on pillows, the tiny baby lying between her breasts. He looked at it in alarm.

'It's all right, David.' Katherine was touching the little head with one finger. 'He's here to keep warm. He's very small, but Mabrooka says he is all right.' She smiled at the village woman, who bowed. Already she was drawing her veil around her face once again. 'You must give her some baksheesh, David,' Katherine went on. Her voice was very weak. 'She probably saved my life.'

Louisa crept out on deck, leaving them alone and took a deep breath of the night air. It must be nearly dawn.

A sound behind her made her swing round. Carstairs was stand-

344

ing there, arms folded. At the sight of him, still dressed in his black robe with its red and gold sash, his head swathed in the elaborate turban she felt a sudden revulsion run through her. His gaze swept over her in disdainful silence, taking in the blood on her gown, her dishevelled hair, her exhaustion and she felt her anger flare at once. 'Don't you want to know how they are?'

He shrugged. 'No doubt you are about to tell me.'

'They are both safe and well.'

'*Inshallah*!' He inclined his head slightly.

'And now I shall leave.'

'Please do.' He turned away without another word.

She made her way towards the stern of the boat where Mohammed was sitting cross-legged waiting for her. Beside him the mooring line from the sandal which bobbed behind the dahabeeyah was tied to the rail. He rose as she approached and bowed to her. 'Sitt Fielding is well?'

'She is well, Mohammed, thanks to you. And the baby boy, too. Will you take me across to the *Ibis* and then come back for Mabrooka, please?' She rubbed her eyes wearily. 'It is nearly day, and I am very tired.'

He turned to pull in the dinghy, then suddenly he let out a cry. Coiled on the boards near him was a large snake. As he moved, it hissed. It lifted its head, the hood extended sideways, and swayed its neck from side to side, its eyes on his face.

'No!' Louisa stared at it for a moment, then she turned to Carstairs. 'Call it off! Are you so evil you would kill another innocent man?'

He was smiling. 'I did not summon it, Mrs Shelley, I assure you.'

'Your assurances are worth nothing.' She stepped towards the snake, her heart in her mouth. 'Mohammed, get in the sandal.'

'No, lady. I cannot leave you.' His face was chalk-white.

'Do it! It will not hurt me.' She stamped her foot and the snake hissed.

Mohammed moved cautiously backwards a step at a time as Louisa reached out for Venetia's discarded parasol, lying near her on a chair. The snake was watching her now. 'Call it off, my lord.' She smiled. 'Would you have me die too, so I can join Hassan?'

He shook his head slowly. 'I did not call it!'

'Then your powers are growing feeble. And they are more feeble still if you cannot dematerialise the evil concoction of your own

345

brain!' She was aware of Mohammed behind her, slowly climbing up onto the side of the boat and over onto the top step of the little ladder. As he let himself down into the dinghy he whispered to her. 'Please, Sitt Louisa. Please. Now save yourself.'

Louisa gave a small smile. 'So, Lord Carstairs. Will you send me into paradise with Hassan?'

Carstairs gave a hiss. As the snake wavered and turned towards him Louisa ran to the side of the boat and scrambled over onto the steps. Within seconds she was in the dinghy and Mohammed was paddling frantically for the *Ibis*.

Behind them they could hear Carstairs' bitter laughter ringing out in the darkness.

Halfway across the river Mohammed rested on the oar. 'Sitt Louisa. I have something for you.' He fumbled in his robe and drew out something small and white. He passed it over to her. 'When I rowed to fetch Lady Forrester I saw it floating in the water. The silk you wrapped it in had caught the air. It never sank.'

Louisa sat looking down at the small damp package in her hands, then she glanced back at *the Scarab* with a slow bitter smile. So, the snake had been far wiser than any of them had known. The scent bottle had been in Mohammed's boat. The gods had not taken it after all.

14

The slaughter block is made ready as thou
knowest
and thou hast come to decay . . . deliver thou
thy priests from the watchers who bear
slaughtering knives
and who have cruel fingers and who slay . . .

The wise one takes a piece of paper. On it he puts the names of the two priests, Anhotep and Hatsek, and he writes their story. Then he writes a warning for the merchant and for the men of Luxor. This is a tale of two djinn who would slay one another if they could and who would kill anyone who touched their sacred vial. This is an holy ampulla, taken from the sanctuary of the temple. Hands that defile it will turn back to dust; the hands of the priests are stained with blood.

By the time the paper is written the sun has gone down and darkness has come over the house of the merchant. The wise one bows and leaves. The merchant struggles with what he has been told. In his hand is a valuable relic of an ancient age. Does he give it back to the gods of yesterday, wrapped in honour and respect or does he take it to the Frangee quarter and sell it for more money than he has ever seen?

He studies the paper deep in thought. The priests grow impatient. They feed on his life force and that of his sons and of his wives and of his servants and they grow stronger than they have ever been since they came forth by day from the tomb of their concealment.

Several boats were waiting at the quayside to take the queues of spectators out to the son-et-lumière at the temple of Philae on its island. The passengers from *The White Egret* took their place in the queues with all the other tourists and climbed into the launches, already staring out in excited anticipation across the dark water with its thousands of reflections.

As Anna and Serena sat down in the stern of the boat Anna found herself next to Andy. She frowned as he put his arm round her shoulder and said, 'No hard feelings, eh, Anna? Have you brought a warm wrap? Apparently the wind off the desert can be very cold after dark while one is watching these things.'

She shifted imperceptibly away from him. 'Thank you, Andy. I'm well prepared for the evening.' She glanced at Serena. In Anna's bag were stowed both the bottle and the diary, in Serena's, statuette, ankh, incense burner, candles. Neither knew how they would manage to get away from the crowds and into the temple sanctuary in the dark, if indeed it would be possible at all. Anna looked round for Toby and spotted him further up the boat. He was talking to the man at the wheel. They were laughing and gesticulating together as though they had known one another for years and it dawned on her for the first time that Toby was speaking Arabic. She still wasn't sure what had happened out there at Abu Simbel but somehow it didn't worry her. Toby had a good explanation for his absence and when the right moment came he would give it to her. That was all that mattered.'

'So, am I forgiven?' Andy was speaking in her ear. 'I only had your interests at heart, you know.'

She didn't know whether he was talking about taking the diary and the scent bottle, or whether he was still referring to Toby, and suddenly she didn't care. She leant forward away from his arm as the boats began to nose away from the landing stages out into the river.

The temple was floodlit, reflecting all its serene beauty into the waters around it. Beside it the Kiosk of Trajan, described so eloquently by Louisa in her diary, stood up to one side of it, the columns delicate, almost ethereal against the midnight blue of the sky, a stunning contrast to the severity of the pylons of the temple itself. Anna caught her breath at the sheer magic of the sight. 'Does it matter that it's not on the actual island of Philae any more? That they have moved it to Aglika?' she whispered to Serena. How could it matter. It looked so perfect. As though it had been there for thousands of years.

Serena shrugged. 'It's Biga Island which was sacred to Osiris that was the truly special place. I think that must be over there.' She pointed out into the dark. 'I think it will be like Abu Simbel. That still had something of the sacred about it, didn't it?' She was staring out across the water. 'Even if it's only the fact that we – the tourists – all go there with a sense of awe. That must create an atmosphere again, mustn't it?'

'I don't think everyone who goes there these days, goes to worship Isis.' Anna shivered, glancing at the bag clutched on Serena's lap. 'I'm scared.'

Serena smiled into the darkness. 'I think the goddess is still here. She'll come. There is nothing to be scared of.'

'And she'll call off her priests?'

Serena slowly shook her head, her eyes on the illuminated stone soaring above the black water. 'Who knows what she'll do.'

As the boats queued to come in turn against the landing stage below the temple the passengers rose to their feet and made their way forward, climbing across the seats, ducking under the awning, passing the throbbing, noisy engine housing as the two-man crew gently eased the boat closer in. They could smell the oil now, the fumes from the exhaust. The noise set their teeth on edge.

349

Anna and Serena quietly hung back, watching Andy inching his way up the boat.

'He'll look for us!' Anna shook her head. Serena looked blank and she had to repeat the words, shouting in Serena's ear against the sound of the engine.

Serena nodded. 'Where's Toby?'

Anna gestured towards the crowd of figures ahead of them.

'Perhaps if Andy sees us with Toby he will back off,' Serena shouted in reply. They were near the front now, and each in turn found themselves being helped up onto the wooden landing stage.

Serena, who had landed first, stood apart from the others and waited for Anna. To her annoyance she could see Andy had done the same.

'We've got to get rid of him, otherwise we haven't a chance of slipping away.' She was glancing around her into the shadows. There was some scrub, some small trees, but the area was well lit and the way to the range of seats where the audience would sit was clearly marked.

'Come on, you two. We want to be near the front!' Andy called.

Anna glanced at Serena. 'You go on, Andy.' She folded her arms. 'I'm going to sit with Toby.'

She saw the anger on his face. 'You are joking?'

'No. No, I'm not joking.' She returned his look coldly.

'You don't believe his story?'

'I don't know what to believe, Andy. And it's none of your business anyway. Please, go on. You follow the others.'

For a moment she thought he was going to refuse, but suddenly Toby was there, waiting at the side of the path. Andy glanced at him in obvious disgust and turned away. Within seconds he had disappeared into the slowly moving queue of people. Toby joined them. 'Do I gather I scared him off?'

'You did.' Anna smiled. 'And that was important because we're going to slip away. We want to get into the sanctuary while everyone is distracted and have another go at calling up the priests.'

Toby glanced over his shoulder. 'You haven't a hope. Look at the lights. And there are men there, ushering people to their seats.' He watched as men and women and children streamed past them. 'Surely it doesn't have to be in the sanctuary? Near the temple will do. What about down there somewhere?' He pointed away to their right below the Kiosk.

'Are you going to come with us?' Serena was clearly becoming agitated.

Toby shook his head. 'Not unless you want me to. This is a women's thing, isn't it? But I'll help you find somewhere and stand guard if you like.'

'We've got to move quickly. Once everyone is seated we won't be able to slip away at all.' Serena was staring round frantically. 'The whole place is floodlit. I hadn't realised the island would be so small. It's going to be too difficult to find somewhere private!'

'It'll be all right.' Toby smiled at her reassuringly. 'Look, follow me down here.' He ducked suddenly off the path between some low bushes. 'See?' he called quietly. 'The shadows are incredibly black where the lights don't reach. It's the contrast. No one will ever spot you down here at the water's edge. It's the perfect place.'

Their feet slipping on the sandy track they followed the narrow path he had found round the side of the island away from the lighted ranges of seats. Clinging to the stony edge of the land below the Kiosk of Trajan they found a strip of bushes and a line of beach. Toby crouched down in the darkness.

'Unless you're unlucky and a stray spotlight comes this way, no one will see you here. They'll be blinded by all the floodlights and once the light show starts everyone will concentrate on that. OK? You've got about an hour, I gather. I'll make my way to the back of the audience and keep my eyes open and I'll come and meet you here, at the end.' He looked round. 'Good luck. Be careful.' He kissed Anna quickly on the lips and turned away. There was a rustle of dried fronds and he had gone.

Serena had already down on the sand, and was fumbling in her bag. 'I don't think anyone would see a candle with all the bright lights around. I'll light it later with the incense. I need that to summon the goddess.' She was talking to herself. She took a deep breath and bit her lip. 'I've brought a scarf to lay out the things on.' Her hands were shaking as she spread out her statuette, her ankh, the incense, the candlestick. Anna reached into her own bag and brought out the scent bottle. Unwrapping it she laid it at the feet of Isis. Then she froze. Somewhere above them they could hear voices suddenly. A shout of laughter rang out across the water.

'They can't see us,' Serena murmured. 'We'll wait until the show starts.' She glanced at her watch in the darkness and shrugged. She could see nothing. 'It can't be long now.' She was fumbling with

351

the matches and swore as the box opened upside down in her hands and the matches cascaded into her lap.

'Take it slowly.' Anna reached over and touched her arm. 'There's no hurry. And we're safe here. Toby's right. No one could see us even if they were looking straight at us.' She paused, looking up. 'Listen, it's starting!'

The lights suddenly went off all over the island. Serena caught her breath. The darkness around them was tangible. The show had begun.

It was hard to ignore the noise behind them. The disembodied voices, the music echoing across the water, the play of lights, weaving history out of the darkness, but the two women kneeling close together on the sand were concentrating on the tiny square of pale silk before them. Serena struck a match and the flame flared, shaking slightly as she held it over the cone of incense. It took three matches to light it, then at last the thin wisp of smoke began to rise. She turned to the candle. Its flame blazed up for a moment, trembled and skittered sideways and threatened to go out. Then at last it steadied and burnt clear.

'Isis, great goddess, I invoke thee!' Serena was speaking in a whisper. 'Hear me great goddess, here in thy island, near thy great temple, hear me and come to our aid. Summon thy servants Anhotep and Hatsek; let them come before us to settle their disagreements and decide on the future of this sacred ampulla with its contents of thy tears.'

She reached forward and picking up the bottle held it up towards the indigo velvet of the sky. Behind them the sounds of music and strange unearthly voices swelled and echoed across the water to the black volcanic cliffs in the distance. Anna shivered violently.

'Isis, send thy servants here! Protect us, guard us with thy magic and send them to speak here, tonight on thy sacred ground!' Serena's voice had risen dramatically. Behind them there was a pause in the sound and the lights dimmed. The island held its breath. A faint flurry of wind touched Anna's face and she saw the candle flicker. Her hand went to the amulet at her throat.

Serena's eyes had closed. She laid the bottle down on the ground and then raised her arms again towards the sky.

Somewhere out across the water a bird gave a sharp cry. They could smell the cold clean air of the desert, threaded with myrrh and juniper and honey from the lighted cone.

A faint light had appeared on the shore a few yards from them. Anna caught her breath. She glanced at Serena and then, quietly, over her shoulder at the temple. She could see the spotlights, tracking arcs against the sky. None was pointing in their direction.

The light near them grew larger. It elongated into the shape of a figure and gradually it appeared to grow more solid. She held her breath. Serena had lowered her arms and crossed them over her breast. She was kneeling, head bowed, waiting.

She's waiting for me to speak. Anna's mouth was dry with fear. She had to speak, to demand of the priest what he wanted. She looked up towards the figure on the shore. It had moved closer. It was standing over Serena. She saw the shadow pass over Serena's face.

Serena's eyes opened suddenly with an expression of acute anguish. 'Traitor!' she screamed. 'You foul traitor!' Behind them the music crescendoed. Her voice was lost in a cacophony of sound. 'The tears of Isis belong to the boy king. They will save his life!'

Anna gasped. An intense pain gripped her head. She couldn't breathe. She could feel her body growing hot and suddenly she was standing up. She could feel herself towering over Serena.

'They belong to the gods! The tears belong to the gods and I shall see they serve no other!' The words were being wrenched from her own mouth.

She saw Serena look up. The shadow figure was wispy and ragged. Another blast of wind from the desert and as the candleflame shrank and trailed black smoke Serena scrambled to her feet.

'Anna!' Her voice was coming from a great distance. 'Anna, be strong! Think of the light! Oh great Isis, protect Anna. Make her strong! Anna! Anna, can you hear me?'

But Anna was far away. Looking up towards the sun she could see it rising high in the sky, a glorious ball of flame in a blue ocean of eternity. She could see the high golden cliffs, the temple entrance, hidden and secret, where the goddess had her home on earth.

Slowly she moved closer to it, drifting on the hot desert wind, listening to the sands whispering across immense distances. In that hidden temple lay all the secrets of eternity, guarded by just two high priests sworn to the service of the gods through life after life for all eternity. She moved closer, sensing the prowling jackal, the

353

sacred desert lion, sworn to serve as she was. And at her feet the serpents of the desert, cobra and viper and asp. In her hand she held a knife, its blade pure gold brought from the deepest heart of Africa to reflect the flame of the sun god and turn it into fire.

'Anna!'

A voice from thousands of years away echoed in the silence. The river in all its beauty licked the shores of the desert, rose in flood and brought green bounty, subsided and rose again.

'Anna! For God's sake!'

For God's sake. The one God, all the gods. Such a simple thing. A few drops of sacred liquid, sealed in a tiny glass container, and washed with the blood of a friend.

'Anna! For pity's sake, can you hear me? Anna!'

She smiled and shook her head. She could see the river now, down there at her feet. The waters are cool, life-giving; they feed the sacred lotus and lap the sands so that the lioness can drink . . .

'Anna!' Suddenly it was as though Anna's head snapped back on her shoulders. A shower of ice-cold water caught her in the face.

Serena was shaking her violently. She let her go to scoop up another handful of water and lobbed it at her, then she caught her and shook her again. 'You didn't protect yourself, you fool! He had you. Hatsek was inside you! I could see his face in yours. I could see his features. I could see his hatred. You would have killed me, Anna!' Serena pushed her away so hard that Anna staggered and fell. 'Have you any idea how dangerous that was?' She was standing over Anna at the edge of the river, her hair awry. Behind them the makeshift altar was scattered, candle and incense overturned, the statue lying on its side.

Anna rubbed her face. It was wet with Nile water. She shivered. 'What did I do?' She stared round, confused. Behind them a light fell suddenly on Trajan's Kiosk illuminating the tall ornate columns. Serena grabbed her and pulled her down into the shadows. 'You were Hatsek, don't you understand! He possessed you, Anna. He took you over!'

'He used my voice? Like Anhotep used yours?'

The sand. The desert wind. The blazing sun. They still filled her head, though the sky above her now was black and sewn with a myriad stars. 'He used my eyes. But he wasn't seeing this.' She gestured around her, confused. 'I saw the temple. The temple where

354

Anhotep tricked him. It was hidden in the cliffs somewhere in the western desert on the edge of the mountains. Anhotep wanted the sacred water of life for the pharaoh, to use it as a medicine. But that was sacrilege. Nothing could have saved him anyway. It was not to be. The history was already written.' She shook her head slowly from side to side. 'The servant of the goddess was a servant of the one God. Of the Aten. It was Anhotep who was the traitor.' She stared up at Serena confused. She didn't know what the words pouring from her own mouth meant any more.

'No.' Serena shook her head. 'No, Anna. That's not true. They fell out. There was treachery and deceit. There was murder which had to be hidden.' She stared down at the ground and then with an exclamation of dismay she dropped to her knees. 'The bottle! Where is it? It's gone!'

Anna shrugged. 'Let it go. The priests have taken it. It doesn't matter. It's better lost. So many people have died –'

Serena stopped scrabbling in the sand and looked up at her. 'What do you mean so many people? How many people?'

'Many. It wasn't just Hassan. There have been generations of people through thousands of years. Whatever was in that bottle, whether they were priests of Isis and Sekhmet or of Amun or of the Aten, the liquid was not something we were supposed to have. Let it go back to the gods.'

She turned and looked at the temple. The sound had stopped. The floodlights had come back on. A ripple of applause ran through the night air. 'It is finished. We have to go. Leave it. Leave it all, here on the island of the goddess.' She bent and picked up the scarf. 'The statue, the ankh, the bottle. Let them sink into the sand and disappear.' She turned towards the palms as a figure appeared out of the darkness. It was Toby.

'How did it go? Did it work?' He looked from one to the other and raised an eyebrow. 'Well? What happened?'

Serena shrugged. 'We've lost the bottle. It's gone.' She stooped and began to gather the other things into her bag. She dusted sand off the little statue of Isis seated on her throne and tucked it away. She wasn't going to leave them behind, she might need them again. Her own offering to Isis, a small gold brooch, had been slipped quietly into the water whilst Anna and Toby were talking. These were the tools of her trade.

'Anna?' Toby touched her shoulder. 'Are you all right?'

Anna nodded silently. She was gazing out into the dark and she didn't look at him.

He frowned, then he turned back to Serena. 'We have to go. Have you got everything?' He glanced around. Then he stopped and pointed. 'There's your bottle. See? It's rolled down there into that dip in the shingle.' He stooped and picked it up. 'Anna?'

She didn't appear to have heard him. In her mind's eye she was still scanning the vast echoing spaces of the desert. He shrugged and looked at Serena.

She took the bottle from him. 'I'll take care of it.' She tucked it into the bag on her shoulder then she touched Anna's arm. 'Ready?'

Slowly Anna nodded. She turned away from the river and when Toby held out his hand she took it.

Behind them the silence at the water's edge was intense. The sounds of the night had ceased. For a while that small part of the island held its breath, then slowly the sounds returned and the water lapped again upon the beach.

Andy was waiting for them near the landing stage. 'Well, what did you think of it?' He smiled at Anna. 'Fabulous, wasn't it?'

Anna nodded. 'Fabulous indeed.' She put her hands to her face for a moment and rubbed it wearily, trying to wake herself up. She was still feeling strangely distant; disconnected.

'Except you didn't see it, of course.' Andy leant close to her. 'Do you really imagine I didn't notice you slip away?'

She stepped back with a frown. She could smell alcohol on his breath.

'Andy!'

'You had to hide in the bushes with lover boy, I suppose! You don't believe me, do you? You don't believe he's a crook.'

'Andy!' Toby dropped Anna's arm and stepped towards him. 'I've had enough of this! Just what exactly are you trying to say?'

'That you are a murdering, lying bastard and you should keep away from decent women.' Andy produced a bottle from the rucksack on his shoulder and took a swig from it.

'Toby, no!' Anna came back to reality with a jolt. She caught at Toby's sleeve. 'Leave it. Don't hit him. That's what he wants –'

She stopped mid-sentence and shook her head. Raising her hands to her temples she stared at him blankly. Something was happening to her again. There were people all round them now. She could see them staring, and whispering to each other as they saw Andy waving the bottle in the air. She could see Ben putting his hand out to Andy and quietly taking it away from him, she could see Omar speaking to them, standing between him and Toby, gesticulating, but at the same time she could see the great white sun, the dazzling red-gold desert, the scene viewed through a man's eyes, superimposed over everything else. Their voices receded. They were muffled.

Her feet were moving slowly towards the boats. Out in the river she could see other boats arriving, bringing visitors for the second viewing of the light show, due to start very soon. She had lost sight of Serena now. And Toby. She stared round wildly. Her eyes wouldn't focus. She could see dunes; wind was blowing the sand across her vision, stinging her face; the sky was a brilliant blue above it, far away. Then Andy was there, beside her again. He was smiling, holding out his hand towards her.

'Please, people. We have to go back to the boat. Cook will have a wonderful supper ready for us.' Omar shepherded his flock closer together. 'Please to hurry up, people. Ibrahim will kill me if you are late for supper!' He grinned and moved away shooing his own bunch of tourists closer together, anxious not to lose them in the dark.

Anna hung back. She shook her head again, trying to concentrate. 'Where's Toby?'

Andy laughed. 'He's probably been whisked away by Interpol. Him and the loopy Serena, both.' He reached across and caught her hand.

'Charley's gone home. Did you know? Invalided out. It was all too much for her. So I can give you my undivided attention, sweetheart. You and that lovely diary of yours.' He eyed her bag. 'Please don't tell me you've brought it with you.'

She tried to pull her hand away. 'Andy, will you leave me alone! I really don't need you pawing at me.' She was finding it difficult to focus again. Harder still to concentrate on what was happening around her.

They were all standing still now, a crowd of people milling round the edge of the temple forecourt, slowly filtering down the steps onto the landing stage where the first motor boat had come alongside. Opposite them, on the far side of the channel, the huge boulders on the island of Biga were black caverns in the shadows of the night, where the lights from Aglika didn't reach.

'Anna!' Suddenly Serena was beside her again. 'Are you all right?' They were nearly at the front of the queue now.

'Of course she's all right.' Andy was still there beside her. 'I'm looking after her.'

Serena pursed her lips. 'What possessed you to bring a bottle of vodka with you?'

He shrugged. 'Cold night. It seemed like a good idea. I gave it to Ben. If you want some you'd better ask him.'

'Ask him!' Serena stared at him, scandalised. 'Have you any idea how much you offend the Egyptians, being drunk like that? You idiot!'

The man supervising the loading of the boat held up his hand. The boat was full. It backed away from the landing stage and turned out into the river as a second boat nosed in towards them.

Anna was suddenly aware that Toby was beside her. She glanced at him and smiled. 'I'm afraid Andy seems intent on disgracing us all.'

'You surprise me!' Toby's voice was grim. 'Well, if he wants to make a fool of himself I suggest he does it elsewhere and somewhere he is less likely to fall in the river!' He took hold of Andy's arm and propelled him away from the edge of the landing stage to where Ben was standing. 'Can you keep an eye on him, Ben? He's not exactly sober and he's being a damn nuisance.' He left him and turned back to Anna. 'And you, Anna, are not looking exactly right, yourself. What happened back there on the beach?' He was speaking quietly in her ear.

She stared at him, frowning. 'It was strange.'

The boat nudged against the platform and one of the crew unhooked the chain across the gap in the rail so that they could climb on board. They made their way between the rows of seats, past the engine and into the broad stern area. Anna sat down in the corner with Serena on one side of her and Toby on the other. She shook her head. 'I think I must be tired, that's all. I feel very weird.' She glanced up. Andy was making his way towards them, grinning. He sat down on a centre seat opposite her.

Ben had followed and sat down beside him with a shrug. 'I think this fellow needs some food inside him,' he commented cheerfully. 'He'll be fine once he's had some supper. Well, what did you think of the show, ladies? Did you enjoy it?' He moved up closer to Andy as more and more people packed in round them.

'It was good.' Anna nodded and smiled.

'Not good.' Andy leant forward and touched her knees. 'She didn't see it, naughty girl. She was canoodling with our rakish ex-con here.'

Toby's face tensed and Anna clutched at his arm. 'Don't rise to it. Please, ignore him,' she pleaded.

Andy was unstoppable. Turning back to Anna he raised his voice to make himself heard over the laughter and chatter and the sound of the engine idling behind them in the central well of the boat. 'So, did you bring that lovely little scent bottle with you to see the show? You seem to be inseparable from it.'

'Yes, I brought it.' She smiled. The engine note changed. The man on the landing stage stood back and raised his hand and the boat began to chug away from the island. Behind them the floodlit temple came fully into view, seemingly floating on the water as they drew away into the broad channel and turned to head back towards the shore.

'And did it perform magic for you? Did your priestly attendants manifest on the island of Isis?' He was grinning broadly.

'They did. Yes.' Anna was tight-lipped.

'So, your magic worked. You rubbed it once twice thrice and the genie of the bottle appeared.' He threw his head back and laughed, enjoying himself hugely.

'It did indeed.' Anna turned away, trying to discourage him.

'So, what happens next?' He sat forward and tapped her knee. 'Are they going to show themselves on the boat? Can you get them to appear at the pasha's party and do a turn for us when we get back to Luxor? Did you hear that, people?' He stood up and raised his voice. 'Anna's Ancient Egyptian ghosts are going to do a turn for us.' He raised his arms above his head and wiggled his hips suggestively.

'Sit down, Andy. You are being a prat!' Ben pulled at his arm.

'They're not going to appear again, Andy,' Anna put in quietly. 'For the simple reason that I left the bottle on the island. It's buried in the sand. Gone for ever.' She looked at him quizzically. 'Luckily for you, no one will ever see it again. Nor will they see whoever it was who guarded it, so let that be the end of it. Please.' Her head was aching again. As she stared at him a gauze seemed to be lying across in front of her eyes. She blinked desperately.

Andy laughed. 'I knew you'd end up losing it. The stupid thing was a fake anyway.'

'It is not a fake, Andy.' Serena suddenly turned on him. 'You're the fake around here. An opinionated, stupid boorish loud-mouthed oaf! I cannot tell you how tired I am of hearing your voice, your opinions, your mockery!' She reached down at her feet and fumbled for her bag. 'For your information, Anna didn't lose the bottle. I picked it up and I brought it back with me. It deserves better than to languish in the sand!' She was groping around inside the bag. 'And if anything can prove just how stupid you are, this can. You are ignorant. You know nothing about antiques. This is over three thousand years old!' She pulled out the little bottle and waved it at him.

'Serena! I had given that back to the gods!' Anna was furious. 'Give it to me!'

'Why? You don't want it, you threw it away! I am going to make sure that it is preserved safely.'

'No, Serena! That bottle has caused the death of dozens of people, perhaps hundreds –'

'Only because they didn't know what it was. We know! We will treat it with the respect it deserves. We'll look after it.'

'Three thousand years old? That?' Andy sat down heavily. He snatched his arm away from Ben with a petulant shrug.

'Yes, Andy. This.' Serena cradled it in her palm. 'This is so sacred. So special.' She sat looking down at it, aware of at least a dozen pairs of eyes on her as the crowded passengers around them waited to see what would happen next. The note of the engine changed as the man at the wheel altered course and for a moment a trail of diesel fumes blew across them, then it was gone and cold clear wind knifed across the boat again. Serena shivered. She looked up at Andy. 'If I give this to you, do you know what will happen?' She was shouting over the noise of the engine and the slap of water against the planking of the boat.

'What?' Andy grinned. He held out his hand. 'Show me.'

'If I give it to you, a cobra will appear, here in the boat. A deadly poisonous, evil snake.' She smiled. 'And it will kill you!'

'That's enough!' Anna leant forward and snatched the bottle out of her hand. 'This has gone on long enough.'

'Show me!' Andy stretched his hand out towards her. 'Go on. Show me the magic snake! I want to see it! Don't you want to see it?' He gestured round the other passengers. 'That would be exciting, wouldn't it?' He stood up once again and balanced unsteadily in front of Anna, holding out his hand.

360

'Andy, you're a fool!' Anna had to raise her voice to make herself heard.

'Give it back!' Serena grabbed Anna's wrist.

'No. No, Serena, I'm sorry.' Anna edged away from her. 'This belongs to another age and to other people. They want it for their gods. Louisa tried to give it to the Nile. Now it's my turn!'

Standing up she turned to face the water.

'No!' Serena's scream echoed across the river. 'Don't throw it away!'

'It's all right, I've got it!' Andy lurched forward, lunging at Anna as she raised her arm and with every ounce of strength she possessed hurled the bottle out into the boat's wake.

Andy missed her arm, staggered off balance and as she fell back into her seat, winded, he clutched at the rail, swayed for a moment, overbalanced and plunged head first over the side.

'Andy!' Serena's scream was echoed by others on the boat as the crew looked back, realised what had happened and threw the gears, dragging the wheel round in a small circle.

'Can you see him?' Toby and Ben were staring at the dark water.

'Torches! Has anyone got torches?' Toby kicked off his shoes and was already standing on the seat, scanning the surrounding river. As several feeble beams hit the water simultaneously behind the now drifting boat, he dived in.

Ben reached over the side, struggling to free one of the old cork lifebelts hanging on the side of the boat. 'Here you are, Toby!' He threw it as Toby's head reappeared. Two other belts followed, hitting the water near him.

'Andy! Andy, where are you?' Serena was leaning out over the side as one of the Egyptian crewmen jumped into the water near Toby.

Suddenly other boats were appearing out of the darkness, circling round them, dozens of passengers craning over the side, staring out into the dark. There was still no sign of Andy as a fast launch appeared and a spotlight suddenly shone out over the scene. Two, then three other men were in the water now, all of them diving.

'The water's pitch-black!' Toby reappeared, shaking droplets out of his eyes. 'You can't see a thing.' He was treading water, turning slowly round, scanning the reflections around him.

Anna turned away from the rail and sat down. She put her head

361

in her hands. 'He's dead, isn't he. And it's my fault! The gods have taken him! I've killed him!'

She looked up at Serena's white face and there were tears pouring down her cheeks.

Serena turned to stare out across the water. 'If it was anyone's fault, it was mine,' she whispered. 'I wound him up. I produced the bottle.'

Several men were swimming with Toby now, diving around the boat. Beyond them another launch had appeared and this time they could see that the men crowding around the bows were dressed in police uniform.

'They'll find him!' Ben sat down next to Anna and put his hand over hers. 'He's a strong swimmer, which I'm not or I'd be over there with them.'

'But he was so drunk!' Serena shook her head.

'I know. But it'll take more than a dunking in the Nile to defeat Andy.' Ben did not sound as though he believed his own reassuring words. For a moment he sat where he was then he stood up again and joined the others desperately scanning the water.

'They won't find him.' Anna looked at Serena. The boat was strangely silent now, without the engine or the cheerful slapping of the water against the bows.

The other passengers were sitting quietly, staring around, numb with shock.

Serena shook her head. 'As you say, the gods have taken him away. He mocked them, Anna, and he paid the price.' She bit her lip.

A slight shock ran through the boat as a launch came alongside and two tourist police officers climbed on board. There was an excited exchange with the boat's captain, then they made their way aft to where Anna and Serena were sitting.

One of the officers sat down next to them. 'This gentleman had been drinking alcohol?'

Both women nodded.

'He was very drunk?' The taller, obviously senior man's English was heavily accented but fluent.

Anna looked up. 'Yes, he was very drunk. He had brought a bottle of vodka with him for some reason. He stood up and,' she paused, feeling the tears returning, 'he went in head first.'

'The water is very cold.' The man shook his head. He stared gloomily over the side. 'Could he swim?'

362

'Yes.' Ben had joined them. 'He swam well.'

'Then it is not good news. He should have come up and shouted.' The officer shrugged. '*Yallah!*' He turned to his companion and after a quick exchange in fast, eloquent undertones, the two men made their way back to the captain who was standing at the wheel of the boat, shaking his head, wiping his hands again and again on an oily rag.

One by one the swimmers were hauling themselves back onto their boats. Anna saw Toby treading water again, looking up at one of the men in the police launch. He shook his head but the man leant over and proffered an arm and she saw Toby hauled out of the water. A few minutes later he was delivered back to their own boat, wrapped in a rug. He was shaking with cold as he made his way towards her.

'He just disappeared. The water is like ink in the darkness. You can see the lights if you look up, but nothing below you. Nothing!'

'It was very brave to go after him.' Anna leant forward to touch his hand. It was like ice.

He shook his head. 'I didn't stop to think. I should have waited. Seen where he came up.'

'He didn't come up, Toby.' Serena had tears streaming down her face. 'We were all watching.'

It was a long time later that the passengers rejoined their ship. The crew met them, solemn-faced, and they were urged to go at once to the dining room. While Toby was whisked away by Omar to be seen by a doctor after his long cold immersion in the Nile, the others trooped obediently to the dining room and sat down. No one had much appetite and it wasn't long before in twos and threes they began to make their way to their own cabins. Serena followed Anna to hers and they sat side by side on the bed.

'It was a stupid accident, Anna.' Serena put her arms round her companion. 'He was drunk.'

'It was our fault. We both wound him up. If I hadn't thrown away the bottle it wouldn't have happened.' Anna was squinting at the wall. There was something wrong with her eyes. She could see the sun again; the sand, the endlessly moving fronds of a tall palm tree.

'No. It could have happened at any second. It could have happened here, off this boat! Andy was like that!' Serena shrugged.

'He was a fool. A great big, stupid, malicious, lying fool . . .' Suddenly she was sobbing violently.

Anna stood up. She shook her head and rubbed her eyes. 'I'll get us something from the bar.' She hesitated, then she went to the door and out into the deserted corridor.

Ibrahim was behind the bar. There were several people in the lounge talking in subdued voices in groups on the sofas around the edge of the room. He looked up as Anna came in and frowned. 'You wore the amulet?'

She nodded.

Ibrahim shrugged. 'The gods are still powerful, *mademoiselle*. I am sorry for Monsieur Andrew but these things happen. *Inshallah*!'

'He didn't deserve to die, Ibrahim.' She climbed onto a stool and leant wearily on her elbows.

'That is not for us to decide, *mademoiselle*.'

'Could I have saved him?' She looked up and met his eyes.

He returned her gaze steadily. 'Not if it was written that this was his fate.'

'I keep thinking we'll hear his voice; that he swam under water and crawled up on the rocks somewhere. That they'll find him alive.'

Ibrahim inclined his head slightly. 'All things are possible.'

'But not likely.'

He shrugged. 'It is the will of Allah, *mademoiselle*.'

'What will happen? Will they cancel the cruise?'

Again he shrugged. 'The police will come tomorrow. And the tour company representative. Omar will meet them. I expect they will ask for you. This is a very small boat. Everybody knew Monsieur Andrew. Everybody is sad.'

She nodded slowly. 'I just want to curl up and go to sleep.'

'You want to take a drink to bed?'

'Yes please. And one for Serena.'

He nodded. 'I bring them to your cabin. You go.' He turned to the shelf behind him, then he glanced quickly back at her. '*Mademoiselle*, do not take off your amulet. Not even for one second. There is still danger near you.'

She frowned. Her hand went automatically to her throat. She wanted to ask why he had said that. But he was busy with his back to her and she realised suddenly that she did not want to know. Not now. She couldn't cope with any more.

Serena was lying on her bed with Louisa's diary in her hands.

'I hope you don't mind. You'd left your bag lying open on the side table and I wanted to read the last few pages. I thought it would help to take my mind off things.'

Anna sat down beside her. 'Good idea.' She sighed. 'Ibrahim is bringing us a drink to the cabin. I suspect he is going to mix a knock-out concoction.' She smiled wearily. 'So, what happened to Louisa?'

Serena sat up and swung her legs to the floor. 'I think you should read it yourself.' She cocked her head at the sound of a gentle knock and opening the door took a tray from Ibrahim.

'There you are. Your knock-out drink.' She put a glass on the table next to the bed for Anna and sniffed cautiously at her own. 'For a Muslim and a teetotaller he mixes a fairly hefty cocktail. Years of catering to the habits of the infidel no doubt.' She paused with a wistful smile. 'Don't dwell on things, Anna. It is absolutely not your fault. It was his for getting stupidly drunk.'

Anna nodded. She could feel the tears very close.

'I'll leave you to read,' Serena whispered. 'We'll talk again in the morning.'

Anna sat without moving for several minutes after she had gone then she reached for the glass. Kicking off her shoes she lay back against the pillows and picked up the diary. Serena was right. There were only a few pages of the close-packed writing left and it would serve to take her mind off the present through what would inevitably be a sleepless night.

The three boats remained at their moorings for several days after Katherine's lying in. Then when she was sufficiently strong to transfer back to the *Lotus* the Fieldings and the Forresters set off once more in convoy on the long journey north, leaving *the Scarab* behind. There had been no sign of Lord Carstairs since Louisa had left his boat before dawn on the day of the birth. Sir John's questioning of the *reis* on the boat had produced no more than a shrug and an eloquent glance towards the heavens. A search had produced no signs of a snake of any size at all.

It was at Luxor that Louisa made her decision.

'I shall take the steamer back to Cairo,' she told the Forresters after dinner on the night they took up their moorings. 'You have been so kind and so hospitable, but I want to see my little boys again.'

In her cabin she began to pack away her painting things. Treece would deal with her clothes, but these were special. They had been packed and unpacked by Hassan. She opened one of her sketchbooks and stared for a long time at his face, the dark loving eyes, the gentle mouth, the hands which were so strong and yet so sensitive.

It was very hot in the cabin and she had pushed back the shutters. On the far side of the river a line of dahabeeyahs were moored against the palm-fringed shore. Most were pointing north. The season had turned for most Europeans and the time had come to make their way down the Nile towards Cairo and on to Alexandria and the Mediterranean coast and the routes back to Europe.

She put down the sketchbook and went to stand looking out at the dusk. The sun hung, a crimson ball, low over the Theben hills, throwing a wash of red across the water.

There was a sound in the cabin behind her, a feeling, no more, that she was not alone. Without turning she knew what it was. 'I have tried to return the bottle to your gods,' she said quietly. 'Each time it comes back to me. What would you have me do?' She wasn't afraid. She went on staring out across the water. Somewhere out there where the mountains turned the colour of blood before they cloaked themselves in darkness lay the temple where these priests had worshipped the gods to whom they had dedicated their eternal souls.

The bottle, still wrapped in its water-stained silk was lying somewhere amongst the paints and brushes on the table top behind her. The cabin was growing dark as the sun slipped behind the hills and the first breath of night air whispered across the water. She closed her eyes.

Take it. Please take it.

The words had echoed so strongly in her head she thought she had shouted them out loud.

Across the river, lamps were being lit on the boats strung out along the shore; the mountains had vanished and one by one the stars were beginning to appear.

Behind her there was a loud knock on the door and Treece came in with a branch of candles. She banged it down on the table. 'Shall I help you dress, Mrs Shelley?' The woman's face was sour. Angry. Within seconds, Louisa knew why.

'Sir John says the steamer is fully booked. There are no cabins available until next week so you'll have to stay with us that bit longer.' She sniffed her disapproval and turned to fetch a ewer of water.

Louisa stood staring after her in dismay. She wanted to leave Egypt. She wanted to close this chapter of her life where every breath of desert air made her think of the man whom she had loved and who had died because of her.

Her gaze fell on the table. For a second her heart missed a beat. She thought the bottle had gone. Then she saw it, small, scruffy in its wrappings, half hidden by a box of charcoal. As Treece had banged the candles down a shower of wax had fallen across the table. A small lump hung from the dirty silk like a miniature stalactite, looking already as ancient as the glass beneath its wrapping.

As she stared at it she knew what she had to do. The next day she would get Mohammed to take her back to the Valley of the Tombs and she would bury the bottle there in the sand beneath an image of the goddess, and she it was who must decide on its fate.

Anna's eyelids drooped. She took another sip from the glass. Ibrahim had put brandy in the drink, but also other things. Strange, bitter things she could not identify. The diary was suddenly heavy in her hands and she let it fall onto the covers, staring sleepily towards the window of her cabin. Even with the lamp beside her

367

bed switched on she could see the stars above the skyline. With a sigh she reached out and turned off the light. Just for a moment she would rest her eyes before she climbed into the shower to soak away the stiffness and pain of the night.

As she sank further into sleep the shadows grew closer and the whispers in the sand grew louder.

She was woken by the sun. Hot. Red. Fiery behind her eyelids. She could feel the abrasive heat on her face, the raw bite of every breath in her lungs, the rasp of sand in her sandals. Slowly she walked towards the entrance of the temple, shaking her head against the haze which seemed to surround her, now crawling across the sand on her belly like a snake, now drifting on the air with the falcon and the circling ever-watchful vulture.

She was drifting, rootless, overwhelmed with anger, then cold with fear as the gods came near and shook their heads and turned away.

'Anna? Anna!'

Voices echoed in her head, then died away, carried on the desert wind from the south.

'Anna? Can you hear me? Oh God, what's happened to her?'

She smiled as the sweet scents of flowers and fruit blew across the sand from the temple buildings. Aniseed and cinnamon, dill and thyme, figs and pomegranate, olive and grape and sweet juicy dates. Herbs from the carefully irrigated gardens, and from the incense rooms, resins and oils.

Her hands reached out towards the dazzling light. She could feel the sticky richness of wine and honey on her palms. Oh beloved land, Ta-Mera, land of the flood and of the fire.

'Anna!' It was Toby's voice, Toby's hands on her shoulders, her arms. 'Anna, what's wrong?' He was far away, his voice an echo across time. Then there were other voices, bright lights in her eyes, fingers on her pulse. She shrugged. They were distant and unimportant. The sun was setting in a blaze of crimson. Soon the stars would shine out across the desert: the great river in the sky, the milky way, mirror image of the river below and, brighter than any other, the sacred star, Sept, the dog star at the heel of the god Osiris.

Then all was dark. She slept. When she woke she felt the cold

368

sweet waters of the Nile on her lips. Voices again, echoing over untold distances, the silence and darkness again.

'Anna!' That was Serena. 'Anna, you're going home.'

But this was home. The home of the gods, the land of the sun god, Ra.

Strange. She was in a car. She could feel the rattle of wheels, hear the blast of horns, smell exhaust fumes, but they were all so far away. There was a strong arm round her shoulders and she leant on it gratefully, her body tired beyond all endurance whilst her brain still yearned towards the desert and the sun.

She slept again. The scream of jet engines was the mighty roar of the cataracts inside her head, the swirling water lit by rainbows beneath the dark Nilotic rock, the lift of the wheels from the tarmac, the free flight of the great falcon from whose eyes the whole land of Egypt could be seen.

Obediently she sipped fruit juice and nibbled a piece of bread. Her eyelids closed. Her head filled again with the shriek of the wind, the fury of a dust storm, and the fierce sword stroke of desert lightning above clouds that would never give birth to rain.

Above her head Serena and Toby exchanged glances and frowned. When the cabin attendant brought more food they waved her on.

The air of England was ice-rimed and sharp. In the taxi Anna stirred. The voice inside her head grew querulous. The being that stared out of her eyes grew restless. Where was the sun?

Anna grew weaker every second.

'I'm sorry to land all this on you, Ma. We didn't know where to take her.' Toby's voice was clear suddenly, his arm, still there around her, guiding her, giving her strength. 'She lives alone, and as we told you, Charley is at Serena's so there is no room there, and I don't know how to contact her family.'

'Take her upstairs, darling.' The voice that answered his was kind and deep, cultured and reassuring. 'Let her sleep. The doctor is on his way.'

She sank down into the soft warm bed and felt the embrace of duck down, the support of fluffy pillows in the cool darkness of an English bedroom.

Bit by bit his grip was loosening, the parasitical hold on her life

369

force was weaker each moment she lay asleep under cold northern skies. Egypt was far away.

The priest of Sekhmet looked out of an English woman's eyes at a strange and alien world and felt sudden overwhelming fear.

15

I am Yesterday and Today; and I have the power
to be born a second time.
Let the decree of Amen-Ra, the king of the gods,
the great god,
the prince of that which hath come into being
from the beginning,
be performed.

The fever that kills everyone in the house of the merchant shocks his neighbours and his friends. His nephew comes to retrieve his treasures and boxes them up to take them to the bazaar. Much money changes hands over the weeks and months that follow. The pretty bottle, fit gift for a lady, with the piece of paper that tells its legend, stands on the shelf and beckons. The priests, strong and angry, fight one against the other in the halls of the heavens and rend the curtains of darkness with their spears.

The merchant who looks after the stall in the bazaar falls sick. His last sale is to a handsome young man whose eyes are alight with love and who seeks a gift for his special lady.

'Anna, are you awake?' Frances Hayward put her tray down near the door and crossing to the window pulled back the heavy curtains so that the watery winter sunshine poured in across the patchwork coverlet. She turned to view her charge. The woman she saw lying propped up on the pillows was pale and very thin, her long dark hair strewn across the sprigged cotton; her large green eyes, opening slowly to view the room for the first time clearly, were deeply undershadowed with exhaustion and strain.

For days now the strange amnesia which had been blanketing her mind and preventing her from functioning on any but the most basic level had been growing lighter. She smiled at Frances as she pulled herself up against the pillows. The room already scented by the bowl of pink hyacinths on the table in front of the window was suddenly full of the smell of rich coffee and toast.

'So, how do you feel?' Frances put the tray on Anna's knees then she sat down beside her. There was a second cup of coffee on the tray and she helped herself to it, her eyes on Anna's face.

Anna shook her head. 'Confused. Woolly. My memory is so muddled. It doesn't seem to be coming back.' She glanced quickly at Frances. Her hostess was a tall woman with wild curly grey hair. She had strong bones and a handsome face. The resemblance to Toby was there, oblique but unmistakable.

She met Anna's gaze steadily and smiled. 'Shall I tell you again? I'm Toby's mother, Frances. You have been here three weeks now. You remember who Toby is?' She raised a quizzical eyebrow.

Anna was playing with a small piece of toast. When there was no response Frances went on, 'You met him on a Nile cruise. You became ill during your last few days there. Toby and your friend Serena didn't know what to do, so they brought you here.'

'And you've been looking after a complete stranger.' Anna crumbled the piece of toast between her fingers.

'It's been a pleasure for me. But I'm worried, my dear. You must have friends and family who are wondering where you are.'

372

Anna picked up her coffee cup and blew gently at the hot steam. The smell cut deep into her brain and she frowned, trying to cudgel her memory. There was so much there, just out of reach, like a dream that slips away even as one wakes up. There were pictures of sand dunes and shimmering heat, of the brilliant blue of the river and the green of the palms, but no faces, no names, nothing to pin anything to. She sipped the coffee again and frowned.

'Toby was wondering whether it would jog your memory if we took you to your house. If you feel strong enough, that is.' Frances was watching Anna's face.

Anna looked up. Her expression was suddenly more animated than it had been so far. 'You know where I live?'

Frances smiled. 'Yes, we know that much! But we couldn't leave you there alone, could we? And we didn't know who to call about you. You told Toby something of your family circumstances, but he couldn't remember any names or addresses.'

They took a taxi across London later that afternoon, Anna wearing a borrowed pair of trousers and an elegant sweater from Frances's wardrobe against the cold March wind. All the clothes in her suit-case were light summer fabrics designed to be worn on a cruise. There was nothing there which would protect her from the south-easterly which was whipping through the streets, rattling billboards, scattering litter along the pavements and whining in the TV aerials far above the street.

The taxi pulled up outside a small pretty terraced house in Notting Hill and they all climbed out. Anna stood surveying the warm grey brick, the square Queen-Anne windows with narrow wrought iron windowbox holders, the blue front door with a half-moon skylight and the tiny front garden. It seemed familiar, yet somehow strangely unconnected.

'It looks nice,' she said with a wry smile. 'Are you sure I live here?'

'I'm not sure of anything.' Toby put his arm lightly round her shoulders. 'See if you've got the key.'

She glanced at him sharply then she rummaged in her shoulder bag and pulled out a bunch of keys.

The house smelt cold and unlived in and there was a pile of

letters behind the door. Stooping to pick them up Anna walked into the living room on the righthand side of the narrow hallway and looked round. The room was furnished with antiques, the sober polished woods set off with colourful rugs and cushions and scarlet swagged curtains which were half-drawn across the windows looking out onto the garden at the back.

Toby reached for the lightswitch. 'Nice house.' He grinned

On a table by the small Knole sofa a light on the answerphone blinked steadily announcing five calls.

'Only five and I've been away weeks.' Anna stared down at it.

'I expect all your friends knew you were away. It's only recently they've realised you should be back,' Toby commented sensibly. 'Aren't you going to listen?' He was standing with his back to the fireplace, his arms folded. 'There might be a clue.'

Anna shrugged. She reached out and punched the play button.

'. . . Anna, dear, this is your great-aunt Phyl!' The voice was loud in the quiet room and indignant. 'Where on earth are you? You said you'd come and see me the moment you got back. I'm dying to hear how you got on. Ring me.'

'. . . Anna? Your great-aunt seems to think you're avoiding her. Ring her or me, for God's sake!' This was a cross male voice. Her father. She recognised it without a moment's hesitation.

'. . . Anna, it's Felix. I got your postcard. I'm so glad you're having a good time. Take care.' That too was familiar. She began to smile.

'. . . Anna? Anna, are you there?' Silence, then a suppressed curse. Female. Unknown.

'. . . Anna? It's Phyllis again. My dear, I'm worried about you. Do please get in touch.'

Toby was watching her face. 'You recognised the voices?'

Anna nodded. 'And this house. It's all familiar. But it doesn't feel like mine.' She shook her head and put her hand to her eyes. 'I feel like a stranger. But I do recognise it all.'

'I'm going to ring your aunt back.' Toby reached for the phone and punched in 1471. After a pause she saw him press the 3 to return the call.

The phone rang for a long time before it was answered. 'Do you want to speak to her?' Toby held out the receiver. Anna shrugged and took it from him.

'Anna? Anna, thank goodness, my darling! I was beginning to think you'd fallen in love with Egypt or found yourself a handsome

374

sheikh or something and decided never to come home!' The voice on the other end paused. 'Anna?'

Anna shook her head. Tears were pouring down her face. She couldn't speak.

Toby took the receiver from her. 'Miss Shelley?' He gave Anna a reassuring smile. 'I'm sorry to interrupt. My name is Toby Hayward. I was on the cruise with Anna. She has not been very well. Is there any chance you could come up to London, or could I drive her over to you? She wants to see you so much.'

He listened for a few seconds, hastened to respond to the anxious questions, reassured and nodded. 'OK. I'll bring her to Suffolk tomorrow. I'm so glad we've made contact.'

He put down the phone. 'She wanted you to go today, but I thought you might be too tired. We'll leave first thing in the morning.' He glanced at his mother who had been standing quietly by the door, studying the room. 'Do you want to help Anna find some warm clothes while we're here?'

Anna was idly picking through the post which was lying beside her on the sofa. She reached for a postcard, studied the picture and then read the back. Then another. At least two of her friends, it appeared, had also been on holiday recently. There were several bills which she automatically discarded unopened, much to Toby's amusement as he pointed out that her good sense had not deserted her along with her memory.

'It's only my memory of the holiday that's completely gone,' she said wearily. 'The rest seems to be here, intact. I recognised my father's voice, and Felix, my ex. I recognised Phyllis.' She shook her head. 'I couldn't recall them spontaneously: it's all been a strange blank when you and the doctor have asked me about things; but when I heard their voices and looked for them in my head they were there!' She broke off. She was looking down at a letter in her hand. It had Egyptian stamps. Her face grew pale.

Toby glanced at Frances. He put his finger to his lips. They both watched Anna as slowly she tore open the envelope. 'It's from Omar,' she said slowly. 'He wants to know how I am?'

She looked up and her eyes widened. The floodgates had opened. A torrent of memory, of noise, of images, of shouting, suddenly poured into her head. She sat down abruptly and stared wildly up at them.

'Oh God! Andy! I remember now. Andy died!'

375

Toby sat down beside her, and put his arm round her shoulders. 'Do you remember what else happened?' he asked gently.

She was staring down at the letter in her hands. 'The scent bottle. The scent bottle of the priest of Sekhmet!' Suddenly she began to sob, tears pouring down her face. She looked up at Toby. 'I remember Andy falling in the Nile. We'd been to Philae.'

Toby nodded.

'Then his body disappeared. There was no sign of it –'

'They found him the next day, Anna –'

'And Ibrahim gave me an amulet.' She put her hand to her throat as though she had only at that moment become aware of the charm hanging on the chain round her neck. 'I'm still wearing it! But it's valuable, I should have returned it to him!'

'No, he wanted you to keep it. He especially told me to tell you to keep it for ever, Anna.' Toby took Omar's letter out of her hands and put it down on the table.

'What happened to Andy?' She turned to him, her eyes blind with tears.

'His body was flown back to London and buried in his family's home village in Sussex. Serena and Charley and Ben all went to the funeral.'

'And Charley?' Anna echoed the name. 'Is she all right now?'

Toby nodded. 'She's fine.'

'So it's just me.' She looked down at her hands. 'It wasn't shock, you know.' Suddenly it was all crystal clear in her mind. 'He needed me. The priest needed me when Charley left Egypt and I let him in. Serena summoned him at Philae and I watched and smiled and was all eager to see what happened and he jumped inside my head! Serena knew how dangerous he was. Ibrahim knew. But I just opened myself up and let it happen! Where is Serena? What has happened to her?'

'Serena has been to see you several times, Anna,' Toby said. 'She's been so worried about you. She tried to explain to the doctor that she thought you had been possessed, but he was not prepared to listen. He patronised her horribly. If I hadn't seen it myself I wouldn't have believed how he behaved to her. I wouldn't have been surprised if she hadn't come back, but she did and she brought someone else to try and help you, but by then you didn't want anyone else poking around in your head and we decided it was better to wait until your memory came back by itself. Ma wanted to bring in a clergyman but Serena said that would make the priest angry.'

Anna shuddered. 'I've been so much trouble to you?' She looked up miserably. 'And it's all my fault.'

'It wasn't your fault.' Frances came and knelt in front of her. 'None of it was. How could anyone have known that these terrible things would happen?' She shivered. 'Come on. Let me help you pack some warm clothes. Then we'll go home. Tomorrow you will be with your great-aunt and things will start to get back to normal for you.'

'Nothing can ever be normal again.' Anna shook her head. 'I killed Andy. With the help of the stupid little bottle.'

'No,' Toby was adamant. 'What killed Andy was a large bottle – of vodka – on an empty stomach! Never, never blame yourself, Anna.'

It occurred to her for the first time that evening to wonder where it was that Toby went after the three of them had eaten together at the small round table in Frances's lower-ground-floor kitchen. She asked Frances only after he had kissed them both on the cheek and run up the area steps, jingling his car keys, to disappear into the frosty London night.

Frances laughed. 'Didn't he tell you? He's staying with someone called Ben Forbes. I gather he met him on this infamous cruise of yours.' She hesitated. 'Toby lives in Scotland, Anna. You knew that, didn't you? After his wife died he didn't want to stay in London any more and he gave me this house. Normally he stays upstairs in your bedroom when he's in town, but he felt very strongly that he didn't want to crowd you.'

'He's been very kind to me,' Anna said thoughtfully. 'I don't know what would have happened to me if he hadn't been there.' She glanced up. 'And I would never have met you.'

Frances smiled. 'I was so pleased he brought you here.' She was busying herself making them both a night cap. 'I expect you have gathered I am a widow. And Toby is an only. I'm just so pleased he and I are friends. I gather he told you about that dreadful time ten years ago?' She glanced up and when Anna nodded she went on. 'He became very defensive after Sarah died; he cut so many people out of his life.'

377

It was the moment to ask questions. To find out more about what had happened. Anna hesitated and the moment passed. 'Will you come with us tomorrow, to Suffolk?' she asked instead.

Frances shook her head. 'No, my dear. I would love to meet your great-aunt one day, but not this time.' She hesitated. 'Toby said you are divorced?'

Anna nodded.

'That must have been sad for you.'

'Not really. A shock at first, to find things weren't as I thought. Then, in the end, a relief. That was Felix, my husband, on the phone at the house. We still speak.'

'And you sent him a postcard.'

Anna nodded again. She accepted a mug of hot chocolate from Frances and sipped it slowly. 'Did Toby tell you the whole story of the trip?'

Frances shook her head. 'I'm pretty sure not. To be honest in the cold light of a London winter it all sounded a bit farfetched. No!' She reached out her hand towards Anna as the latter opened her mouth to protest. 'I'm not saying it didn't happen. Clearly something awful did happen. I'm just saying I found it hard to picture it all. Andy's death was sufficiently dreadful for me. Perhaps that's all I can cope with at this stage.'

Anna nodded slowly. Her fingers groped inside the neck of her blouse and closed round Ibrahim's amulet. 'I would like to go and see his grave,' she said. 'Take him some flowers. Tell him I'm sorry.'

Frances glanced at her. She hesitated, obviously trying to decide how to respond. 'Anna, my dear, you weren't in love with Andy, were you?'

'In love with him!' Anna was shocked. 'No, of course I wasn't!'

'I just wanted to make sure.'

There was a long silence. Anna was groping for words, unsure of her ground, aware suddenly of a huge misty gulf in her memory. 'Did Toby not tell you about Andy and me? How he was trying to get hold of my great-great-grandmother's diary?'

Frances nodded. 'He told me. He told me a lot of things, but he left some out as well.'

'Oh?' Anna stared down into her drink.

'Things which are none of my business, such as how you two feel about each other.'

Anna could feel her cheeks colouring. 'I know how I feel about him.'

'You're fond of him?' Frances glanced up and catching Anna's eye she smiled. 'In love with him?' She waved her hand in front of her, the fingers crossed.

'I think I might be.' Anna shrugged. 'But we've had such a short time together and that time was difficult!'

Frances snorted. 'That seems like an understatement! I won't ask any more, my dear. Just know that I'm so pleased Toby met you.' She reached across the table and squeezed Anna's hand.

Anna went over that short conversation again and again in her head as she lay in the bath luxuriating in the mixed oils of rose and lavender she had found on the shelf above it and a smile came slowly to her lips. Wrapped in a huge soft towel she climbed back to her attic room and wandered round for a while thinking about the visit to her great-aunt next morning with Toby.

The diary lay on the small table in front of the window. She stood staring down at it, frowning. She had promised that she would give it to Frances to look at tomorrow while they were out, but in the meantime were there not one or two pages left that she still had not read herself?

The last thing she remembered doing on the boat was putting down the diary on the bed in her cabin and lying staring at the ceiling, overwhelmed with fear and a strange, alien rage.

She reached for the book thoughtfully. Had he really gone, the priest who had invaded her head, or was he merely biding his time? She shuddered and moved her head cautiously from side to side as though testing it, then she looked down at the book in her hands. In the last section she had read Louisa was planning to go out to the Valley of the Tombs to bury the scent bottle which had turned out to be a sacred ampulla, at the feet of Isis.

It was dawn when Louisa and Mohammed mounted their donkeys and turning their backs on the river, headed westward across the rich, densely planted fields. They rode in silence, unencumbered by pack animals or companions, watching the dull clear light grow stronger by the minute. As the first shafts of sunlight were throwing long shadows ahead of them across the ground they had already reached the edge of the fertile ground and were heading out into the bright heat of the desert.

'Where will you put the bottle, Sitt Louisa?' Mohammed looked over at her at last. 'Which tomb do you want to go to?'

Louisa shrugged. 'Somewhere quiet and hidden so the bottle can rest in peace. I need to find a picture of the goddess Isis so it can lie near her.' Her donkey stumbled suddenly and she grabbed at the saddle to steady herself. 'That is all I want to do. Then we can go straight back to the boat and forget it.'

He nodded gravely. The path had narrowed as they reached the mouth of the valley. He glanced round at the dark entrances in the cliffs. He was not a dragoman. He did not have Hassan's knowledge and experience of the valley. Reining in the donkey he shook his head. 'Do you remember where to go?'

She stared round her, hoping that Mohammed would attribute the tears in her eyes to the glare of the early morning sun striking off the glittering rocks. Her memories of this place were so closely tied to Hassan, every rock, every shadow bore the imprint of his face, every echo the sound of his voice.

Finally she urged her donkey on. There were other visitors in the valley this time, groups of travellers with their own dragomans staring round, or emerging into the daylight full of wonder at what they had seen.

They stopped the donkeys near one of the entrances. Mohammed slid from the saddle and helped Louisa to dismount then he reached into his saddle bag for candles. He shivered. 'I do not like these places, Sitt Louisa. There are bad spirits here. And scorpions.'

And snakes.

The word hovered unspoken between them. Louisa bit her lip and forced herself to move forward, leading the way. 'We won't be here long, Mohammed, I promise. You have the spade?'

They had brought a small spade lashed to the saddle of his mount so she could bury the bottle in the sand. He nodded. Swiftly he moved in front of her and she saw he had his hand on the hilt of the knife tucked into his belt and it gave her some comfort as they climbed the path towards the dark square in the dazzling rock of the cliff, to think that he was armed and prepared to use the knife to protect them.

They reached the entrance, panting. Mohammed peered in. 'Is this the right place?' She saw him make surreptitiously the sign against the evil eye.

She nodded. Somewhere inside she would find a representation of the goddess with her strange characteristic head-dress of a solar disc and throne, her hands clutching the ankh, symbol of life, and her staff.

She reached into the bag hung around her shoulders for the bottle, still wrapped in the water-stained silk. 'It won't take long,' she repeated. She stepped ahead of him into the darkness, hearing the rasp of a match behind her as he lit the candle in its little lantern, seeing the shadows run up the wall. Here they were, the pictures she remembered so clearly, the bright colours, the dense endless stories told in strange indecipherable hieroglyphics, the ranks of gods and goddesses stretching into the shadowed darkness.

'Sitt Louisa!' His strangled cry echoed into the silent depths of the tomb.

She spun round.

He was standing at the entrance almost where she had left him, still in the sunlight, flattened against the wall, frozen with terror. In front of him she could see the swaying head of the cobra.

'No!' Her scream tore into the shadows as she hurled herself back towards the cave entrance. 'Leave him alone! No! No! *No* . . .'

As the snake struck she threw the bottle at it and then went for it herself, grabbing at it with her bare hands. It thrashed for a moment in her grip – warm, smooth, heavy, and then it had gone. She was staring down at her empty fingers.

Mohammed slid to his knees, sobbing. 'Sitt Louisa, you have saved my life!'

'It didn't bite you?' Suddenly she was shaking so violently she too could no longer stand and she found herself on her knees beside him.

'No.' He closed his eyes and took a deep breath. 'No, *Lillah*! It did not bite me. See!' He held out the width of the full trouser leg and she saw the mark of the fangs and the long trail of the poison which had run down the cotton below the hole.

There was a rattle of stones below them and they looked down to see two men scrambling up the path. One, dressed in Egyptian robes, had a drawn blade in his hand. The other was a European.

'We heard your screams.' The taller man when he spoke was obviously English. He stared round the tomb entrance as the two Egyptians spoke to one another in quick agitated Arabic.

'It was a snake.' Louisa looked at him gratefully. 'I think it's gone.' She scrambled shakily to her feet.

'Did it bite anyone?'

She shook her head. 'It missed, thank God!' She closed her eyes.

The bottle had gone. There was no sign of it on the path, in the tomb entrance, on the track down the steep hillside at the base of the cliff. It had vanished with the snake.

She accepted their rescuers' offer of rest and refreshment, then she and Mohammed reclaimed their donkeys and headed back towards the river.

They arrived back hot and dusty to find the boat in turmoil. One of the travellers planning to return north to Cairo had fallen sick and a berth had been found for her on the next day's steamer. There was very little time if she wanted to take it up. She must pack her belongings, say her farewells and allow her trunks to be loaded into the launch and moved over to the larger boat without delay.

Later she was glad it had all happened so quickly. There was no time for retrospection. Barely time for goodbyes. Mohammed and the *reis* wept as she left the boat for the last time, as did Katherine Fielding who had, to her delight named her baby Louis after her. Venetia offered a cold cheek with barely a smile, David Fielding and Sir John both gave her huge bear hugs. Augusta took her hands and squeezed them. 'Time heals, my dear,' she said gently. 'You'll forget the worst times and remember the good ones.'

It was strange, travelling with the constant sound of an engine and the splash of the paddle wheels as a background to her thoughts. There was no need to be at the command of the fickle wind. The river banks with their moving panorama of palms and lush crops, the shaduf, lifting the water endlessly from the river to the fields as they passed, the plodding water buffalo, the donkeys, the fishing boats. She watched them all from the deck, her reddened eyes hidden by smoked-glass spectacles, sketched, wrote a line or two in her diary to bring the account of her visit to Egypt to an end and she slept.

She reached London on 24th April. A week later she was reunited with her sons. It wasn't until the 29th July, on a hot afternoon as she worked in the cool tree-shaded room that she used as her studio at the back of their London house, that she opened the first of the boxes of Egyptian canvases and sketchbooks and began to pull them out one by one. Carefully she stacked them round the walls studying them critically, allowing herself for the first time since her return to remember the heat and the dust, the blue waters of the Nile, the dazzling glare of the sand and the temples and monuments with their carvings and paintings and mementoes of a long-dead past. She paused to stare out of the window at the garden square outside her house. Her world, the English world, was predominantly green, even here in London. The desert and the Nile were nothing to her now but memories.

She stooped to pick the last canvases out of the box and frowned. Her old bag was there. She must have used it to wedge the paintings in place. She pulled it out and stared at it ruefully. The bag had accompanied her on all her painting trips. Even now there were brushes and some paints left inside. She put it on the table and rummaged inside to retrieve them.

The scent bottle was still wrapped in the stained silk, tied with ribbon. She stared down at it for a long, long time, then slowly she began to unwrap it.

She had taken the bottle out of the bag. She had thrown it at the snake. Surely she had. She remembered it being in her hand. She remembered looking down at it as she stepped out of the sunlight into the shadow of the tomb.

Dropping the silk to the floor she stood looking at it as it lay on her palm. Then she shivered. Once again it had returned. Could she never be rid of it? 'Hassan.' She whispered the name quietly. 'Help me.' There were tears in her eyes as she turned to the Davenport at which she was accustomed to sit and do her correspondence.

383

Opening the lid she slid out one of the drawers and reached inside to touch the small lever that activated the secret compartment. She laid the bottle inside it and stood looking down at it for a moment then she touched her finger to her lips and pressed it lightly on the glass. The piece of paper telling its story, she had left tucked in her diary, still in her writing box and unlooked at for months. One last look, one last thought of Hassan and she pushed the secret drawer back. It clicked into place and she quickly shut the lid of the desk.

She would never touch the drawer, or her journal again.

'Did you know all this when you gave me the diary?' Anna was sitting next to Toby in Phyllis's sun-filled sitting room.

Phyllis shook her head. 'I always meant to try, but somehow with my bad eyes I never got round to reading it.'

'So you didn't know about the bottle when you gave it to me?'

Phyllis shook her head. 'I would hardly have given it to you, sweetheart if I'd known its history!' She was indignant. 'You were a little girl. As far as I knew it had lain in that drawer ever since Louisa put it there. The Davenport came to me through my father, of course, and I knew nothing of the paper in the diary. Even if I'd known it was there it would have meant nothing to me. None of us can read Arabic.'

The three of them sat in silence for several minutes. In the hearth the fire crackled cheerfully, filling the room with the scent of apple logs.

'What happened to Louisa in the end, do you know?' Anna asked at last.

Phyllis nodded slowly. 'I know a bit. My grandfather as you know was her eldest son, David.' She paused thoughtfully. 'She never married again. And as far as I know she never went back to Egypt. She moved from London sometime in the 1880s, by which time she must have been in her late fifties or early sixties, I suppose.

She bought a house down in Hampshire which she left to David when she died. I can remember going there when I was very small but it must have been sold before the last war. She went on painting, of course, and became a very well-known artist, even in her lifetime.'

'Did she ever keep a journal again?' Toby asked suddenly.

Phyllis shrugged. 'Not as far as I know.'

'I'd love to know if she ever thought about Egypt again,' Anna said wistfully. 'What must she have felt like when she found she still had the scent bottle after everything she had been through to try and get rid of it? And why did she hide it? Why didn't she destroy it as soon as she found it? Why didn't she throw it in the Thames? The sea? Anything! But to keep it close to her. Wasn't she afraid the priests would come back? Or the serpent?'

Phyllis sat back in her chair and stared thoughtfully down at the fire. The cat on her knees stretched luxuriously and kneaded the thick tweed of her skirt for a moment or two before falling back to sleep. 'I'll tell you what I have got. There is a box of Grandfather's old letters upstairs. His own to the family and those from his brother John mostly. I don't remember there being anything particularly exciting but you can have them if you want them. Toby dear, could you go up and carry them down for Anna?' She gave him instructions on where to find them and watched as he left the room. Then she smiled. 'You hang on to him, darling. He's a very nice man. Are you in love with him?'

Anna blushed. 'I like him.'

'Like?' Phyllis shook her head. 'Not good enough. I want to hear that you adore someone. And that someone adores you. He does, you know. He doesn't seem to be able to take his eyes off you.' She sobered abruptly. 'What really happened to you in Egypt? I don't think you've told me everything. I'm sorry about that unfortunate man drowning. But there's more, isn't there. Do I gather you were ill?'

Anna nodded slowly. 'Not ill exactly. I'll tell you what happened. Did you know the scent bottle was haunted? I know that sounds crazy. Impossible. But it's true. It was guarded by two Ancient Egyptian priests who were rivals for its ownership. They appeared on the boat and scared me witless so I did something very stupid. I had made friends with a woman called Serena Canfield. She is an initiate of some kind of a modern day Isis cult. She summoned up the priests to try and send them away. A sort of spirit disinfection. But I let one of them get inside my head. I went a bit mad for a while after Andy died. If Toby hadn't taken care of me I don't know what would have happened.'

'Anhotep and Hatsek.' Phyllis repeated the two names softly.

Anna wondered for a moment if she had heard correctly. Her eyes widened. 'Then you have read the diary?' she accused.

'No.' Phyllis shook her head slowly. 'There is a painting of them, here, in this house. Their names are written on the back.'

Anna stared at her. She had gone completely cold all over. 'Where is it?'

'I never liked the painting but I knew it must be valuable. It's probably worth a fortune at today's prices so I kept it, but I put it in the back store room.' She turned as Toby reappeared with an old school tuck box in his arms. 'Put it down there. Thank you, my dear.' She frowned as Anna made for the door. 'Darling, wait. Be careful! Toby, go with her.'

'Where? Where are we going?' Toby hurried down the long passage after her leaving Phyllis sitting by the fire, her face buried in the cat's fur.

'She's got a picture of them! In the freezer room. I don't believe it! She's got a painting of the priests!' Anna pushed open the door of the kitchen and led the way inside. It was a large kitchen, warmed by an old cream-coloured Aga, the scrubbed oak table littered with books and papers, the dresser hung in equal number with colourful mugs and ancient cracked tea cups. For a moment she stood still, staring at the door between the dresser and the sink. 'It's in there.' She swallowed. Her hand went to the amulet at her throat. 'Toby, it's in there!'

'There's no need to look at it.'

'There is. I've got to see it. Don't you see, I've got to see if they looked the same to Louisa!' She stared round the room, focusing on the vase of winter jasmine on the dresser. She found she had reached for Toby's hand, trying to steady the beating pulse in her ears.

'You're safe, Anna. The bottle is at the bottom of the Nile.' Toby put an arm round her shoulders. 'It's just a picture. We can ignore it. Go back to the fire and look at the letters. Put the kettle on again and top up the teapot. Go home.'

She shook her head. 'I've got to see it.' Taking a deep breath

386

she walked over to the door and opening it she reached for the lightswitch. The room was small, lined with shelves of tins and jars and boxes on three walls and almost filled by a large chest freezer on the fourth. Above that there were hooks, carrying string bags, onions, garlic, old saucepans and baskets. She stared round and for a moment she didn't see the picture. Then she spotted it, half shrouded by a net of potatoes. The frame measured about two feet high by about eighteen inches across. It showed two tall dark-skinned men standing in the desert against a sky the colour of sapphires and framed by a huge acacia tree. One was dressed in white linen robes, the other wore an animal skin draped over his shoulder and round his waist. Both wore strange head-dresses and carried tall staffs and were staring out of the picture towards the viewer with an expression of intense concentration. Toby turned from studying the picture to look at Anna. She had gone as white as a sheet.

'That's them,' she whispered, 'just as I saw them.'

'OK. That's enough.' Toby pulled her away. 'Come on. Back to the fire.' He switched off the light and shut the door behind them.

'Why haven't I seen it before?' She shook her head. 'I've been in that room a hundred times. Opened the freezer, fetched things from the shelves. Since I was a child!'

'Perhaps it wasn't there before. Or as it was half hidden perhaps you just didn't notice it. After all, it meant nothing to you then.' He followed her back along the passage to the sitting room.

Phyllis was sitting on a cushion on the hearth rug in front of the fire, the open box beside her. The cat had taken over full custody of her chair. She glanced up as they came in. 'Did you see it?'

'How long has it been hanging there?' Anna threw herself down on her knees beside her great-aunt.

'Oh, my dear, I don't know. Thirty years? I can't remember when we put it there. It used to give me the creeps, so one day I went and hung it in there out of sight!'

'Then why haven't I seen it before?'

'You have. You just never noticed it.'

'But don't you see? If I'd seen it I would have recognised them. I'd have known who they were.' She slumped back on her heels, her hands to her head.

Toby sat down beside her. 'Anna, an awful lot of people can see something every day of their lives and not look at it,' he said gently.

387

'Especially if you didn't find it interesting. After all, you had no reason to notice it, did you? It meant nothing to you until you actually went to Egypt.'

'Unless I noticed it, and stored it away in my memory like some hidden nightmare to bring back later. Going to Egypt reminded me in some strange subliminal way. What do they call it? Hidden memories? Perhaps I made it all up. Cryptomnesia? Created the whole thing out of my imagination.' She stared at them both hopefully.

Phyllis shrugged. 'I've found the early letters,' she put in quietly. She held out some envelopes fastened together with white tape. 'See if there is anything interesting.'

With shaking hands Anna drew the first out of its envelope. She read it quietly and passed it to Phyllis with a smile. 'They are very early. Your grandfather is still at school in this one.'

She opened another, then another, slowly relaxing as she became immersed in the gentle day to day activities of a Victorian family. It was ten minutes later that she let out a little cry of surprise. 'No! Oh God, listen! This letter is dated 1873. It's from John. That's Louisa's younger son. "Dear David. Mother is not well again. I called the doctor, but he has no clue what is wrong. He orders her to bed and commands us to keep her still and warm. On her orders I went to the studio to fetch her a sketchbook hoping to keep her in bed drawing. Imagine my astonishment when I was confronted by a large snake! I had no notion what to do! I slammed the door and called Norton."' She looked up. 'Who was Norton? "We went in very cautiously and found nothing. It must have made its way through the window which was open and out into the street! It must have escaped from the Zoological Gardens."' Putting down the letter she stared into the fire. 'The snake came to England,' she said bleakly. 'It followed the bottle.'

'Does he say anything else?' Toby was frowning. She shook her head. 'We did not tell Mother in case it alarmed her.' She gave a short laugh. 'How wise!' She leafed through some more letters. 'No, nothing else. These are from Cambridge. Then the army. There is no mention of home. No, wait.' She held up another letter in excitement. 'This is Louisa's writing.' She opened the folded sheets reverently and was surprised to find there was a lump in her throat. It was like rediscovering an old friend.

There was a long silence as she scanned its pages. When she

looked up her face was pinched and drawn. 'Read it.' She handed it to Toby. 'Read it out loud.'

'"I have painted a picture of my persecutors in the hope of getting them out of my head. They haunt my dreams even now, so many years after my visit to Egypt." Who is she writing this letter to?' He looked up.

'It is addressed to Augusta. The Forresters were living in Hampshire. Perhaps that's why she moved there.' She shivered. Hugging her knees she stared into the fire. 'Go on.'

'"Last night I dreamt about Hassan. How I miss him still. Not a day goes by without him appearing at some point in my memories. But I dread his two companions in my thoughts. Will they give me no rest? They beg me to take the phial back to Egypt. If I were strong, perhaps I would do so. Perhaps one day one of my sons or grandsons will take it for me."' Toby broke off, staring at Anna. 'That's you. Her great–great–granddaughter. You took it back.'

She nodded. 'But something went wrong. I didn't know what I was supposed to do. I didn't do it right.'

'You left the bottle in Egypt.' Phyllis untied another bundle of letters. 'That was the important thing.'

'And sacrificed a man's life.'

'No, Anna. The fact that Andy died as the bottle went into the Nile was pure accident. He was blind drunk.' Toby folded up the letter and put it back in its envelope. 'In fact, although it is probably no consolation, I have read since that it was considered very good fortune to die in the Nile, as one was taken directly by the gods. But remember, there were no priests and no snakes in that launch.'

'No?' Anna smiled quietly. 'The priest of Sekhmet was in my head, Toby.'

Phyllis frowned. 'We haven't talked about you, Toby.' She changed the subject adroitly. 'Come on. Let's have all the details. What do you do for a living?'

Toby smiled. Sitting up straight he gave a mock salute. 'I'm afraid I paint, too.' He shrugged helplessly. 'Not as famous as Louisa, but I have had several exhibitions and I can earn my living at it. I am also lucky enough to have inherited a bit of money when my father died, so I've been very spoilt. I'm a widower.' He hesitated, glancing at Anna. Then he shook his head and went on. 'I have a mother, no brothers or sisters, alas, but an uncle who is at the consulate in Cairo, hence my contacts over there. I do not work for the CIA or the Mafia. I am not wanted by the police as our poor late friend Andy seemed to think. I have a house in the Scottish borders and another in London which is where my mother lives. My passion, at least until recently, has been travelling and painting. Mostly I go on my own, but sometimes I've been known to do daft things like travel on the Orient Express just for the hell of it, or go for a cruise on the Nile. I've supplemented my income by writing two travel books, both quite well received.' He grinned. 'If I write about our last cruise it will, I fear, have to be fiction and I shall launch myself as a thriller writer or no one will believe it!' He shrugged. 'That's it, really, except to apologise for abandoning Anna at Abu Simbel. I never got the chance to explain what happened and why I wasn't there when she needed me.' He shook his head. 'I met a friend of my mother's who was on a different cruise. She was on her own and just after I had spoken to her she was taken ill. That was why the tourist police were looking for me. It was at her request. By the time I'd sorted her out, Anna had got on the bus and gone.'

Anna smiled. 'Being kind to ladies in distress again. It's a good excuse. You're forgiven.'

'Good.' Phyllis climbed to her feet with a groan. 'Well, dears. I think it's time for a stiff drink. You take these letters away if you want them. And the picture.' She paused. 'No? All right. I'll keep your priests on ice, as before.' She laughed. At the door she paused and looked back. 'Did I tell you, Toby? You've passed muster. I think you'll do.'

Anna grinned. 'She hated my ex,' she said quietly. 'And most of my old boyfriends, so you are honoured.'

'I'm glad.' He moved forward and leant down to kiss the top of her head. 'But this is going a bit fast, Anna. I'm not offering marriage. At least, not yet –'

'And I'm not looking for marriage. Not ever!' she retorted sharply. 'I'm an independent lady, looking for a career in photography. Remember?'

He nodded.

'But don't tell Phyllis. Not yet. Don't spoil her fun.' She glanced up at him and raised an eyebrow. 'OK?'

'OK.' He nodded. 'Sounds fine by me.'

*   *   *

They arrived back in London very late, but lights were still burning in the basement of the house as they let themselves in. Frances was sitting at the kitchen table, reading. She glanced up at them. 'Have you had a good day? I'm dying to hear all about it. But first –' She stopped for a moment and they both saw a frown hover between her eyes. Then she went on. 'I've been riveted by your diary, Anna. I've hardly moved all day.' She stretched wearily. 'And I've got something very odd to tell you. I don't know how you're going to take it.'

She watched as Toby carried the tuck box in and set it on the floor. 'Sit down, both of you.' She closed the diary and sat staring at the old worn cover on the table before her for several seconds. They sat down, one on each side of her, glancing at each other in concern, then they both looked at her expectantly. Anna felt a sudden worm of unease deep inside her. Frances's attractive face, usually so tranquil, was etched with worry.

'The villain of the tale. Roger Carstairs. Do you know what happened to him?'

Anna shrugged. 'He's never mentioned again in the diary after the Fieldings' baby is born. I gather he was quite famous in his day. Serena knew a bit about him. And even Toby had heard of him.'

Frances glanced at her son and nodded. 'He was famous. He left Egypt in 1869 and travelled to India and the Far East. He was away for about five years then he surfaced again in Paris. He lived near the Bois de Boulogne in a rambling old house which had once belonged to a French duke.'

Toby frowned. 'How on earth do you know that?'

Frances held up her hand. 'He married a French woman, Claudette de Bonville and had two daughters. One of them was my mother's grandmother.'

There was a stunned silence as Toby and Anna stared at her. 'You are descended from Roger Carstairs!' Anna said incredulously.

'I'm afraid so.' Frances shrugged. 'He had two other children by his first marriage, of course. They stayed in Scotland. The elder, James, inherited the earldom, but it died out as neither he nor his brother had any children.'

'And what happened to Roger?' Anna was staring at Toby. He seemed as stunned as she was.

'He disappeared.' Frances shrugged. 'Rather apt, really. It was thought he went back to Egypt. I was looking through the family papers and records this afternoon. He left France under a cloud after five years with Claudette and travelled to Constantinople. Then he moved to Alexandria where he stayed a couple of years. Then he moved on. As far as I know he was never heard of again.' She turned to Toby. 'Before you ask why you didn't know all this, a: you have never been interested in family history and b: my parents would not allow his name to be mentioned in the house. I'd forgotten about him until he turned up in Louisa's diary. Claudette took the children to Scotland in an attempt to get his estate to help her. She was destitute after he left. The brothers refused to give her anything and she came south to England to see Roger's sister. She seems to have been a nice person. She helped them settle in England and in the end both girls married Eng-lishmen.'

Anna was staring at Toby in silence.

'I'm glad you ditched the bottle.' He raised an eyebrow. 'Or you really would have suspected me of coveting it!'

'You haven't inherited his powers, I hope.' Anna forced herself to smile. She shuddered.

'No, I haven't.' He was looking at her closely. 'Apart from liking snakes. This has upset you, hasn't it? Anna, it was more than a hundred years ago!'

'I know. I know it's a weird coincidence. I know it's not logical. It's just that I've lived in Louisa's head for so long.' She closed her eyes, stunned by the sense of despair which had swept over her.

'I'm sorry, perhaps I shouldn't have told you.' Frances looked at her with concern. 'But I had to. I didn't want there to be any secrets between us. I thought – I hoped – you'd be intrigued. It is such a strange twist to your story.'

Anna stood up. She walked over to the small cane sofa under the window and threw herself down on it. 'Serena says there is no such thing as coincidence.'

Toby glanced at his mother. 'In that case, maybe this is our chance to make amends. Maybe it is my karma to try and make up for the unhappiness he caused Louisa.'

'And the other evil things he did?' Anna was hugging herself against the cold which had enveloped her even in the warm kitchen. She was shivering.

'A lot of people's ancestors did evil things, my dear,' Frances put

392

in gently. 'There has to be a place for forgiveness in history. That is what Christ teaches us. And although Roger Carstairs might have been an evil man, my grandfather, who was also Toby's ancestor, don't forget, was a rector in a village in the midlands, a much loved and respected man who did an enormous amount of good in the world. He found it hard to live with the memory of his grandfather. He prayed for his soul every day, or so we were told. So there is balance. Our blood is not wholly tainted.' She stood up and smiled wearily. 'Now, if you will excuse me, it's very late. I'm going to bed. Goodnight, my dears.'

Toby and Anna watched her go in silence. It was Toby who spoke first as the door closed behind her. 'Well, that was a bit of a facer. Of all the things in my past I felt I might have to explain to you and talk my way out of, descent from Roger Carstairs was not one of them.' He stood up and, going to the cupboard under the worktop brought out a bottle of whisky. 'I need something a little stronger than hot chocolate at this point, I think. Would you like one?' He reached two glasses down from the shelf over the sink. 'Ma's right, you know. It doesn't matter.' He poured out half an inch of whisky in each glass and passed her one. 'No, I didn't mean it doesn't matter. Of course it matters. But it doesn't affect us. It doesn't, does it?'

Anna shook her head slowly. 'Of course it doesn't. It's just that his memory resonates very powerfully in my head at the moment. It's all tied up with the fear and anguish I felt. It's tied up with the deaths of two men who lived three thousand years ago! It's tied up with Serena and Charley. Everything.' She put down the glass untouched and put her head in her hands.

'It wasn't a good holiday, then?' Toby looked at her quizzically.

She laughed in spite of herself. 'No, it wasn't a good holiday! Although it was memorable and I saw some wonderful things and met some wonderful people.'

'I wish I could confidently think I was one of them.'

She scanned his face for a few seconds. 'You are one of them.'

'Even though you are now seeing me in a black cloak with a pointed hat and a death-dealing magic wand, with a basket of pet snakes who kill at my command?'

'Even though I'm seeing all that!' She stood up. 'I'm going to go to bed, Toby. I'll take my drink up with me. It's been a tiring day, going up to Suffolk and everything.'

'OK. Perhaps we can look at some more of those letters, tomorrow?' He nodded at the tuck box.

'Perhaps.' She walked to the door, then she turned. 'Toby, I want to go back home tomorrow. Your mother has been incredibly kind and hospitable but I'm well now and I do want to be under my own roof. You understand?'

'Of course.' He couldn't hide his crestfallen expression.

'It's not because of Carstairs. I need to pick up the threads of my life again.'

He nodded. 'Will I be a part of that life?'

She hesitated. 'I am pretty sure you will, if that's what you want. But I need time. Too much has happened.'

'Sure. You'll have all the time you need.' He got up to open the door for her. As she passed him he leant over and kissed her cheek. 'Meeting you has been the best thing that's happened to me in a very long time, Anna.'

She smiled. 'I'm glad.'

It was only after she had gone that he realised she had not said she felt the same.

Her little attic bedroom was very comforting in the light of the bedside lamp with its flower-sprinkled shade. She kicked off her shoes and stood staring round, sipping the whisky. She felt safe here. Nurtured and cared for in a way which had not happened to her for a long time, perhaps since she was a child. She liked Frances enormously and she trusted her. She liked Toby. Perhaps she even loved him. So why, suddenly, was she filled with such misgiving?

She walked over to the small chest of drawers which did duty as a dressing table and peered into the mirror. Her face was thin and drawn and she looked pale, even to herself. Her face was shadowed of course, with the light behind her. She frowned.

The sun had come out. It was so bright now, shining obliquely across her features, that she had to screw up her eyes against the glare. The reflection cleared a little. She could see cliffs; a bird flying slowly against the sky; a palm frond tapping against the window . . .

'No!' She spun round, sending her whisky glass flying. It hit the corner of the chest of drawers and shattered, sending whisky showering over her hairbrush and make-up. She closed her eyes and took a deep breath. When she opened them again the room looked the same as usual. Warm. Shadowed. Safe. With shaking hands she picked up the glass and put the pieces in the wastepaper basket. She was mopping up the whisky with tissues when there was a tap at the door. 'Anna? Are you OK?' Toby called softly.

She bit her lip. Tears were beginning to prick beneath her eyelids. Silently throwing down the wadded tissues she went to the bed and lay down, pulling the pillow over her head.

'Anna? Are you asleep?' There was a pause then she heard his footsteps padding back down the stairs. Ten minutes later she heard his car start up in the quiet street and drive away.

When she woke it was still dark outside. The lamp was still switched on and she was holding the pillow tightly in her arms. She was fully dressed and the room smelt disgustingly of stale whisky. With a groan she hauled herself out of bed and looked at her watch. It was four in the morning. Undressing, she crept downstairs to the bathroom, flushed away the whisky-sodden tissues and ran herself a deep warm bath. She hoped the sound of running water wouldn't wake Frances but she had to wash away the stench of fear which seemed to cling to her skin, the hot grittiness of desert sweat, the misery which clung in her pores. She lay there a long time, staring at the pale pink tiles behind the taps then at last she climbed out and wrapped herself in a towel. The landing was quiet outside the bathroom, the door to Frances's bedroom closed. Upstairs she opened the window wide, letting in a blast of cold night air then at last she turned off the light and climbed into bed.

It was after ten when she woke. She dressed quickly and ran downstairs to find the house empty. In the basement there was a note on the kitchen table: 'I thought I'd let you sleep in. I'll be back at lunchtime. F.'

Thoughtfully she made herself some coffee then she went back upstairs to the ground floor sitting room. There was no sign of Toby. No message. She reached for the phone book and found Serena's number.

'I hoped I'd catch you. I wanted to thank you for coming to see me.'

'How are you?' Serena sounded cheerful. Anna could hear distant music in the background. She recognised the Classic FM jingle and then the opening bars of Beethoven's Sixth Symphony.

'Serena, I'm going home this afternoon. Will you come round and see me there? I'll give you the address.'

'Something is still wrong, isn't it?' Serena's voice was warm. Concerned. Comforting.

'Yes.' Anna managed to swallow her tears. 'Something is still very wrong.'

Toby and Frances returned together at lunchtime with pâté and cheese and bread and a bottle of Merlot. They were not surprised to find Anna's case ready-packed in the hall. 'I'll drive you back after lunch. Toby gave her a glass of wine. 'We're going to miss you.'

She smiled. 'I'm not going far. And I hope you're both going to come and see me often.' She hadn't realised how formal it sounded, hadn't meant it to sound quite so final, until she saw Frances glance at her son. His face was bleak.

He forced a smile. 'You won't be able to keep us away,' he said. The words did not sound as though he believed them himself.

None of them ate much and less than an hour later he was driving her across London, her case in the boot, her bag, her camera, her guidebooks, lying on the back seat of the car.

He managed to find a parking place almost outside her door. 'Fate taking a hand,' he said wryly. 'It's determined to hurry you back to your own life.'

'Toby –'

'No.' He raised a hand. 'I'm a great believer in fate. What will be, will be, and all that. Come on.' He pushed open his door and went round to the back of the car.

Anna climbed out and walked slowly to her front door leaving Toby to follow with the case. Late snowdrops and the first crocus were crowding the narrow bed under the front window and winter jasmine shone yellow across the London bricks. The windowbox held a straggle of winter pansies, nearly over now, clearly showing that their owner had not been there to look after them.

She reached for her keys. 'This isn't goodbye, Toby.' She turned and faced him on the step. 'There are things I have to work out by myself.' She took his hands. 'Please, be there if I need you.'

'You know I will.'

She reached up and kissed him on the lips. Then she turned and hefting the case in by herself she closed the door behind her.

He stood for several seconds staring at it blindly, then he turned away.

On the other side of the door Anna stopped too. She dropped the case and her bags and took a deep breath, fighting back her tears. It was there again. The sunlight behind her eyes. In the narrow dark hall of a west London terraced house she could feel the heat of the desert sun on her face and smell the rich drifting smoke of *kyphi*, incense of the gods.

Biting her lip she glanced at her watch. Soon Serena would come and perhaps then they would be able together to chase away this intruder in her head for good.

She stooped to pick some letters off the mat. Amongst them was a small parcel. Throwing the letters on the side table she stared at the parcel. It had Egyptian stamps. She turned it over and over in her hands then she carried it into the living room and tore it open. Inside was a typed letter and a small bubble-wrapped packet.

The letter was from the Luxor Police Department.

> The enclosed artefact was found in the hand of the deceased, Mr Andrew Watson, when his body was recovered from the Nile. It was later established that the item belonged to you and that it had been imported without licence. It has now been established that your ownership is not in doubt . . . I hereby return it . . . Please acknowledge your receipt of the same . . .

'No.' She shook her head. 'No. Please, no.'

She put the packet on the table and stared at it. Then she turned and ran to the front door.

'Toby!'

She scrabbled frantically at the lock and pulled it open. 'Toby, wait!'

His car was pulling away from the kerb.

'Toby!'

She ran towards the gate but already, with a quick glance over his shoulder he had spun the steering wheel and with a hand raised to acknowledge the car which had paused to let him out into the stream of traffic, he drove away. He had never looked back in her direction.

'Toby!'

397

She stood staring after him, feeling more lost and frightened than she had ever felt in her life. 'Toby, come back. Please. I need you!'

Her hand dropped to her side, then slowly she turned and walked back towards the house.

As she climbed the steps she could already hear the distant call of chanting across the sand, smell the *kyphi*, feel the heat of the sun god, Ra, as he lifted over the horizon.

At the traffic lights in Notting Hill Gate Toby frowned. He drummed his fingers on the wheel. His head was strangely full of odd sounds, sounds he had never heard before: the plaintive chanting of distant voices, echoed by a harp and what sounded like the low haunting notes of an oboe, floating over vast distances.

He shook his head, puzzled.

Toby!

The call came from far away.

Toby, come back! *Please*!

He frowned.

That was Anna's voice.

He jumped as the car behind him hooted angrily. The lights had changed and he had not seen them. He stared into the mirror, dazed, then suddenly he made up his mind. He spun the steering wheel full circle and swung the car round with an angry squeal of tyres.

Seconds later he was speeding back towards her house.

'Anna! Anna?' He left the car in the middle of the road, the door open, the engine running.

'Anna! Open the door!' Running up the path he hammered on it with his fists. There was a slight click and the door swung open. She had not closed it properly when she walked back into the house.

'Anna?' Toby stared inside. 'Where are you?'

The hall was deserted, the door into the living room ajar. Pushing it back, he threw himself into the room.

'Anna!' He skidded to a halt.

The room smelt of Egypt. Of heat and sand and of exotic incenses.

The shadow was all around her.

'Anna, fight it, sweetheart! I'm not going to let him have you. Anna, look at me! I love you!'

398

He grabbed her hands and spun her to face him. 'Anna!'

She blinked, frowning. 'Toby?'

'I'm here, sweetheart. It's all right.'

She was coming back to him. The shadow was fading.

Gathering her into his arms he kissed the top of her head.

'It came back, Toby,' she stammered. 'The bottle. Louisa couldn't get rid of it and neither can I. I threw it in the Nile but Andy caught it. He had it in his hand, Toby. Andy brought it back!' Sobbing, she glanced at the table where the little bottle stood amidst its wrappings on the polished mahogany surface. 'I'll never be free.'

He stared at it thoughtfully. 'There are a lot of things we can do, Anna. We can give it to the British Museum. We can send it back to Egypt. We can throw it in the Thames. But whatever happens, we're going to face this together.'

She looked up at him. 'You mean it?'

'I mean it. You are not alone. You'll never be alone again unless you want to be and you are going to be free of Anhotep and Hatsek. I guarantee it.'

As he kissed the top of her head he glanced up. On the shining wood of the table, scattered amongst the wrapping paper he could see the fragments of dried resin, smell its cloying scent. As he watched more appeared on the carpet at their feet.

Anna looked up at him. 'Serena is on her way,' she murmured. 'She'll help us, I know she will.'

Toby tightened his arms around her. 'Of course she will. And don't forget, I have the blood of Roger Carstairs and of my reverend great-grandfather in my veins. That must give me some start in the spiritual stakes.'

As she looked up at him he smiled. 'Courage, my darling, their combined shades have given me an idea. If I stand over that little bottle with a large hammer in my hand, I think the priests of Ancient Egypt are going to start listening to what we have to say to them for a change, don't you?'

The goddess Isis is with thee and she never leaveth thee;
thou art not overthrown by thy enemies . . .

Let the servants of the gods sleep in peace . . .

Author's Note

In common with many people, I suspect, my expectations of Egypt were so enormous that I was, in a way, almost reluctant to go there. Supposing it was not as wonderful as I hoped? Supposing the visit was a disaster and all my dreams and fantasies were shattered? I have Carole Blake to thank, both for the suggestion as a possibility rather than a dream that we embark on the adventure, a first for both of us, and for being a wonderful companion on the trip which ensued; we had such a good time!

The boat in which we sailed from Luxor to Aswan was very like the *White Egret*, although, I'm pleased to say, nothing sinister happened while we were on her – although I did see a ghost in the passenger's lounge! Perhaps that gave me the idea that ghosts too could go on cruises!

Within ten minutes of setting off from the airport towards the centre of Luxor I knew that there was going to be an Egyptian novel. I was entranced and from that moment on, Egypt was everything I expected of her and more. The atmosphere, the history and the memories were all there to be found if one looked, in spite of the crowds.

I already had a great many books on Egypt and I bought more, but those which helped me most with the Victorian sections of this story were the accounts of two of the intrepid ladies in whose mould Louisa was set. I do recommend *Letters from Egypt* by Lucie Duff Gordon and *A Thousand Miles up the Nile* by Amelia Edwards to anyone interested in Egypt's nineteenth-century past and of course no one should go through life without looking at the wonderful magical lithographs of David Roberts.

Rachel Hore and Lucy Ferguson helped bring me back down to earth in the editing of my manuscript – to both of them as usual my grateful thanks. My visit was short and so packed with experiences that I may have remembered some things wrongly. If so it is my fault alone.

I made my own offering to Isis at Philae. Maybe, like a coin in the Trevi Fountain, that will ensure that one day I return to Egypt. I hope so.

BE